Praise for
ECHOES

"Ms. Grady has delivered a story so fascinating, you'll want to read it in one sitting." —*The Best Reviews*

"A definite thumbs up for dramatic suspense and a plot that keeps you on the edge of your seat." —*Romance Junkies*

"Erin Grady is an author on the rise!"
—*The Romance Reader's Connection*

"*Echoes* is a beautifully romantic suspense novel . . . Ms. Grady delivers a spectacularly dark paranormal romantic thriller. Next Erin Grady book, please!" —*Joyfully Reviewed*

"Secrets, peril, and eerie revelations make this debut paranormal thriller stimulating reading. Those who love the parallel story technique will thoroughly enjoy watching this two-tiered story unfold." —*Romantic Times BOOKclub*

"Wow, right out of the blue and just when you least expect it, a knock-out novel of romantic suspense . . . Far above the general run of romantic suspense."

—*All About Romance*

Whispers

ERIN GRADY

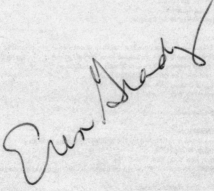

BERKLEY SENSATION, NEW YORK

THE BERKLEY PUBLISHING GROUP
Published by the Penguin Group
Penguin Group (USA) Inc.
375 Hudson Street, New York, New York 10014, USA
Penguin Group (Canada), 90 Eglinton Avenue East, Suite 700, Toronto, Ontario M4P 2Y3, Canada
(a division of Pearson Penguin Canada Inc.)
Penguin Books Ltd., 80 Strand, London WC2R 0RL, England
Penguin Group Ireland, 25 St. Stephen's Green, Dublin 2, Ireland (a division of Penguin Books Ltd.)
Penguin Group (Australia), 250 Camberwell Road, Camberwell, Victoria 3124, Australia
(a division of Pearson Australia Group Pty. Ltd.)
Penguin Books India Pvt. Ltd., 11 Community Centre, Panchsheel Park, New Delhi—110 017, India
Penguin Group (NZ), Cnr. Airborne and Rosedale Roads, Albany, Auckland 1310, New Zealand
(a division of Pearson New Zealand Ltd.)
Penguin Books (South Africa) (Pty.) Ltd., 24 Sturdee Avenue, Rosebank, Johannesburg 2196,
South Africa

Penguin Books Ltd., Registered Offices: 80 Strand, London WC2R 0RL, England

This is a work of fiction. Names, characters, places, and incidents either are the product of the author's imagination or are used fictitiously, and any resemblance to actual persons, living or dead, business establishments, events, or locales is entirely coincidental. The publisher does not have any control over and does not assume any responsibility for author or third-party websites or their content.

WHISPERS

A Berkley Sensation Book / published by arrangement with the author

PRINTING HISTORY
Berkley Sensation mass-market edition / April 2006

Copyright © 2006 by Erin Grady.
Cover design by Brad Springer.
Interior text design by Kristin del Rosario.

ISBN: 0-425-20963-6

BERKLEY® SENSATION
Berkley Sensation Books are published by The Berkley Publishing Group,
a division of Penguin Group (USA) Inc.,
375 Hudson Street, New York, New York 10014.
BERKLEY SENSATION and the "B" design are trademarks belonging to Penguin Group (USA) Inc.

PRINTED IN THE UNITED STATES OF AMERICA

10 9 8 7 6 5 4 3 2 1

For Lynn, who rode into town and said,
"First we drink, then we fix the problem."
You saved more than just the day.

And to Hailey and Taylor who
gave up their mother for many long weeks.
I love you both.

ACKNOWLEDGMENTS

I would like to thank Alicka Pistek of the Alicka Pistek Literary Agency and Susan McCarty of Berkley (who I will greatly miss), for their support, editing, and exceptional insights which helped make this story complete. Thanks to my husband, for everything. To Lynn Coulter, for every single step of the way; to Judi Barker and Rebecca Goude, for speed reading a first draft; to Charles and Betty Grady, Debbie Kapfer, Margarita Vianco, and Val Swanson, for stepping in and taking my kids so I could have time to write. And thanks to my family, friends, and readers who continue to support me. I will be forever grateful.

chapter one

BRENDAN thought lying to Analise's mother would be the trickiest part, but that had been a piece of cake. Analise told her she was spending the night at a friend's and she was such a good kid, her mom never even questioned it. No, the biggest challenge had been keeping it a secret all the way there. He'd never considered how hard that would be. But that was the way he was. He never saw the big picture, never realized he wasn't seeing it, until it was too late.

He'd been obsessed with the town they were headed to for weeks now. Maybe it was the *way* he'd found Diablo Springs that had him so intrigued.

He'd been hauling a load of sod to Phoenix, taking the same damn road he always did, when he'd seen the sign, DIABLO SPRINGS, NEXT EXIT. Thing was, he'd driven that stretch of highway a dozen, maybe two dozen times, and never seen the sign before. It was like this time it was meant to be. Stupid, but there it was.

He'd spent the whole next day on the Internet, researching. He learned that once the town had been Apache land, but when silver was discovered in the Tombstone Mountains the Indians had been driven off. After that it had become a hive for outlaws and home to infamous prostitutes. As he'd read the history he'd found himself wishing he'd been alive in those days, picturing himself with a pistol strapped to his leg and a rifle to his saddle.

There'd been a natural hot springs there that the Apaches had used for sacred ceremonies. It was a sure bet the miners and bandits hadn't used it for the same. Despite its reputation as the kind of place to get either screwed or killed in, Diablo

Springs had become a tourist town at the turn of the century. Unbelievable. Rich socialites had played cards shoulder to shoulder with the rough and ready crowds of desperados. They went through sheriffs as fast as they did bullets.

And then, for no apparent reason, the springs just dried up. The town did too. Brendan searched for hours, trying to find out just why. But no explanation was offered.

Bringing Analise here, just the two of them, was one of his crazier ideas. He had this image in his head of how happy she'd be when he told her he'd found the town where her mother grew up. For some reason, it had been this deep, dark mystery in Analise's house. Where they came from, who her dad was, why there were no family pictures on the bookshelf in the front room. . . . And the more her mother refused to tell her, the more Analise became determined to know.

Well now she would, because Brendan had found it. Tomorrow they would have to "face the music" as his old man liked to say. They'd have to tell her mother that Analise was pregnant. But tonight, they'd be sleeping under the stars in the back of his pickup, and life would be good.

"We're almost there," he said.

She smiled, but he could see she was confused, wondering where *there* was.

Overhead thunder rumbled and the sky churned— masking the last glimmer of day. Lightning spidered across the surface and threatening clouds rode low, rasping against the parched and cracked desert floor, charging the air with electricity. He drove straight through the tiny town, wanting to see the old hot springs before it was fully dark. Beside him, Analise peered out the window, a frown pulling her brows together.

"What is this place?" she asked.

For an answer, he reached over and lifted her arm. A charm bracelet hung from her wrist. Her mother had given it to her last week for her sixteenth birthday. The bracelet was old, and it had been the unique assortment of dangly trinkets that had fueled Analise wondering about where she came from.

"This is Diablo Springs, honey," he said.

If anything, her frown deepened. He'd been so excited to bring her here—he'd even called it a late birthday surprise. But now, seeing it through her eyes, it didn't seem so special, such a great idea. The big picture, once again, eluded him. In the long shadows and the gathering storm, the entire place looked eerily forsaken.

"Diablo Springs," she said. "Are you kidding?"

"No. I found it the last time I went into Phoenix. I know you've been curious about it."

"Curious, yeah, but . . . I thought we were going someplace, you know, like a hotel."

Brendan swallowed hard. Of course she'd thought that.

LESS than a quarter mile of open scrub and cactus stretched between the road and the place where the old springs once flowed. A bridge and walkway had once made a path to the hot pools, and guests of the Diablo Springs Hotel had made the short journey by foot. In the pictures he'd seen, decking had been built up around the springs where bathers could sit and dangle their feet into the water. Now it was all overrun, devoured by the hot sun and burning grit of the desert. Only the bridge remained intact. As he pulled closer, he could see what was left in ruins around a black sinkhole. The railings were splintered and busted and stuck up from the remnants like broken bones.

Following the road to the huge indentation in the ground, he watched the horizon devour the last glow of sunlight. In the fresh dusk, he stopped, hopped out of the truck, and went around to help Analise down. She was so small and fine boned—he couldn't touch her without wanting to protect her. And now, with the baby coming, he had that much more to worry about.

The air was thick and close, hinting at the heat that morning would bring. The low scrub crept right up to the sides of the dirt road, looking like it might try to take it over very soon. Beyond, a wild assortment of spiky and thorny desert plants sprawled out over the abandoned grounds, some blooming with wild pinks and corals. Not a blade of grass was in sight.

The land was tough, barbed, dead inside. Abandoned and hard to love. He felt an instant connection to the place.

"So I looked it up on the Internet," he said. "This used to be like some Wild West town, not as big or famous as Tombstone, but pretty bad. Outlaws and gunslingers. No one major got shot down, to make it, you know, legendary. But people came here because of the hot springs. Used to be right here."

He pointed to the black ravine ahead. It had shocked him the first time he'd seen the pictures of it. It looked as if a giant lightning bolt had plunged sideways into the flat earth, leaving a hole straight to hell. Dry now, like the crackling air. Hard to imagine it had ever held healing waters.

Analise looked at the dirt fissure, unimpressed by its history. She turned away from it and stared out at the silhouetted town. A few lights twinkled in windows as night worked its way into homes. Her expression, her reaction to his surprise, wasn't at all what he'd imagined.

He reached in the back seat and pulled out a blanket, which he spread over an unlikely patch of even ground. As he smoothed it down he discovered a miniscule sprouting of what looked like grass. Grass, even here. Feeling somehow betrayed by it, he twisted it until its grasping roots snapped and then hurled it into the gaping hole.

"Sit down, honey. I brought us a little picnic."

Analise gave the blanket a nervous look. She held herself stiff as a doll, seemingly undecided about which way to face. The town and the ravine were like warring poles and she the metal pin in between. Brendan frowned.

"I don't like it here, Brendan. Let's go."

God, he was such an idiot to have brought her here. It was nothing but dirt. Just like him.

"Go where?" he said bitterly. "Maybe to the Ritz? You think I got that kind of money?"

Analise looked instantly contrite, which only made him feel like a bigger shit.

"Brendan, I'm sorry. This was a great surprise. I do want to see it all, but it's getting really dark."

"So?"

"It's . . . I mean . . . Don't tell me you don't feel it?"

In fact, as she spoke, pointing out the clustering darkness, he realized he did feel it. The entire place seemed strangely . . . disturbed. The air held a tension, a feeling of violation, a sense of hostility. Brendan shook his head. Freaking himself out like a kid in a haunted house, that's what he was doing.

"You afraid of the dark now, honey?"

Her smile was small and forced.

He got up and went to the truck where he rummaged for his flashlight, hoping its batteries were still good. He turned it on and a pale, buttery beam chased back the shadows. It waned after the initial burst, but held.

"Better?" he asked.

Analise nodded without much conviction. "I guess."

"Apparently, this used to be built up," he said, hoping to distract her with some facts about the place. "You can still see some of the decking," he went on, aiming the pathetic beam of the flashlight at the ruins. "And right over there, see that big house? That used to be the saloon and whorehouse. So what I read, was, there's a myth that the whole place is cursed and one day it just dried up."

"What dried up?"

"The hot springs," he said, irritated.

"It's creepy," Analise said, looking fearfully at the dimming glow of the flashlight.

It didn't matter that she was right, it made him mad. "Do you know what I went through to get here?"

Tears made her eyes shiny and luminous. "I know, I'm sorry. It's just . . . I'm scared, Brendan."

"You're scared of everything. You—" He stopped suddenly and scanned the area around them. He'd heard something.

"What?" Analise said.

"Shh." He stood, searching the darkness. The feeble glow of the flashlight reached only a foot or two in front of him. Past that it was all huddled shadows and looming shapes. He strained with the effort to hear. The quiet folded in and stretched out in a hiss. Then a slight, slithering sound reached his ears. Like dirt spilling into an empty hole.

In unison, he and Analise looked to the ravine. He took a step closer.

"No. Brendan, no. Let's just get out of here."

He waved her off and took another step. As if frozen, Analise watched. The sound came again. Loose soil and rock sliding down the side. As if something were climbing up.

"What do you see?" she whispered.

Brendan shook his head and moved closer to the edge of the hole. A rock joined the slight avalanche of dirt. It clicked and thumped down to the bottom. Analise made a whimpering sound that cut him to the bone. She'd been telling the truth earlier. This place . . . it wasn't right. Nothing felt right. The unrest hovered like a layer of dust in the heat.

More rocks, the earth slide increased. As if something had lost its foothold and slid back a few feet, causing the hole to cave in around it.

Brendan was almost to the edge. His flashlight crawled over the terrain then inched up to the piled dirt circling it. The blackness around him seemed more complete because of the tiny rent he and his light put in it. He acknowledged the fear that threatened to buckle his knees even as he refused to give in to it.

He stopped a few steps from the lip of the opening.

"Brendan," Analise said, her voice a shaky whisper in the uneasy night.

He leaned forward, trying to peer down into the pit without actually going to the rim. He couldn't see a damn thing. More dirt shifted and skipped down in the depths. Dirt he'd dislodged? Or—

"Brendan, please come back. Please?"

A deep and dank odor wafted up toward him. Like something dead and long ago rotted had escaped its sealed chamber. What the hell was it? Another step and then suddenly a rush of air blasted out in a gust that lifted his hair and scared a shout right out of him. After it, the scrabbling sound raced up the ravine wall. Brendan staggered back, shouting again as he stumbled. Behind him Analise began to scream.

"Run!" he hollered, racing past her to the truck.

She didn't even know from what, but she didn't stop to ask. She followed him and jumped in as he threw the engine into reverse. Her door slammed shut, nearly clipping her foot, which had barely had time to clear the running board. He cranked the wheel and the truck fishtailed before spinning around and out the way they'd come. Shaking and crying Analise turned in her seat and looked back.

"What do you see?" he demanded.

She was sobbing, too hysterical to even answer. He tore his gaze from the road and looked in the rearview mirror. A pale light seemed to hover over the pit. What was it? A face? But it glowed, not like skin but—suddenly it shifted and looked at him. He screamed like a girl and Analise joined in.

"What is it?" Brendan shouted. "Is it following us?"

"I don't know," Analise sobbed.

Brendan had the pedal to the floor and the truck felt like it had wings as it flew across the desert, barely staying on the excuse for a road. It hadn't taken them this long to get there, had it? Shit, was he lost? Had he gotten turned around? Where was the moon? Where was the fucking *town*?

"Why did you bring me here?" Analise was crying over and over. "Why, why?"

He turned in his seat and looked back. Nothing following, and yet . . . A glimmer . . . The town. How had the town ended up on his right? Didn't matter, as long as he got there. He cranked the wheel, his instincts telling him he was backtracking while his eyes told him he was headed the right way.

"No," Analise shouted. "You're going back."

He opened his mouth to tell her she was wrong, but now he was completely disoriented and his headlights picked out the gaping ravine ahead. At seventy miles an hour they were going in.

He twisted the wheel hard left, taking the truck into a crazy spin at the edge of the abyss. He felt the wheels lose traction. Felt the pull of gravity trying to suck them down. The back end hovered for an instant over the great nothingness of it, and then slowly, the truck began to slide down.

chapter two

SOME say destiny is unavoidable. Some say a person's whole life is determined before he or she is even born. Reilly Alexander didn't buy into that, which wasn't the same as saying he didn't believe it. When he looked back on his life, it seemed fate had done more than drive him around; it had plotted out a specific course that brought him here, now, to a bookstore in Los Angeles where he would meet his destiny.

"We've put your table right up front," the Barnes & Noble manager told him.

"Thank you."

"I think you'll have a good turnout. Your book has been selling quite well for us."

This was his fourth book, and he still couldn't get used to hearing that it wasn't complete crap. Maybe he'd never get used to hearing it. A part of him still believed that it was his nefarious and disastrous venture into the music business that brought the readers to his books, not the writing. Not *his* stories, but *the* story of a failed rocker turned literary genius. He smirked to himself at that. Yeah, right.

But fans did come. The women as often as not asked to touch the tattoos on his arms—the bolder of them asked if he had any others he might share. The young musicians came because they thought some of his luck would rub off on them—it mattered not that his luck in the music business hadn't been the best. The others . . . he still hadn't figured out what drew the others. All in all, though, he ate well, traveled in fair style, and lived a life of quasi-fame. In honesty, more than he'd ever expected of himself.

He ran a hand over his nearly shaved head, still expecting the shoulder-length shag he'd worn until a few months ago when he'd decided it was time to cut even that from his life. The impeccably dressed manager he followed to the table hadn't said a word about Reilly's appearance, but it was there in the look that skimmed his Flogging Molly T-shirt and faded blue jeans. In the beginning, when the first book had come out, he'd tried the dressing-up bit and felt like an even bigger idiot and imposter. The slacks and button-down had fit his image like panty hose and a sunbonnet.

"Just let me know if you need anything," the manager said before going about his business. A cold beer would be nice, but Reilly refrained from asking and simply thanked the man. All he could hope was that the next two hours went fast.

During his college years Reilly had made his living as lead singer and songwriter of a band called Badlands. When the group broke up after three years and one hit single, Reilly had been left with a bit of fame and little fortune. Individually, each of the band members had branched out and failed to produce anything worth listening to. Reilly had resorted to writing songs for others until he'd finally settled down and pounded out the novel he'd been thinking of for years.

Four books later and, apparently, he was doing well enough to warrant a fifth. Of course the scandal over his last book hadn't hurt his sales any. The girl he'd been dating claimed he'd sexually assaulted her as part of his research for his writing. It was bullshit, but when did that matter to the media?

Riding the infamy tide with Badlands had taught him not to believe his own press—good or bad. They loved his books today, but only if he had something better to provide tomorrow. His problem of the hour was, he didn't. The channel of ideas he'd been surfing had suddenly disappeared and left him lost and in a panic over what next. Was it time for yet another career change?

The signing started like clockwork with a steady trickle of readers who had fished his other titles off the shelves and now wanted his signature on the new one. It never quite felt real to scrawl his name on the title page, but he tried not to let it show. After a while there was a lull and Reilly sat back to take a swig of water and catch his breath. A moment later a young man wearing faded blue jeans, a Badlands T-shirt, and a camera around his neck came up to the table. Reilly immediately took note—he hadn't seen one of his old band's shirts in years. It made him feel nostalgic for a minute. He guessed the wearer to be in his late teens, early twenties, too young to ever have been to a Badlands concert, but who knew? He had blond hair, blue eyes, and a build that spoke of hours devoted to the gym. He reminded Reilly of an actor, but he couldn't remember who.

"Mr. Alexander?"

Reilly nodded, hiding a wince at the "mister."

"I'm Zach Canning. I'm a freelance reporter for *Spin* magazine."

"I think you're in the wrong place, buddy. This is a book signing."

Zach grinned. "Had to do a bit of convincing to get here, too."

Reilly raised his brows at that. "Here's a news flash for you. The assault case was dismissed. She just wanted to get in the limelight long enough to be discovered. I hear she's making porn flicks now."

Zach nodded sagely. "Yeah, that had to suck. That's not why I'm here though."

"Good." But Reilly's relief was short-lived.

"I'm doing a feature on One Hit Wonders. You know, where are they now?"

"They're all in hiding," Reilly said. He knew for a fact that one or two of his own one-hit disaster group would probably shoot the smiley Zach Canning for his efforts to out them.

Zach sat on the edge of Reilly's table and picked up a copy of his latest book, *Master Piece*.

"So is this based on your life?" Zach asked.

Reilly gave him a steady look. "It's about a maniac who stalks groupies and murders them."

Zach nodded, still wearing the idiot smile.

"So no," Reilly said patiently, "it's not about my life."

The kid let go a snort of laughter. "Good thing, huh?"

Good thing Reilly didn't make Zach a one-hit wonder, but a woman's voice interrupted them.

"Excuse me?"

Reilly looked away from Zach to a petite and very old woman standing at his table. Fine–boned and birdlike, she stood tall despite the fact that she was obviously well into her golden years. Her skin was the color of toffee—not black, brown, or white, but a mixture of all three that defied racial claims. It was papery-thin and yet unwithered. The lines fanning from her eyes were deep, speaking of untold years, but the eyes themselves sparkled like black diamonds. She wore pink lipstick—a young girl's color, but she managed to carry it off. Perhaps it was the white-toothed smile. A turban in bright African colors wrapped around her hair and a long flowing tunic matched it. Black pants with precise creases covered her legs and black sneakers completed the outfit. Reilly stared at the athletic shoes with a bemused smile. The words *super granny* came to mind, but he kept them to himself.

Behind her in a bizarre cluster stood a hodgepodge of humanity that Reilly couldn't have dreamed up and fictionalized if he'd tried. Like some kind of comic book depiction of a crowd they huddled together, some extremely tall and others excessively short, some unnaturally thin and others uncommonly fat. Their clothes crossed the spectrum from white gauze to fuchsia, tie-dye to black satin. One man wore white gloves and a priest's vestments. Either this was the weirdest book club on the planet or they'd been beamed down from a circling vessel. The group watched the old woman with avid interest.

"Is there a circus in town?" Zach asked, oblivious to the offensiveness of his remark.

The woman simply stared at him until Zach eased himself off Reilly's table and shifted uncomfortably. She continued to stare until he hung his head in shame. Reilly grinned. He had to admire a woman who could do that with just a look. He'd known a few of them in his lifetime.

"You are Nathan Reilly Alexander?" she said, her voice strong and clear.

No one called him Nathan. If it wouldn't have been such a pain in the ass to do it, he'd have had the name removed from record. "It's Reilly. Reilly Alexander."

He reached for the book she held out and opened it to the title page.

"You can make it out to Chloe LaMonte," she said. "Your guide to your destiny."

He paused, pen poised over the page. "Come again?"

"You've been waiting for me, haven't you?"

Reilly gave her a slanted look and a head shake. "Can't say that I was."

"You haven't been thinking of fate, of your destiny? Of where you go from here?"

He wanted to scoff, but of course he couldn't. He'd been doing more than thinking about it. He'd been dwelling on it. He wrote, "To Chloe, enjoy the book," signed it, and handed it back to her. She took it with a strange smile.

"Don't you wonder why I'm here?"

"Sure. Why are you here?"

"There's a town called Diablo Springs," she said, her voice rich and melodic. A trace of an unidentifiable accent teased the ends of her words. "It was a notorious place once. Do you know how it got its name?"

Reilly nodded. "Some people say it was named for all the outrageous lies people told about it. Some say not."

"That's right. I've even heard it's haunted."

She got a faroff look in her eyes and became so still that every hair on Reilly's body stood on end. For a moment he thought of pushing away from the table and bolting, but the idea of it was ridiculous enough to keep him rooted.

As if hearing his thoughts, she snapped her attention back to him. "Others have said it's home to spirits that will never find peace. You are familiar with this place, of course."

"Obviously you know the answer to that."

She nodded. "I've been called there."

"Then you should go."

"I've been called to bring you. I'm leaving tonight."

Beside him, Zach said, "Do you know this lady?"

"Listen Ms. LaMonte—"

"You may call me Chloe."

"Chloe, I don't know what you've heard about Diablo Springs, but I can pretty much guarantee that it isn't true. It's just a dried-up old town."

"A ghost town, but only the ghosts know it."

"If you say so."

"Aren't you curious about who is calling me?"

"The ghost of Christmas past?" Zach asked.

"Carolina Beck."

That got Reilly's full attention. "You're friends with Carolina Beck?"

"Her spirit."

"She's dead?"

"I'm not sure."

Reilly leaned forward, intrigued now. "How is she calling you?"

Chloe leaned in, "How did I know you would care?"

A pale man appeared at Chloe's side, younger than she by about twenty years, but still graying at the temples. Tall and skeletal, he struck Reilly as a hybrid of a vampire and Abraham Lincoln. Where Chloe was color, he was transparent. He put a protective hand on Chloe's waist and a watchful eye on both Reilly and Zach.

"You're looking for your next story," Chloe went on. "You're worried because you can't find one. It's a question of destiny, but you can't see what's right under your nose."

"And you can?" Reilly said.

"You're part of this story, Nathan Reilly Alexander."

"And just what kind of story would that be?"

"A ghost story, of course."

chapter three

GRACIE leaned back from her PC and stared at the brochure she'd created for a distance education program. The banner read, "See the world from the other side of the textbook." It was the kind of program she'd longed to go on when she'd been in college. But by then she'd had a baby, a job, and more life experience than she cared to remember.

She saved the file and shut down her computer. Tonight the house seemed cavernous, though in reality it was just a tiny one-story bungalow built in the giddy days following World War II. San Diego was filled with them. Apart from the two bedrooms—hers and her daughter, Analise's, there was a nook that doubled as an office, a living room/family room, and a kitchen with enough room for a dinette. The yard was small, but Lake Murray, where she could walk her pair of horse-sized dogs, Tinkerbelle and Juliet, wasn't far off. Their third dog, a petite Yorkie named Romeo, sat on her lap while she worked. Gracie absently scratched behind his ears.

She supposed she should get used to the silence in the house. Analise was sixteen, and soon she'd be off to college. She was an honor student with gifts that ranged from math to music. First-chair orchestra, accelerated calculus; she'd have her pick of universities. Gracie would miss her, but she was so proud.

Standing, Gracie stretched. All three dogs did the same. Analise was at a sleepover tonight at her girlfriend's and Gracie had worked away the hours without realizing how late it was. Now she was stiff and suddenly exhausted.

She headed for the bathroom and a hot bath, snagging her book on the way. Chin deep in suds, she sighed. The hot water and absolute quiet lulled her. Her mind drifted until she gave up on the book and just relaxed, eyes closed, slipping low in the tub so only her face remained above the water.

She'd been a single parent since she was seventeen, but now that the demands of raising a child had lessened, she thought about herself. What would she do with all the years before her? She was only thirty-three. Maybe she'd find someone, but so far the only men she'd dated had proven to be either unreliable or unsatisfactory in other ways. Maybe she hadn't given them a chance. Maybe she—

The scream brought her straight up in the tub. Suds clung to her skin, making a crackling sound as they evaporated. What had she heard? The echoes of the sound seemed to hang in the air around her. But who could be screaming? Though muffled by the water, the sound had seemed to come from inside, not out.

On the rug next to the tub, the three dogs stood at attention. Juliet gave a low growl that lifted the fine hairs at her nape.

Gracie climbed out of the bath, wrapping herself in her big terry robe. She peered at the clock on the nightstand. Eleven.

The dogs escorted her to the hall. She paused at Analise's door and listened, though she didn't expect to hear anything. Analise was gone. The darkness and shadows seemed to fold one over the other as she quietly turned the knob on Analise's door. Awareness crystallized the stillness in the house.

She took a step forward into Analise's bedroom, feeling sick with an inexplicable dread tightening inside her. On any given day, a chaos of jeans, peeled off and left inside-out, shirts discarded with sleeves half in, half out, shoes kicked off, stray socks, and hair things would have littered the floor. But tonight it was spotless. All week Gracie had noticed little things that seemed out of character for Analise. Her hair styled out of her face, her makeup less severe, a smile in the morning instead of a grouchy mumble. But none of it sent up the kind of red flag the clean room did. Something was going on.

A sound came from the front of the house and both Juliet and Tinkerbelle spun around with bared teeth and deep growls. Romeo joined in, late on the uptake but determined to be as fierce as his giant counterparts.

Was that a door? Gracie thought as she strained to hear beyond the yapping animals. They sounded frightened, and Gracie realized she was scared too. She just didn't know why. The pair of big dogs made menacing forerunners as they inched down the hall.

The growls became fiercer with each step, and Gracie braced herself for the dogs to attack, but they only waited, their next moved hinged on hers. The hallway had never seemed so long, so dim, so cut off from the rest of the house. They moved toward the darkness at the end like soldiers in a tunnel. She felt the ridiculous need to call out "hello" or "who's there?" but managed to control it. As the family room came into sight, the shadows seemed to shift, as if cast by a moving light. Tinkerbelle gave a deep, warning woof and Juliet joined in a discordant harmony.

Gracie rounded the corner quickly, three dogs at her feet, snarling with fur standing in a ruff of fury. The room was empty. Of course it was. The front door remained closed, the windows shut tight. But Gracie's first relieved sweep of the room slowed and the nagging fear amped up.

Without warning, Juliet launched herself at the front door, barking like a rabid wolf. Tinkerbelle charged just a half step behind and Romeo hopped between them. Over their ruckus, Gracie heard a sound, a scratching at the door. Slowly she approached as the dogs frothed in their excitement and fury. Dry-mouthed, Gracie pressed her eye to the peephole.

Another eye stared back from the other side.

Gracie screamed and lunged away, tripping over the dogs and sprawling on the floor. They barked frantically, circling in search of their attacker. From outside Gracie heard a sound that had no place on this earth. It was a shriek, inhumanly high-pitched and loud. It raced through her blood like ice. She stayed frozen, still on the floor, caged by her fear. Romeo hopped in her lap and the girls crowded around, suddenly silent and trembling.

What was out there?

Feeling lead-limbed, Gracie stood and inched back to the door. The dogs circled her legs, whining with each step closer she took. Her heart thundered against her ribs and she felt dizzy with the thought of putting her eye back to the peephole. Her palms were damp as she pressed them on either side and then she looked.

The porch was empty, lit by the bright light outside the door. A strong wind blew the branches of the giant eucalyptus tree in the front yard, making a rustling sound as it swayed through the dangling limbs. There was nothing else, no one outside.

She took a deep breath. Of course there wasn't.

But then the wind dragged the limbs of the eucalyptus to and fro, and for a moment, for an instant, it seemed that someone stood beneath it. A woman . . . a small and bent woman . . .

The telephone rang, startling a scream out of Gracie. She spun around and stared into the kitchen where the phone hung on the wall. A red light blinked with each ring, like a warning signal in the darkness.

Late-night calls never brought good news, but it might be Analise, wanting to come home instead of sleeping over at her friend's, and Gracie was suddenly desperate to have her daughter close. She looked once more out the peephole, seeing clearly that the only thing out there was her imagination working overtime. Still, relief was far away.

Apprehension lodged deep in her chest and made the simple task of crossing to the phone monumental. The caller ID displayed an unfamiliar number, with an all-too-familiar area code. Arizona.

Diablo Springs. The realization hit her like a hammer.

Her hand shook as she pushed the talk button. The man's voice on the other end stirred a memory, though she didn't place it until he told her his name.

"Eddie Rodriguez?" she repeated with both confusion and disbelief.

"Yeah. Remember me?"

They'd gone to grade school, junior high, and high school together. How could she forget? But why was he calling her? And why now, in the middle of the night?

"Listen, Gracie, I've got some bad news. I think you'd better come home."

"Home?" Gracie reached for the edge of the counter and braced herself. Diablo Springs was a lot of things to her. But it wasn't home.

"It's your grandma. . . ." Eddie paused, took a breath. Unconsciously Gracie did too, steeling herself for his next words. "I'm sorry. There's no easy way to say it. Or explain it for that matter. Gracie, your grandma's dead."

The words rolled over her like a numbing tide.

"Are you there?"

"Yes. I'm here."

"Okay." He stopped again and this time it made Gracie's heart lodge somewhere in her throat. "There's more," he said finally.

Gracie swallowed, feeling as if she were sealed in an airtight silo that filtered every sound but her thumping heart. She stared at the front door, thought of the eye staring back, of the woman standing outside, looking frail and bent, like an old woman.

"More?" she prompted, her voice rough and deep.

"Is—Gracie, do you have a daughter?"

chapter four

.

REILLY had always thought Diablo Springs looked like a Hollywood rendition of the town that time forgot. With the lightning storm giving it a strobe effect, the town seemed to loom up like a spooky relic in a bad horror flick. Ironically, when he'd lived here, he'd thought the world ended at the town's borders. He was right, he realized now, just not in the way he'd thought back then.

Beside him in the passenger seat, Zach Canning began fiddling with the radio for the hundredth time in as many minutes. Finally he picked up a station that had to be broadcasting from Phoenix. A staticky voice told them to grab a hump and ride the camel—apparently the slogan went with the KMLE call letters. Smiling triumphantly at having found a station at last, Zach sat back. But a second later, earth-shaking thunder chased the signal away.

"Welcome to Diablo Springs," Reilly said.

End of the world, here we come. . . .

Reilly glanced in his rearview mirror at the minivan following him. Chloe, the Abraham Lincoln/vampire look-alike, and the guy dressed like a priest were in the van. He wondered if they were as freaked out by the weather as Reilly was by the turn of events that had unfolded in just one short night.

The clouds had gathered during the drive from Los Angeles, and each mile east had brought them deeper into brooding skies and quaking thunder. Now the storm seemed to hover just over Reilly's SUV like a twelve gauge with a tight trigger.

What had he been thinking coming back here? What had

possessed him to go home, pack his bags, and hit the road with complete strangers? Chloe said he needed a story, and God knew it was true. But no story—short of discovering Elvis was alive and living in Burbank with JFK—was enough to warrant the impulsive journey. No, it wasn't the bait Chloe had dangled that had him behind the wheel now.

If he was honest, he had to admit that he'd been brooding about the trip for many weeks—months even. Since Matt died. Chloe walking into the bookstore with her entourage of weirdos and her bizarre claims that she'd been called to Diablo Springs by spirits was interesting. And he couldn't pretend that he wasn't intrigued by the fact that she'd shown up to take *him* with her. How could she know that the mere mention of Carolina Beck would pique his curiosity like it had? He was betting she didn't know why. She couldn't know what his relationship to the old woman was. Just like she couldn't know what his relationship to her granddaughter, Gracie Beck, was. She couldn't. And yet, here Chloe was and she seemed to know a hell of lot more than she let on.

But even that wasn't compelling enough to send Reilly across the desert.

He'd been a coward three months ago when Matt died. He'd gone on with life without pause, taken business as usual without caving into the loss or indulging in grief. There hadn't even been a service. Digger Young, whose family had owned the mortuary business in Diablo Springs for at least a hundred years, cremated his brother and shipped his ashes and a bill to Reilly in LA. The ashes were in his suitcase now, on their way back.

He'd pretended his brother's death was a tragedy that didn't really affect him. But each day since, getting out of bed had been a little harder. Going to the computer, a bit more difficult. Facing himself in the mirror, a lot more painful.

He'd lost weight, lost his drive. He quit caring about anything. Last week he'd shaved his fucking head. Next week he might move onto something more permanent— like maybe shave a few years from his life. The fact of the matter was, he needed to bury his ghosts and Matt was only one of them.

He'd made the decision to come in a split second, because he knew if he thought about it, he'd talk himself out of doing it. And every survival instinct he possessed was telling him now or never. Deal with the shit or let it bury him so deep he'd never come out.

Chloe LaMonte was merely the resounding clap that began the avalanche—the instigator of a collapse long in coming. Reilly either came home and faced his past or he would self-destruct. Simple as that.

The thing that ate at him though, was he was pretty sure Chloe knew it. In fact, he'd bet on it.

He couldn't say why she'd walked into the bookstore, but he'd swear there was more to it than chance or fate or spirits whispering their secrets in her tiny old ears. She had an agenda and once he got his own shit together, he intended to find out what it was. In the meantime, though, he'd saddled himself in a no-win situation. Not surprising. He was the master of getting himself into no-win situations.

"You ready to talk yet" Zach asked, turning off the hissing radio in disgust.

Reilly had been silent and stoic the whole way, though he'd agreed to let Zach accompany him and conduct his interview. In some delusional part of his head, Reilly had decided bringing Zach would be a good thing. Reilly would go to Diablo Springs, deal with his messed up issues, write a brilliant novel about the experience. And Zach . . . Zach would write an article about the fascinating road trip he'd taken with literary genius Reilly Alexander. The publicity from it would please his publisher, boost book sales, and they'd all live happily ever after.

Except Zach wasn't interested in writing about Reilly Alexander, author. He wasn't even interested in writing about Reilly, ex-Badlands lead singer. Zach wanted to dig up dirt. What Zach wanted, Reilly wouldn't give. And like a coon dog on a scent, Zach wouldn't quit until he had Reilly treed.

"I told you, man," Reilly said. "I'm not spilling my guts to you or anyone else."

"You'd spill to Oprah. Everyone spills to Oprah."

"Yea, well, if Oprah ever has me on and I spill, you can say I told you so."

"That's cold, man."

Reilly wasn't really worried about Zach tripping him up. He wasn't a man to cave under pressure. But what if now that they were in Diablo Springs, Zach found other sources? What if he caught another scent? What if he realized Reilly hadn't come because of the crazy woman in the minivan behind them?

Reilly didn't say anything for a minute and then he asked, "Why do you care, anyway? Why the hell do you give a shit about me and my brother?"

"You guys were great. Badlands could have had it all."

"Not even close. Cut the crap, Zach. What do you really want?"

Zach gave him a look across the dark cab. "I want to know how someone can have it all and just piss it away."

Reilly tightened his grip on the wheel. Fair enough.

He turned after the Circle K and made his way into downtown Diablo Springs. The view temporarily distracted his passenger and Reilly had a moment of reprieve.

"Christ," Zach said, peering out the window. "People live here?"

Reilly shrugged, trying to smile though it wasn't really funny. People did live here, though why in hell, he didn't know.

"There's not even a stoplight," Zach said in the same tone of voice he might declare an alien landing at the corner.

"There's one," Reilly said.

"I can't believe this is where you grew up."

"Believe it. I lived right down Rough Street. Fourth house on the left."

He stared at the house he was raised in, now boarded up and overrun with scrub and, most likely, rodents and bugs. This was the desert and no place on earth was more hospitable to vermin. He'd written a number-one single and two bestsellers about the things that creeped and crawled across the hot sands of Arizona.

Zach snorted. "What a dump."

"Yeah," Reilly said, "what a dump."

He pulled up to the curb in front of the Diablo, where they'd be staying for the next few days if Chloe could be believed. She said she'd spoken to Carolina Beck just yesterday and confirmed reservations for herself, her disciples, and Nathan Reilly Alexander. Zach was the only surprise it seemed. And yet, she didn't really seem that surprised at all. That irked him nearly as much as her continued use of "Nathan."

Lightning sizzled and sparked above them, turning the windows into glowing eyes of malice. The giant mesquite in the front swayed dangerously and smacked the house with sagging branches. Rock and cactus made a hostile and skeletal garden of the front yard and tumbleweed bounced its way past them to lodge in the neighbor's fence.

Reilly glanced at his watch. It was nearly two a.m., but lights blazed at the house. A welcoming sight in a town that gave desolation new meaning.

He and Zach stepped from his Jeep.

"What is this place?" Zach asked, standing beside him.

"It used to be a hotel . . . saloon . . . casino . . . fine dining . . . brothel . . . ," Reilly said. "Kind of one-stop shopping for the outlaw in need."

"Is that a fact," Zach answered, suitably impressed. "A whorehouse. Cool."

The oppressive heat was intensified by the brooding storm overhead. It felt like they'd stepped into a damp electric blanket with a buzzing short deep within its circuitry. In the distance the ruins of the old hot springs stuck up like black bones against the gray-green sky. There were flashing lights out there—police cars, it looked like. He frowned, wondering if the Dead Lights had lured another victim into the caverns of the dried-up springs.

"How do people survive in this?" Zach wanted to know.

"You're lucky it's night." Reilly looked away from the flashing lights to watch the younger man swat at a rash of black gnats buzzing around him. "If the sun were shining, you'd be fried before you reached the porch."

Zach looked like he believed it.

"Hell, this is pleasant," Reilly went on, enjoying his cocky companion's discomfort. "When I was a kid, we didn't even have air-conditioning."

"You're shitting me?"

Reilly laughed and shook his head. He glanced back at the vehicle that had followed him out of Los Angeles, watching the old woman and her two companions pile out of the minivan. Between the vampire/Abe Lincoln look-alike, the white gloved priest, and Chloe, he couldn't say which of the three was the strangest.

"Welcome to Diablo Springs," he said.

The air held a fetid smell that brought home a million memories. Hot summer nights swimming with his brother, Matt, in Danny Green's aboveground pool. They'd frozen water in milk jugs and floated them in a vain effort to cool it off. They'd slept on cots in the backyard, braving the bugs for the chance of a breeze. They'd learned the sun could be an enemy. And so could a lightning storm.

As Reilly grabbed his bag from the back of the SUV and looked up at the rumbling, mottled sky, lightning split the clustered darkness, and the sharp scent of sulfur joined the loamy smells in the air. The rain seemed to evaporate before it reached earth, leaving a thin steam that made the skin sticky and the air thick.

The trio huddled beside their van like preschoolers outside a haunted house. Then Chloe LaMonte stepped from the circle and headed toward Reilly. She moved with the grace of a 1950s movie star, her steps very sure, especially for a woman of her age. Her eyes glowed like embers in the muted light.

She stopped at his side, followed closely by the vampire guy Reilly guessed to be her bodyguard or an adopted son . . . or maybe her significant other. Hard to say. He easily topped Reilly's own six foot two and looked like he might never have seen the sun. He wore a plain black T-shirt and black cotton slacks. Next to the colorful Chloe, he looked like he'd missed his own funeral. He wished he could remember the guy's name.

"Nathan," Chloe said in her soft, mysteriously accented voice. "Do you feel them?"

"Christ, they're eating us alive," Zach said, swatting at the bugs.

Abe the vampire frowned at Zach, but Chloe didn't even spare him a glance. "I know you do. You sense them. You've always sensed them."

"I sense we're going to get hit by lightning if we don't get inside."

Her grin was smug. He gritted his teeth.

"We're late," she said, unconcerned with his prediction. "Not too late, but late. Let's go in."

Reilly gave one more glance at the flashing police lights out at the dried-up springs and then followed Chloe and Abe up the walkway. The priest and Zach fell in step behind him.

Chloe paused on the porch, looking at him expectantly as he joined her. "No one home?" he asked.

She gave a shrug that managed to look European and convey absolutely nothing. "You go first," she said. "You'll have to face . . . is it Faith?" She tilted her head to the side and narrowed her eyes. "No, it's Grace, isn't it?"

"Gracie?" Reilly glanced at the front door and then back to Chloe, more disturbed by Chloe mining the name from his memory than anything the peculiar woman had said up to this point. He hadn't seen Gracie Beck in years—not since the night he'd lied to protect his brother. How many nights since had he wished he could do it all over? Do it right? But there were no do-overs in life.

Chloe gave him an enigmatic smile. "Gracie, yes, of course. You didn't really think you were through with her, did you?"

Reilly was flat-out dumbfounded. "I think you've got your wires crossed, Chloe. Gracie hasn't been back to Diablo Springs since she ran off. And I never really knew her that well in the first place."

"Perhaps," she said, her tone contradicting her words. "Why don't you find out?"

"Who's Gracie?" Zach asked, looking between Chloe

and Reilly. When neither answered, he looked to Abe. "Who's Gracie?"

Reilly gave a tight smile and shook his head. Chloe was baiting him. She had her little psychic antennas out looking for ways to scam him. Sure, he'd been thinking of Gracie Beck. Hell, this had been her house. But there was no way she was in it. As far as he knew, Gracie hadn't set foot in Diablo Springs in seventeen years.

"Do we know who's dead yet?" Zach asked.

"Give it a break, Zach," Reilly said.

Chloe waited for him to open the door, making it clear that it was by her decree he entered first. That too pissed him off. He didn't like people making decisions for him. Never had.

Frowning, he rapped on the door, waited, knocked again. When no one answered he tried the knob. He hadn't expected it to be locked and it wasn't. Diablo Springs wasn't the kind of place anyone robbed. If the residents had anything worth stealing, they would have long since sold it to get out of town.

The door swung silently open. Somewhere behind them, not far from the ruins, lightning struck with a crack and a hiss, releasing a torrent of raindrops that finally broke through the vapors. It seemed they should sizzle as they hit the brimstone below. That was all the invitation any of them needed to get inside.

They filed through the door in twos, like kids using the buddy system for their field trip. Reilly dropped his bags and closed the door.

Every light in the house seemed to be on, but there was no sign of life anywhere. Reilly called out, "Is anyone home?" but only his echoing voice bounced back to answer.

"God, it's hot in here," Zach said.

"The Lord's name is not an epithet," the priest said, giving Zach a look that might possibly turn him to stone.

Reilly didn't wait to hear what Zach had to say in return. He advanced into the sitting room in front of him, feeling like he was stepping back in time.

"It has changed, no? Since the last time you were here?" Chloe's voice came deep and melodic.

"I only made it past the porch once."

"But you would have seen had it been this?"

He had to say he would have.

He remembered the house as being bright and cheery, TV-mom clean and neat. There'd been a serviceable sofa of everyday blue and a matching chair in front of a console television set. Nondescript, outdoorsy paintings had adorned the walls and blue-checked curtains covered the windows.

All of that was gone now. A scene from the old West had taken its place.

He'd told Zach the truth. The Diablo had once been a saloon as well as a house of ill repute. Scars on the floor defied the renovation from saloon to boardinghouse by clearly marking the path the large bar must have taken in front of the western wall. He wondered why Carolina had never had it repaired. Even though the bar and stools and tables were gone, Reilly could still picture what it must have looked like all those years ago, filled with smoke and drunks and cowboys shooting the moon.

To the right were stairs leading up to the bedrooms. Straight ahead was a swinging door into the kitchen. The décor now leaned heavily to Victorian—as ironic as it was fitting. Chintz upholstery and tiny crystal lamps communed in front of the stone fireplace. Dainty tables on spindly legs displayed doilies and ornately framed pictures. The wood was dark, the curtains heavy, and the atmosphere cloying.

"Wow," Zach said, coming to stand at his elbow. "This is some place. It still looks like a whorehouse."

Chloe's expression tightened and her eyes narrowed. "If I were not a woman of honor, I would be hexing you young man."

Zach waved his hands in mock terror. Chloe turned her back to him and advanced into the room. Her black sneakers brushed the floor in an eerie whisper.

Ignoring her, Reilly moved deeper into the sitting area,

still picturing how it must have looked a hundred years ago, filled with unsavory men and sleazy women.

"Who do you think all these pictures are of?" Zach asked, circling around behind Reilly—giving Chloe a wide berth despite his show of mockery.

Reilly stared at the yellowed photographs in their antique frames, not recognizing anyone.

"Think they're the whores?" Zach whispered so Chloe wouldn't hear.

An old-fashioned portrait hung above the enormous stone mantel on the fireplace. In it, four women sat at a table in front of a bar. Sunlight spilled through the cloudy windows and pinned them all in place like butterflies on a board. Beyond their circle of light, a scattering of dusty and disreputable men watched, as if picture-taking were the most interesting thing to behold. A large black woman stood in the background, her eyes cold even from the distance.

The women in the center seemed to be in various stages of dress and of different ethnic backgrounds. A pale and freckled young woman stood between two other girls, both creamy dark with liquid eyes. None of them looked old enough to be in such a profession. The last sat in the center, features unremarkable except for her light eyes, which looked nearly translucent in the faded picture. Though she was as young as the others, she looked out of the glass with a steady, weighted stare. A woman, not a girl.

There was something hauntingly familiar about her but it took a full minute before he realized what it was. She looked like Gracie Beck. She looked a *lot* like Gracie Beck.

He stared at the picture as a knot of conflicting emotions tangled inside of him. He didn't feel Chloe approach until her breath fanned over him. "Do you know why you're here?"

Like a spider, her words crept across his skin. He jumped and brushed at his ear, turning to face her angrily.

"I know I'm getting sick of this little guessing game of yours." He'd been raised to respect his elders, and his sharp tone embarrassed him, but Chloe LaMonte would try the patience of a saint and Reilly was hell and gone from sainthood. He wanted to get away from her. Suddenly he wanted to get away from *here* regardless of the fact that he had come by his own free will. The air was thick and muggy, the storm loud and isolating.

"I'm going to open some windows," he said, despite the storm, despite the fact that outside was nearly as hot as in. Easier said than done, however. He tried one, then another, but neither would budge. Frustrated, he moved to a third when a loud whirring came an instant before the sound of air blowing through a vent.

Air-conditioning. Miracles did happen. He looked around for the thermostat and found it by the kitchen door. It seemed anachronistic in its surroundings, but Reilly was relieved it existed at all. He crossed to the control, nearly laughing when he saw it fixed at ninety-five. Leave it to Carolina Beck to install air, but refuse to keep it turned low enough to cool. He moved the lever to sixty-five, hoping she wouldn't go nuts when she found out. *Sorry, Carolina, but this is hard enough without being steamed alive.*

The sound of a siren approaching startled the entire group. Zach went to the window and looked out.

"There's a police car out there," he said.

Reilly opened the door and watched a uniformed man step from his car and hurry up to the porch. When the officer raised his head and looked at Reilly, his mouth fell open.

"Son of a bitch," he said.

Reilly silently echoed that. Though a couple of years younger, Reilly knew him well. It was a small town and they'd all gone to school together. Eddie Rodriguez had been a local hero, star athlete, and, last Reilly heard, he'd been given a scholarship to UCLA. Eddie should have escaped Diablo Springs long ago. But here he was with a sheriff's uniform and a shiny badge.

"How the hell are you?" Eddie said.

It seemed a ridiculous question after the bizarre night and Reilly couldn't help the humorless laugh he gave. "Well I could use a drink."

"You and me both, but I'm here on business. Mind telling me what you're doing here?"

The direct switch from personal to professional threw Reilly off, but he recovered and said, "Actually, I'm trying to figure that one out myself." Reilly's answer came across more insolent than he'd intended. But why was it Eddie's business what he was doing there?

Eddie's friendliness seemed to fade a bit as he looked past Reilly to Chloe and the others. "You with them?"

Chloe stepped forward and stopped at Reilly's side, setting her hands on his arm in a proprietary manner. "Rather, we are with him."

"No," Reilly said. "You're not."

Chloe smiled. "Nathan is looking for his next story. He thinks he'll find it here."

Eddie's eyes narrowed at that. "What makes you think so, Reilly?"

"Wait a minute. Rewind. They"—he jerked his thumb at the small group—"are the story. I mean, look at them."

Only the priest appeared to be offended by the comment.

"We have reservations, Officer," Chloe said, looking concerned and anxious—two things Reilly knew she wasn't.

"That may be, but chances are you'll need to find another place in the morning. Carolina Beck died tonight. We found her body out by the ruins."

Reilly heard the news, but couldn't quite process it. He looked at Chloe and she stared back, pulling him into the deep wells of her eyes, pulling him into the subtle blackness at their core. She'd known.

"That's not all we found, either," Eddie said. "I'll be damned if I can explain it, but that's not all."

Chloe's eyes glimmered and a sad smile curved her pink lips. The question formed in Reilly's mind, filling him with an unsettling mix of curiosity and outrage. What else did she know? But before he could ask, the front door swung open with a bang and a burst of rain. A woman rushed through.

Reilly stared as the night surpassed strange and hit downright unbelievable. It was Gracie Beck.

She'd always been tiny—even before he'd filled out and shot up to his six-two height, the top of her head had barely reached his chin. She was still small, but age had rounded the sharp angles of her shoulders, added fullness to her breasts, smoothed the slope to her waist. She wore khaki capris that followed the curve of her legs and a black T-shirt. Reilly's eyes were drawn to the rain-soaked fabric pulled gently across her breasts. He could just make out the faint outline of a lace bra.

She still didn't look like she could live off the land for more than a day or two, but there was flesh now, where once there'd been little but skin and bones. Her soft brown hair was drawn back in a ponytail, but a few wisps escaped to frame her face. The eyes were still gray, the color of a turbulent ocean, overflowing with the kind of secrets that would drive a man insane with wanting to know. But gone was the cocky defiance that had marked Gracie Beck from the cradle. Gone was the devil-may-care smile that had teased him into wet dreams as teen. In its place was a somberness that had no place on a mouth so soft.

She scanned the room quickly, eyes widening as they moved from one stranger to another. She frowned when she saw Reilly—as if finding him among this group of misfits was the most incredible of all. He knew how she felt.

"What . . ." she began.

And then she saw Eddie and dismissed them all without a word.

She crossed to the sheriff's side, grabbed his arm, and demanded, "Where is she?"

chapter five

IT had felt like the dead of night when Gracie pulled into town. She'd bypassed Diablo Springs' tiny municipal building, which was dark and still. From the corner she'd seen the Diablo, lit up like Christmas morning, and the patrol car parked in front, bubble light swirling red and blue against the night. She'd stepped inside the front door expecting to find Eddie Rodriguez waiting, but what met her eyes was something entirely different.

For a moment an utter sense of displacement stopped her. Nothing was the same. Not the furniture, the pictures, the curtains. Not the strangers crowded inside. She tried to sort through her confusion as she stared at the clustered group of people. A man who looked as if he'd neglected to remove his Dracula costume after Halloween, an older, light-skinned woman wearing an African turban, and a priest of all things. Rounding out the group was a young man with the classic good looks of a model or an actor. And, nearby, most bizarre of all, Reilly Alexander.

"What . . ." She couldn't even think of what she wanted to ask. It was like a nightmare that kept morphing from one psychotic scenario to another.

She shook her head and fixed her attention on Eddie. He, at least, was supposed to be here. "Where is she? Where is my daughter?" she asked. Her voice cracked with the necessity of asking.

"She's fine, Gracie," Eddie said, taking her shoulders in his reassuring hands. "Dr. Graebel checked her out. She has a bump on her head and she's shook up, but no permanent damage. He's got her over at the clinic and is going to bring her here as soon as he gets the boy settled in."

The boy? Brendan? Brendan brought her here. Why?

"How is he?"

"Hard to say. Doc's got some tests going—he isn't conscious yet, but so far Doc can't figure out why. I'm sure he'll tell you when he gets here with Analise."

"I'll go get her," Gracie insisted. "I don't want to wait to see her."

"Gracie, she'll be here in a few minutes."

From the porch she heard her dogs barking like maniacs. She'd tied them there before coming in. Gracie pivoted and stepped outside.

"Tinkerbelle, Juliet, heel."

Both dogs obeyed immediately, sitting with ears pricked and shamed faces. Romeo trotted to her side and sat on his hind legs.

"Stay," Gracie commanded them and they contritely did as they were told. The three tracked her with their eyes as she left the porch, but neither moved so much as a hair.

When she came back inside, it seemed like the whole room had responded to the authority of her voice. The priest and the good-looking young guy both stood attentively. The old woman was smiling at her, though Gracie didn't know why. Dracula waited close at her shoulder, protective as any watchdog she'd ever seen. Reilly was beside Eddie, watching her like she was a ghost.

Gracie wanted to ask about her grandmother, but not with an audience, especially one as strange as this group. In fact, why were they here? Why were they all gathered by the door at this late hour?

"Eddie," she said, lowering her voice and turning her back to them. "Who are all these people? What are they doing in the Diablo?" In the middle of the night, dressed for a masquerade?

Eddie looked blankly back. "Your guess is as good as mine. Reilly brought them."

Reilly'd had his mouth open since she'd walked through the door. Eddie's comment shut it.

Gracie hadn't seen Reilly since she'd left Diablo Springs. He was taller now, more broad-shouldered and narrow-hipped—a bigger man than she'd remembered him being—but she could have picked him out of a crowd. Sure, he was a little older, a little harder. A lot less boy, a lot more man. He wore a sleeveless T-shirt that showed a golden tan and the thick corded muscles of his arms and shoulders, faded Levi's, and flip-flops. A Chinese symbol was tattooed on his right forearm, and a series of them made a chain around his left bicep. His hair was just shy of shaved and a five o'clock shadow darkened his jaw.

The sight of him slammed into her already overloaded emotions. He was like the song that would forever remind you of a tragedy. Where were you when the earth stopped turning? Standing face-to-face with Reilly Alexander, she thought.

If it wasn't for her concern about Analise, the news of her grandmother's death, and the unfolding drama of this never-ending night, she couldn't have looked him in the eye. But it seemed that tonight she was insulated by shock and grief. Nothing could surprise her. At least that's what she thought until the spry old woman opened her mouth.

"The sheriff is right, Gracie Beck. We are here for Nathan," she said. "He's looking for a story."

"A story?" Gracie repeated, not following the mysterious woman's meaning. Frowning, she turned to Reilly, who looked like a bad boy caught peeking up the teacher's dress.

"I—" he began, but the woman cut him off.

"You see, your grandmother had a very strong spirit. She called to me. I, in turn, called to Nathan."

To the best of Gracie's recollection, Reilly hadn't been called Nathan by anyone but his mother, ever. So who was this woman? And what was her connection to him?

"I'm sorry. How rude of me not to tell you," she said, answering the question that Gracie had yet to voice. "My name is Chloe LaMonte. And these are my disciples."

"*I* am not a disciple," the priest said. "I am clairvoyant, but not a follower of spiritual sacrilege."

Chloe ignored him and went on. Her voice was clear and strong, tinged with a compassion that seemed misplaced, considering her motives. "We have been studying Diablo Springs for sometime now. There is a psychic phenomenon here that is beyond anything I've ever experienced. It's incredible, really. Like a vibration. I'm surprised even you can't feel it."

The "even you" comment irritated Gracie, but she was too tired to react. Too tired to even feign politeness. She turned abruptly away from Chloe and asked, "What about Grandma Beck, Eddie?"

Eddie glanced over her head at the group of people. "Maybe you folks could find your rooms?"

"Rooms? They're staying here?"

Chloe answered, "We have reservations."

"Gracie," Reilly said. "I'm sorry about this. I didn't know you'd be here. I didn't know about your grandma."

"How could you? It only happened tonight."

"She knew," the good-looking young man said, pointing at Chloe.

Reilly touched Gracie's arm and nodded toward the closed kitchen door. "Why don't we go in the kitchen? I'll try to explain"—he looked at the group in the living room—"this."

Gracie gave a curt nod and motioned for Eddie to follow. Stepping onto the porch, she untied the dogs, who dutifully trailed her to the kitchen. The small group in the front room parted for them to go by. Knowing how sweet the Great Dane and Labrador-mix dogs were, Gracie sometimes forgot just how intimidating and *big* the animals were. The expressions on the nervous visitors' faces as they passed were a quick reminder.

Before they took their seats, she addressed Tinkerbelle and Juliet.

"Friend," she said.

The dogs scanned back and forth between Reilly, Eddie, and Gracie, their expressions seeming to say, "We don't think so."

"Friend," she repeated, then gave Reilly a brief hug,

feeling unbelievably self-conscious as she came into contact with the warmth of him. The hug she gave Eddie was more heartfelt. He patted her on the back and pressed a kiss to her hair, murmuring how good it was to see her, under any circumstances. Satisfied, the dogs relaxed beneath the table, but Reilly didn't look anywhere near at ease with their watchful eyes following him.

Gracie sat down next to him and Romeo hopped in her lap.

"Why are you and those people here?" she said.

Reilly exhaled heavily and shook his head. Then, with obvious reluctance, he told them about his signing and Chloe's approach.

"I couldn't believe she'd know your grandmother. Chloe's . . . out there. And Carolina was as down to earth as they come."

"So you just jumped in your car and followed that woman here?" Gracie said.

Reilly nodded his head, but she sensed he wasn't telling her the truth. Not all of it anyway. No surprise there.

"You drove all that way for a story?"

"Well—"

Furious, Gracie stood. "Well I hope my grief makes good copy." He opened his mouth to say more but Gracie held up a hand. "I'm going to see if I can find my grandmother's reservation book. If I can't, I don't care if it's the storm of the century out there. All of you are gone."

She stomped out of the kitchen. As if attracted by the radiation of her anger, the lunatics in the front room turned and watched her pass. On the table in the entry was the leather-bound book Grandma Beck had always used to record the comings and goings of the Diablo's temporary residents. Gracie opened it and fanned the pages until she came to the last with writing on it.

There, under a page with today's date, was Grandma Beck's scrawl. *Bill Barnes, all rooms.* Then after that, *Sold Out!* Underscored twice. And then in small penciled-in numbers, as if it were a secret mission, she'd written, *Paid in advance. Check with bank. Wire transfer??? Full price.*

Damn it. Worse than reservations, they'd already paid. And they'd filled every room, which meant Gracie and Analise, when she finally got there, would be sharing quarters in Grandma Beck's room.

Reluctantly, she faced the group watching her. "Who is Bill Barnes?"

Dracula stepped forward. Surely not?

"She didn't take credit cards, so I had Bill wire the payment to her bank account," Chloe said. "She was very suspicious about it."

"Why didn't you just pay her when you got here?"

"Because I knew you'd throw us out."

Chloe's dark voice and unsettling declaration sent a deep unease through Gracie. She didn't like Chloe La-Monte. Not at all.

"I still might."

"No, you won't. Not in good conscience and you are a person guided by your conscience."

Gracie wanted to spite this woman and damn the consequences, but Chloe cut her off before she could form thought into action. "She called to us," Chloe said softly. Again Gracie heard that ring of compassion. "All the way across the desert, we heard her. All of us."

"All of you?" Eddie repeated, staring from one face to another.

"She is angry."

Gracie was angry too. How dare this woman come here with all this mumbo jumbo gibberish?

"Listen, I don't know who you are or what—"

"I am Chloe LaMonte," she said patiently. "A vessel of the spirits. I am here to help your grandmother find peace and move on."

"My grandmother is dead. She doesn't need your help." Gracie was shaking with anger.

Bill Barnes touched Chloe lightly on the arm and murmured something in her ear. Chloe nodded. "You're right, Bill." She looked at Gracie. "We think it's best if we discuss this in the morning. Would you be so kind as to tell us what rooms we're in?"

Gracie glared at her, wishing with all her might that she could tell them to take a hike, but the rain was hammering down now, coming in sluices that roared through the rain gutters on the roof. Thunder shook the house as the wind rattled the windows. And Chloe was right, she was a woman guided by her conscience, damn her. She'd have to be heartless to send them out in this when she knew there wasn't another place to stay for at least fifty miles, and she was too exhausted to be heartless tonight. But that didn't mean she'd be nice.

"Up the stairs and to the right. To the left are family quarters. Stay out of those."

With that she turned on Eddie who stood just outside the kitchen, Reilly at his side. The dogs remained where she'd left them, but they were on their feet and watching through the open door.

"Eddie, it's been more than a few minutes. Where is Analise?"

As if in answer, headlights shot through the windows and climbed the walls as a car approached. Gracie went to the porch and stared through the pouring ran as Dr. Graebel got out and ran around to the other side. Sheltering his passenger, he hurried them both up to where she waited. When he lowered the umbrella, Analise stepped forward into her mother's waiting arms.

chapter six

May 1896
Somewhere in Colorado

THE first scream carried across the plains like the howl of
an October wind. It brought my head up and around. I was
on all fours, trying to pull some deadwood free from a tan-
gle of roots. As the sound settled around me, I perched up
on my knees like a prairie dog to see over the waving sea
of grass, but that didn't help much. All I saw was more of
the same.

I figured it must have been a crow or buzzard I'd heard.
There'd been plenty of each on the way, and I hated them
both. In fact, today I hated just about everything and everyone.

I'd been mad for days, ever since my daddy came home
and said we were pulling up roots and running away. He
hadn't said "running," but that's what it was all the same. I
wasn't old enough to argue, but I was old enough to be mad
about it. I hadn't even gotten to say good-bye to Charlotte or
Willie Johnson, who'd been acting like he might want to be
more than friendly with me. Seventeen was only old enough
to do a woman's share of chores, not speak my mind.

The fact that we were running like cowards bothered me
as much as anything. I'd begged my daddy not to testify in
court about the holdup, but of course he didn't listen. Men.
The bank sure didn't deserve his loyalty, but he'd given it
all the same. And look how it had paid him back. Momma
had tried to sway him as well, but then he'd gone all
Stonewall and decided that, as the man of the house, he'd
say where and what and why things got done. Even at my
age, I was woman enough to know life wasn't fair.

We were five days from Alamosa now, and I was still madder than a hornet. I didn't like walking day in and day out. My momma looked like she was carrying a litter of babies, though we both prayed just one would come out. Even though her ribs must have felt like they were ready to burst, Momma still took in the scenery like she'd been blessed to even step foot on God's green earth. I couldn't see it that way. Not when I was sleeping on the hard ground with bugs sure to be creeping and crawling over me all night and my bed at home as empty and neat as could be.

I picked up another stick, shifting the bundle in my arms and giving myself a splinter in the process. That only spurred my mad.

And then I heard the next scream.

This time, there wasn't any doubt. That was no bird. I rocked back on my heels, looking over the swaying seed-pods toward our camp on the other side of the hill. The sun arced low in the sky, dragging shadows out with the wind. A gun fired, and an instant later a gray puff of smoke wafted upward.

I scrambled to my feet, dropping the wood I'd been gathering as I raced without thought toward the sound. More gunshots cracked the dusky blue day, followed by a triumphant whoop of glee that made my blood run cold. Indians? Was it Indians?

I dropped to my knees at the top of the hill and scooted up to look over. My skirts tangled about my legs and ripped when I didn't heed them. Belly flat to the earth, I peered down at our camp. Five men on horseback rode circles around it, firing pistols into the air just for the fun of it, I guessed. Not Indians. These were white men, men who looked like they'd not seen a bath for many years. They seemed to be playing a game of some sort, turning and riding and darting around. I couldn't see beyond the wagon, though, to what was at the center of their sport. I cupped my hands to my eyes to block the glare of the setting sun and searched for my momma and daddy, grandma and brother. Had they gone to gather wood or hunt? Were these bandits robbing us while they were gone? But even as I thought it, I recognized the flaw in my thinking. It was Momma I'd heard scream. I was sure of it.

The men down below laughed and shouted happily to one another as they raced around. I made my eyes squinty, trying to make out features through the dirt and dust that caked their faces. Who were they? Why were they here?

I scanned the far hillside, praying the rest of my family was there, on the other side, watching with the same horror I was. Over the fire, a pot of stew Momma had set to cook still hung and the fresh breeze brought the smell of it to me.

Momma, where are you?

Johnny's toys lay atop the quilt Momma and I had sewn when he was born. Beyond that . . .

A wave of sickness hit me. Beyond Johnny's blanket, Grandma's wheelchair lay on its side, wheels peeking out from behind the crates we'd unloaded when we set camp. I stared, one part of my mind jamming like gears in a windmill as another part spun out of control. Why was Grandma's wheelchair all tipped over? And where was Grandma?

A rider suddenly charged up the hill, and I quickly ducked down.

He shouted out to the others. "Lonnie, Jake, come on. Let's git."

"Ain't done," one of them hollered back. "Not by far we ain't. And I'm hungry. I'm going to sit me down and have some of this fine stew Mrs. Beck done cooked up for us."

The rider muttered something and then reined his horse around.

Lonnie . . . Jake . . .

I flattened myself to the earth, inhaled the dark scents of dirt and worms, and tried to batten down my fear. Lonnie and Jake . . . The Smith brothers. I bit hard on my lip to keep from crying out. The brothers were identical twins, just a year older than my seventeen, and they were murderers. Cold-blooded murderers. Last month my father had stood as the only witness to their thievery and murderousness and convinced a jury to hang the two men.

A movement from the opposite hillside caught my eyes. Daddy and Johnny, running toward the wagon. My daddy held his rifle in one hand, Johnny clung to the other. They'd heard the gunshots, as I had, but from their angle, they couldn't see the men, now gathered at the fire. I wanted to stand up and shout, wave my arms and warn them, but if I did . . .

My daddy's footsteps slowed as he stared at something out of my sight. What? What did he see? He stilled, Johnny at his side, and stared. Just stared.

Then slowly he pushed Johnny back, pointed at a boulder. Johnny didn't want to do what Daddy ordered. I could see it in his posture. In the defiant tilt of his head. He was eight, but tried to act eighteen. At last he crouched down where he'd been told and Daddy cocked his rifle and advanced on the camp.

No, I breathed. No, Daddy.

One of the men, maybe Lonnie, maybe Jake, looked up, as if sensing the approach. He reached for his gun and pulled it free of the holster. In my mind I could hear the metal clear the leather. Time seemed to slow down. I felt each beat of my heart, watched paralyzed as my daddy advanced on the gang. What could I do? If I stood, they'd kill me. I knew they would. But if I didn't, my daddy would certainly die. I tried to make my legs move. Tried to get to my feet. But I was frozen, flattened on the hillside like one of the stones beside me.

The man with the gun sidled up to the wagon and then peeked around. Daddy saw, took aim, and fired. The shot splintered into the wagon and sent wood shards flying in all directions. It made a loud boom that echoed across the open plains and hills. A yelp broke from my lips, but I clapped a hand over my mouth to mute it. The man with the gun howled and grabbed at his eye.

Fast as lightning the other men reached for their weapons and rounded the wagon. Daddy got off another shot, but that was all. The four men fired with abandon and my scream lodged in my throat as Daddy's body danced with the impact. They riddled him full of lead, moving forward as they fired like the mindless killers they were. The sloping foothills around me sucked up the sound and threw it back in resounding echoes that seemed to pierce through me. I covered my ears and shut my eyes, but I couldn't block out the sound or the tears squeezing through my tightly closed lids. I couldn't erase the image of my father's body jumping in a death jig of gunfire. Suddenly the shots stopped. I opened my eyes. Daddy lay still and broken on the ground, arms and legs askew in angles no arms or legs were ever meant to be. One of the outlaws raised his pistol and put a final shot in his head.

I prayed as hard as I could that Johnny would remain behind his rock. But even as the sobbing plea lodged in my throat, I saw Johnny emerge from his craggy hiding place, heard his scream, a tormented sound filled with more humiliation, anger, and agony than a child could ever endure.

To my horror, Johnny broke from behind the boulder and charged across the clearing. The sound he made matched the anguish trapped inside my breast. His screams reached up to the heavens and tore a hole in them. But they didn't stop what came next. The army of four turned like soldiers and opened fire.

"No," I cried. Yet the word came dry and silent, a fiery whisper that burned and crackled in my throat. "No," I tried again, but it was too late. Now both my daddy and brother lay flat on the ground in a twist of blood and gore. The same filthy killer who'd put his gun to Daddy's head now did the same to my brother. The vibration of the shot traveled through me like a quaking of the earth. Hot tears streamed down my face, but still, I couldn't move.

The man twirled his pistol like a gunslinger, grinned at his friends, and then joined them back at the fire. They ransacked the kitchen crates for plates and spoons, laughing as they scooped Momma's stew onto their dishes. They sat in a circle, joking and laughing as they fed themselves, ignoring completely the crumpled, bloody bodies of Daddy and

Johnny. I watched it all, shaking with disbelief and sobs as silent as my screams.

I scanned the craggy knolls around me, looking for Momma. Where was she? Hiding? Or didn't she know? Maybe she was close to the river? There, the shots might not have been heard. How would I face her when she came back to find her husband and son murdered while I'd done nothing to help?

I begged God for forgiveness I didn't deserve while I watched the men and tried not to think of why Grandma's wheelchair was overturned, where Momma might be, or the poor wasted bodies of my little brother and beloved daddy. The horrible men glutted themselves on the stew for interminable minutes, and then one of them moved to the back of the wagon and urinated on Grandma's wheelchair. This, this horrible act of disrespect finally loosed my immobile limbs. I stood without thinking, but then another man's head whipped around, and I dropped to my belly with such force I knocked the breath from my lungs.

Excited voices came and then the sound of horses. They'd seen me.

On all fours I scrambled down the hill, trying at once to keep low and move fast. I looked behind and saw that the grass was flattened where I'd lain on it. In a full panic I stood straight, hiked up my skirts, and tore across the open grassland. Ahead were bushes and beyond a smattering of pine trees leading into the foothills. I made it to the first of them just as the men crested the hill behind me. My heart hammered against my ribs and my constricted lungs fought to bring in air. Silently I crept back and back until I reached a tree with low branches. I crawled beneath the skirt of its boughs and then up two, three limbs. Overhead the branches grew tight as a cage. I could go no higher. I stayed as still as I could, peering through the pine needles. The wind teased through the trees, disguising my movements. The riders came down the hill, following the tracks I'd left until they reached the place where I'd stood and run. From that point they worked their way back and forth, bickering as they rode, one calling the other stupid, the other retorting in kind.

They entered the trees and circled between the pines. I stood still as time, waiting for them to see me. The man my daddy had hit with the splinters from the wagon stopped at the tree next to the one where I hid. The side of his face was puffy and bloody, the eyelid swollen nearly shut. Still, if he moved, if he looked straight on . . .

My heart thudded in my chest, and the terror I'd held down threatened to swoop up and out in a never-ending scream of fear and pain. My eyes streamed with the effort to be silent, to be still. The man coughed and spat, his face coming up and around to where I huddled. I closed my eyes and silently whispered my last plea for forgiveness.

"Jake!" one of the others shouted. "Anything?"

To my left, Jake answered, but I dared not turn my head to look. I dared not move. Another of them shouted something from beyond the trees.

"She's gone," the bloodied man beside me said. "I say let's git too. Ain't nothing she can do out here but die."

The truth of that added another layer to my horror.

The four of them gathered close to the trees, and I trembled with the effort to remain motionless. They conferred for a moment that lasted so long my hands felt numb and my legs weak. And then single-file they rode out. As the last man spun his horse around, I caught one clear look at him.

It was Lonnie Dean Smith all right.

I bit hard on my lip, choking back the sob. I stayed where I was until they'd left the cove, until they'd ridden up and over the ridge. Unmoving I stared at their tracks. Is that how they'd found my family? Followed our tracks from our front door? But how were they free? I'd seen the brothers taken away in handcuffs to await their execution. How were they here when they should be in jail? Locked up. Ready to hang?

My daddy had known they'd break free. He'd known that they'd come for him. That's why he'd wanted us to leave as we had, in the dead of the night with only a wagon full of possessions. Daddy had known the Smith brothers wouldn't hang. He'd known they'd hunt for him. He hadn't known how quickly, though, or with what determination.

The horses were on the move again, and I cowered in the pine as they passed back down the valley toward the trees where I hid. They came close enough that I could have reached out and touched them as they passed by. The last man towed Daddy's two horses behind him. Both animals were ladened with supplies they'd pilfered.

I made myself as small as I could, waiting for the moment they would see me. The earth shook as they rode past and then quieted as they continued onward. Warily I looked after them. A dust cloud followed them up the next hill and then they disappeared down the other side.

Branches pulled at my hair and snagged my clothes as I scurried down from the tree. My hands were sticky with sap, and my arms were scratched and bleeding. I hit the ground, wiggled out from under the boughs, and then raced toward the camp, silent lest my voice carry and bring them back. Great billowing waves of black smoke rose up from the valley where we'd stopped. As I reached the hilltop, I saw our wagon ablaze and all our things burning like midnight torches. I half-ran, half-stumbled down the other side to the inferno.

"Momma!" I shouted. My daddy and brother still lay where they'd been gunned down. I ran to them, touching their bloodied and broken bodies with shaking hands. Most of Johnny's face had been blown away, half of Daddy's head. There would be no miracle of survival for either.

I stood, my hands red with their blood. "Momma!" I cried again. "Grandma!"

No one answered. Holding my apron up to my face, I circled the hot flames to the place where I'd seen my grandmother's wheelchair. Now I saw what had been hidden before, my grandmother's wasted body, bloody with gunshots, sprawled on the ground. I dropped to my knees beside her, sobbing, my eyes streaming with tears from grief and pain and smoke. The ground near Grandma's gray hair was wet, and I realized with sickening rage that the man I'd seen had been urinating not on Grandma's chair, but on her body.

"No!" I screamed at the sky.

I still hadn't found my mother. Quickly I stood and hurried to the far end of the wagon, where the smoke was like a black wall holding me back. I saw a foot sticking out from behind the wheel. Dropping to my hands and knees I crawled under the smoke to where my mother was sprawled in the dirt. Her dress was ripped down the front, her swollen, pregnant belly sticking up to the sky, her skirts bunched to her waist, her privates exposed and legs splayed at an awful angle. She'd taken a bullet to the head and another to her stomach. Sobbing, I smoothed my mother's clothes down to cover her nakedness. I collapsed on the ground next to her and curled myself into a tight ball of misery. I didn't know what do. I wiped my tears with my bloody hands and cried out at the pain that burned inside me. I was covered in blood, but I was alive when everyone I loved was dead.

The wagon, weakened by fire, gave an ominous groan, lilted to the right, and then shuddered in warning. Before I understood what that meant, it collapsed on top of my mother's body. I scrambled back just in time to avoid being crushed by burning wood.

They were all dead. Everyone but me, who'd been too cowardly to save them. I wanted to curl up and die beside them, let the fires burn away my anguish, but I was too yellow for even that. I scooted back as the flames burned hotter and higher. My eyes streamed, my lungs burned, and my heart ached. Then the wind shifted, and the flames moved to the long grasses on the outskirts. In a blink they caught like tinder and exploded into an inferno. I stood as the wind swept the fire along, realizing in moments I'd be trapped.

Instinct kicked in when the urge to survive did not. Keeping my apron to my face, I moved to the railings at the back of the wagon where my daddy kept one shotgun hidden and loaded for me and my mother. She'd probably been going for it when the Smith riders attacked. I didn't have time to search for more bullets. From my father's dead body, I took his heavy hunting knife. And then my feet were moving away as my mind stayed with my family.

The fire chased me, happily making sport of this run for

my life. With each pounding step, I thought of my mother, my brother, my father, my grandmother. Their names alternated in my mind, keeping time with my steps. My chest felt as if it were held tight in a vise, a clamp determined to squeeze the air from my lungs and the blood from my heart. I raced to the shallow river and splashed across, the wet cold bringing me from shock into the full realization that whether I lived or died depended on what I did next.

chapter seven

DR. GRAEBEL gave Gracie a very detailed report. Her daughter had been in a motor vehicle accident, but seemed to have been extremely lucky to have walked away with very few injuries. She had scratches and a bump on her head they'd want to watch, but other than that she was fine. Gracie didn't accept the doctor's diagnosis until she'd held Analise and inspected her injuries herself. He was right, though. Analise seemed unharmed, just shaken by the experience. She kept apologizing, for being there or for something else, something worse. Gracie didn't know. But tonight wasn't the time to question her. Not when they were all so tired and anxious. Gracie couldn't stop hugging her, kissing her, telling her she loved her. And for the first time in a long time, Analise let her.

Arms around her daughter's shoulders, Gracie made her way into the front room and sat on the love seat beside Analise. The psychics were out of sight, upstairs finding their rooms. Their footsteps sounded like an elephant stampede from downstairs. Gracie hoped by some miracle they'd all disappear in the morning. After his quick briefing on Analise's condition, Dr. Graebel left to go back to his other patient, Brendan, who was still under observation. He promised to update them in the morning.

As soon as he was gone, Analise curled into Gracie's body and began to cry. Eddie and Reilly stood by, neither looking like they knew just what to do. The kid with the Hollywood looks inched closer to the two men. A camera hung around his neck and his hands moved up to hold it and then back to his sides several times, as if he were trying to decide whether or not he'd get away with taking a picture. Gracie gave him a hard stare, letting him know in no uncertain terms that he wouldn't.

Reilly seemed to notice her fixated attention and turned to the young man. "Go to bed, Zach."

"But—"

"Go upstairs, find an empty room, and go to bed."

Spoken like a father to an errant child. Zach looked less than willing to go, but finally conceded the stare down and went upstairs.

Gracie brushed the hair back from Analise's face and murmured soothing words to her as she cried. Tears of relief slid down Gracie's cheeks as well as she held her daughter. Only now could she admit to herself just how frightened she'd been.

After a while, Analise's sniffles quieted and Eddie spoke. "Analise, do you think you could talk to us about what happened tonight?"

Her lashes were spiky and her eyes shiny from tears. She looked so young and defenseless that Gracie thought her heart might break. She'd spent her life trying to shelter Analise from pain and fear, yet here she was, captive to both all the same.

"I don't remember what happened," Analise said in a thick voice.

"Why are you here, honey?" Gracie asked, thinking that might be a good place to start.

Analise bit her lip and looked down. "Brendan brought me as a surprise. For my birthday."

"You lied to me about staying with Karen."

Analise nodded. Gracie let it go.

"Why did Brendan think a trip to Diablo Springs would be a birthday surprise?" Eddie asked.

"He knew I was curious about where I came from. Who my dad is." She glanced at Gracie and quickly away.

"But how did he know about Diablo Springs?" Gracie asked, steering away from that topic.

Analise held up her wrist and jingled her bracelet. It had been Gracie's and before that, her mother's and her grandmother's. Gracie didn't really know how old it was, but she'd given it to Analise for Christmas last year. Analise twisted it around until she found the charm she wanted and held it apart from the rest. Gracie felt numb as she stared at the small state of Arizona engraved with the words *Diablo Springs*.

"Brendan said he saw a sign for it the last time he went to Phoenix and he knew it had to be the same place. He said my grandmother lives here. Does she, Mom?"

More tears burned Gracie's eyes. She didn't want to answer that question, but of course, she had to. "Lived. I'm sorry, Analise. She died tonight."

"Tonight?" Analise whispered.

Gracie nodded.

"Where?"

Gracie frowned at the question. "I don't know." She looked at Eddie. "I don't even know what happened to her yet. I don't know how she died."

Eddie avoided her eyes for a moment and sat down opposite them. "Let's start at the beginning," he said.

Frowning, Gracie nodded. Reilly stayed in the background. Gracie glared at him, letting him know that he wasn't welcome. He looked back, unmoving.

"What time did you get here?" Eddie was asking Analise.

Analise sniffed and wiped at her eyes. "I'm not sure. The sun was just setting, though. It got dark really fast. I didn't like it out there, but Brendan had read something about the old hot springs. He was so excited that I didn't want to, you know, be a bummer. Then we . . . then we heard something."

"What?" both Eddie and Gracie asked at the same time.

"I don't know. It sounded like something . . ."

Analise swallowed and tears began to slide down her face again. Gracie could feel her daughter trembling and wrapped her arms around her.

"It's okay. You're safe, honey."

"It sounded like something was in the hole."

"The springs?" Eddie said sharply.

She nodded. "And then Brendan went to look. I told him not to. I was so scared. It was so . . . I told him to come back and then all of a sudden he shouted to run. We got in the truck and started to drive and we saw the lights. We thought it was the town, and we turned, but we couldn't find the way and . . . and . . ."

She glanced from one face to another, as if expecting someone to be able to fill in the blanks for her.

"That's all I remember."

Eddie nodded, looking over her head at Gracie. "You did fine, sweetheart. You did fine."

"I'm so tired."

"We all are. Gracie, why don't you put her to bed then come back down. I still need to talk to you," Eddie said.

Gracie nodded and helped Analise to her feet. "I'm sorry, Mom," she said.

Gracie tried to smile as she led her daughter up the stairs. But she'd lived in Diablo Springs too long not to be shaken by Analise's story. Her daughter had seen the Dead Lights over the springs, that much was certain.

But what had they heard in the dark?

chapter eight

UPSTAIRS in the hallway, Analise said in stage whisper, "Who is that guy with the tattoos, Mom?"

"Someone I used to know."

"Yeah, well he looks at you like he doesn't want to be a 'used to' anymore."

Gracie stopped the, *really?* before it got to her lips—but just barely. Schooling her expression, she said, "No, he doesn't. He looks like that all the time. It doesn't mean anything."

Gracie ignored the glance Analise gave her and kept walking. She paused and took a deep breath as they turned left toward Grandma Beck's room, thoughts of Reilly and how he was looking at her banished. "As unbelievable as it is, turns out Grandma Beck leased all the rooms tonight. We'll have to share hers."

"I don't want to sleep in her room," Analise said, her voice thick with emotion. "She died. Tonight."

"I don't think she died in there, Analise."

"It doesn't matter. I won't sleep there."

Gracie brushed her hair back from her face and counted to ten. The past few hours felt like they'd lasted weeks. "There were only the two rooms up here that were for us," she said wearily. "Hers and mine, and I doubt mine is still kept." She stopped at the door to what was once her bedroom and opened it. Her "See?" died on her lips as she looked inside. The room was exactly as it was when she'd left. Not even dust had moved in to change it. Gracie gripped the door frame, staring at this metaphor for her relationship with Grandma Beck with a feeling akin to dizziness. She'd thrown her out, but preserved the memory of her.

Analise entered with a look of wonder, for the moment her fear forgotten. There were posters of David Bowie, the Go-Go's, and *Dirty Dancing* on the walls and a twin bed with a bright purple comforter butted up to a table in the corner. A picture window overlooked a huge mesquite in the front yard. In the daylight they would be able to see the ruins from here. Now it was just a dark void in the distance. A vinyl beanbag chair sat next to a stereo with a turntable. There was still an album on the post and three stacked beneath. The last she'd listened to was *Scandal.* She remembered singing "Goodbye to You" as she'd stormed from the house. Attached were headphones the size of an airplane operator's. Yearbooks and photo albums stood in line on her bookshelves, along with her favorite stories from kindergarten up. She'd always kept her books. *Green Eggs and Ham* shared a row with *Are You There God? It's Me, Margaret,* and *The Stand.* She'd taken only what she could carry—everything else she'd left behind. Until she walked through the door at that moment, she hadn't realized how much of herself that included.

"I can't believe she kept all this stuff," Gracie murmured.

Analise gave her a troubled look so filled with questions that Gracie couldn't quite meet it. Numb, she led them to the next door. Like the downstairs, Grandma Beck's room was entirely different now. Did it reflect the changes that had gone on in her life after Gracie left? Once it had been bright and airy, holding only an oversized bed with a wicker headboard, matching dresser, and rocking chair by the window. Gracie could picture Grandma Beck in total peace and concentration as she read her steamy romances, rocking away the hours in the quiet and solitude.

Now the room was filled by an enormous mahogany dresser, a chest of drawers, a nightstand, and a rolltop desk. The narrow double sleigh bed seemed disproportionately small compared to the other pieces. A cream chenille bedspread covered it in graceful lines and two rose-colored toss pillows perched on top, but still it seemed to huddle apologetically against the wall. More of the ornate framed pictures of people she didn't know covered every surface of the dresser and chest, layered four and five deep on yellowed doilies. The room smelled of beeswax and roses, smells Gracie would forever associate with her childhood. That, at least, was the same.

"See, it's not big enough for both of us anyway," Analise said.

"Okay. I guess that makes sense," Gracie said, feeling the same irrational reluctance Analise had expressed about sleeping here.

Silently Analise went back into Gracie's old bedroom with Tinkerbelle and Romeo following close at her heels. Both dogs would take up their usual posts at the end of the bed. Tinkerbelle would wait until Analise went to sleep, though, before she made the jump from the floor to the mattress. She thought she was sneaky.

Ever faithful, Juliet followed Gracie back downstairs where Eddie and Reilly waited. The house felt unbelievably hot down here—much warmer than it did upstairs though it should have been the opposite. Or maybe it was her anxiety that made it feel so warm. Her grandma was dead. She didn't even know how yet.

"Can we try to open some windows?" Gracie asked Reilly as she entered the front room. He sat on the couch but looked completely out of place on the floral chintz—a biker in a flower garden. Eddie remained in the same spot as when she went upstairs . . . by the window, watching the storm rage outside.

"Tried that. They're either painted or nailed shut. They wouldn't budge, but I cranked down the air, so it should be cooling off." As he spoke, Reilly stood and moved to a thermostat on the far wall.

"Grandma Beck has air?" Gracie exclaimed. "I don't believe it."

"Would it make it any more believable if I told you she had it set at ninety-five when I walked in?"

The first smile since the nightmare had begun curved Gracie's lips. How typical of Grandma Beck.

Reilly muttered something as he stood in front of the control. "Did you see anyone over here?" he asked Eddie.

Eddie shook his head.

"Well the temp's turned back up. One of Chloe's disciples had to do it. Probably the guy who looks like he's out of blood."

"You talking about Bill Barnes?" Eddie said, looking at his notepad. "He does look like a vampire, doesn't he?"

Gracie took a seat on the sofa and Juliet sat attentively at her feet. She'd agreed to treat the men as friends, but she obviously didn't consider them trustworthy. Smart dog. Where Reilly was concerned, there was no trust.

"Eddie, what happened out there at the springs tonight?" Gracie said.

Eddie took his time responding. He flipped through his notebook, as if he might find the answer written there. Finally, he closed it and stuffed it back in his pocket. "I don't know what happened. All I can tell you is what I saw." He looked at Reilly and then back at Gracie. "You care if he stays?"

"Are you going to write this up in your story?" she asked.

"I'm here as a friend."

"Oh, friends, are we?" She didn't wait for him to reply. "Go ahead, Eddie."

Outside, the storm slammed fiercely into the house, making the hanging pictures tremble against the wall. A thunder and lightning crescendo dragged out the momentum, hushing the room with its ferocity.

"From what I got earlier, your daughter and this Brendan kid arrived just after seven. Mac Conner came out when he saw the sirens and told me he'd seen them drive through town."

Gracie and Reilly looked up in unison, both with the same bemused expression on their faces.

"I'd forgotten what it's like to live in a town so small a strange vehicle is noticed," Reilly said.

Eddie frowned. "Yeah, well. We know our neighbors here."

"No offense intended."

Eddie sniffed. "Mac said they were speeding. That's why he noticed."

"I've talked to Brendan about driving fast," Gracie said. "He doesn't listen. I think teenagers are missing the connection between their ears and their brains."

Reilly stifled a grin but not before Gracie saw it. She didn't have to ask why. She sounded like a mother. Well that was fine. She was a mother.

"The sun set about seven fifteen. I was at the Buckboard, having dinner. At about seven thirty my radio went off. Monica over at the municipal office said Carolina Beck had called in, all upset and shouting. Said there was trouble out at the springs. Said to get my ass out there right now."

"She said that?" Gracie asked. "She said 'ass'?"

"According to Monica she did."

"I never heard her use so much as a 'darn.'"

"Yeah, well . . . who knows. Maybe Monica threw the 'ass' in for effect. However it happened, I jumped in my car and went straight there. That was just about the time the storm blew in. It was lightning like there was a short in the sky. I haven't seen a storm like this in years. Hell, the rain alone is enough to dance about. We're going on a ten-year drought."

"Eddie . . . my daughter?" Gracie prompted before he could go on too long about the drought. She'd heard it enough times to know the subject of drought in a conversation could last almost as long as the drought itself.

He nodded. "When I got there I didn't see anything. Not a damn thing. Then as I was turning, I saw the truck perched at the edge of the ravine where the springs used to be. Lights were out, and it was so dark, I almost missed it. So I backed up and aimed my headlights and that's when I saw your grandma."

At last. Gracie braced herself. "Are you going to tell me what happened to her, Eddie?"

Eddie made a face and scratched the back of his neck,

looking for all the world like he didn't know how or what to say that would describe what happened next.

"Before I could get out of the car, I saw the truck start to rock. Still couldn't see anyone in it, but it looked like it was shaking." He lifted a hand and made a back-and-forth motion. "Then Carolina, she shouts at it. I couldn't hear her over the wind and the thunder, but she was screaming like a banshee. Then right in front of my eyes the lightning just snaked down and got her." He looked up, shaking his head as if he still couldn't believe what he'd seen. "Just nailed her, Gracie. She didn't stand a chance. I came running but there wasn't nothing I could do. By the time I reached her, it was over. She was dead. Then I looked back at the truck and I saw the kids in the front seat. They were staring out and . . ." He paused, his face a picture of utter disbelief. "They weren't looking at me or your grandma. It was like they were looking through us. Like they were seeing something I couldn't. I don't know how else to explain it. I tried to get to them, to get them out, but it was like the wind was against me and lightning was hitting all around. I thought I was going to be laid out next to your grandma in a minute. I could see the kids, though. They just screamed and screamed and then the truck went over." He whistled and made another gesture. "It all happened so fast."

"Oh my God." Gracie whispered. It was almost too horrible to believe. Her grandmother wasn't the first Beck woman to lose her life at the old springs. Gracie's mother had died there when Gracie was just an infant. And now it had nearly taken Analise as well.

"I jumped on the horn and called for help," Eddie was saying, "and then I got my winch and fed it out into the hole."

Eddie stood and paced a few steps. "It was damn quiet down there. Can't explain that right either. It was like being inside a vacuum. I couldn't hear the storm. Couldn't hear the kids. Couldn't hear nothing. Like being in a tomb. I ain't ashamed to tell you I was spooked, 'cuz I sure as shit was."

"How did you get them out?" Reilly asked.

"The truck caught not far from the edge. Don't know how or on what yet, but it was just dangling. I was scared to death I was going to tap it and it would just go. I got to your daughter's side first, Gracie. The boy was unconscious, but she had enough wits left to help me get her out. About that time, backup came and we pulled Brendan up too. That's what happened, I guess. It was just an accident, really. But with your grandma out there struck dead and the kids screaming . . . Well, I guess it kicked my imagination into overdrive. Because it didn't feel like any other accident I've been to, and I've been to a lot, small town or no."

The seriousness of his last words left both Gracie and Reilly silent. She wanted to ask, what *did* it feel like, but the look on Eddie's face was answer enough. He'd been shaken by it, and Eddie Rodriguez was not the kind of man who was easily shaken.

chapter nine

AFTER Eddie left, Reilly and Gracie stood in the entry-way, silent, each absorbing his strange tale. Reilly didn't know what the hell to make of it. Eddie had been freaked out—delusional in Reilly's opinion—scaring himself in the dark like a little girl. For once, though, he'd kept his opinion to himself. He didn't think he'd win any gold stars for his effort, but he didn't get kicked out of the room, either. Small, but a victory all the same.

He took a step forward and the horse-dog pricked its ears, watching him with a predatory look. Now *there* was something to be scared of.

He wanted to talk to Gracie. He wanted to ask about her life, about the years since she'd left Diablo Springs, but he knew this wasn't the time. Still, the questions and the deep desire for the answers gummed up his reactions and made it difficult to know what to say to her right now.

"So," he said after a moment of silence. "What do you think about Eddie's story?"

Gracie shook her head. She looked numb, her eyes glazed, like she'd chased a couple of downers with a beer. "I think I'm too tired to think. This has been the longest day in history."

He nodded. "You look tired. I mean, you look good. But tired."

"You had it right the first time."

"No, really. You look good."

Tired, stressed-out, and road worn, she looked better than most women did fresh and ready to paint the town. Her eyes darkened, as if she'd read his mind, but the look she gave him was cold and angry. He couldn't blame her. A hundred years couldn't erase what he'd done . . . what he hadn't done. He might apologize for it, if he thought it would make a difference. He didn't.

"Your daughter really resembles you," he said.

"I don't think she'd appreciate that, but thank you."

"So where is your husband?"

He'd meant to ask in a more roundabout manner. Maybe start with a casual, *Does she look like your husband?* or *Can you see her father in her?* But somewhere in the passage from thought to words, the question became what it was: blunt and insistent. It was none of his damn business, but when had that ever stopped him?

"I don't have a husband," she said.

And then she turned and began switching off lights, followed closely by her canine sentry. She checked the door and then started up the stairs. End of conversation. He got it.

"It's wild being back here, isn't it?" he said, picking a safer topic as he followed her and the enormous dog up.

She glanced at him from over her shoulder. "It's hell."

There was no subtlety to the subtext that went with her words. Her eyes said it all. She hated his guts and wanted him out of her house. Who could blame her? If he'd known she was going to be here, if he'd known about her grandmother, her daughter, maybe he wouldn't have come. Maybe. But he hadn't known, and now that he was here, now that he'd heard Eddie's wild account of what had happened at the ruins, he had no intention of leaving.

He didn't believe in all the psychic bullshit Chloe was dealing; the only spirits in Diablo Springs were being poured at the Buckboard. Yet, his instincts told him that there was a story here and even though he'd admitted to himself that he was here to settle his past, if he happened to stumble over inspiration and a viable story—hell, he'd take it.

So what if Gracie Beck didn't want him to write it? His name was already blackened as far as she was concerned. Nothing he could do about it now. Obviously she hadn't moved on—honestly, he never thought she would. She had every right to think he was shit. But he was going to stay until he got what he wanted—whatever that might be.

"What happened to your music, your group?" she asked, lowering her voice as they reached the upstairs landing where everyone would be asleep.

He looked up, surprised that she'd known about it, surprised that she'd asked. "Basically we sucked."

"You had one hit."

"*One* being the operative word."

He paused, wavering between letting the casual conversation continue or grabbing the bull by the balls and bringing up the one topic that he knew was on both their minds. He went for the balls.

"Matt's dead."

The look on her face made him wish he'd thought it through better. Well, she had to know, and there was no nice way of saying it. Better to get it out in the open than dance around it for however long they were together.

"He's dead?" Her voice managed to sound injured and impregnable at once.

"Shot himself out at the springs a few months ago."

She didn't say, "good," but she thought it. He knew she thought it. And even though she had the right, it pissed him off. His brother had been an idiot. He'd been selfish and, God help him, he'd done things . . . he'd done horrible things. But he wasn't born that way; he hadn't begun as a monster. There was no explaining that. It sounded like a bleeding-heart excuse even to him. It was the truth, though. The bad in Matt had been forged, not inherent.

"He'd only been back in town for a few weeks. He spent most of the past ten years behind bars." Robbery, assault, parole violations. Matt couldn't live by the rules. He couldn't even acknowledge their existence.

Her eyes widened, but there was no sympathy in them. Again, he didn't expect there to be. Reilly rubbed the back of his neck, looking anywhere but at her face. An awkward pause filled in the shadowed spaces between them. He figured the best thing he could do was leave it at that. But he couldn't. He caught his lower lip between his teeth and glanced up at her from beneath his lashes, still wanting to say something—something that wasn't so damned volatile. But there were no words that could make up for the bad blood between them.

He followed her to a door at the end of the hall where she stopped. The horse-dog waited at her feet, watching him with a cold and steady look.

"Gracie." He reached out as he said her name, but the dog advanced with lightning speed and a low growl. Reilly took a hasty step back.

"Juliet," Gracie reprimanded in a harsh whisper. "No. Friend. Friend."

She stepped forward and wrapped her arms around Reilly's middle in another of the meaningless hugs she'd given him earlier. The warmth of her body came through the light embrace. Her hair smelled of coconut, her skin of something sweet and sensuous, a scent he knew he'd be thinking of long after she left. The tension in her body seemed to travel like a current to his and suddenly he wanted to wrap his arms around her and hold her tight against him. She pulled back, looking at him with a mixture of hurt and anger that somehow he understood.

She let go and went into her room without a word. The horse-dog shot him another dirty look before following. Reilly remained where he was, staring at the painted door as it closed in his face.

"Christ," he muttered in the darkness. He should just cut his losses and get the hell out of Dodge now, before he dug himself any deeper. But he wouldn't. That much he knew for certain.

GRANDMA Beck's inner sanctum was one Gracie had rarely breached in the seventeen years of living here. Carolina Beck had been an intensely private woman, known by all, yet truly known by none, least of all her granddaughter.

As Gracie closed and locked the door, she couldn't help feeling like a trespasser. The room was freezing cold and after the sweltering heat of downstairs it brought gooseflesh to her arms and shivers through her body. She looked around for the vent, thinking this explained why the rest of the house hadn't cooled. Obviously all of the air dropped into this room and went no farther. Maybe if she closed the vent a little, it would force the cool air to the rest of the house. But the outlet had to be behind one of the heavy pieces of furniture, because she couldn't find it anywhere else.

Frowning, she gave up her search. Trying to keep her mind blank, she stripped and remade the bed, pausing for a moment with the old sheets in her hands. They smelled of Avon's Skin So Soft lotion, which her grandmother had used since the beginning of time. The scent pulled her back to when she was young and Grandma Beck had held her and loved her. Tears blurred her eyes as she dumped the sheets in the laundry basket.

The clock on Grandma Beck's nightstand read three a.m. After making up the bed with a clean set of sheets she found in the linen closet, Gracie put on the oversized T-shirt and boxers she slept in and laid down. Juliet circled a few times, looked up sheepishly, and then tried her luck for the end of the bed. Exhausted and still reeling from the traumatizing day, Gracie didn't scold her. Not tonight. Tonight she was grateful for the company.

She reached for the small bedside lamp and paused, hand halfway to the dangling chain, as a trickle of unease slid down her spine. Juliet lifted her head and gave a low growl as Gracie let her gaze slowly track the room. Shadows bathed the corners in twilight and cast stark silhouettes against the bulky furniture. The rain continued to pound the roof and the thunder boomed at irregular intervals. But the room was as still as only the hours after midnight can be.

And yet . . . She sat up, leaving the light on. Her skin pricked, her senses honed in to identify the source of her anxiety. It felt like . . . She was being watched.

Juliet's growl trailed off, but she remained alert, her attention fixed on the corner by the window.

"What do you see?" Gracie breathed.

She slipped from beneath the covers, shivering in the plunging cold of the room. Juliet got to her feet as well, but remained on the end of the bed, still focused on the corner. Standing on the mattress, the dog was nearly as tall as Gracie, and she was comforted by that until Juliet's growl became a snarl full of teeth and menace. What was there? What did Juliet see?

She waited, watching for something to move. This was ridiculous, a squeaky voice in her head tried to insist. She was alone. Yet, the feeling buzzed through her, undeniable. She thought of earlier that night . . . the scream that she'd heard muffled by her bath . . . the eye staring back from the peephole . . . the figure she'd seen under the old eucalyptus tree.

Slowly she circled the room, each footstep eclipsed by her own elongated shadow as it crept across the floor and climbed the walls. She approached the corner that Juliet had under surveillance with something akin to terror. But closer inspection revealed dust and nothing else. Still, she felt the invisible eyes stalking her. She shook her head, silently berating her imagination. But imagined or not, the sensation of being hunted felt real. Suddenly, the hairs at the back of her neck rose, and she pivoted around.

The corner was no longer empty.

Juliet's snarl became a fierce bark as she hurled herself off the bed at the man who'd appeared. In the same instant, Gracie shrieked and tried to run. But her feet tangled in the braid rug and sent her flying into the bed.

Time seemed to slow to each ticking second. The mattress bounced as she fell on it, Juliet's nails clicked wildly against the floor as she lunged for the corner, and the man vanished. Gone in the same heartbeat he'd appeared. Gracie stared at the place where he'd been, unable to process what she'd seen, what was no longer there. Juliet was having the same problem. She circled and sniffed in a frenzy, whining when she found nothing to explain what had happened.

In the next instant the bedroom door flew open. Analise rushed in, her long legs bare beneath the pajamas Gracie had packed for her, followed a step later by Reilly. His shirt was off, the top button of his jeans was undone, and his feet were bare.

"What happened?" he said at the same time that Analise asked, "Are you okay?"

Gracie couldn't catch her breath, let alone answer. She stared at the corner. There was nothing—no one—there now. But there had been. A man. She'd seen him as clearly as she saw the alarmed pair standing in front of her. At the doorway, Chloe and her two disciples gathered with curiosity. Chloe moved to the front, Bill Barnes on her heels. The turban was gone and her white hair stuck up in thin, frizzy tufts. Gracie tacked on ten years to her previous estimate of Chloe's age.

"Mom?" Analise asked, staring at Bill and Chloe with wide eyes. Her shock was no wonder since they'd been upstairs by the time Analise arrived at the house, and no one had bothered to warn her about them.

The fear in Analise's voice brought Gracie back from the edge of her own terror. She looked at the frightened face of her daughter and found her voice. "I'm fine. I tripped on the rug and fell," she said.

"He was here," Chloe whispered, and Gracie could swear she heard fear in her voice.

"Who was here?" Analise asked.

Gracie gave Chloe a pointed look. "Could you excuse us, please?"

Chloe nodded quickly, but she stayed where she was, the yearning to enter too strong to deny. And yet she was afraid. Gracie knew it. Bill pulled her away and guided her and the priest back down the hall. She heard Zach's voice as they met him on the way and Bill telling him to go back to bed.

Gracie tried to smile at her daughter. "Everything's okay," she said. "Those people are Grandma Beck's boarders. You don't have to worry about them."

Analise looked back and forth between the bed, the corner of the room, and the open door.

"Go back to sleep, honey. I'm sorry I shouted—it's been

such a long day I guess my nerves are shot." Analise looked desperate to believe her. "Go on. Tomorrow will be a busy day. We'll check on Brendan first thing. Go to bed."

With a reluctant nod, Analise turned to the door. Before she stepped through she came back and gave Gracie a tight hug. "You get some sleep too."

"What was Chloe talking about?" Reilly asked as Analise shut her bedroom door.

Gracie shook her head and presented a blank face, but the corner mocked her with its emptiness. If she told him what she'd seen, he'd think her crazy. Not that she cared what Reilly Alexander thought. But was she sure she'd seen a man when she knew it was impossible that one had been there?

"Hey," Reilly said, his voice deep and soft. He placed a warm hand against her cold arm. "You're shaking."

Gracie nodded, trying to look anywhere but at his bare chest, which looked smooth and silky except for the line of hair that led down his flat belly to his jeans. His skin was the color of honey, golden and warm. He looked tired and disheveled, but at the same time watchful and prepared. For what? she wondered. The shadowed jaw and nearly shaven head gave him a tough-guy look that went deeper than the image. There was a hard edge to Reilly Alexander. She remembered it well.

"It's freezing in this room," he said.

"I know."

"All the air must be coming through in here. Maybe the other vents are blocked. Did you try closing it a little?"

"I can't find it."

Juliet trailed him as he circled the room, searching for the source of cold air. "It must be behind the dresser or desk."

"Must be," she agreed. She stayed perched on the edge of the bed, watching him. His back was muscled and sleek, like the rest of him. It tapered from broad shoulders to trim hips to long legs. Another small tattoo was at the base of his neck, this one a miniature sunburst. It looked Aztec or Mayan. His back flexed as he pulled the desk away from the wall to look behind it. Finding nothing, he pushed it back and looked behind the dresser. Watching him, her fingers curled into her palms. His skin would be warm to the touch, warm enough to distract her from the fear that still lingered low in her belly.

He turned suddenly, as if hearing her thoughts, and Gracie felt a wave of heat flood her face and neck. What was wrong with her? Reilly was the last man she should be thinking about. She was here to collect her daughter, bury her grandmother, and then leave Diablo Springs behind forever. Not get mixed up with Reilly of all people.

"I don't see the vent either," Reilly said, coming to stand right in front of her. She had to tilt her head and look up the length of his bare chest to meet his eyes. The position was intimate in itself—she sitting on the bed, he standing in front of her. His top button was undone and white boxers with a pattern of tiny penguins peeped out. She nearly smiled at that. Who'd have pictured such boxers on a man like Reilly Alexander?

"Are you sure you're okay?" he asked.

"It's been a long day," she said. "I'm jumping at my own shadow."

He scanned her face, searching for the lie in her voice. He didn't find what he was looking for, but he nodded.

"I'm just down the hall if you need anything," he said.

Yeah, right. Like she'd turn to him for help.

He flicked those dark eyes over her T-shirt and bare legs, a new light in their depths when he looked back into her face. For an instant she expected him to say something baiting. Something as sexual as the gaze that steamed over her body. But he only stared at her for another moment and then left.

She sighed and flopped back on the mattress. Juliet crawled up beside her and nudged her nose against Gracie's arm.

"What did we see?" Gracie asked the dog.

Juliet didn't answer. Instead she circled at the bottom of the bed before lying down. Her eyes, however, remained watchful.

Gracie glanced once more at the corner before slipping back under the covers. It was empty of course, and the feeling of being watched was gone. Still, she kept the lamp turned on. Sleep played an exhausting game of tug-of-war with her anxiety. She kept starting back awake, looking to the empty corner. And then another thought crowded into her overactive mind. Before changing, she'd locked her bedroom door. How then, had everyone been able to enter when she'd shouted?

chapter ten

AT six a.m., Gracie gave up trying to sleep. She showered and dressed, going through the motions of drying her hair and brushing her teeth. Grandma Beck's toiletries were neatly lined on the vanity beside the sink. Gracie unscrewed the caps and smelled the lotions that had been a staple of her life. For a moment, the grief she'd kept at bay was more than she could bear. So many wasted years, years when she'd missed Grandma Beck so much. And now it was too late. Too late to make changes. Too late to do anything but mourn.

The hallway was silent when she stepped out—all of the interlopers remained behind closed doors, slumbering in the smoldering heat of the great house. On the way downstairs, she paused at her old room where Analise still slept to let the dogs out. Tinkerbelle and Romeo jumped down and followed her and Juliet to the first floor.

The heat downstairs hovered just around sweltering, as close to hell as Gracie hoped she'd ever come. Beyond the confines of the house it had to be cooler, but the storm had gained momentum during the night and the rain raged down in torrents. Still, with sweat already pooling at the small of her back, outside seemed the lesser of two evils. She opened the front door and stepped onto the porch. The wind blew gusts of pouring rain beneath the shelter and the sky looked like an angry bruise in shades of green and black. Like a lid, the clouds held the heat down on the earth, making it feel like a tropical island instead of a desert wasteland.

She stayed on the porch while the dogs braved the rain to do their business. In the distance she saw the wasted remnants of the bridge and the decking that had once circled the hot springs. She'd seen pictures downtown in the municipal building that showed the springs during its heyday when merry turn-of-the-century socialites lounged on that same deck next to the healing waters. Then the springs had vanished, the beginning of the end, more or less, for Diablo Springs. But somehow the town held on despite the fact that its one redeeming attraction had dried up.

She heard footsteps behind her and turned to see Reilly coming out with two coffee cups in his hands. The sight of him brought a low vibration deep in her abdomen. He'd always had that effect on her. When she'd been twelve and he fifteen she'd thought he hung the moon. He didn't notice that she existed until the summer he came back from his first year at college, though. The summer when life as she knew it had ended, when he had betrayed her in ways she'd never imagined possible.

He handed her a cup and said, "I didn't know how you liked it so I took a guess at cream and sugar."

"Good guess," she said.

He wore a T-shirt with a picture on the front of an American flag in the clutches of a pissed-off eagle and dark blue board shorts. He smelled shower fresh and looked rested, though she knew he couldn't have slept many more hours than she. The scruff of beard remained on his face, matching the stubbly length of his hair. He was a grown-up now, an adult with a career and a future. But he still looked the part of the bad boy who'd raised hell with his brother all those years ago.

He took a seat on the porch swing and stretched his long legs out in front. Gracie thanked him for the coffee and nervously perched next to him. They swung gently for a moment, watching the storm while the dogs raced around in the rain.

"What kind of dogs are those?" he asked.

"Great Dane and Lab mostly. Who knows what else? Rescue dogs."

"They're big."

"Good protection."

He nodded. The Yorkie, Romeo, tippy-tapped up the stairs and came to sit at her feet. His fur was damp, and it looked like one of the girls may have rolled him in the mud. In general, he looked disgusted with the situation.

"You're up early," she said after a moment of silent swinging. With each move back and forth, his leg brushed against hers. The contact made her feel jittery.

"Too hot to sleep. Your room stay cold?"

"Yes. I almost froze to death."

"Sounds great. Maybe I'll sneak in there tonight."

He'd said it lightly, but the layer of tension that seemed to exist between them twisted and tightened the words into something more. He moved and his arm touched hers, sending an electric current through her. She stood suddenly and took an agitated step away.

"I saw your house when I drove in last night," she said, hoping to distract them both from the sudden intimacy of the rain, the porch, the seclusion. The attraction she couldn't seem to deny no matter how much she wanted to.

Reilly's jaw tightened and a flush crept up his neck. "Kind of fitting, what's happened to it."

Gracie didn't comment on that. She didn't think he'd appreciate her agreement. "I knew you'd moved on. I mean, I saw you in the paper when the . . ." She trailed off, feeling her own face start to burn. She'd seen him in the paper when he'd been accused of assaulting his girlfriend. Guess it ran in the family.

"The case was dismissed," he said wearily, as if he'd had to offer the explanation so many times he no longer cared if anyone believed him. "She was just after the publicity."

Gracie shrugged. "Anyway, I thought . . . well, I knew *you* were gone, but I expected Matt to still live here. I mean, if he were still alive. I never thought he'd leave . . ."

She trailed off, feeling insensitive and idiotic—and angry for feeling either. Reilly stared at her for a moment like he was reading her mind.

"Matt pretty much burned all of his bridges," he said at last. "After the band broke up, he came back for awhile. Arnie Schmidt hired him as a mechanic, but then he got caught stealing. After that no one wanted anything to do with him. Arnie didn't press charges, but he didn't keep it a secret either."

"And why did you come back, Reilly?"

The blunt question caught him off-guard and Gracie had a moment of childish triumph. She didn't want to have a friendly conversation with Reilly Alexander. She didn't want to feel attracted to him or aware of his nearness and the clean scent of his skin. She wished she could call up some of the cold rage she'd felt last night. But somehow his closeness had dispelled her anger, leaving her feeling confused, vulnerable, and defensive.

"This is my hometown too," he said.

She let out a breath of disbelief. "And you just decided to come back for a visit, is that it? In the middle of the night? With complete strangers?"

Reilly stood and paced a few steps away. The red stain was back on his face. "Why I'm here is my own business."

"Not when you're staying in my grandmother's house. Not when your little visit just happens to coincide with mine, and with my grandma's death. With what happened to my daughter."

"I had no way of knowing—"

"Really? Because last night your little friend Zach said Chloe knew my grandma was dead."

Reilly didn't have an answer for that.

"So which is it?" Gracie demanded.

"She said that Carolina's spirit had called her, had called both of us."

"And you believed that?"

"No. I thought—I *think* Chloe is a crazy lady."

"So why did you bring her here?"

He ran a hand over his head and a strange look flashed across his face, as if he'd expected to find hair where the shaved stubble was. He used to have beautiful hair, Gracie remembered. But somehow the shaved look suited him too. Fit the lean, hard man he'd become.

"I didn't know you'd be here," he said at last. "I swear I didn't think she was telling the truth about your grandma. I came because I had to come. There's no other way to explain it."

In spite of herself, she wanted to believe him. The look in his eyes begged her to believe him.

"So Chloe tells you that you're being called back to this place and you suddenly feel compelled to go? But her telling you and you coming are unrelated? Is that what you're saying? Because if you ask me, that sounds every bit as crazy as what Chloe is spouting."

Reilly shook his head. "Christ," he mumbled. "I can't explain it to you, Gracie."

"Why?"

"Because it's personal."

"*Personal?* And this invasion of *my* privacy isn't? You act like this is all some coincidence. Some big misunderstanding. Well, I don't like coincidences, Reilly, and I'm not buying that we're all here at the same time by accident. Chloe wants something. You want something. I want to know what that something is."

Reilly turned away from her, but not before she saw the haunted look in his eyes. When he spoke, his words were deep with emotion. "All I want is to bury my brother. That's the only reason I'm here."

"What?"

"It's the truth. I have his ashes upstairs in my room."

"But you said . . . last night you said he'd died months ago."

"He did."

"Why didn't you bury him then?"

He hunched his shoulders. "I couldn't. There wasn't even a service. No one cared that he was dead and . . . I couldn't do it alone. So I didn't do it all."

Gracie stared at him, trying to process this new piece of information. She didn't doubt that he was telling her the truth. She could see it in his face. But she still came back to the simple question of why now? Why after all this time would he pick last night, the same night her grandmother died, her daughter was injured, and Gracie ended her seventeen year boycott of the town? And how did it all connect to Chloe LaMonte?

"I've been procrastinating, hell *avoiding,* coming back here, Gracie. Because even now, I don't know what . . . how . . ." He cleared his throat. "Chloe throwing out the hook and reeling me in, it was just an excuse. A slight of hand, you know? Watch Chloe and the Clowns on the way and maybe it won't hit me what I have to do while I'm here."

Gracie shook her head, unconvinced. He sounded sincere, but she knew better than anyone that Reilly Alexander was a liar.

He took a small step forward, his hands bracketing the words he struggled to find. "Gracie, insane as it sounds, maybe Chloe was right about one thing though."

"And what is that?"

"My coming, you're being here . . . There's history between us. You know that."

"Is that what you're calling it? History?"

Her words had enough bite to leave marks. Reilly stiffened and his hands dropped to his sides. She'd wanted to hurt him, but now that she had she wished she could take the words back. And that made her angry with herself. What was wrong with her? Didn't she remember what this man had done to her? She forced herself to take a step forward, forced herself to say the words that felt like stone in her gut.

"What did you expect, Reilly? Did you think you could just waltz in after all these years, bring me coffee, hold my hand? Look under my bed for monsters and I'd just pretend the past never happened? That I'd want to be friends? That I'd think it was *history* we shared?"

A nerve jumped in his clenched jaw. "No. I told you, I didn't know you'd be here."

Her breath was coming in jerky gulps and she realized

she was dangerously close to tears. "I don't trust your friend Chloe. And I certainly don't trust you. I never will."

His shoulders hunched, as if in defeat. Again she felt the warring emotions inside her. Offer comfort, hurt him more.

"Would it make a difference if I said I was sorry?" he murmured. He gave her a guarded look that only increased her tension.

"Not a bit. You had your chance to be a stand-up guy with me, Reilly. You blew it."

"Well, I am sorry, Gracie. If I believed in God, I'd be on my knees begging for forgiveness. But God never really had a lot to do with my life. Matt's either. I don't think the Almighty would be any more forgiving than you are."

"Am I supposed to feel sorry for you?"

"No."

He moved closer, invading her space. Making her feel naked in the tank top and short skirt she'd felt confident in earlier.

He lowered his voice, but his anger still simmered on the surface. "I don't want your sympathy. I don't expect you to like me. But I am sorry. I swear to you, I am sorry for what I did."

They stared at each other in the weighted silence. Gracie's eyes burned, but she refused to let him see that she hurt. There were no words that could make up for what had happened that night all those years ago. She'd been raped by his brother. And afterward, when the sheriff went to arrest Matt, Reilly had lied and given him an alibi, knowing what he'd done.

A lot of time and a lot of water had passed beneath the bridge the two of them had once crossed. Her wounds had healed, but the scars would remain forever. She wasn't a girl anymore. She was a woman. A woman who knew better than to think a man like Reilly Alexander was anything more than what was on the outside. She'd never trust him. He sounded sincere now, but he'd sounded just as sincere all those years ago when he'd lied to the sheriff too.

"It was a long time ago, and I really don't care if you're sorry or not," she said, lifting her chin and staring him in the eye. "I moved on, haven't thought about you in years. But just don't think you can play me, Reilly. It's not happening. We aren't friends. Never have been, never will be. Got it?"

"Loud and clear."

"Good."

She gave a low whistle to the dogs who dashed from the yard to her side. Juliet paused beside Reilly and gave him a questioning look. Reilly reached down to scratch her ear. She let him, but before Gracie could think her a traitor, she gave her fur a violent shake, spraying Reilly with mud and dirty rainwater from head to toe. With a cold smile, Gracie marched through the door, and nearly plowed into Bill, who hovered in the shadowy entrance nearly invisible in his black-on-black attire.

She jumped and clapped a hand over the scream that nearly burst from her lips. Bill looked like she'd scared him just as much. He seemed paler than last night, but his eyes glowed like small, round coals pitted in the translucent pallor of his face. He glanced anxiously up the stairs then back at Gracie. Had the high priestess of weird sent him to spy on her?

"Don't trust the boy," he said softly.

From the corner of her eye, she saw Reilly move toward the door. She gave him her back.

"Don't trust the boy," Bill whispered again, more urgently this time.

"What are you talking about?"

"Bill," a familiar voice called from upstairs.

Bill straightened, like a puppet on a string. But there was nothing puppet-like about the look he gave her. It was at once demanding and beseeching. The black wells overflowed with the urgency of his thoughts, drawing Gracie deep into them. And then he seemed to fade into the background and disappear.

chapter eleven

DR. GRAEBEL'S house doubled as Diablo Springs' only medical facility. It was located not far from the Diablo—nothing in the tiny town was that far. But the short drive was not pleasant in a car with three wet dogs. Gracie had wanted to leave the dogs back at the Diablo, but they'd whined and barked and worked themselves into a frenzy before she'd managed to shut the door and make it down the hall. She didn't want Grandma Beck's bedroom to be in shreds when she returned so she'd relented.

The storm had at once quieted and increased so that the rain seemed to waterfall from the sky instead of simply pour, and the descent acted as a muffler to all other sounds. The thunder and lightning had retired for the time being, although the sky looked every bit as black and ominous as it had in the wee hours of the morning. It was just after eight when they pulled up to the clinic—only hours since Gracie had burst through the front door of the Diablo. It felt like days.

Analise had been quiet since waking up and she sat stiffly in her seat. The short drive down Rough Street to the clinic should have taken less than five minutes, but with the streets nearly flooded, Gracie dared not go too fast. As it was, they could have walked it quicker than they drove it.

"Is this ever going to stop?" Analise asked.

"It doesn't look like it, does it? I can't remember it ever raining for so long here. I hope it lets up long enough for us to bury Grandma Beck."

Saying the words brought a wash of uncomfortable and unresolved emotion. As if the death of her grandmother wasn't as important as getting her into the ground. But that's how she felt. She didn't want to be like Reilly, carrying around his brother's ashes because he couldn't bring closure to Matt's death. Now that she had Analise safely with her, she just wanted to collect Brendan, put her grandmother to rest, and get the hell away from Diablo Springs. And everyone in it, she added silently. Especially Reilly Alexander.

She parked in front of the clinic and cracked the windows for the dogs, knowing the seats would be wet and the dogs even smellier when they got back. The entire trip could be summed up in the same way—one unpleasant thing to counteract a dozen worse. Together they raced to the front door, arriving drenched all the same. Dr. Graebel looked tired and drawn when he let them in.

"How is he?" Gracie asked, glancing curiously at Analise who hung back in silence.

"I think he'll be fine." He cleared his throat, indicating the room to the right with a nod. "He's in there. You can take him home."

Gracie thanked him and led Analise into the room. Brendan was a gangly young man, tall and rangy with corded muscles and sun-baked skin. His hair was beach blond and his eyes a clear sky blue. He was a product of harsh raising and hard outdoor work.

A white bandage circled the top of his head. It looked unnaturally bright against his deep tan. Bruising seeped out from beneath it, discoloring the skin around his temple and right eye. One arm was in a sling, but not a cast. He was dressed and sitting in the hard plastic chair next to the bed, deep in concentration. When he heard them enter, he looked up, frowning worriedly when he saw Gracie, but his face brightened when Analise stepped in behind her.

He reached out for her hand and she hurried to his side and took it. "I've been so worried about you," he said, pulling her fingers to his lips.

The gesture seemed old-fashioned and for a minute Gracie wondered at it.

"I was worried about you too. They wouldn't let me stay."

He gave Gracie an accusing glance, though the decision had been made before she'd arrived. She found herself defensive under his censure, a strange impulse wanting her to say as much, but she held it back. He'd brought her daughter here, knowing she'd lied to Gracie about her whereabouts. Injured or not, Brendan was on Gracie's shit list.

"Are you all right?" he asked Analise, looking deeply into her eyes with touching concern that softened Gracie's outrage.

"I'm fine, I guess. It was scary."

"I can't really remember what happened," he said.

"Me neither. I guess we got turned around and almost drove into that pit out there."

"They should have filled it in a long time ago," Dr. Graebel said.

Gracie silently agreed.

"You sure you're okay?" Brendan asked Analise.

For a moment, Gracie was moved by the distress in his eyes. They were young, but he really did love her. She hadn't been in favor of his dating Analise. He was two years older than she, already out of school, and making a living, though a hard one. Still, he was responsible and he treated Analise like a queen. And Analise, to her credit, was a bright young girl. She was an honor student who'd been a never-ending source of pride to Gracie. Forbidding her to see Brendan had become a trust issue between them, and faced with Analise's steady dependability, Gracie hadn't felt it was fair to deny her that faith.

To her knowledge, until last night, Analise had been true to her word. Her grades hadn't been affected, Brendan returned her by curfew, and Gracie saw what Analise liked— loved—about him. He was good to her daughter. Until, that was, he'd absconded with her and brought her here, of all places. To the one town Gracie never wanted Analise to know about.

"Turned around . . ." Brendan was saying. "I remember thinking I saw the town." He squinted, as if searching for the memory. It seemed he seized on some image, his eyes widening then narrowing again.

"What's wrong, Brendan?" Analise asked.

He shook his head, and the strange expression vanished. "I was just really worried about you."

Again, Gracie thought of how much he cared, worried that such an intense relationship should come so early in Analise's life, reassured herself that all young love was intense. And usually fleeting.

Brendan's next words, though, sliced through the warm feeling and turned her blood cold.

He moved his hand to Analise's abdomen and asked, "What about the baby? Is the baby okay?"

chapter twelve

REILLY sat on the front porch, notebook and pen in hand, his mind an absolute blank. On the first page he had several lines, begun but not completed. Scratched out in anger. He couldn't string a sentence together to save his soul. Frustrated, he sat back and ran his fingers over his shaved hair. Christ, what was he doing here? He'd more than stirred up unsettled emotions in Gracie Beck. He'd resurrected his own beasts and they nipped and gnawed at his insides.

He should go upstairs, pack his bags, and get as far away from this place as he could. Matt wouldn't have wanted Diablo Springs to be his final resting place, anyway. Their life here had been hellish. But even as he thought it, he knew it wasn't true. It *had* been hell, but Matt had always yearned to fit in. Only in death would he be able to, and Reilly wouldn't take that from him.

Frustrated, Reilly stared out at the gray world, his thoughts as dark and streaming as the weather.

Zach stepped onto the porch a few minutes later and broke the trance the rain had created. He wore grunge jeans and a T-shirt advertising some kind of sour drink with the slogan SUCK THIS across the chest. His blond hair was combed back and Reilly suddenly remembered the name of the actor he resembled. McConaughey. A young Matthew McConaughey.

He had a determined look on his face that told Reilly there would be no dodging his questions this morning, as he'd done last night. He wasn't surprised. Honestly, Reilly had expected him to be more demanding sooner. Granted they'd been in Diablo Springs less than twelve hours, but it occurred to Reilly that Zach didn't appear to be in any great hurry to get his interview and return to civilization. In fact, while Reilly had been sitting out on the porch *not* writing his book, a lot of things had occurred to him.

It could be that Zach was just one of those "go where the wind takes me" kind of people. But Reilly didn't think so. There was something off about Zach Canning. Thinking about it now, Reilly realized he'd sensed it from the beginning. A smarter man would have listened to his instincts and stayed the hell away from the reporter. Reilly had invited him on a road trip. Jesus.

Zach took the only dry chair and pulled out a pocket-sized tape recorder. "You going to make up another bullshit excuse or are you going to talk to me?" he asked, turning it on.

"That depends," Reilly said, willingly setting his writing and knotted frustration aside. "Are you going to tell me what the hell you're really doing here or are you going to keep playing me for a fool?"

Zach grinned, giving his recorder a pointed look. "What? You think you're on *Punk'd* or something?"

"No, but I don't think you work for *Spin* either."

"Freelance, dude. I work for no one."

"Right."

The two stared at one another for a long moment. Zach's expression didn't change a bit.

"Look, man," Zach said. "You don't want to answer my questions, that's okay. But why'd you drag my ass across the desert if you were going to say no?"

"You *begged* me to bring you," Reilly said.

"For an interview. For a story. Not because I like cactus and old women."

Reilly took a deep breath and nodded. Maybe the kid was on the level. Maybe Reilly had been keeping secrets for so long, he was suspicious of anyone asking questions. "What do you want to know?" he said at last.

"Well let's start with the freak show. What was it Chloe said that hooked you in? Was it the broad she mentioned that locked the deal?"

"She wasn't a broad."

"Whatever."

"She was Gracie's grandmother."

"So what's she to Creepy Chloe?"

"I don't know. But when she wakes up, I plan to find out."

"There's got to be a connection."

Reilly nodded. He'd been dwelling on that for most of the night.

"What about the granddaughter?" Zach asked.

"Gracie?"

Zach nodded, raising his brows in suggestive manner that didn't sit well with Reilly.

"You stay away from her."

Zach gave a short bark of laughter. "What are you? Her father?"

"She's a decent woman," Reilly said.

"My mother is a decent woman. Gracie's nothing like her. So why do you think her kid was out there?"

Zach jutted his chin in the direction of the old springs, abruptly changing the subject.

"I don't know. Sounded like a freak accident."

"Shit, yeah," Zach said. He looked at Reilly with a dark stare. "Lot of that going around."

"Meaning?"

"Well first Madam Madness and the Ghouls show up at your book signing with a message from the dead—at a book signing for chrissake—and then we find out the old lady here got struck by lightning while her grandkid and boyfriend were sucked into a hole. That's about as freak accident as they come."

"How do you know about that?"

"I listened, man. You think I really went to bed when you told me to?"

"You're a dick, you know that?"

Zach shrugged. "Better than being a pussy."

Reilly narrowed his eyes and thought it might feel good to break Zach's nose. Zach's grin faltered and Reilly had the satisfaction of seeing a glimmer of fear in the cocky reporter's eyes.

Zach made another abrupt subject change. "So what do you think she wants?"

"Chloe?"

"Yeah. She's gotta want something out of this. And I'd bet my balls it ain't a message from the other side."

Gracie thought Chloe wanted something too. Reilly glanced at the house, where Chloe still slept, and then back at Zach.

"What do *you* think she wants?"

"Money."

"Money?" Reilly repeated blankly. "There's no money. Did you look at the town when we drove through? Poor is a step up for the people who live here."

Zach shrugged. "Old places like this, they have secrets." He gave Reilly a knowing look. "Don't they?"

"You seem to have all the answers. You tell me."

Zach shrugged. "You said it yourself, the Diablo used to be a happening place. Maybe there's a buried treasure or some shit like that."

Reilly laughed. "You think Carolina Beck would have been taking in boarders if she was sitting on a treasure?"

"Maybe. Old people are weird that way."

Reilly just shook his head. Zach was an idiot.

"Is that why *you* are here? Because you think there's a fortune buried in the backyard?"

Zach shrugged. "Maybe there is, maybe there isn't. What I do know is something's going down here. I can feel it. My instincts tell me it's going to be good and I'm the only reporter in a hundred mile radius."

"So you're waiting to exploit it, whatever it is?"

"You got it." Zach sat back, a self-satisfied smile on his face. "So tell me, what was sweet Gracie so upset about this morning?"

"What is it you do? Lurk in every shadow?"

"It's my job."

"Bullshit."

Zach grinned again. "She doesn't like you much, does she?"

"You know what? This interview is over. Take your fucking questions and shove them up your ass."

"Oh, hit a nerve."

Reilly was on his feet when a sound howled across the rain-drenched distance and pierced the tension on the porch. High-pitched, inhuman, it seemed to moan and keen at the same time. The unnatural wail halted his rush of anger and iced down his temper in a split-second.

"Holy shit," Zach whispered. "What was that?"

It came again, this time louder, more insistent, echoing in the stormy murk. Both men turned in place, as if searching for the source. But Reilly knew where it came from. He'd heard it before.

"What the hell is that?" Zach demanded again.

Just on the horizon, a faint glowing began. It hovered for an instant over the gaping black of the dried-up springs and then it split twice, until there were three lights that throbbed with a sickly brightness. The eerie keening vibrated with the pulsing lights until watching them, hearing them, was like having something hot and acrid smoking inside his head.

Zach clamped his hands over his ears and clenched his eyes. "What the fuck?" he shouted. "What is it?"

"Dead Lights," Reilly murmured. "It's the Dead Lights."

The shrieking intensified, coiling a tension into the air that tightened with each painful second. Then, as suddenly as it started, the shrill moaning simply stopped. An instant later the pulsating lights vanished.

Stunned, Zach lowered his hands. His lips moved silently over a question he didn't seem able to form. He turned shocked eyes on Reilly.

"What—"

But before he could finish a door slammed loudly inside the house. And then another door banged shut, the sound echoing like a bomb. Reilly stepped inside, Zach on his heels. He'd cleared the threshold, had a split second to register that there was someone standing in the shadows, and then the front door shut with force enough to rattle the house.

Zach was saying something, but Reilly couldn't hear him because every door in the house was slamming over and over. The thundering booming traveled down like repeating artillery. *Bam, bam, bam.*

And then silence.

Frozen in place, Reilly and Zach watched as the knob on the front door turned and then swung quietly open again.

chapter thirteen

May 1896
Colorado

I turned slowly. In every direction the mountains reached up and sealed me down in the scrub. I had survived the violence of the outlaws, but I would not survive this. Once I'd waded across the shallow but fast river, I'd left behind the flames that had chased me from my family's burning camp, but I could not give up my run. The vision of my mother, slaughtered, crushed beneath the burning wagon, unborn baby dead inside her . . . It would haunt me forever. I knew I would always remember her, not as I'd known her alive, but as she'd been in death.

So I ran. I didn't know for how long or how far. The sun had arced across the sky and night had fallen more than once, but time had no meaning in the place of pain that I existed in. I didn't know where I was, how to get back to where I'd begun. My only thought had been to flee, like a coward. I'd taken my daddy's shotgun, lifted his hunting knife off his cold body, and I'd run. I didn't even know if there were bullets left in the rifle. At least I knew how to shoot it, though not very well. I even knew how to load it, if I'd had more bullets. But at that moment I didn't care. The knife hung in the pocket of my skirt, sheathed in its heavy leather. It felt like an anchor, pulling me down into the depths of this horror. It had banged into my leg as I charged across the desolate valley between the foothills, punishing me for my weakness with each step I took. My thigh would be black with bruises. I was glad of it.

Dusk hung heavy in the sky again, like a gray velvet curtain with a tiny, intricate pattern of rhinestones glimmering in the weave. I knew later the stars would be like diamonds glittering so bright they hurt the eyes. Where would I be when they came out? Where was I now? I hadn't seen another living soul or even a sign of life since I'd left the camp.

I'd never known a sense of direction. My daddy had teased me relentlessly that I couldn't tell east from west. As the silvery light crept over the lavender sky, my eyes caught on a wisp of smoke in the distance that had been invisible to me before. Had I run in circles? If I followed that smoke, would I end up back at the camp?

There would be nothing to find but death, and yet it was a destination. A place where other travelers might stumble upon me. Now that I'd slowed, the steady thumping of the knife against my leg brought tears to my eyes, but I didn't remove it from my pocket. The rifle seemed to weigh a thousand pounds, and my hand and arm cramped as I gripped it. Grief was a hitch in my side, making each step so painful that I didn't want to take it. I didn't want to see what was left of my family and yet, a part of me welcomed the pain. A part of me knew I deserved to see them. If I'd done something to help, they might still be alive.

No, they would not. I would just be dead as well.

Though it was a voice of reason in my head, it angered me. I should be dead.

I was so thirsty my mouth felt like ash and my insides were hollow with hunger. I'd slept on and off, when exhaustion had literally brought me to my knees, but I was still so fatigued that putting one foot in front of the other was a monumental effort. Perhaps another day in the rising heat without food or water would find me joining my family anyway.

I reached the hilltop and looked down into a wooded valley. Aspen and cottonwood trees grew wide and sprawling in the pocket of lush vegetation. As the last of day leeched from the sky, it took with it all color from the world below. The trees looked black against the gray, the ground another version of darkness. The trail of smoke drifting up, white against the shadowed landscape.

This was not where my family had camped. Pine trees scattered darkly over the foothills, but the grove where I'd hidden was nowhere to be seen. I could not make out where the fire burned, but I realized it was not the smoldering ashes of my family I saw. It was a campfire and on it, the smell of food.

It took only an instant for me to understand. Suddenly rage overwhelmed me, adding power to my exhausted body. The Smith Brothers. I'd stumbled across their camp. The taste of vengeance rose up inside me, bitter on my tongue. I wrapped my hand around my daddy's shotgun and once again, I began to run. I bolted through the trees with branches snagging at my hair and ripping at my clothes, but still I did not slow.

As I drew closer I could hear voices, but not the deep drawl of any of the Smith riders. These were women's voices.

Confused, I paused. Why would women be out here with murdering outlaws?

In shadowed twilight I crept closer. I could smell the fire—made of cow pies by the noxious odor—long before I could see the flames. At last I was near enough to see the flicker of fire and the people sitting around it. Three women, clothed as I was in traveling dresses of indistinguishable browns and grays, sat comfortably by a fire. One of the women was Negro, another a mix of races I couldn't discern, but she looked to have been made from a golden wax, and a third looked of the Irish with a mane of rust-red hair and skin pale even in the elements.

The Negro and Irish women were sewing as they listened to the golden woman speak. The firelight caressed her skin, giving her a bronzed hue. Her teeth flashed white as she smiled. She seemed to be telling a story and the others hung on her words, pausing with needles poised for the next stitch as she drew the tale out.

Beyond her, another Negro woman, this one large and lumbering and black as the night, moved about the fire. She wore a handkerchief tied around her head and an apron that seemed to glow in this world of black and white. She didn't give the speaker the attention the others did, but she listened all the same as she fried bacon and tended something else that smelled heavenly. My stomach growled so loud I feared they'd hear me.

They camped beside a wagon with a tarp strung from the side to posts pounded into the ground. I crouched, watching them, afraid to step into the open. What were they doing out here, alone, without men to protect them? The women of Alamosa did not venture too far from their men—perhaps theirs were close by. Could they be with the Smith Brothers?

I stayed hidden in the underbrush that surrounded their camp, moving in a steady circle until I'd made my way to the other side. I heard the sound of water and saw a stream to my right. My thirst drove me to the banks where I drank until I made myself sick. Moments later I was heaving the cold water out again. I lay beside the stream until I had enough strength to rinse my mouth, take a few small sips, and then move back toward the women's camp.

I didn't see a corral for horses or any livestock that might pull the wagon. Were these women stranded? Perhaps victims of thievery? I thought of the Smith Brothers again. Had they been here? The laughter I'd heard said no, but people had a way of rising to the occasion when tragedy struck, and they had each other to see them through.

When I looked back to the campfire, the golden woman had finished her story. She sat beside the young Negro who looked, upon closer inspection, much younger than my seventeen. The larger woman still hovered over her skillets, scorched skirts perilously close to the fire, but the redhead was nowhere in sight. Their laughter drifted back to me, waking an ache so deep it hurt. There had been laughter at our campfire each night when Grandma, burdened though she was by her wheelchair, and Momma and I would clean after our meal.

A snapping twig to my right caught me unaware and I spun around. I was face-to-face with the redhead. She gave a shout of surprise, eyes round as saucers, skirts bunched around her waist, knees bent in a squat. She stumbled backward and fell on her bare behind. Embarrassment rooted me to the spot. I looked away, sputtering an apology.

"Saint Mary and Joseph," she exclaimed in a lilting Irish brogue as she struggled to stand, yanking up her drawers and down her skirts at once. In an instant the women from the camp had surrounded us.

"Where you come from?" the large black woman exclaimed.

I opened my mouth to answer, but the Irish woman interrupted me. "You're head to toe in blood, lass. What are y'doing out here?"

The big one had a knife in her hand, the kind my mother used to bone chicken. She waved it at me.

"She trouble. You get, trouble."

The girl I'd guessed to be younger than I pushed forward. Up close she looked no more than fifteen. A light rash of blemishes made a T of her forehead and nose, but it was her luminous eyes and dark lashes that gathered the attention. She would be an incredible beauty when she matured.

"She scairt," she said. She laid a gentle hand on my arm and said, "Don't be scairt. We won't hurt you. I'm Chick."

I stared uneasily from one unfamiliar face to another. Who were these women? Why were they out here in the middle of nowhere?

"She look like somebody been at her wit a whip. Somebody after you?" Chick asked.

I shook my head.

"She looks hungry, is what she's looking," the Irish one said.

"Don't be feeding her like no stray dog," the hefty one said. "Mis'r Tate see you doin' that he'll have your hide."

"That Athena," Chick said softly of the woman waving the knife. From her tone I understood that Athena was the ruler of this small band of women.

"He wouldn't dare lay a hand on her," the woman who looked dipped in gold said, moving nearer to me. Up close, her skin was the color of light molasses and it gleamed in the weak light. I had thought Chick lovely, but this girl . . . woman . . . was breathtaking. She shined like a luminary. Her hair was cut very short, almost masculine, but there was nothing male about her curving figure and gleaming beauty. She spoke with fine grammar, not like the other girls.

"Best not let him hear that talk," Athena said, still waving the knife. She glared at me with a hatred that went deeper than our short acquaintance. I didn't know what I'd done to earn it, but I was smart enough not to ask. "He have your hide," she told the golden girl. "Honey or no Honey." Another pointed look at me, as if I had caused some great trouble by stumbling in half starved and desolate.

"Why don' she talk?" Chick asked Athena, whose expression became harsher by the minute. I thought I'd better say something before she ordered me away.

Swallowing my fear, I asked, "Are you stranded?"

"Stranded?" the Irish one repeated. "No, girl."

"Then where are your horses?"

"M'sr Tate got them," Athena said suspiciously.

"Do you . . . have you seen the Smith Brothers?"

"Who?" Athena demanded.

"Lonnie and Jake."

"Don' know no Lonnie and Jake. You get hit in the head?"

I didn't think so, but I'd fallen enough times during my mad dash that I could have.

"Why you covered wit blood?" Chick asked, reaching a hand out, but not touching me.

I wasn't ready to answer that. I wasn't certain I could trust them.

"My name is Ella," I said. "I'm lost."

The golden girl approached and laid a gentle hand on my arm. "Are you hurt?"

I shrugged and tears filled my eyes. I didn't want to cry, but I didn't want to be lost and alone in the world either. Whether it was wise or not, I couldn't pretend that I was not in desperate need of help.

The golden girl said, "Bring her over to the fire. Let's get her cleaned up."

Even though I wanted that, wanted the fire, a taste of whatever smelled so heavenly, a rest . . . I could not so easily forget the fear and apprehension that I knew would never leave me.

"Why are you out here? A group of women . . . alone?" I heard the words, knew I'd formed them, but hardly recognized the directness, the hard tone. They seemed to have come from another girl than the one who'd woken up just a few days ago, mad at her father for taking her away from her friends. But I would never be that girl again.

The women looked at each other. No one answered.

I stood my ground, yet inside I was shaking. It was part fear, part anticipation. If they told me they were the women of the Smith brothers, I don't know what I would do to avenge the deaths of my family. I didn't think I had the courage to hurt them . . . but I would not eat the food or lay in the blankets by the fire of the men who had destroyed my life.

The silence stretched. Finally the golden girl whispered, "What terrible thing happened to you, child?"

Despite my resolve, her kindness and apparent ignorance of the horror that had befallen me was my undoing. "My family—" I hitched in a breath. "My family has been killed by outlaws."

This made Athena pull in her neck turtlelike. She looked around with big eyes as if expecting the outlaws to charge them at any moment. It wasn't an unreasonable assumption. I wasn't certain they wouldn't.

"I thought you were them."

"You thought we was them? What was you gon do? Kills us?" Athena asked, hands on her hips and scorn on her face.

I raised my chin. "Yes."

That caused looks to pass from one woman to another.

The redhead said, "Well, now, you can see we're no such thing as outlaws. Why don't you put your gun down, lass? Won't be no need of it."

I followed her glance to the rifle still clutched in my hands. I'd forgotten about it."

"'Less they followed her," Athena said.

They each of them glanced out at the scrub and brush. "They couldna made it past the Captain," the redhead said.

This seemed to be enough reassurance for them all. I did not have such faith in this captain, whoever he was. One man would not stand against the Smith Brothers.

The golden girl approached me. "That Honey," Chick whispered. "Honey Girl, cause she's sweet and creamy—that what Aiken say."

Honey Girl reached for my hand and guided me closer to the fire. Chick followed, chattering to my back. "They call me Chick, on account I'm small and soft. I told you that Athena. She take care of us." The big woman glared at me so there'd be no misunderstanding that *I* was not one of *us*. "And this Meaira. She from Ireland."

The last said with a soft awe. I felt it too. I knew that my daddy thought immigrants were a sea of trouble that flowed steadily on our shores. My family could trace its heritage back to England. Our ancestors had come over a hundred years before, which, according to my father, no longer made us immigrants. "We're settlers," Daddy was fond of saying. The distinction was not quite clear to me, but I was sharp enough to understand that somehow the distinction existed. I imagined for Chick anything beyond the ocean was a wonder.

The woman called Honey Girl had a dark sadness in her eyes, but she smiled at me and gestured that I sit on one of the crates by the fire. The look spoke of deep loss. Would I have that same look in my eyes should I stare in a mirror?

I sat hesitantly while Chick bustled over to the spider frying pan that sat in the fire. She picked up a long-handled fork to turn the bacon and Athena snatched it out of her hand. I noticed she walked with a pronounced limp.

"Don't mess wit my skillet."

"No, Athena, I surely won't do that."

Chick gave her a guileless smile that softened Athena's expression. She gently touched Chick's cheek. "Go on and sit yourself down."

Chick scurried over to sit beside me. Meaira came with a bowl and a rag. She began dabbing at my face. When I didn't wince, she asked. "Is this your blood?"

"Some." I didn't tell them it belonged to my mother. I couldn't put my thoughts around the words. Did not want to conjure the memory. But there it was anyway, hovering just at the edge of my mind. I felt hot tears filling my eyes again, and I clenched my teeth hard to fight them back. I was a coward, not a crybaby. But they wouldn't heel. They spilled over and streamed silently down my face. One plopped onto my hand and mingled with the dried blood there. I must look a sight. The thought made the tears come faster. Meaira put her arms around me from one side and Chick from the other and the two strange women held me while I cried.

LATER they fed me and I ate under Athena's fierce eyes. Why she disliked me so, I didn't know. But she watched the horizon fearfully—I assumed for the murderers to swoop down on us. I watched for them as well. I spent a restless night with the women, tossing and turning, starting to wakefulness in the grips of nightmares. Chick was there beside me, her luminous eyes full of compassion. On my other side lay Honey, who set her cool hands on my face and murmured comforting words in her sweet tone. Somehow I made it through the night.

Dawn found us back around the fire drinking Athena's coffee. I offered to help with breakfast and she gave me a withering stare. I didn't know if she resented the implication that she might need help, or if it was just me she took exception to. I thought it was probably me, but I still didn't know why. She made breakfast from last night's meal and then the camp became a hive of activity. I felt useless in the midst of it and tried to help. Chick kept a steady conversation, telling me that soon Aiken and the Captain would be here.

"Who are they?"

This question stilled all the women. They stared at me, then from one to another, none of them answering.

"A businessman, the Captain is," Meaira began, hesitantly. "You understand?"

I nodded, though I didn't think I did. "My father was a businessman. He was a banker."

This produced another round of stares. "That not the kind Captain is," Chick said. "He work the tables. You know. Cards. He won hisself a saloon."

I raised my brows at this. My father had been a player of cards, although my mother had disapproved. Perhaps if he'd ever won she'd have considered it a business venture as well, but unfortunately he had not been very skilled. He understood the rules of gambling, but not the concept of the game. He'd taught me when I was only eight and by the time I was ten I could beat him every time. He'd often joked that he wished he could smuggle me in with him. Many a night my entire family had settled around a table with a deck of cards and my daddy's hope that practice would make perfect. For me it had, but for Daddy . . . I bit my lip, knowing he would never learn to win now.

"And Aiken," I asked. "Who is he?"

"He the devil," Athena said, turning her back on me and the conversation.

"The devil," Meaira scoffed. "What will she think? No lass, not the devil. A man of business, he is."

Athena snorted and jabbed a finger at me. "Well he ain't gon' be happy to see her."

The devil and a gambler who thought themselves businessmen. I still didn't know where the women fit in, but Athena's words inspired them all to move faster in their efforts to be packed up and ready.

It was close to nine in the morning when Honey stood up and shielded her eyes from the bright sun. The camp was tidy, and the women waited in a circle around the dying fire.

"Captain's coming," she said.

"Is Aiken with him?" Meaira asked, looking very hopeful about the prospect of the devil's arrival.

"Just the Captain," Honey said. Meaira's disappointment had a pale and shaken air to it. I wondered at her relationship with Aiken.

I looked but saw nothing of either man. Honey must have excellent eyes or a sixth sense where the Captain was concerned. After a few minutes of staring, I made out a spec on the horizon. Possibly a man on a horse, but how could they be certain it was the man they called Captain?

The declaration of his imminent arrival had a galvanizing effect on the other women, however. Apparently they didn't need to see him to believe it. They all began to move about with feigned casualness, as if they'd risen on a whim to dust off their skirts or straighten the already neatly stacked crates by the wagon. But the tension hung thick in the camp. Athena clicked her tongue and looked around like a soldier at her troop.

Honey disappeared into the back of the wagon. When she came out, she'd touched up her makeup and changed into a dress that looked very fine for camping. Meaira slouched on a crate dejectedly. I noted the dark circles under her eyes and a grayish cast to her skin. She did not look well in the least.

Chick fussed with her hair and adjusted her dress over her underdeveloped breasts. Even Athena, though unconcerned with her appearance, busied herself around the fire. She retrieved her skillet from a crate and started cooking. By the time the Captain came into sight, the bacon was popping and Athena began cracking eggs in beside it.

He was a big man riding an enormous horse. The mount was a mottled blend of grays and white with brown mixed in at intervals as if by mistake. My brother would have known the name of it. He would have run out to meet the rider, hopping alongside as he admired the horse. I swallowed thickly.

The Captain's saddle was worn, dark leather. A workingman's saddle, not a fancy tooled thing as my daddy's boss at the bank had. The Captain wore boots and dark pants with a gold strip down each leg. They were faded pale and the cording sapped of color until it looked more lemon than golden. His work shirt was grayed as well and buttoned casually up over a broad chest. He wore no jacket. The hat on his head was low, keeping his face in shadow.

On the saddle behind him hung a string of rabbits. He untied them and dropped them by the fire.

Athena picked them up and said sweetly, "Thanky, Captain."

He gave a half nod and backed up his horse. As he began to turn, the angle shifted and the shadows cleared from his face. For the first time, I saw him full on. He had eyes the color of the Mississippi River—all muddied browns and swirling greens. Dark, yet glimmering with light and current. I recognized him, of course. He was one of Lonnie and Jake Smith's riders.

I'd seen him once in town, before the trial. I'd been coming out of the dry goods store as he went in. We bumped into each other and for a moment he held my arms between his big hands. I remember looking into those eyes, seeing the ebb and flow of the powerful tide of emotion and hot-blooded man thoughts that swept across his face. I'd felt the sensation of his look as it skimmed over me and lingered on my breasts. I'd never seen a man like him before. He was hard and weathered, his face tanned. He smelled of a fresh bath and his cheeks were smoothly shaven but for the blond-gold mustache that curled over his lip.

He had held me longer than was necessary, and I didn't protest, as I should have. My hands were pressed against the hard warmth of his chest and his heart beat steady beneath my palm. My imagination took flight with thoughts of him pulling me tight against the solid breadth of him. Bending me back over his arms as he kissed me. I didn't really know what he might do next. I had an idea of what went on between barnyard animals, but no clue how that really applied to humans.

He'd smiled at me then and the look had a hint of devil-may-care. It took my breath away while at the same time making me smile back. His attention focused on my mouth, and it seemed he was as fascinated by me as I was of him. He'd even leaned forward, ever so slightly.

That was when my mother noticed us. She'd already walked out of the door, pushing Grandma's chair and chattering about the new fabric she'd purchased. Apparently she hadn't realized I wasn't at her side.

"Sir, kindly release my daughter," she snapped.

He'd dropped his hands instantly, tipped his hat at us both and stepped aside. I allowed my hands to trail his chest as I lowered them. He recognized the gesture for what it was. Even though I'd never been so bold with a man before, I wanted him to know that I liked his touch. I succeeded.

My mother angrily grabbed my arm and marched me home where my father told me who he was. Sawyer McCready. A Smith rider.

He narrowed his eyes at me now, noticing for the first time that I sat near the fire. I held my breath, wondering if he recognized me as well. He didn't say a word, just silently cut his eyes from one woman to another as he sat astride that huge horse.

"Captain," Honey said, moving up to his side and setting her hand on his thigh. She had long, slender fingers, slightly darkened at the knuckles, but smooth as the rest of her. "This young woman found her way to our camp last night. Her family has been murdered."

Those eyes snapped to me again and I felt them drilling into me. I inched my hand down to my pocket and eased it in. My father's knife lay heavy and warm against my legs. It wasn't the shotgun—they'd taken that from me last night—but it would do. My fingers closed on the smooth metal, and I slowly pulled it out, keeping it hidden in the folds of my skirts. He was still watching me and I knew I would have to act fast before he figured out why I looked familiar.

Hands behind my back, I pulled the knife from its leather sheath and I charged. I'd moved so quickly and unpredictably that everyone was frozen into stillness. No one thought to stop me. It didn't occur to me that they might. I was focused only on one thing—this man had helped slaughter my family. One way or another I would be dead soon, either by starvation or murder, but I would be a coward no more.

I didn't hesitate as I took a running leap off a crate and hit him square on as he sat horseback. I knocked him off balance and ruined any angle I had at bringing my knife down in a fatal blow. We fell off to the other side and my blade glanced his arm. He cursed and rolled with me, the weight of him far too much for me to fight. That didn't mean I wasn't going to try. I kicked and bit and swung wildly with my knife until he got me pinned on my back, both hands captured by one of his. I had the satisfaction of knowing he was breathing heavy as he looked down at me. I stared defiantly back and saw the dawning of recognition.

"Ella," he said.

He remembered my name, though my mother had only said it once. For a moment this distracted me. He'd remembered my name. But I remembered why I wanted him dead.

"You murderer! They were good people," I shouted. "You killed them. You killed them as they ran." I was shrieking, but I couldn't stop. I screamed at him again and again. "Murderer."

He wrestled the knife from my hand, easily twisting it out of my grip as I cried out with rage. He sat astraddle my pinned body, looking at the long wicked blade I'd nearly skewered him with. His expression crossed between disbelief and anger. I waited for him to bury it to the hilt in my heart—I welcomed it. He looked at me, those muddy eyes cold, and then he backed off and stood. I flipped over and took off running. I heard him curse again, and the others scream in surprise. I hiked up my skirt and ran for all I was worth. I didn't know if he was following me or not until he tackled me, sending me sprawling on the ground, my mouth full of leaves and dirt.

He roughly turned me, lying on me to keep me pinned to the ground. "I don't know what you're talking about," he shouted at me, his face inches from mine. He was hurting me.

"My parents," I shouted back. "My brother. My grandmother. Why? They were leaving. They were leaving."

I was sobbing, hysterical with fear and anger and hurt.

"Go ahead and do it," I told him. "Spill my blood like you did theirs."

"Who are they? Your parents? Who were they?"

The correction caught and silenced me. "My father was Conrad Beck."

Sawyer knew the name. I saw it in his face. I waited for him to deny it, though, expecting only lies from the likes of him.

"I don't ride with Smith anymore. Not for almost a year." He stood up and reached down to offer me a hand. "I didn't kill your family."

I didn't believe him. I'd heard Lonnie sit on the witness stand and swear he hadn't touched Louise Franklin, even though more than five witnesses saw him rape her before he'd murdered her. I hadn't believed him either. Just because I didn't see him do it, didn't make him innocent.

I didn't take Sawyer's hand. I stayed where I was, glaring my hate. He stared back at me for a moment and then daringly turned his back and walked away. He had my knife, but my rage was far from gone.

"Get the hell out of here," he said over his shoulder.

That stopped me. I looked around at the same desolate nowhere I'd journeyed through for days without seeing another sign of life. I didn't know where I was now any more than I had last night when I'd stumbled over the women. Where would I go? What were the odds of me finding another camp, another living soul who would help me? My father had taught me enough about gambling to know they weren't good.

Sawyer didn't wait to see what I would do. He showed me his back, which I thought both brave and foolhardy considering I still wanted to kill him. When he reached the camp, the women fussed around him, tending to his wounded arm and bringing him food.

I put my face in my scraped and bloody hands, wanting to sob until all the pain inside had come out. But what good would that do me? I wouldn't stay out here like a hungry dog waiting for scraps. I wouldn't let him see that he'd broken me. Wincing, I pushed to my feet. My knees were as skinned and torn as my hands and my ribs felt bruised and battered. But my anger fueled my steps. I followed the stream that I'd found last night with a determination rooted deep in my desperation.

The long steps between afternoon and twilight gave me too much time to think. Sawyer's words played through my mind, keeping time with my progress. He said he hadn't ridden with the Smiths for over a year. Was it true? I hadn't actually seen him among the riders who had killed my family. Nor were the murderers with him now. And the women . . . they'd been genuine in their surprise when I'd asked about the Smith brothers.

Sawyer had ridden with them once, though. And if not a murderer, it at least made him a thief. An outlaw, all the same.

The tears I'd refused earlier would be denied no longer. They burned my eyes and slid down my cheeks but they did not slow my steps. I didn't know what I would do now, but somehow quitting would mean that I'd failed my family even worse than when I'd let them die. My mother had always said I possessed an inner strength that would keep me going when times were hard. I hadn't believed her, but now I felt her whisper to my heart, "You can do it, Ella."

The words of encouragement didn't slow my tears, but my steps became more certain. Maybe I *could* survive this. But all around me only open terrain and encroaching darkness waited. I was scared. I couldn't pretend otherwise.

I let myself cry as I followed the widening stream to nowhere. Huge, quaking sobs shook my shoulders and made me stumble. I howled with grief and moaned with heartache as I plowed determinedly forward. I cried so loudly that at first I didn't even hear the hoofbeats of the approaching horse. It was not until the animal came to a stop abreast of me that I noticed it. Although it was full night now and only the black silhouette showed, I knew who the rider was. Sawyer McCready. Captain McCready.

I slowed to a stop, staring at the powerful man and horse. My face was wet with tears, my shoulders still shaking with my anguish. But I managed to hold my head up and glare at him.

"I hope you brought my gun and knife since you've sent me out here to fend for myself," I said.

His mouth dropped open with shock. The reaction brought me a flush of satisfaction. Then he said, "*You* attacked *me*."

"I was just protecting myself."

"Yeah, well so was I."

I heard him click his tongue and the horse came closer. He stopped beside me and looked down.

"You're going to get yourself killed out here," he said, his voice dark as whiskey.

"Why should you care?"

In the silence that followed, I bit my tongue. He was right—I *was* going to get myself killed. If a bear or mountain lion didn't decide to make a snack of me, then perhaps Indians or even the Smith brothers would see me dead. But I'd go down fighting, as my daddy used to say.

"I didn't murder your family, Ella, and I'll be damned if I'll have you out here dead weighing on me. I'll take you back to camp. Tomorrow we'll be moving on and when we get to a town, you can find your way home from there."

My nose was running and I had no handkerchief. Feeling foolish, I lifted my skirt and wiped it. I thought I saw a flash of smile, but it was gone so quickly I might have imagined it.

"Why would you help me?"

He looked down, shook his head, then met my eyes again. "Because I'm a damn fool. Because I know what Lonnie and Jake are and you shouldn't never have had to see it."

The truth of his words made me want to start crying fresh tears, but I bit my lip and nodded.

"You got nothin' to fear from me," he said. "But I ain't going to sit out here all night trying to talk sense into you."

That made me want to snarl back, but for once I managed to hold my tongue. I looked around at the clustered darkness, the black woods in the distance, the deep valleys between the foothills. Swallowing, I looked back to his shadowed face, wishing I could read him. Wishing I knew what to do. How could I trust this man? How could I not?

"Come on, Ella. It's late."

He kicked his foot free of the stirrup and reached down a hand. With a deep breath, I took it.

chapter fourteen

THE storm rose up like an angry beast and consumed Diablo Springs. At least that's how it felt, driving through the flooded streets to her grandmother's house. Or perhaps the storm was inside Gracie, swamping her hopes and dreams for her daughter, dredging the past from the valleys of her mind, and floating it to the surface.

In the backseat, squished in with the dogs, Analise huddled against the door, and Brendan, looking confused and somehow innocent, sat directly behind Gracie. She wondered at Analise's distance from Brendan. Had the dogs forced her away, or was there trouble in paradise?

She met Brendan's eyes in the rearview mirror, but they revealed nothing of what was going on in his mind. She wanted to hate him, to throw him out of the car, to call him names. But like the storm, her anger simply roiled and ebbed in torrents, bogging her down with indecision and frustration. By the time she reached the house, her nerves were stretched beyond endurance.

They raced through the onslaught of wind and rain to the shelter of the porch. There, they found Reilly sitting quietly, a notebook opened to a blank page on the bench beside him. He looked from one drawn face to another, but didn't ask any questions.

"Go gather your stuff," Gracie told Analise. "We'll leave as soon as you're ready." To Brendan she said, "You can wait out here."

Brendan nodded and sat down opposite Reilly.

The house was extremely quiet when she entered, no far-off rustling sounds. No voices coming from the other room. The stillness was both complete and unnerving. Where was everyone?

She followed Analise up the stairs, stepping into the arctic cold of Grandma Beck's room with more reluctance than she could control. She couldn't wait to get out of here. Unresolved or not, she wanted to leave Grandma Beck and her godforsaken home behind.

She was glad now that she'd been too tired to unpack last night. It took her only a few moments to gather her things and zip up her bag. Juliet kept watching the same corner she'd guarded last night, but today there were no warning growls to add to Gracie's anxiety. As Gracie turned to pull her bag off the bed, Analise stepped into the room.

They stared at each other in a pained silence. Gracie didn't know whether to shake her or wrap her arms around her daughter. It hurt to think of her pregnant. She hadn't even realized Analise was having sex, though they'd talked about it a hundred times or more. She'd always told Analise that if she reached that point, no questions asked, Gracie would get her on birth control. Analise had dutifully nodded and mouthed words that Gracie had wanted to hear. Not even thinking about it, Mom. Saving myself for marriage. I promise I'll tell you.

Lies. Lies all of it. How many other lies had she told? How many other nights had she not been with a girlfriend? Rage welled up inside Gracie. If Brendan had been foolish enough to follow them up, she would have slapped him. How dare he ruin Analise's life this way? She'd been an honor student, scholarship bound. Now she was a teenaged statistic.

"Mom," Analise said, her voice breaking. She looked at the floor and then back up. Her round wet eyes could have been staring out of the face she'd had at two, when she'd skinned her knees or gotten a splinter. She was a baby herself—how could she be approaching motherhood?

"I'm sorry, Mommy," Analise said.

Gracie's bottom lip began to tremble as she stared at the dejected form her daughter made.

"I know."

Gracie opened her arms and Analise stepped into them. Her hot tears slid down her cheeks to mingle with Gracie's as she rocked her back and forth.

"When we get home," Gracie said, pulling back. "We'll talk about it. You have options, Ana."

Analise nodded, but what she said was, "Brendan and I have already worked everything out. We're going to get married."

Married? Gracie pulled in some air as dots swam behind her eyes. *Married?* "Analise, you know I think Brendan is a nice boy. But you're too young to get married."

"I'm too young to have a baby too Mom. But I'm doing it anyway."

She said it with a finality that let Gracie know adulthood was perhaps not so far away. Still, she'd chain herself to the chapel door before she'd let Analise sashay through it in a wedding dress at *sixteen*. The baby she couldn't change, but if it took the last breath in her body, she wouldn't let Analise compound it with an even bigger mistake.

"We'll talk about it when we get home. Okay?"

Analise nodded, but the determination in her eyes didn't waver. Gracie's footsteps felt heavy as, bags in hand, she led them back down the stairs and onto the porch.

"You're leaving," Reilly said when they came out.

"Yes. As soon as I stop at the mortuary."

Like Dr. Graebel's clinic, the Diablo Springs mortuary was actually little more than a converted section of the undertaker's home. She'd tried calling, but got a strange ring that made her think his phone line was down.

"You're going to Digger Young's?" Reilly asked, frowning.

She nodded once.

"You're taking them?" he asked, looking at Brendan and Analise.

"Yes."

"You sure you want to do that?"

"For God's sake, Reilly, no, of course I don't want to. But he's got Grandma Beck's body and I want things settled. I want to go home."

He didn't seem surprised by her outburst, why would he be? But something had changed since that morning. She'd said his apology was too little, too late. But the fact was, she'd heard the honesty behind it. Against all reason, she believed that he truly was sorry. And though forgiveness seemed far off, so did the act of betrayal. She was a different person now. Perhaps he was too.

"You know Digger's been living out there running the business all these years, right?" Reilly said. "I hear he's certifiable now."

"I can deal with him."

"What makes you think so?"

She raised her shoulders and brows. "What makes you think I can't? I'm not a little girl anymore who needs someone to look after her, okay? I appreciate your concern, but I can handle a visit to the mortuary on my own."

"Damn it, Gracie, would you quit trying to show me how tough you are and just listen to reason? He's a nut case that lives miles from anyone else and spends his days and nights with dead bodies. You just shouldn't go alone. I'll take you."

"And that's supposed to make me feel safer?"

"Maybe not. But it'll make me feel better."

"I guess I didn't make myself clear this morning, Reilly—"

He made a sound and shook his head. "You did. Forget I said anything—sorry I butted in. You want to go to Digger's house by yourself, go ahead. I won't even offer you a ride."

"I don't want to go," Analise said.

Gracie stared at him, still angry, but she knew she should welcome his offer. There was history between her family and the Youngs. Bad history. Over the years she'd heard stories about Digger and the family business—a business run by multiple generations of men who took on the name Digger after their predecessor died. Stories that would make a young girl's blood run cold. And even though she knew most of them were small-town rumors with no basis in fact, if she was honest, she didn't want to go see him alone. She didn't want to go at all.

Rumors about the fiendish morticians weren't the only kind that had circulated in Diablo Springs. There were more personal tales involving her mother and the current Digger's father. Some of those stories blamed his father for her mother's death. Some of them blamed him for Gracie's conception. None of them had an ounce of proof to back them up. But there wasn't an ounce of proof to refute them either. Whatever the truth, Grandma Beck had hated the Youngs and Gracie, by default, had grown up with a suspicious fear of them. Stepping into their lair was up there with having all her teeth pulled without anesthetics.

She took a deep breath and let it out.

"Where is everyone?" she asked.

"They piled into the bat-mobile and went to the Buckboard for something to eat."

"Why didn't you go?"

He looked at his feet and shook his head. "Thought I'd wait for you."

There was nothing duplicitous in his tone or expression, and she found herself taking his words at face value. It was stupid of her to feel so raw about something that happened years ago. It was done and over.

As if reading her mind, he said softly, "I'm not the worst thing that could happen to you, Gracie."

That brought her eyes up and around to lock with his. He stared back, unflinching.

"No. No, you're not."

Which was far from being the best thing, but she didn't say that. He pulled his keys from his pocket and waggled them with a pointed look. "My Jeep is probably better in this weather."

She turned to Analise, noting how pale she looked. "Maybe it would be better if you and Brendan stayed here while I go to the mortuary."

But she really didn't want that either. She'd grown up here, but somehow in the passing years the house had changed, changed into something no longer familiar. Something she didn't trust with her loved ones.

"I have a better idea," Reilly said. "Why don't we drop them at the Buckboard. They can get something to eat."

The way he said it raised Gracie's antenna, but before she could question him, Brendan said, "That sounds great. I'm starving."

He grinned widely, looking pleased with himself. He reached for Analise's hand and brought it to his lips. Once again the gesture struck Gracie. She'd never seen him do it before this morning. It seemed so out of character.

"How about you, Sugarbear?" he said. "You and the baby hungry?"

Reilly's eyes widened at that, but to his credit, he didn't comment. Analise's face flushed red. She looked like she wanted to slug Brendan, but she held back. Gracie wanted to hit him as well. What was wrong with him? Did he really feel the need to broadcast the pregnancy to everyone? On the tail of that thought came a slap of reality. Like it or not, it couldn't be ignored or kept secret.

"That's settled then," Reilly said, avoiding Gracie's eyes.

"What about the dogs?" Analise asked. "They'll be scared if we leave them behind."

"If everyone is gone, they'll be fine locked in the kitchen. I promise," Gracie said. Analise looked like she might argue, but in the end she kept quiet and followed her mother back into the storm.

THEY piled into Reilly's Cherokee and took off. Reilly had to drive slowly and navigate around places where the water had risen so high it flooded the road out completely. He was glad of the lifted body of the SUV and the traction it had.

"I can't believe how much the water in the streets has risen just since I drove to the clinic," Gracie said, staring worriedly out the window. "If we don't leave here soon . . ."

She left the rest unsaid. Watching the rain pour from the sky, Reilly thought *soon* might be too late. He was worried they wouldn't make it back from Young's.

The Buckboard had been the only restaurant in town for as long as Reilly could remember. The doors were unlocked at six and they served breakfast until ten, when the bar opened. After that it was burgers and sandwiches until midnight or whenever the last of the customers staggered out. On special occasions, Ernie Ives, the owner, would add some variety and more red meat to the menu, but for the most part the residents of Diablo Springs made due with the usual fare. Reilly and his brother had worked in the kitchen for summer jobs, drank their first beers at the bar, and brought their first dates there for dinner. Reilly had a fond memory of Corrine Murray giving him head in the men's room his senior year. Ah, the good old days.

He pulled to a stop at the entrance and Brendan and Analise got out.

"Be careful," Gracie told them.

"We will," Analise said.

There was a tension between Gracie and her daughter that was thick enough to cut. It didn't take a genius to guess it had to do with the baby. The kid who'd brought Analise to this isolated place—both figuratively and literally—looked placidly out of big blue eyes, innocent and unaware of the strain around him. He was either the world's greatest actor or he truly didn't realize the chaos he'd caused. Reilly didn't know what to bet on.

They waited until the two had disappeared inside before pulling away.

"So, you're going to be a grandma," he said, grinning at the look that crossed her face.

She nodded. "I just found out this morning."

And he was the jerk who was rubbing it in. He felt like apologizing, but he'd been doing too much of that. Instead, he said, "Too bad. She's pretty young. Can't be, what, fourteen? Fifteen?"

Gracie stared at her clasped hands. "She's sixteen."

Reilly looked away from the road to stare at her. She took a deep breath and met his eyes.

"Yes," she said, before he had to ask.

It felt like an avalanche started somewhere inside him. It rumbled and crashed, gaining momentum as it brought realization down through his mind. It was seventeen years ago that Matt had raped her . . . and that meant . . . Analise was Matt's daughter—a child seeded in violence. And Gracie Beck loved her anyway.

He felt a sudden burn of tears in his eyes and quickly looked away. He didn't cry, hadn't even shed a tear when they'd told him Matt was dead. But this . . . this caught him like a sucker punch below the belt. It stole his breath, left him feeling exposed and vulnerable—two things Reilly never let himself be. It made him want to lash out, but not at Gracie. She'd already suffered enough grief from him and his brother. He cleared his throat, willing away the ache in the pit of his stomach.

"Did your grandmother know? About the baby?" he asked, swallowing around the lump in his throat.

Gracie shook her head. Reilly exhaled, wanting to ask more questions but not be responsible for the answers.

"Is the baby why you left like you did?"

She looked at him then, her eyes round and sad. "She threw me out, Reilly."

"Because of the . . . because you were . . ."

"Raped?"

The word brought forth a mental picture of how she'd looked the morning after, battered, emotionally and physically beaten. Sitting across from her at the sheriff's office, he'd wanted to help her. But he didn't.

Just the night before he'd seen her at the barn dance the McGees held every year. She'd moved through the room like smoke, dressed in a short skirt that gave tantalizing glimpses of thigh. She'd been a kid when he'd left for school, but she'd been all grown up when he came back that summer.

"I saw you at the dance that night," he said. "I think that's the first time I ever noticed you—as anything besides the kid that lived down the street, I mean."

"It was." She looked down at her fingers. "I was trying to make you notice me. I thought you were the homegrown hero—a sure ticket out of Diablo Springs. That backfired, didn't it?"

The sound she made was almost a laugh, but it was too bitter to be humorous.

He swallowed, feeling the confession coming up the way the avalanche had gone down. It hollowed him out, demolishing any obstacles or objections that might have kept it in.

"I knew Matt had a thing for you, but I didn't know what . . . I didn't know how bad it was. You were on fire that night and there wasn't a guy in the room who wasn't wondering what you were wearing under that skirt."

Her lips thinned and her eyes turned hard. "So I was asking for it?"

"No," he said quickly. "Hell, no. That's not what I meant. I just—Christ, I goaded him, Gracie. I told him you were going to be mine. And you acted like it wouldn't be a bad thing."

Unbelievably, he was blushing. He could feel the stain of red heat creep up his neck.

"I think I drove him to the edge. It's my fault, what happened."

She stared at him, eyes steady, their color matching the turbulence outside the window. "You believe that, don't you?"

He nodded. "Matt spent his whole life watching out for me. Since we were little. You know about my dad, right?"

"They used to say he was cruel."

"They were being nice. He was a sadistic bastard. He did things . . ." Reilly stopped. He wouldn't go there. Even she couldn't expect him to go there. He shot her a quick glance and saw that he didn't need to. She knew. Whether by rumor or assumption, she knew.

"Matt always took for both of us."

"He was alone, though, when he took from me."

He shook his head. "I've used that reasoning a million times since. But I knew better. Matt wasn't ever leaving Diablo Springs. He died here. He died of it. And there I was the hot-shot golden boy, coming home to glory. He was proud of me, but he wouldn't have been human if he hadn't been jealous. And then I had to take the one thing he had that was good."

"What was that?"

"His fantasy about you."

Reilly glanced at her again, expecting to see the full blast of her fury, of her scorn. But what he saw there made that ache inside him bellow with agony.

She said, "What happened—what he did—it was like a ticking bomb. It might not have happened that night. And maybe he wouldn't have had you there to lie for him. But it would have happened. Do you understand?"

Reilly nodded but he wasn't positive he did.

"I went out with him once. He asked me a hundred times before he finally wore me down and I said yes. We went to the movies and as soon as the lights went out, his hands went to town. He scared me so bad I ran all the way home. After that things got worse."

She took a deep breath and looked out the window. "You didn't drive him to it. He was already there."

Reilly shook his head, but inside a heavy weight shifted and eased back. He wanted to thank her, but he couldn't make the words come out. He was afraid of what would follow them, what else he might confess. Angry with himself, he reached over and turned the air up a notch. The sound of it blowing filled the car.

After a moment, he picked up another thread of the conversation, a safer one this time, or so he thought. "Why did your grandma throw you out then? You said it wasn't because of—" Once again he couldn't force that harsh word out. When had he become such a coward?

"She found me on the front porch. It was pretty obvious that I'd been raped. Matt had on this black T-shirt and black jeans and he'd been hiding in the bushes when I came home. I didn't seem him until it was too late. I remember he pulled his shirt up so the collar covered the bottom of his face. I don't know why because I knew who he was and he knew I knew, but he kept it up the whole time. Maybe he was ashamed to show his face. I don't know. Grandma came out after it was all over and I was crawling up the steps. Matt was already halfway to the springs. When she saw him . . . this shadow tearing across the ruins all dressed in black . . . I can't explain it, Reilly. It was like she caved in from the inside, out. I was curled up crying and she started running through the house shouting. She kept screaming 'aching, aching.' I didn't know what was going on. I didn't know what to think."

Reilly clenched the steering wheel, picturing her crumbled on the front porch. Even as he'd lied for Matt, that image had been burned in his mind. Since then, Reilly had been with his share of women, some nice, some vindictive, some downright mean, but he'd never understood what made Matt want to hurt someone, someone like Gracie Beck.

"She took me in and cleaned me up. She kept saying it was her fault. I don't know why, she wouldn't tell me more. I guess when something like that happens, everyone feels to blame. Everyone but the person who did it."

Reilly knew that Matt had felt the burden of his guilt, but he'd never convince Gracie of that. He didn't try.

"I thought she'd call the sheriff, but she said it wouldn't help. The only thing I could do was get away. The next thing I knew, she'd packed me up."

Reilly couldn't even imagine how she'd felt being thrown out after surviving a rape.

"I finally convinced her that I knew who'd done it. It was like she was certain that some stranger had swooped into town just to hurt me, but once I got through to her that it was Matt, she was furious." Gracie paused and took a deep breath. "You know what happened after that, though. Sheriff Greene hauled Matt in and you gave him the ticket out."

Guilty as charged. She didn't wait for another apology.

"That pretty much sealed my fate. Next thing I knew, she was shoving a suitcase full of money in my hand and giving me the keys to the Plymouth."

"Money? Where'd she get the money?"

"I have no idea. We sure didn't have much of it around the house when I was growing up."

"She never explained why she wanted you to go?"

"No. She just told me to get away from Diablo Springs and never come back."

chapter fifteen

DIGGER Young lived in the same residence his family had occupied for nearly 150 years. It was an incredible house, especially by Diablo Springs' standards. Different from any other place on earth. The Youngs had started as carpenters who were more or less recruited into the casket business and, with it, the mortuary trade. As a home to carpenters, the hand-tooled magnificence of the place shouldn't have been surprising, but the house itself looked too maudlin for opulence. Each generation had added their touch, like globs of dough on a pie. Carved balustrades climbed up and up, embossed with capering squirrels and soaring birds. The porch roof was made of the finest wood, teak and unending. Elaborately carved vignettes and rosettes adorned the wide front door and continued up to the trim where the dainty sculpting went all the way around like decorations on a cake.

And yet overall, the house seemed ominous, hunkering. A place that surely had cobwebs dangling in the corners and strange smells wafting through the rooms. There was something monstrous about it.

Reilly took the winding drive to the far side where the entrance to the mortuary was. For all the elaborate decorations at the house's front door, this entrance was plain to the point of obscurity. A white sign with YOUNG MORTU-ARY in black letters hung above a smooth white door and that was it. It was stark and cold, and as she stared at it through Reilly's windshield, Gracie was overwhelmingly grateful he'd insisted on coming with her.

She was also glad they'd talked on the way. Their

circumstances hadn't changed at all, but somehow everything else had. She felt the tight grip of anger that had been
knotted inside her ease up. Seventeen years was a long time
to bear that kind of burden. She'd mistakenly thought she'd
shed it years and years ago, but now she realized she'd only
hidden her rage and pain deep within. Now that she'd dug it
up, she found it could no longer hurt her. She could let it go.

"Ready?" he asked.

Not at all. Truth be told, she didn't want to go in there.
"Ready," she answered.

He put an arm around her as they dashed together to the
porch that wrapped around the entire house. When they
reached the shelter there, they stood for a moment, looking
at the lakes filling in the valleys of the desert. Despite the
heat, she shivered as Reilly tried the knob of the mortuary
door. When he found it locked, he used the miniature
knocker in the middle. No one answered. He knocked
again. Gracie's hands clenched in frustration. As much as
she dreaded this, she wanted to get it over with.

"Let's try the other door," Reilly said.

They followed the porch to the front door of Digger's
home and Reilly knocked again. They heard a shuffle,
something heavy being moved and then silence. They
looked at one another as they waited. After a moment there
was another sound, scraping, furtive.

"I don't like this," she said softly. Understatement of the
century. So much for her brave words earlier.

The door swung open suddenly, as if to startle away a
kid playing ding dong ditch. Gracie let out a yelp and from
inside the house, Mike "Digger" Young did too.

When she'd left Diablo Springs, Digger had been in his
prime. The seventeen years since had added a smattering of
gray to his hair, a distinguished flair of white to his temples,
and character lines to his face. He had bright blue eyes that
seemed electric beneath his dark brows and his hair was
neatly trimmed, his cropped beard groomed to perfection.
From the neck up he appeared suave, dignified. The image
stopped at his worn red cotton button-down and faded
Wrangler jeans, but there was still something devastatingly

attractive about him. Rumor had it that her mother had been crazy about Digger's father at one time, though he was twenty years older than she'd been. If his father had half of his looks, Gracie could see how her mother might have willingly entered a relationship with a man so much her senior.

He leaned closer to the torn screen on the ornate door and frowned. "She's not here," he said.

"What?" Gracie asked.

"I said, she's not here. I don't keep them here. It's just lies that I keep them here."

A cold chill that had nothing to do with the hot, wet wind covered Gracie in goose bumps.

She inched closer to Reilly and said, "I'd still like to make arrangements for her burial if possible. We tried to call first, Mike. Your phone must not be working."

"Don't have one. And it's Digger. Won't answer to nothing else."

"You don't have one? But there's a number in the book."

"I know. Doesn't mean I have to answer to it." He glared at her for a moment.

"Digger," Reilly said. "Can we come in?"

Digger's eyes bugged out a little and he looked over his shoulder and back. "In here? You want to come in here?"

Before Reilly could answer, Digger gave a harsh laugh. He had the whitest teeth Gracie had ever seen. They looked nearly artificial against the dark beard and the dim lighting. Despite her determination not to, she looked for resemblances between herself and this man who might have been her brother. But she saw nothing familiar in his face. The callous sound of his laughter ended abruptly and he opened the door wider.

"Daddy's probably pissin' himself knowing you're coming in his house," he said.

Gracie hesitated, one foot on either side of the threshold, a knot of anxiety tightening in her stomach. Reilly's hand moved to the small of her back, whether to urge her forward or support her, she wasn't sure. Digger took it all in and gave another bark of laughter.

"I meant in his grave. He never did get over your momma. Never did."

She had no comment on Digger's devotion to her mother. Everything she knew was hearsay. Grandma Beck had refused to talk about Gracie's mother's relationship with Digger but the rest of the town was happy to offer their theories.

With more reluctance than she'd admit to, Gracie stepped through the door. The smell hit her immediately. It was dark and sweet, like fruit that had spoiled. Cloying. She looked around for the source, but everything inside was immaculate—she'd been wrong about the cobwebs. There wasn't a speck of dust in sight. The room was packed full of furniture, though. Wooden, all of it. Carved rocking chairs, unfinished oak tables. Stools, lots of footstools, and straight-back chairs. Beneath that heavy, tainted sugar smell lingered the scent of freshly cut wood, sap, and pine.

"Sit down, sit down," he said, suddenly jovial.

He pulled a couple of the straight-backs from the clutter of furniture and set them in a tight circle just inside the door, seemingly unaware of how strange that was, to huddle in the entryway.

"I don't get visitors much," he said.

Shocking, thought Gracie, but kept that to herself. She'd expected some level of hostility from him. Between the scandal over her mother's death and the undertaking business, Digger was the kind of man people talked about. He was rarely seen in town, even more rarely seen with others. Until a few moments ago, Gracie had never known him to smile. Beyond the circle of his kingdom, Digger was like a ghost.

"I hadn't spoken to Grandma Beck in a long time. I'm afraid I don't know what provisions she made for . . . for . . ." Gracie breathed in, trying to fight down the emotion. But all she accomplished was filling her lungs with that cloying scent. "I'm not sure what arrangements to make, to be honest, but I wanted to talk about the options."

"Do you want to see her? She's still fresh. Haven't fixed her up yet if you know what I mean."

The last wasn't a question. Gracie swallowed hard. Reilly reached for her hand and kept it clasped in his.

"You just said she wasn't here," Reilly pointed out.

Digger frowned. "'Course she's not here. She's in the mortuary. Told you, I don't keep them here. It's just lies that I keep them here."

Gracie frowned. "Her—she's next door?"

Digger nodded. "Unless she got up and walked out."

Gracie stood so suddenly her chair tipped and nearly fell over. Reilly righted it as he stood beside her.

"Do you want to see her?" he asked softly. Digger watched with undisguised interest.

Gracie's voice seemed to have left her, but she managed a nod.

Digger stood and carefully returned their chairs to the jumble they'd started in. Without a word, he led them through the front door, around the porch, and to the mortuary entrance. He pulled a large key ring with only two keys on it from his pocket and opened up. The door swung back on a stillness that seemed to mock the flailing storm beyond the porch shelter. Digger gestured for them to go inside.

"You'll want to brace yourself," he said in the same tone of voice he might have told her there was a sale on eggs at the grocery store.

She nodded and followed him through the reception area where three chairs and a love seat were gathered, waiting for the next group of mourners. A black velvet curtain portioned off a viewing room to the left. Digger went straight, through a utilitarian door that led down an L-shaped hall. At the end was a metal door with a red Do Not Enter sign.

Digger looked at Gracie one last time before pushing through to a stainless-steel room with counters, two tables in the center, and a huge drain in the floor. The embalming room. One table had a sheet-covered body on it. Gracie's stomach clenched tightly and Reilly turned her to face him.

"You don't have to do this, Gracie," he said.

"Yes, I do."

She heard rustling and knew Digger had uncovered the body on the table. She tried not to breathe too deeply as she faced her grandmother's corpse.

Digger was right. She'd needed to brace herself. But not for the reasons Digger might have imagined. She'd needed to brace for the rush of emotion that hit her like the storm outside. It came from everywhere and nowhere at once. Carefully she approached the still form that had once been a living, breathing person. She stood over Grandma Beck and felt the tears fill her eyes as memories she'd thought forgotten swirled through her mind.

It wasn't the grisly death she saw as she looked down; it was the remembered life. Grandma Beck was a little woman who always gave the impression of being larger than she was, though on tiptoes she barely reached five foot two. Her hands were tiny, delicate things that now lay crossed over her chest, as if in defense. Her eyes were mercifully closed. The soft shadow of her lashes on her cheeks and the relaxed expression on her face made her look like she might be sleeping. Like she might, at any moment, sit up and tell Gracie she was sorry and that she loved her. Only the ashen pallor of her skin let Gracie know that wasn't going to happen.

As she stared down at her, Gracie felt another chunk of the wall she'd built between her past and her present dislodge and disintegrate. She brushed at the tears streaming down her face and gave a sad laugh. Reilly was silent at her side.

"I didn't realize how mad I've been at her. I mean, I knew I was hurt and I was angry at first. But I thought I'd gotten over it. I thought I'd moved on. I didn't realize . . . until just now, looking at her . . . she was hurt too. She had to be hurt too. She loved me. It wasn't easy for her to send me away."

"You thought it was?" he asked.

She nodded. "I had myself convinced that she never really cared. That she was glad to get rid of me. But when I look at her, I can remember her touching me." The tears fell faster. "Holding me and taking care of me."

"Maybe she thought she failed you, Gracie. Maybe that's why she sent you away."

Gracie looked into his face, grateful for that bit of insight. "I'll never understand, I guess. Not everything. But why she chose to do what she did—it wasn't because she didn't love me."

Reilly gave her a gentle smile.

"She was a stubborn old bird," Digger said meanly. "And she'll be joining them, sure enough."

"Joining who?" Gracie asked.

"The Dead Lights. I seen it already. She ain't going away."

Gracie exchanged a look with Reilly. "I don't know what you're talking about."

"Sure you do. You seen 'em." He looked at Reilly. "I know you have. They're all out there, wandering them springs. Oh, folks pretend it ain't so, but don't see none of them out that way at night, do you? Just me. Just old Digger. Been a Digger Young watching the Dead Lights for over a hundred years."

"The Dead Lights are just an illusion, Digger," Reilly said. "A weird fluke of the old springs and the night air."

"Yeah, you believe that. But when they come thumping at the Diablo, you'll mark my words. And they will. She knew 'em. Drove her crazy in the end."

Gracie had heard enough. "Did she want to be buried here, Digger?"

Digger laughed. "No. She didn't trust a coffin to hold her down. She wants to be cremated and spread out at the springs."

chapter sixteen

GRACIE sat quietly beside Reilly as he navigated the flooded roads, Digger Young's words playing over in her mind. *She knew 'em. Drove her crazy in the end. . . .* Was it true? Was that how her grandmother had come to be out at the springs in the middle of a storm? And why would she want her ashes spread out there? It made no sense at all.

Gracie rubbed the gooseflesh on her arms. At last the rain had defeated the ovenlike heat, reducing it to warm instead of bake. But it wasn't the cool air that made a shiver creep over her. It was the memory of Digger's voice, deep and insinuating. *"When they come thumping at the Diablo, you'll mark my words. . . ."*

"I hate this place," Gracie said, staring out the window at the gray and turbulent world. To her, Diablo Springs would always be covered in gloom—whether with storms of the past or of the present, it didn't matter.

"I don't blame you. I hate it too," Reilly said. "This town is just one big, bad thing waiting to happen."

Amen, Gracie thought.

Reilly glanced away from the road for a moment. His eyes were dark and serious. "What do you think about what he said? About your grandma?"

This morning she would have been angered by any question from him. But her resentment had waned. He'd opened a dam and let so much out that she felt almost light in the aftermath.

"Do you remember much about her, Reilly?"

"Some people thought she was crazy."

"She probably was. Having Analise . . . I can only

imagine what it must have been like for her to lose my mom. You don't want to outlive your children. I don't know what she was like before it happened though. I just remember she was always secretive. She'd never talk about the past. To this day, I don't have a clue who my grandfather—hell, who my dad was."

"There aren't any men in your family at all."

She'd thought it enough times, but hearing it spoken, hearing it spoken *here*, sent a chill down her spine. "She used to say we were cursed."

Saying it made her blush. "I know it sounds stupid. But I used to believe it. After the rape, I was convinced. She was so frantic about getting me out of town that I thought if I stayed I'd be struck down where I stood."

"Like what happened to her?"

She looked at him.

"I'm sorry," he said. "I don't think before I speak. Talk about curses."

"But you're right. And after I was gone, she never let me come back. She returned my letters—even pictures of the baby. I tried calling, but she wouldn't talk to me. I was devastated." She looked down at her clenched hands, blinking back a well of emotion that threatened to overflow. "Still am, I guess."

Her last night in Diablo Springs had culminated in a trauma she'd never fully recovered from. Now, in retrospect, she could see that the events leading up to it had been building her entire life, but she couldn't explain that. How would she begin to put into words the sense of hysteria that had somehow always been near the surface, like flowing water beneath thin ice? For as long as she could remember, her grandmother had been looking over her shoulder—not watching for the normal hazards of childhood and adolescence—searching for something only she understood. Gracie had been left in the dark, sensing the paranoia but never comprehending its source.

She looked away from her hands at Reilly's profile. He held himself stiffly, his hands tight on the steering wheel as he drove the flooded roads.

"Do you still feel cursed?" he asked.

She shook her head. "Not really. Actually, I've been blessed in so many ways. I've got a terrific kid and a great job. A good life."

And she found she meant it. Even with this latest life-altering news of a baby, she and Analise would weather it. Together. She could offer her child this much . . . which was more than she'd ever gotten from her own family.

"What do you do?" Reilly asked, interrupting her thoughts.

"I'm a graphic artist," she said, with a hint of pride. "I work at the university—San Diego State."

"Sounds like you like it."

She nodded. She loved her job. "How about you? When did you start writing?"

"After the group broke up. I started with songs. It took me a while to commit to a book. Never been very good at the commitment thing."

"You never got married, settled down?"

"Never even came close. I guess I haven't stayed in one place long enough. And I guess I never thought settling down was that great a deal. Didn't do much for my folks. How about you?"

"I was close a couple of times, but it never worked out."

The silence that followed had a hot edge to it. Gracie didn't quite know how or why, but she recognized it for what it was.

Clearing her throat, she said, "Thank you for taking me today. You were right. I wouldn't have wanted to be at Digger's alone."

He cocked a brow in her direction. "You mean you're glad I'm here?"

"Let's not get carried away."

He grinned and made a right on Main Street.

"Stop looking so smug," she said.

"I'm not."

"Yes you are. I can feel it."

He pulled to a stop at the one and only traffic signal in Diablo Springs and waited. Beside him, Gracie curled her fingers into her palms. The warm dampness outside seemed to heighten the scent of his cologne, his skin, his heat. The combination chased a new perspective into her mind. There'd been a time, before that night, when she would have given anything to be alone with him.

She glanced at him again to find him staring back at her. The rain battered the roof of the Jeep, coming down in a solid, pounding cascade. The fury of it isolated them inside, obliterating everything beyond the capsule of time. The light remained red, though they were the only car at the signal. Outside the gutters overflowed and pooled back into the street.

She could feel tension emanating from him, like a low hum only she could hear. Maybe it was coming from her as well. His hand slid over the back of the seat, coming to rest just inches from her face. She chewed on her lower lip, looking at him with a desire that caught her completely off guard. In less than twenty-four hours she'd gone from hating him to . . . to wishing he'd touch her. How had that happened?

"What do you want, Reilly?" She'd asked a similar question this morning. But this time her voice made the words different. The accusation was gone. In its place was a genuine need to know.

"I thought I came for Matt. But right now, I'm not so sure."

Maybe she should have been bothered by that, but she understood what he meant.

"What are you thinking?" he asked, something deep as the darkness of his eyes in the question.

"I was thinking, people come into your life for a reason. I just don't know what yours is yet."

"Let me give you a hint," he said.

And he leaned across the seat and kissed her. He didn't hesitate, didn't pause a moment to give her the chance to pull back. And that was fine, because she didn't want to. Still, her senses were shocked by the hard demand of his mouth, her emotions rocked by the mystery of him and the strange fulfillment just touching seemed to give her. She took a surprised gulp of air and felt as if she'd breathed in a part of him—an essence that fired through her bloodstream and made her arch forward into his embrace.

Her hands came up to his chest, her fingers curled into his shirt. And she kissed him back. Hungrily. He made a low sound in his throat that triggered a million reactions inside her body.

Overhead, thunder rumbled ominously and lightning snaked down with a fiery hiss. It struck the dangling traffic signal with a loud boom that pressed hard against her eardrums. Gracie let out a shout of surprise, pulling back just as the light exploded, shooting shards of smoking metal in every direction. Reilly grabbed Gracie and pushed her down as a chunk of metal hurled toward the windshield. It hit like a detonation and spidered the glass.

Stunned they looked up at the exposed wires that smoked and sizzled in the rain. A blackened hunk of the signal lay on the hood. To the right the pole that had held the light began to sway.

"Oh, my God," she said.

He hit the gas and the SUV jumped forward, parting the water on the street as they plowed through. The hunk of metal on his hood clattered and thumped its way across and off. Behind them, the pole listed to the right and then crashed to the street where they'd been stopped.

chapter seventeen

REILLY pulled into the crowded parking lot of the Buck-board Bar and Grill, but he didn't cut the engine. He turned in his seat and watched her for a moment. What was he thinking, Gracie wondered? What was *she* thinking? The sound of the wipers swishing back and forth sounded un-naturally loud.

He leaned forward and kissed her again, the taste of him still new and exciting in ways she couldn't describe or deny.

"We're not finished," he said against her lips.

She wanted to say, thank God, but she kept it to herself. Reluctantly, she pulled away.

Together they raced to the front doors of the Buckboard. Even if they hadn't already been soaked, there was no way to do it without getting wet. The water gushed through the gutters and sloshed over the walkway. She'd hoped it would cool her blood, but she felt like she was on fire.

They entered the Buckboard on a gust of wet air that swirled into the restaurant like a mist. The parking lot had been full, but inside it was downright crowded. The entire building was long and narrow, built when the population had been under five hundred. The bar was old and battered. It ran lengthwise for maximum occupancy, but even then, no more than ten or fifteen people could belly up at any given time. Behind it was a fake, but ornate, antique mirror that reflected the drinkers and eaters at the scattering of tables in the din-ing area. Old-time pictures covered the walls, showing gun-slingers and turn-of-the-century dignitaries—the few who had braved the heat to visit Diablo Springs during its hey-day as a resort.

A couple high-topped tables took up the space between the bar and the eight or nine dinner tables. At the far end, a miniature stage and stamp-sized dance floor implied that some nights drew enough business for a two-step and a local band. Now they both were empty.

Smoke made a haze of the air, mixing with the yeasty smell of malt and spilled booze. The lighting was dim, the shades open to show the spectacle of the storm outside. Reilly rested his hand on the small of Gracie's back, offering support and laying claim in one small gesture. Gracie scanned the faces around her looking for Analise. She spotted her, sitting in the corner with Brendan. A frown tightened Gracie's mouth. Chloe LaMonte and the ever-present Bill sat with them. At another table she saw the young man who'd come with Reilly.

"Come on in, folks," a wild-eyed waitress in a jean skirt and tank top said as she balanced a tray of beer mugs.

She took a half step away and then turned, pointing at Reilly. "Oh, my God," she exclaimed. "Reilly Alexander?" She rushed up, switching the tray to her left hand and giving him a hug with her right. "How are you?" Before he could answer she turned to Gracie. A second of silence passed between them and then she let out another screech. "Gracie Beck! I never thought I'd see you again."

Her name popped into Gracie's head at that moment. "Corrine Murray," Gracie said. "Wow, look at you. You look great."

She did look great. The years had been good to Corrine, filling out the bony girl into a curvy woman. She'd always had a bright smile and almond skin. Now she accented her dark eyes with shadow and the dusky lips with lipstick and the overall effect was wowza. They'd never been close friends, but she'd always liked Corrine.

"It's busy," Gracie said.

"Christ almighty, this isn't busy, it's insane. I'm usually doing my nails in between customers." She looked at Gracie for a moment. "I was sorry to hear about your grandma Beck."

There was little sincerity in the sentiment, but it made sense to Gracie. Though she didn't know why, Grandma Beck had never liked Corrine, even when she was a child. Grandma had felt that way about a lot of the kids in her school. She wouldn't have had any friends if it had been up to her grandma.

"Thank you," Gracie said.

Someone gestured for her and Corrine nodded back. "Go ahead and find a table. I'll be right with you."

As they approached the table where Analise sat, Gracie felt a tightening in her stomach. Familiar faces turned like beacons to watch her pass through. It had been years, but she recognized nearly all of them, even those whose names had been erased by time.

"Blast from the past," Reilly mumbled as he put on his own smile and wave show.

They stopped at the table where her daughter sat. Chloe perched on the edge of her seat, directly opposite Analise. She held Analise's hand, palm-up as she stared down at it with fixed concentration.

"What's going on?" Gracie asked.

"She's reading my palm," Analise exclaimed, bright-eyed.

Gracie couldn't help the feeling that gripped her as she watched Chloe peering into her daughter's hand, "reading" her future. She couldn't put her finger on it, but she knew the woman was up to something. And it couldn't be good. She also knew that such a person could easily use a palm reading to try to manipulate a vulnerable young girl in the name of her future. For this reason and others she hadn't had time to analyze, her voice was sharp as she said, "I asked you to stay away from my family."

Chloe looked very different from the old, white-haired woman who'd stepped into Gracie's room last night. Today she wore a brightly colored tunic that billowed from an empire waistline and floated down to her lap. Blousy sleeves gathered at her wrists and covered part of her birdlike hands. A pair of royal blue pants matched her athletic shoes today and another brightly patterned turban covered the thinning white hair. She'd put on makeup with a heavy hand that accented the dark pearls of her glittering eyes. Gracie wondered if it also hid the shadows beneath them.

"Do you know why you resent me so much?" Chloe asked. As always, her voice was melodic. But this morning her smile was slight and somehow sorrowful. Not quite pitying, but full of compassion.

"Intrusion," Gracie said. "I resent the intrusion."

Chloe nodded, lowering her eyes. "That's fair enough. But you should know I wouldn't be intruding if it wasn't necessary. You think I'm a joke. You think I'm here for some"—she waved a small hand in the air—"nefarious purpose, but that isn't why I've come to this place. I have my own ghosts, Gracie Beck. And I want them laid to rest."

She glanced at Bill in a gesture that was at once commanding and helpless. He rose and held her chair as she stood. She gave one last searching look at Gracie, and then she moved away. All eyes watched her part the sea of white faces. She walked with a regal grace that somehow transcended the rubber-soled shoes.

I have my own ghosts . . .

What the hell did that mean?

"Hey," Brendan said loud enough to silence the tables nearby. Chloe paused and looked at him. "What about me?"

The sight of him caught Gracie by surprise. He'd changed just since this morning, though she couldn't put her finger on how. He was still the same blond-haired, blue-eyed young man, and yet something was different about his eyes, about the way he stood, the way he watched. Was it the weight of responsibility that straightened his back and squared his shoulders? The reality of a baby and mouths to feed? A part of her hoped so and a part of her wanted to die from the knowledge. Her baby was having a baby and this boy would be a father.

Chloe hesitated, appraising him with something like wariness. He thrust his hand out to her and Gracie sensed her recoil, though she didn't move a muscle.

"Another time," Bill said softly. He guided Chloe to a seat at a table near the empty dance floor.

"You didn't let her finish," Analise complained. "She didn't finish reading my palm."

"I don't want her around you."

"Why?"

Corinne chose that moment to approach their table and take their order, saving Gracie from an explanation she didn't have.

"Do you know her?" Corrine asked, looking over at Chloe with a frown.

"Not really," Gracie answered. "She's staying at the Diablo."

"She gives me the creeps. She said she can read me. She said she knows why I'm outside the circle. What crap."

Gracie nodded.

"She also said if I went home I'd find my wedding ring, but I had to do it now. You think she's for real?"

"I don't know. I doubt it."

"I've been looking for it for a month."

"But why would you have to go home now to find it?"

Corinne shrugged, still looking back at Chloe. "She's nuts. Anyway, what'll you have? Menu hasn't changed much. Burgers or burgers."

Gracie was surprised to realize she was hungry. Very hungry. She and Reilly ordered burgers. It was an easy choice.

"What did they say about your grandma?" Analise asked when Corrine had left.

"She wanted to be cremated. She wants her ashes spread at the hot springs."

Brendan's eyes widened. "You're kidding?" he said.

All three of them looked at him. "No, why?"

He laughed softly. "Just a creepy place to spend eternity, that's all."

His words seemed weighted, but with what, Gracie didn't know.

"I have to go to the bathroom," Analise announced. She stood and Brendan stood as well. Analise frowned at him. "I can find it on my own."

He smiled and took her arm anyway. She looked for a moment like she might jerk it from his grasp, but after an exasperated sigh, she let him lead her to the rest rooms. Did he plan to stand outside the stall while she went? Gracie and Reilly sat in silence for a few moments after they'd left, maybe both pondering the same question.

After a while Reilly asked, "Why do you think she wanted her ashes spread out at the ruins?"

"I don't know. Maybe to be close to my mother . . ."

The thought had been in Gracie's head ever since Eddie told them where Grandma Beck had died.

Analise chose that moment to reappear at the table. "Why would that be close to your mother?" she asked.

Gracie's eyes fluttered down and she bit her lip. "What happened to your mother, Mom?" Analise asked again. "You told me she died when you were born."

"I told you she died when I was a baby." Analise had assumed it was during childbirth and Gracie had never disillusioned her.

She took another sip of her soda before meeting her daughter's curious gaze. Brendan looked on with an expression she couldn't read.

"My mom died out there too. At the hot springs," Gracie said at last.

Analise's eyes and mouth rounded to Os. "How?"

"I don't really know. It's a dangerous place."

Gracie looked away, not wanting to explain about her mother. Too raw after the visit to the mortuary to invite any more painful memories.

"C'mon, Mom. What happened to her?"

Gracie gave a soft, humorless laugh. Analise had been trying to pry the lid off Gracie's past for months now, ever since she'd given her that charm bracelet and told her it was a family heirloom. She'd wanted Analise to know that somewhere they had history. She hadn't wanted it to be here and now, though.

So far Gracie had managed to sidestep the direct questions, but there was no way around it now. She would have to tell the story—she owed it to Analise. And perhaps it was time.

"I'll tell you what I know, but it's not much, Analise. To this day no one really knows what happened to my mom."

Gracie paused, searching for the place to begin. It wasn't easy because there was no beginning or end. The story was a series of events that might or might not have been connected. Hard to explain that to someone sitting on the edge of her seat waiting for a tale to be spun.

"What I know for certain is that she was at the ruins and I was with her. It's not known how she got out there, though. I was just an infant and it was August so it had to be scorching hot. She certainly wasn't taking a walk, but no one knows for sure what she was doing."

"I think it's haunted out there," Analise said.

Gracie looked at her daughter's pale face, wanting to ask why, but not really wanting to know the answer.

"What Grandma Beck told me was that she just disappeared one night."

"What about your dad? Where was he?"

Gracie sighed. "I told you I don't know who my dad was, Analise."

"Yeah, you've been a wealth of information," Analise said.

From his expression, the sarcasm caught Reilly by surprise, but not Gracie. Analise was whip-smart and since she'd hit the teenage years, she'd had no qualms about cutting someone to the bone with her wit. But Gracie couldn't reprimand her for it this time. She was only speaking the truth. In her own way, Gracie was every bit as tight-lipped as Grandma Beck had been.

"My mother dated a local man named Michael Young. Everybody called him Digger because his family owned the mortuary—still does. We went to see his son before coming here. From what I'm told he was a very nice man but he was older than my mother. Quite a bit older. When she got pregnant, everyone assumed he was the father, but she'd never tell who it was for sure."

"Why?" Analise asked.

"People said she was afraid Grandma Beck would make her marry him and she'd decided she didn't like him enough for that. My mom was a grown woman by that time, though. Old enough to decide who she was going marry, I'd think. Again, no one ever knew for sure what the reason was."

Brendan leaned forward and said, "Kind of a pattern, wouldn't you say, not knowing who your dad is?"

It wasn't true. Gracie knew who Analisa's father was. She just never saw what good could come of sharing the knowledge. She went on as if Brendan hadn't spoken. "She'd quit seeing Digger long before I was born and he never made any claims that he was my father—that I know of anyway. He was a widower and he was raising a son from that marriage. Generally people thought he was a respectable, if strange, guy and if he was my father, he would have done the 'right thing.' Which, I guess, is what my mom was worried about."

Gracie thought about what the "new" Digger had said today. His father had never gotten over Gracie's mom.

"How old was his son?" Analise asked.

Gracie thought about that for a moment. Mike junior had been a man in his forties when she'd left Diablo Springs. "I guess he was close to my mother's age. Maybe a little older."

"That's gross," she said.

"Anyway, I was only a few months old when my mother disappeared. No one saw her leave the house and she never came back. They combed the town, the hills, and the ruins searching for us after Grandma Beck discovered we were gone. Diablo Springs gives small town new meaning in case you haven't noticed. Every available man, woman, and child was out there beating the bushes looking for us."

"But they didn't find you?"

"Not at first. After a couple of days, the sheriff started questioning people. He went to Digger's house and found that he was gone too. His son hadn't seen him since around the time my mom and I vanished."

Analise's eyes rounded.

"So the story goes, on the fourth day Grandma Beck just woke up from a dead sleep, grabbed her hat and shoes and started walking out to the ruins—still wearing her nightgown. She was like a woman possessed, is what they say. The people who saw her followed her. By the time she got to the ruins, the sheriff was there and trying to talk her down. He figured she'd gone crazy with grief and was going to throw herself into the pit or something. She walked right up to this sinkhole and pointed to it. She told the sheriff that her daughter was in that hole and if he wanted to live to see another year, he better get her out."

Analise said, "And did he?"

"Find her—us? Yes. They dug into the sinkhole and it opened onto a cavern and my mom was in it, unconscious. She was holding me. She'd kept me alive by nursing me until I'd drained her dry. She died on the way to the hospital without ever regaining consciousness."

Gracie inhaled, forcing down the rise of old guilt and hurt. Rational or no, she'd always felt her grandmother blamed Gracie for killing her mother and had never forgiven her for it.

"What about Digger?" Brendan asked.

"He was never seen again. No one knows what happened to him."

"How did your grandmother know where to find you?" Analise asked.

Gracie rolled the tension from her neck and swallowed around the lump in her throat. She hadn't thought about this, hadn't hurt about this in nearly twenty years. But the old sting of it burned at her eyes. "I don't know."

"Don't you?"

They all turned quickly to find Chloe standing right behind Gracie.

"It's not polite to eavesdrop," Gracie said.

"What do you mean?" Analise asked.

Chloe gave a look that almost spoke of apology. Almost.

She said to Analise, "When you were out there last night, did you sense that things were not . . . right? That in that place, everything is very wrong?"

Analise nodded. "It felt like I had things crawling on me. But there weren't. I kept brushing my arms, though. And then Brendan got really mad at me."

Brendan looked at her, his face placid, but his eyes were hard. "I wasn't mad, Analise."

"Yes you were."

Chloe interrupted before Brendan could answer back.

"Your family is connected to this town, connected by history and by blood." She looked to Gracie. "It called you back."

"No, Eddie Rodriguez called me back."

"Ask Brendan how he found this town," Chloe said, her voice gentle and patient.

All eyes turned to Brendan. He smiled. "Wasn't hard."

"He saw it when he was driving to Phoenix last week," Analise said.

"And how many times have you made the drive?" Chloe asked.

Brendan shrugged. His eyes looked like ice, fractured from the cold. "Dozen, maybe more."

"Yet I'm willing to guess that you'd never seen a sign for Diablo Springs before."

He shifted, a frown pulling at his brows. For a moment it seemed the mask slipped and the Brendan Gracie knew peered out. The thought caught her by surprise. Why would she think that? The boy in front of her *was* the Brendan she knew. And yet . . .

"Nothing that happens here is by chance," Chloe said. "Diablo Springs wanted you to find it. Wanted you to bring them here."

"That's crazy," Brendan said. Gracie agreed.

"Are you sure it's not you that's making things happen?" Reilly, who'd been very quiet up to that point, asked Chloe.

"You mean earlier?" she said.

"What happened earlier?" Gracie asked.

Reilly shook his head. "Nothing."

"We don't know," Zach said, appearing at the other side of the table.

Apparently there was no such thing as a private conversation at the Buckboard. Zach pulled up a chair and squeezed in between Gracie and Reilly. Reilly gave him an annoyed look, but Zach's interest seemed focused on Gracie alone.

"We saw the Dead Lights. And maybe ghosts in the house."

"I didn't see any ghosts, in the house or anywhere else," Reilly said, giving him a hard look.

Zach made a sound of disbelief. "Sure you didn't. You probably didn't hear the doors slamming either." Zach turned back to Gracie. "I saw a man, standing at the bar."

"What bar?" Reilly asked.

"What man?" Gracie asked, wishing her tone held the same note of skepticism as Reilly's. But the memory of the man she'd seen in her room last night was too fresh for her to discount what Zach was saying.

"I don't know who he was. I saw him and then he was gone."

"What did he look like?" Chloe asked, reaching behind her for a chair. Bill anticipated her need and pushed one forward.

Zach frowned. "He wasn't much taller than me, not much bigger. But he looked hard. You know. Someone who works outdoors, with his hands."

The copper hue of Chloe's skin took on a yellowish cast.

"You're saying you saw a ghost long enough to describe him?" Brendan said. He gave a snort of laughter. "That's bullshit."

Reilly nodded, but Gracie read something in the way he avoided her eyes that made her question his reaction.

Analise glared at Brendan. "I believe Zach. The whole house is creepy. You can't remember what happened to us last night, but—"

"But what? You do?"

"I remember being scared."

"You're always scared."

Analise closed her mouth, looking hurt and angry.

"We saw the Dead Lights first," Zach said. "Then all the doors just slammed. No reason. Just bam, bam bam." He repeated the word loud enough to make her jump. "When we came in to see what was going on, I saw the man at the bar—just for a second, but I know what I saw."

"Is that true?" she asked Reilly. "Why didn't you tell me?"

"You wanted me to tell you that the air-conditioning came on and blew the doors shut? Zach's been watching too much TV."

Zach smacked the table with his open palm. "You're a liar."

"Watch who you're calling a liar, Zach," Reilly said in low voice.

Before Zach could argue, someone else approached their table. It was Bud Bowman, the town's only lawyer, standing beside them in a dated three-piece suit and worn dress shoes. Bud had been more than the family attorney, and when she was growing up, Gracie had always suspected that he'd loved Grandma Beck. She remembered that Bud had always personally brought papers to the Diablo and often stayed to dinner. And he always had cinnamons in his pocket. He smiled at Gracie.

"How are you?" he asked.

Gracie shrugged. "Hanging in there."

"I know this is a hard time. Carolina will be sorely missed. After the storm clears, I'll bring her papers by so you can settle her estate."

"I'd appreciate that."

"You going to inherit it all?" Brendan asked.

"I don't know," Gracie said, not wanting to think about that. She had enough emotional baggage from this town without adding the Diablo and all its secrets to it.

"You let me know when it's a good time to settle matters," Bud said gently.

There would never be a good time to handle it, but she couldn't say that to him. Bud started past their table and then stopped beside Zach, frowning.

"What happened to Hollywood?" he asked in a surprised voice.

"The studio gave me the week off," Zach said, grinning.

"Ah," Bud answered. He smiled at Gracie again and then donned a black raincoat and stepped out into the storm.

Zach put his elbows on the table with an ear-to-ear grin. "People think I look like Matthew McConaughey," he said. "I told the waitress I was."

"You do, kinda," Analise told him.

"My ass," Brendan said.

Their food arrived and they sat back so the big, burly man with a dirty apron and a three-day beard could set their cheeseburgers on the table. Gracie wondered what had happened to Corrine.

"Jim?" Reilly said with surprise. "How the hell are you?"

"Ass deep in orders and my fucking waitress has disappeared."

They looked around just as the door opened and Corinne walked in from outside, dripping rainwater. She stood just at the entrance, swaying, looking strangely out of place. As if she'd just woken from a dream.

"Corinne," Jim hollered at her. "Get your ass over here and serve this food. I'm backed up in the kitchen without doing your job too."

He lumbered back through the swinging doors, a man with orders to fill, without ever looking at her. If he had, he would have seen the greenish black bruise around Corrine's eye. Her tank top was torn and smeared with something reddish. The rain had diluted it and run through it, making it look tie-dyed.

Chloe stood and without a word, Bill escorted her back to the table by the dance floor. She'd looked frightened, but Gracie couldn't say of what. Instead she watched as Corrine moved slowly to their table.

"Corrine, what happened?" Gracie exclaimed.

"What the hell does it look like?"

Gracie drew back, stung. Corrine swung her angry eyes to Reilly. "Why'd you bring all those freaks here? Huh? Why?"

Reilly didn't have an answer.

"Jesus," Corrine said. She pulled up one of the chairs and covered her face with trembling hands. No one spoke for a moment.

"Corrine?" Gracie tried again, reaching out to touch her arm.

She lowered her hands and looked at Gracie. As long as she lived, Gracie would never forget the pain she saw in her eyes.

"You know what she said?" Corrine demanded. "That bitch? Do you know what she said?"

Somehow Gracie knew who she was talking about. "Chloe?" Gracie asked.

"Bitch," Corrine spat. "For no reason, she just comes up to me and says, 'Go back and find it. You won't know until you do.'"

Corrine sniffed, lifted the hem of her tank top, and stared at her shirt, shaking her head. Gracie watched her, knowing without being told what the red stuff was.

"I thought she had a screw loose," Corrine went on, "so I just ignored her. But she kept on and when I finally asked her what the hell she was talking about she tells me my ring. My wedding ring. 'Go home,' she says, 'go home and you'll find it.' I told her if I was going to find it, I'd find it later as well as now. But she went all crazy on me. Said it couldn't wait. Said it would be gone if I waited."

"That's where you've been? You went home?"

Corrine glared at her. "Yes. She got me in a knot about it. All I could think was that someone was going to rob my house while I was at work. Like she'd had some kind of vision or something. So I snuck out and raced back to my house."

"And now you know where it was?" Gracie said, feeling like she was being led into a trap.

"That wasn't what she meant I'd find. I walked in on my husband boning the babysitter in our bed. He'd told me he had to work a double shift at the hardware store. He wasn't supposed to be home."

"God, Corrine. I'm sorry."

"Not as sorry as he is."

Corrine looked over her shoulder as a gust of thick, wet air came in. Gracie looked too. Eddie Rodriguez stood in the entry, scanning the occupants. He paused when he saw their table. He took off his hat and came over.

"Took you long enough," Corinne said.

He nodded, watching her warily. One hand was at his hip, poised just above his gun. His beige uniform was drenched dark brown from the rain.

"You going to shoot me?"

"Not unless you make me."

Corrine gave a bitter laugh at that. "Is he dead?"

"Not yet. He's at the clinic waiting on an ambulance to take him to Tucson."

"Tell me Doc Graebel didn't sew it back on? Shit."

Eddie winced, shaking his head. "You ran it through the garbage disposal, Corrine."

She smiled the coldest smile Gracie had ever seen. "Oh yeah."

Moving with careful calm, Eddie pulled out his cuffs. "I need to take you in."

"I know," she said. She took off her apron and set it on the table and then she held out her hands. "I always wanted to be handcuffed by you, hoss."

Eddie turned her and locked the bracelets on each wrist. "There were easier ways to go about it. All you had to do was ask."

"Where's the fun in that?"

With everyone in the bar watching, Eddie led Corrine out the door. Gracie sat in silence for a moment, not sure she could believe what she'd just heard.

"Did I get that right?" Reilly asked.

Gracie nodded, glancing from him, to the openmouthed expressions on the faces of her daughter and Zach. Only Brendan seemed undisturbed by what had happened. He wore a peculiar smile that made her skin prick and her nerves buzz. Suddenly she wasn't so hungry anymore.

"What did he mean about the garbage disposal?" Analise asked.

No way was Gracie going to explain the Lorrena Bobbit connection. The less said about what had just happened, the better.

"We've got to get out of here," she said.

chapter eighteen

May 1896

THE ride back to camp with Sawyer would be imprinted in my memory forever. My emotions had been drawn and quartered, until I didn't know what feeling went with what part of me. I sat behind Sawyer on his powerful horse, lulled by the rolling motion of its gait, my face was pressed into his back. He smelled of horse and sun and river-washed cotton. Familiar smells that mingled pleasantly with his own scent. Against all reason, I was comforted.

My tears had doused my blood lust, and I began to think that I'd acted out of judgment rather than rationale. I hadn't seen Sawyer with the Smith brothers and he would have been hard to miss on his enormous horse. And why would he be riding alone now if he was with them? More to the point, why wouldn't he have simply killed me when I'd attacked? He'd have witnesses to verify he'd acted in self-defense should it ever come under the scrutiny of the law. But he hadn't taken my life. Instead he'd helped me.

My arms were around his waist and only the anchor of his solid body kept me from sliding to the ground. His chest rose and fell with his steady breathing. His voice was gentle when he talked to the horse, but he did not speak to me, nor I to him. What would I say? Perhaps I was wrong to have tried to slit your throat and thank you for not cutting mine?

When he deposited me back at the camp, Chick and Meaira were there to help me. Honey brought me food. Athena fussed around Sawyer and then cared for his horse. I heard his deep thank-you and the hint of a smile in her welcome. I'd only heard her use that tone with Chick. After he'd eaten, Sawyer took his bedroll and moved to the other side of the fire. The rest of us slept beneath the tarp by the wagon. It seemed exhaustion took all of us, or maybe it was the sense that we weren't alone this night, that there was someone to watch over us. Ironic, that the someone was Sawyer McCready. When I awoke the next morning, he was gone.

WE ate a cold breakfast of biscuits and bacon and then finished packing the camp to move out.

They did not speak of Aiken Tate, and I could only guess at their relationship. Where had he been all this time? Was it possible that he might not return at all? Meaira paced and watched the horizon with a desperation I only partly understood. We were stranded with a wagon and no horses. But it seemed she was anxious about more than that. She was agitated and irritable and snapped at the others for no reason until at last she stalked off to sit by herself. After a while, Honey joined her. I didn't know what had happened to have her so upset.

Chick went to work on a party dress she'd been sewing. She was very proud of her efforts, but her skill did not quite match her enthusiasm. Darning and sewing the family's clothing had been my chore since I was ten, and I could stitch a suit of armor if the need called. I feared that her feelings would be hurt should I offer to help, but she was more than happy to let me fix her clumsy stitches and embellish her gown. The cotton fabric was not so fine as the cut and style of the garment, but the dark rose color would look lovely against Chick's skin.

"Where will you wear such a dress?" I asked her as I stitched in tiny beading to the gathered bust.

Chick turned her round eyes on me, considering before she answered. After a moment she lowered her voice and said, "Athena say don't tell you our business."

"This dress is your business?"

Chick shook her head. She leaned forward and spoke softly. "It what I wear when the men come."

I tried to keep my expression blank, but my surprise must have shown on my face. Chick looked for Athena and saw her down by the river, bent over her washboard. Honey and Meaira sat on the small hillside not far away. Watching for the Captain or Aiken, I thought.

Satisfied that no one could hear, Chick said, "You cain't tell I said."

I shook my head. "I won't."

"We's fancy girls." She gave a nod, her expression prideful. "Not yet. Now we work the fields, wherever Aiken tell us."

I didn't know much about fancy girls, but I'd never thought of them as field laborers. I said as much.

Chick laughed, covering her smile with her hand as she did. "I mean we's *in* the fields, not working them."

I still didn't understand and I felt embarrassed and stupid under her knowing eyes. I was older than she, but not so world-wise.

"Aiken, he take us from place to place. He got us, but he don't have nowhere to put us, see? Not anymore. Used to be we was in Atlanta, but Aiken got run off. Now sometime we not even in a town. Just someplace where men be."

There was no hiding the horror I felt at her words.

"Ain't so bad," she said. "He gots a tent and the men is nice. Usually." She looked down, picking a long blade of grass and pulling it apart with her fingers. "Sometime theys old," she said. "Sometime they smell even though Aiken make 'em take a bath."

"Why do you do it, then?" I asked.

"What else I gon' do? It not as bad as working cotton. My momma did that. She die 'fore I was ten. Aiken take me in then and I do dishes and scrub floors 'til I was older. Some nights my hands be bloody from it."

"And now . . . Aiken . . . is . . . ?" I didn't know how to word it.

"He own us."

"Slavery isn't legal anymore, Chick," I said, thinking perhaps it was possible she didn't know this.

"Murder neither, but it still get done."

Her words brought forth a rush of images . . . my grandmother's broken wheelchair . . . my brother. Chick squeezed my hand, pulled me back to her.

I said, "Why don't you run away?"

Chick looked at me and her eyes were much older than her thirteen years. "I got no place to go." She shrugged. "Nothin better waitin' for me later. I can do this here, elst I can do it in some town for someone else who maybe treat me worse. I don' want to work no crib."

I didn't know what she meant.

"See, the old whores, theys in the cribs. That what they call the place they work. Cribs. They nasty, but once a whore get used up, that's all that left them."

"Is that—this kind of work—your only choice?"

Chick shrugged. "Athena, she used a work all day, half the night for people who barely gave her enough to eat. Least here we goin' somewhere. We ain't hungry. We better off than most."

I didn't know what to say.

"'Sides, I like it when they choose me. The young ones always do. Me and Honey. They likes us best."

Again, I knew my face had betrayed my thoughts. Chick dropped her eyes and spoke to the ground between our feet.

"Athena say you cain't know how things is for us. She think you look down on what we do. Think us trash."

"No, Chick," I said, touching her hand. "I don't understand it, but I could never think anything but good of you." And it was true. Chick was sweet and kind and despite what I'd just learned, I thought her innocent. Someone who needed to be taken care of. But that was foolish of me, I supposed. It was I who was naïve and needed to be cared for.

"You ever work for someone?" she asked.

"For my family but no, not for someone else."

"Folks treat their dogs better than a person who need help. Just cuz we ain't slaves don't make us people to

them. Aiken, he ain't good, but he better than a lot. And
things gon' get lots better soon," she said suddenly,
fiercely. "Now Captain 'round. He give us a place. He take
care us."

"Does he . . . own you as well?"

She shook her head. "I wish he did. First, he didn't want
nothing to do with us, but Aiken, he smart. He show him
we be good for the saloon. We be real good."

"How did Sawyer and Aiken become partners?"

"I don' know. Honey, she think Aiken trick him. She
think Aiken cheat Captain. She say Captain a good man.
Not the kind to join the likes of Aiken Tate."

"If he wasn't above joining Lonnie and Jake Smith, I
don't think his standards are as high as you imagine."

"Honey smart. She say he good, he good."

If I was honest, a part of me agreed.

I asked, "How about the others, Chick. How did they
come to be with Aiken?"

Something over my shoulder caught her attention and
froze her expression into wide eyes and open mouth. I
looked. Athena stood right behind me. Her eyes seemed to
blaze with anger as she looked from Chick's guilty face to
mine.

"He comin'," she said.

I turned around and looked to the horizon. Honey and
Meaira did the same. Meaira stood, wringing her hands as
she watched. There was a hunger on her pale face that confused me. She looked feverish. None of the others seemed
to notice, nor was there welcome in their seeking eyes or
any of the caged excitement that had preceded the Captain's arrival.

Honey stopped in front of where I sat. "I hope you don't
plan on attacking Aiken like you did the Captain," she said.

I shook my head.

"That's good. You don't want to make Aiken mad."

I set Chick's dress aside and stood, joining the uneasy
vigil that awaited his appearance.

"You do what he tell you," Athena said, her voice dark
as maple syrup.

I'd prepared myself for a man larger than Sawyer, more menacing than ten Sawyers. But Aiken Tate was a petite, dapper man. He had bright blue eyes and a smatter of freckles across his nose. He wore a small hat that perched jauntily on his head and a three-piece suit in gray pinstripe. He was dusty, but looked more a businessman than the devil I'd been warned about.

On a lead attached to his saddle were two other horses that looked to be of stock breeding. Work horses. I'd wondered what drew the wagon. Now I knew. It made no sense to me why he took them rather than leave them with the wagon, but I had to assume he had a good reason for what he did.

He swung off his horse and Chick dutifully went to take the reins. Athena had a plate of biscuits and bacon waiting and moved quickly to serve him. There were no niceties accompanying her efforts, however. Just as there was no string of rabbits for her stew.

Aiken's small, bright eyes buzzed over and lighted on me like a bee to a flower. "Well, well," he said, smiling to show a mouthful of crooked teeth. Still, there was something vaguely charming about the lopsided smile and the sparkling blue eyes. If it weren't for the apprehension that seemed to flutter between the other women, I might have liked him on sight. "Who are you?" he asked.

My mouth was dry as I answered. "Ella Beck."

"Ella. That's a pretty name for a pretty lady."

His voice was not deep, like Sawyer's, but it was pleasant. Everything about him was pleasant. "What brings you to our humble quarters, pretty lady Ella?"

"I'm lost. Saw— Captain McCready has agreed to take me to the next town with you."

Aiken's smile widened. "He's a good man." He looked around, then asked, "Where is he?"

Meaira stepped forward, laying a hand on Aiken's arm. "He said he'd ride ahead and meet up with us tomorrow. He said we should start as soon as you got here. Did everything go okay in town?"

There was something in the intensity of her gaze that I

couldn't decipher. Aiken ignored her question as he moved to sit on the crate and eat. I realized that though at first sight I'd thought him a small man, my impression had been erroneous. He gave the illusion of being slight, but in fact he was of solid build.

Meaira followed him like a dog expecting scraps. "Aiken?" she said, her voice edged with need. "Did . . . Do you . . ." She couldn't seem to get it out. Aiken gave her a few more tortured seconds of trying before reaching in his pocket and pulling out a small bottle.

He held it out but when she reached for it, he pulled it back. "You have to make it last," he said.

She nodded. "I will. I promise. I will."

Her eyes fixed intently on the bottle. He held it away for another moment before finally handing it over. Meaira's smile lit her face. "Thank you, Aiken."

Athena said, "Everything ready for us to go," and gave Meaira a look I didn't understand.

Aiken nodded. "We got a good twenty-five miles to go today. There's a boomtown sprung up between here and Diablo Springs. I hear they ain't seen a woman for months out there. We'll be more'n welcome to settle aside them all." He nodded at Athena. "Get the wagon harnessed and let's get a move on."

I saw Meaira quickly disappear in the wagon. After a few moments, she came out again. As I moved to help with the last of the crates, I watched her. She seemed strangely disoriented.

"Laudanum," Honey said from beside me. "Aiken keeps her stocked."

As if hearing us, Meaira hung her head and turned away.

We moved out within the half hour. Athena drove the team from the wagon. The rest of us walked alongside. Aiken rode up ahead, leading the way and keeping the pace.

When my family left Alamosa, I'd walked as well. After the first week my legs had become strong and my body had adjusted to the toil. We'd had to strap my grandma to the back in her chair because the terrain was too rough for her to wheel over. I'd walked beside her, describing the scenery for her as we moved forward. She would comment on my description after we passed. It became a game for us, me stretching my mind for new ways to say green or wide open or breathtaking, Grandma, trying to envision it from my narrative alone.

Thinking of it now brought a lump to my throat and the grief that I'd yet to acknowledge swamped me. I didn't cry tears, but I mourned with every step. I'd lost my entire family. I was alone in the world.

It was early afternoon before Aiken allowed us a break. Athena started a fire and warmed last night's beans, but there was no room for hunger in the blackness of my soul. I took water and moved away from the others. I felt Aiken watching me with his bright eyes, but he didn't say anything. When we moved on again, I fell in step, but I was numb and silent. I'd escaped the Smith brothers, survived the wilderness on my own for days, faced off with a man to be reckoned with, but now that I was somewhat safe, I wanted to give up. I wanted to lie down and die.

Hours later, it was Honey who came up beside me and handed me a biscuit with a nonchalance that had me accepting before I realized it.

"I used to want to die," she said softly.

I took a bite of the biscuit. It was days old and hard, but my stomach rumbled gratefully as soon as I began to chew. "Do you still want to?" I asked. My voice was scratchy.

"Naw, not anymore." She turned those chocolate eyes on me. "Surviving is all a person can control."

There was a twisted logic in what she said, more in what she didn't. If I gave up now, the Smith brothers would have succeeded in wiping out my family, and succeeded with my blessing.

"I miss my family," I said.

"Me too. But giving up won't get them back."

How she knew what I was feeling, I didn't know. But I was grateful for her words.

"Captain says he'll take you to town with us. Make sure

you get there safe. After that, you decide what happens to you. Give up, and you let them own you. Your momma wouldn't have wanted that."

No, she wouldn't have wanted that at all.

She left me then, to finish my biscuit and make up my mind. In the end, there really wasn't a choice. I picked up my feet and joined the others.

chapter nineteen

THE boomtown was more a grimy gathering of tents and lean-tos than anything like a township. They camped close to the shores of a river and scattered all around them was the refuse of the makeshift settlement. In all, I guessed there were about thirty tents. The mud was so thick that the wagon's wheels sunk in and the horse's legs were three-quarters caked with it. We hopped onto the wagon that Athena drove in an effort to keep our shoes from being sucked off our feet. Filth had never known such luxury. I had never known such filth.

There were no buildings constructed, but a tent with one side open was clearly functioning as a saloon and another as a place to eat. A Chinese man stared out as we passed, watching us suspiciously. The saloon was brimming with business and dirty, drunken miners hooted and laughed as they indulged themselves in liquor. One man stepped out and urinated in the middle of the street. When he saw us, he stood holding himself in one hand, a startled grin on his face as he waved with the other. He slipped in the mud as he hurried to tell the others what he'd seen.

The stench was beyond my powers of description. It was apparent that man and beast alike used whatever space was available to relieve themselves. The remains of meals past were thrown into the widening path of mud that bisected the row of tents. Bones and skinned carcasses lay in between. A few dogs ran beside us, barking and snarling.

I looked at Honey, but she wouldn't meet my eyes. Chick stared out with a blank expression. Meaira watched as if through a cocoon of her own making. What must they be thinking? What must they be feeling, knowing what the night had in store? How could they . . .

Aiken stopped his horse and spoke to a man who'd flagged him down. I heard Aiken say "bath" and the other look as if he'd been slapped. They conversed for a few moments more before Aiken rode away.

"He told them," Meaira said, staring at the squalor with a placid expression.

"Told them what?"

"Take a bath is what he makes them do," she said. "They won't be liking it, but they'll be doing it."

I was overwhelmed with relief, though I wouldn't be one that had to endure their foulness. I couldn't bear thinking of sweet Chick, lovely Honey, or dazed Meaira, touching any of these barbarians.

"Is it always like this?" I asked.

Chick shook her head. "No. This bad."

Aiken moved us to a clearing upwind that had not been contaminated by their waste. In the growing darkness, we set up our camp. This time, though, we added a canopy, anchored by four corner poles with one in the middle that held the canvas up like a spire. Long sides flapped in the wind and brushed the ground.

No one had spoken since arriving and the silence rode heavy on the air. The other women avoided looking at me, but I was acutely conscious of their thoughts. A part of me wanted to shout, to stop what we were doing. I wanted to herd the women back into the wagon and rein the horses into a gallop. But none of them seemed as concerned with what the night held in store as I was. According to Chick, this was what they did and they did it by choice. Though they'd told me Aiken was the devil, it didn't seem to me that he had threatened them in any way to participate in the upcoming festivities. I assumed they would be paid for what they did, but what price would be enough?

A table with folding legs came from the wagon to be set up in the center of camp. Meaira and Honey opened chairs around it. Four thin, rough mattresses that I'd not seen before came from a trunk. Athena beat them with her broom and then laid them out in the tent.

It was full dark by the time Aiken declared himself satisfied with our work. We could hear the men in town brawling at the river as they took turns bathing in the muddied water. I didn't know how clean they would be once they arrived at the camp. I hoped for the others' sakes, they used soap. Two who were very eager had been scrubbed and waiting for nearly thirty minutes while we finished setting up. They stood like school boys in their Sunday best, hair slicked back, faces scrubbed. Clothes brushed, if not clean or fine.

A light breeze moaned through the night before dancing across our camp to catch at the billowing sides of the tent. Inside, hanging panels had been strung up to divide it into compartments, each with a pallet on the ground. Athena opened a chest and white sheets were brought out to cover the sagging, stained mattresses. Then the girls turned attention to each other, fixing hair and making up. I sat numbly to the side, wondering what I would do once it all began.

Aiken whistled as he shuffled cards at his table and dealt a hand of solitaire. A cigar hung from his lips, the smoke drifting up on the night air to mingle with the other scents. I dreaded what would come next, but the waiting was painful in itself.

"Are you ready for us?" one of the scrubbed school boys asked.

Aiken flicked a glance over the camp and then nodded. "Yes, sir, we are ready."

Aiken shook both their hands, ushering them forward. The two were young, younger than I even, and they were eager. Without ado they asked how much for a tumble. Aiken looked surprised. He proceeded to talk the two young men into circles for a few minutes, denying that the girls would even consider selling their bodies for money. They were young, chaste girls who'd had their share of bad luck, but he, the good Samaritan, was taking them to San Diego where they would enter a life of servitude for the

Holy church. I watched Aiken with a sick fascination as he weaved his tale like a web around them. The men were obviously distressed to think of the beauties becoming servants of the church and they did their best to convince Aiken it was a mistake. One even offered to marry Honey and relieve Aiken of his burden.

Chick leaned close to me. "He do this every time," she said.

"Why?"

"You see."

After he'd worked them up, he found out what they were willing to pay and then offered to make an exception, allow the boys private time to converse with the girls for a price that was two dollars less than they'd offered.

"I'm a charitable man and I can see how you are both fine young gentlemen who wouldn't think of hurting my girls. I can see where you are pained by the rigors of life. Is that how it is?"

Two cents wouldn't rattle in either of their heads, but they nodded and tried to look as if they understood what he was saying.

"I will take your money, but only to put it to the good of feeding and clothing these fine, upstanding women. Now who is it you would like to . . . speak to alone?"

They both pointed at Honey, then, seeing each other, one switched and pointed to Chick.

"Now I can't let those two beauties go for such a pittance. Why not Athena? She is older and won't miss the flower of her innocence."

Of course this wouldn't do. I watched with a numbness that defied my sense of disbelief. Aiken was the maestro of manipulation. Beside me, Chick smirked.

After much conversation, during which Aiken dazzled them with his use of the English language while keeping them in a befuddled act of negotiation, they seemed to reach an impasse. Aiken drew it out even more until finally the two men "convinced" Aiken to take their money— nearly double what they'd originally offered—and Aiken called Honey and Chick over.

He introduced the girls and in a fatherly manner handed them off in kind to the young men.

Honey didn't look at any of the others as she led her young man into the tent. Chick smiled shyly at hers, who turned a dark shade of red. I heard him say it was his first time as she took his hand. She told him not to worry, she knew what to do.

Honey's boy was nervous and she had to work at his confidence. Her voice soothed and drifted out of the flapping walls of the tent. Chick's partner was eager and quick. She'd returned to her seat before Honey's had even begun. I wondered if her young man would feel cheated, but the look on his face spoke of rapture. I thought I might be sick. But others had already arrived and they crowded around, eager to be chosen. Athena and I sat off to the side, each silent until even she was called upon to perform inside the tent.

Our campfire became a beacon and the men gravitated toward it. Not all came for the women. Some came for the cards that Aiken dealt, others were just curious. Some tried to beg and borrow enough to visit with one of the girls. Some tried to win the fee gambling.

While they waited for their turns, Aiken entertained them at the card table and proceeded to cheat at faro. From where I sat I could see the extra cards he'd hidden beneath the table. He was quick and skilled, and I might not have recognized his game had I been on the other side of the deck. He let them win most of the time, and as the perfect host, he ordered Athena to bring his whiskey when she emerged from the tent. He charged heavily for the honor of sharing his bottle, but no one seemed to mind. Sounds of grunting and the musky scent of carnality carried on the hot breeze, which lifted the edges of the tent like skirts and afforded quick peeks into the goings-on inside. I could smell their arousal and sense the excitement buzzing through the men.

I'd been in the shadows, tucked as far away as I could get from everyone else, but when Athena began to serve drinks, someone noticed me.

"I'll take her," a man with short black hair and clean-shaven cheeks said, pointing at me like I was a horse in a corral.

Aiken cocked his head to look at me and I held my breath for a moment. "Sorry, sir. She's not one of the girls," he said.

"She looks like one to me."

"She is a beauty. Can't say that I've ever seen so fair a face. But she is from a finer breed than my others."

"That's what you said about them too," another man interjected. "You's just saying it so as you can charge more."

Aiken's smile made my skin crawl.

"Were that the truth, sir, I would have you call me out. But I'm willing to wager this young lady is of yet untouched. What price can a man put on such virtue?"

I jumped to my feet. "I'm not for sale."

"No, dear, for your price would be well over what any man here could pay."

"Who are you to say what we can or cain't pay?" the first man asked. "I got a bag full of gold in my pocket and a mine that's spittin' out the nuggets."

"He do," a voice agreed. "I seen it with my own eyes."

"I am not for sale," I repeated.

Aiken said, "You heard the little lady. She will not give herself over to the likes of you."

His words were inflammatory and he knew it. Offended, the man said, "I'm as good as any man. Better than most. I'm good enough for her."

"The lady says she's not for sale," another said.

"She thinks she's too good. I'll show her ain't no woman too good for me. I'll make her come around."

I saw the warring mixture of excitement and disgust on the face of the man who'd spoken on my behalf, and I understood what was happening. I'd become a challenge.

"I think she'd like me better," a new voice said and a big burly man stepped through the crowd.

"She ain't gonna get the chance to know. She gonna want only me after she had me once."

"I am not having anyone," I said clearly. "I'm lost and the Captain has promised me safe escort to a town."

He'd promised me no such thing, but he had agreed to take me.

"She's a spitfire all right," Aiken said. "It'd take more than one man to tame her. It's a shame she's not willing to let a single one try."

I watched with horror as the idea of it went from one to another. Honey, Chick, and Meaira were in the tents and the gusting breeze brought more than quick glances at their activities. It scented the air. I was young, but I knew nothing was as dangerous as a mob of men. My daddy had told me stories that had made my blood run cold.

The black-haired man shook his head and walked away, but the other men moved in closer. I thought quickly. I picked one out of the crowd who looked to be unsure. "I could be your sister," I said to him. "Or yours," to another.

My words hit some of them like cold water but before I could feel relief, the burly man pushed through and said, "You couldn't be mine. She's got a face like an ass."

Laughter burst out all around him and then animated talking. I tried to force my point again, but no one was listening to me now. The burly man moved in and took my hand. "I'll be as gentle as you let me be, darlin'," he said to the delight of those behind him. Another man leaned in and told him to loosen me up good.

I didn't wait for what came next. I began to fight. I hit and scratched and kicked and pulled and screamed. Honey rushed from the tent at the sound of my voice and turned on Aiken.

"You can't do this," she told him, eyes wide.

"I told them no. I told them twice she was a lady."

I twisted and bucked in the burly man's arms. It looked like I might get help from the crowd, but those who moved forward were held back by those who wished to be next. I couldn't believe what was happening. Had these men lived like animals for so long, they'd ceased to be part of humanity as I knew it?

He'd nearly made it to the tent with me screaming and struggling for all I was worth. He didn't wear a gun, but my hand brushed a knife at his waist. I tried to reach it, I tried to pull it free, but he trapped my arms, smiling grimly as he hauled me closer. Honey was there, trying to pry me free, begging the man to take her instead, telling them all they could have her if they'd just leave me alone. But no one was listening. My struggles had become a point of fascination. I could see it. None of them were able to look away. I screamed, though I knew it would do no good. It was all happening too quickly. It seemed hours since he'd grabbed my hand, but only a few seconds had passed. If I could just slow him down . . . It was then that a horse charged into camp.

From the corner of my eye, I saw the rider, a man nearly as big as his mount. Though his face was in shadow and his clothes covered in dirt, I recognized Sawyer McCready immediately and I cried out his name. A part of me acknowledged that I was praying for rescue from a man who was possibly as disreputable as Aiken, but I only knew that I was glad to see him. He pulled his gun and fired into the air.

The sound echoed loudly and a sudden, stunned silence fell over the small crowd.

"Captain," Aiken exclaimed, pushing out of the throng to stand beside Sawyer's horse. "I am powerful glad to see you."

Sawyer ignored him and spoke to the man who held me captive. "Let her go," he said.

The burly man stared Sawyer down. Having fought to capture me, he wasn't going to set me free on command. "She's mine," he said.

"I'm not yours," I said.

"Let her go," Sawyer repeated. His tone was low, his words hard.

The man hesitated and Sawyer leveled his gun. For a moment, no one moved and then slowly, his hands loosened. I jerked free of him and Honey gathered me up, pulling me out of reach before he could change his mind. But I could not just crawl away. My rage was too much. I turned on him, slapped his face, not once but twice, staring at him like the trash he was. I saw something flash in his eyes. Something that spoke of a man who might once have lived inside him, a man who would have been shamed by what he'd done. And then it was gone. He slapped me back. The blow knocked me sideways and I staggered. Only Honey kept me from falling. White spots mixed with red and danced behind my eyes. Sawyer's gun was cocked before they cleared.

"Fool," Honey muttered as she dragged me away. I didn't know if she meant me or the burly man.

Aiken moved in closer to Sawyer and spoke in low tones. Sawyer listened, watching the crowd with his gun still in hand. After a moment he nodded. Aiken faced the men, his crooked smile flashing.

"Drinks on me, boys. Let's get back to having a good time."

And just like that, it was over. I couldn't believe it. The men moved away and Honey sat me down on the crates. I was shaking and I was terrified.

"Honey, there's still business to do," Aiken said, his voice steady and commanding. "Don't want the boys restless."

"You'll be okay, now," she said to me, though I didn't think she believed it any more than I did. Quickly she moved away and a moment later she led the burly man into the tent. I clenched my eyes against the sight.

Someone touched my shoulder and I jumped, opening them again. Sawyer squatted down in front of me. His fingers were gentle as he tipped my chin and stared at my face. My cheek throbbed and my eye was swelling.

"You're going to have a shiner," he said. But his voice was not steady and I sensed that the sight of my battered face upset him more than he would show.

"Thank you," I said. "Thank you."

He nodded once and stood. I looked up the long length of him and though just yesterday I'd tried to plunge my knife into him, right then I wanted nothing more than to be in his arms. As contrary as I was to think it, I wanted him to shelter me from this barbaric world that had somehow become mine. I watched the swirling colors in his eyes as he listened to my thoughts. It seemed he might reach for me, answer my silent request, but Aiken chose that moment to approach.

"Captain," Aiken said, clapping him on the shoulder. "Lucky for us you showed up. A mob's an ugly thing. There was no backing them down."

He stared at me when he said it, and I recognized the threat in his eyes. I looked to Sawyer who was nodding. He believed Aiken.

"You pushed them to it," I said fiercely, locking eyes with Sawyer. "He encouraged them, told them they'd have to fight me."

"Fight both of us," Aiken said, laughing loudly. The sound filled the camp and I remembered that I thought him pleasant when I first met him.

"She's understandably rattled by what happened, Sawyer. She's confused. I never would have done such—"

At that moment, six men on horseback rode in at a gallop, stopping Aiken in midsentence. They pushed through the small crowd of miners without care of who might be in their way. One man jumped just in time to avoid being trampled.

"Is this a party?" one of the riders asked. "Thought I heard a gun, but it looks like a party. I don't recall getting my invite, though."

I recognized the voice and turned my head to gaze at him full on.

"I said, is this a party?" Lonnie Smith repeated. He had his gun in his hand.

chapter twenty

IN complete silence, Reilly drove Zach, Gracie, Analise, Brendan, and a hell of a lot of tension back from the Buckboard. It could have been the ominous storm that silenced them. It was sure doing a number on Reilly. The water had risen past the gutters and now entire streets were flooded. It was more like a hurricane than a storm in the desert. He'd never seen anything like it in all his life.

But that wasn't all that kept them quiet.

Gracie sat in the front seat beside him. The feel of her almost close enough to touch, the scent of her hair, her skin . . . she'd bypassed his brain and embedded herself in his senses. He'd never had a woman get under his skin so quickly and completely. Granted, he'd known Gracie for a long time, but what he was feeling had nothing to do with old acquaintances and everything to do with the scalloped lace he could almost see outlined beneath her T-shirt. If he closed his eyes, he could imagine the contrast between the white lace and her skin, the way the light would play off her body, the shadows, the curves . . . He gave a mental groan. Without even trying, she'd turned him into a teenager with a perpetual hard-on.

He forced himself to concentrate on the roads. Driving through the rivers in the streets was like plowing through Jell-O. It gave, but not willingly. He saw Eddie's deputies and volunteers out sandbagging the few business doorways in a vain effort to keep out the water. He obviously hadn't wasted much time dropping off Corrine at the municipal building before racing over here to help with the work.

That was Eddie, always there to help a neighbor, no matter what. It was no wonder he'd grown up to be a cop.

As they drew near, he flagged them down. Reilly pulled to a stop and hit the button for the passenger window as Eddie came up to it. He wore a bright yellow poncho but rain still streamed down his face as he leaned his forearms on the door and looked in at them all.

"Good to see you. Saves me a trip out to your place, Gracie."

"Why were you coming?" she asked.

Eddie wiped at his face and said, "If this doesn't quit we're going to be flooded by midnight. I should have started warning people in town earlier, but I was worried about the folks farther out on lower ground. Now it's too late for you all to get out—valley's flooded all the way to the highway. Good thing most people in town have a second story, but some don't."

In a town with a population of less than four hundred, only about fifty lived within the city limits. Most had properties farther out. Farms, ranches. They lived in a place like Diablo Springs because they didn't want to be too close to their neighbors, but they did like to know who was living next door. Most had family properties that stretched back generations. Like the Diablo.

"I'm going to be sending folks where it's safe if I find them. You people at the Diablo need to stay put where you are. Don't try to get out of town. It's too late for that. I don't want to be called out to rescue you later. Or look for your bodies either. Is that clear?"

Crystal clear.

"Yes, Eddie."

He looked at Reilly. "The Diablo should be fine, up like it is. We'll load you up with some sandbags just in case. No more rides into town until it's over though."

Reilly nodded grimly, put the SUV in park, and started to get out.

"Hold up a minute," Eddie said, stopping him. Eddie went to the cruiser parked nearby, got something out of the trunk, and came around to the driver's side. Reilly rolled down the window and Eddie handed him a folded rain poncho like the one he wore. He pulled it on and together he and Eddie loaded up the back of the SUV with sandbags. Zach, he noticed, didn't offer to help. No surprise there.

When Reilly got back inside, Zach was leaning over the backseat, talking to Gracie.

"I've never been in a flood before," he said.

Reilly heard, *"I want to bang your brains out during the storm."* He slammed the door and eased the over-weighted SUV back onto the road.

"Me neither," Analise said from the back seat.

Zach moved his hand so he was touching Gracie's hair. "My dad was in a flood when he was a kid. He used to talk about all the stuff they'd find in their yard after the water dried up. You know, things that floated down from other people's houses—weird stuff like plates and couch cushions, even found a wallet that turned out to belong to someone who drowned."

Reilly saw Gracie's mouth tighten. Drowning in a flood was not exactly a topic he would have chosen.

Analise didn't seem to mind though. She asked him a question Reilly didn't hear and just like that, Zach came down with a sudden case of diarrhea of the mouth. He spoke with animation, waving his hands, occasionally managing to touch Gracie in the process. Reilly was willing to bet it wasn't by accident. Zach segued into his own personal anxiety over the storm, throwing in that he couldn't swim.

"You're a California boy," Reilly said. "How can you not swim?"

Zach gave a shrug. "Just can't."

He went on to explain in greater detail, but navigating the curving road made it too difficult for Reilly to listen and drive. Reilly finally tuned him out. It wasn't until he saw Gracie's hand reach up and touch Zach's face and then Zach capture her fingers and hold them that Reilly's attention snapped back to them.

"Do I feel hot?" Zach asked. "I've got the chills."

The Jeep went through a lake-sized puddle that jerked at his wheels and forced Reilly to concentrate on the road.

Beside him, Gracie was telling Zach, "You should go to bed when we get back. You're probably coming down with something."

Zach still had her hand. Reilly wanted to reach over and slug him. His knuckles were white from the effort not to as he made the turn onto Main. Gracie let out a sigh of relief when the Diablo came into sight.

"The water's not up to the steps yet," she said. "Thank God."

Reilly echoed that.

"Can I have my hand back?" she asked Zach with a smile, gently tugging her fingers away.

Reilly watched out of the corner of his eye as Zach reluctantly released her. He and Loverboy were going to have to talk.

Reilly parked and stepped out into the pouring rain. He still wore the poncho, but that didn't mean he wasn't getting wet. That wasn't why he was irritable and edgy though. He wasn't used to being responsible for anyone but himself . . . or Matt. He wasn't used to caring about anyone else either. So how'd he get saddled with this three-ring circus climbing out of his Jeep? And why was he feeling like he'd fight a pack of lions to keep them safe? Well, at least part of them. Zach he could use as a distraction while he got the rest of them to shelter. The thought cheered him a little.

Reilly opened Gracie's door and held out a hand to help her down. He smiled at her. She hesitated for a second and something in her eyes made him think she was reading the chaotic emotions flashing through him. She smiled back.

"Be careful," he said as she hurried up the walk. Mentally he slapped himself on the forehead, hearing Zach's annoying taunt in his head. *What are you, her dad?*

Analise jumped out the back door and advanced on her mom without waiting for Brendan. As she followed Gracie to the porch, he heard her say, "God, Mom. Think you could have flirted with him any harder?"

Gracie glanced back, startled. Her eyes flew to Reilly and he realized she thought Analise was talking about him, though they'd barely exchanged a word. He thought he'd been the only one to feel the thick sexual tension between them. Maybe Gracie felt it too.

He quickly looked away as she said to Analise, "I didn't . . ."

"He's like, my age, Mom."

"Ah," Gracie said pausing on the porch, and there was a wealth of understanding in the sound. Reilly stood aside for Brendan to step out and used the excuse to watch her again.

"Zach's not your age, Analise. He's probably nineteen, maybe twenty."

"Too young for you."

"I'm not trying to date him," Gracie said. "And even if I was, why is it your business? You're going to be married and away in a few months anyway."

A stricken look crossed Analise's face, mirroring the expression on her mother's. Instinctively Reilly knew Gracie wanted to take the words back, wanted to apologize and comfort her daughter. But she couldn't. She'd spoken the truth. And it hurt her as much as it had Analise.

Zach was the last to make it out. As he stepped into the rain, Reilly said, "Why don't you help me with the sandbags?"

Zach looked incredulous. "I'll get all wet."

"So? You won't melt."

Zach looked like he was dying to make a smart-ass comeback, but something in the look on Reilly's face made him reconsider. Silently he followed Reilly to the hatch in the back and pulled a bag off the pile.

"I told you to stay away from Gracie," Reilly said, hefting two of the bags out.

"I didn't hear her complaining."

"Yeah? Well I'm doing it for her. Are you hearing me?"

"I hear you. I just don't know why you think I'd care. She looks at you like she wiped you off her shoe. Me, she likes."

Reilly stared at him, feeling like steam must surely be

coming out of his ears. "She doesn't like you, she's just being nice. Christ, you're not much older than her kid."

"I am too. I'm twenty-five."

"Well you look twelve so stay the hell away from her."

"Zach," Gracie called from the porch. She looked from one to the other of them. A shadow passed across her eyes as if she guessed the essence of the tension between the two men. "If you think you have a fever, staying out in the rain is hardly the cure."

Reilly would have punched him right then if Gracie hadn't been watching. Zach started up the walkway and then glanced back. Reilly met his eyes, expecting him to be smug. But what he saw there wasn't satisfaction. It was anger. Anger that seemed to match his own. It lit something in Reilly like a fire. He followed him up and dropped the sandbags on the porch. It was time to set the matter of Gracie Beck straight for once and for all. Zach dropped his bag too, made a little "bring it on" gesture with his fingers, and followed Gracie into the house. It was junior high immaturity, but somehow it still got to him.

They stepped through the front door to smells of cooking wafting from the kitchen. The strong aroma of roasting beef, fat crackling in the heat, spices baking until they released their perfume hung in the air. It distracted him for a moment and set off an alarm of unease.

"Who's cooking?" Analise asked.

"I don't know," Gracie answered looking at the closed door. Instantly Reilly knew what she was thinking. *Why weren't the dogs barking?*

The rain had drenched them all and now Gracie's T-shirt was nearly transparent. Scalloped lace. His imagination hadn't done it justice. He looked away to find Zach staring at her too. Reilly brushed past him to follow Gracie to the kitchen.

The room seemed dimly lit without lights on, though it was still early afternoon. Reilly flipped a switch. Nothing happened. He tried again. He was about to say the power was out when the light flickered on, then off, then on again. It wasn't out yet, but soon.

Gracie moved in, making a sound to call the dogs. He heard one whimper before he saw it cowering beneath the table. A second head popped up and then the little one jumped from behind his cowering girlfriends.

Gracie scooped Romeo up. "He's shaking." The two big dogs came out, tales tucked tight between their legs, eyes big and round. Gracie squatted down. "They're all shaking."

Reilly crossed the kitchen to the oven. With each step, his gut filled with a deep disquiet. He held a hand over the stove. Cold. He opened the oven door. "It's empty."

"Of course it is," Gracie whispered, holding the trembling dogs against her.

Reilly swallowed and moved to her side. The oven was empty, but the scent of meat was so strong that it made the air moist and heavy. He could smell onions and carrots simmering in the juices of beef.

"Maybe the damp has brought out old smells," Reilly suggested.

He knew that neither one of them really bought it, but what else could explain the smell of cooking in the cold, dark kitchen? And why were the dogs so frightened?

"Hey," he said, squatting down beside Gracie. For once the dogs didn't growl. "It'll be okay."

She nodded, but didn't look convinced.

"The storm probably scared the dogs. Hell, it's scaring me."

She nodded again and rose to her feet. He did the same. In the dimness of the kitchen, her eyes looked huge and worried. It seemed that the weight of the world was on her shoulders and she was determined to carry it without faltering. Between her grandmother dying, Analise's pregnancy, and having to deal with all the dark memories Reilly had stirred, it probably felt that heavy.

"Gracie, you'll get through this. We'll get through it together."

"I wish I could believe that. But I don't know what to do next. I mean, where do I start? How do I help my daughter bring a child into the world when every bone in my body is screaming mad about it? Her whole life is about to change, and she doesn't have a clue. And what about all this stuff?" She spread her arms wide to encompass the kitchen and everything beyond. "I'm going to have to go through her things. I can't just board it up and leave it, but what do I know about what she has? What she'd want kept? I don't even know who those people are in all those pictures."

Having started, she seemed unable to stop. Reilly did the only thing he could. Listened.

"I don't know where all this furniture came from or why she's got this place set up like something out of a *Gunsmoke* set. It makes no sense. Nothing about it makes sense. What am I going to do with this stuff, Reilly? When all I want to do is pack up my kid and get the hell away from here?"

Tears glittered like crystal in her eyes, but she didn't cry. She just stood stiff and angry as she looked around her. Reilly took a step closer, invading her space and bringing his body within touching distance.

The rain and heat brought the perfume off her skin, so it drifted light as a thought to him. He cupped her cheek with his palm and tilted her face up, looking down into the soft gray of her eyes. "One thing at a time, babe. You can't do it all at once. Right now, we're stuck here. Nothing we can do about it. We'll find some candles. Light a fire in the fireplace and turn the house into a sauna. It'll be fun."

She smiled and he felt good knowing he'd done that. He stepped a little closer, bringing his other hand up so that he framed her face. "Then we'll pick a chest or a closet or whatever, and we'll start going through it. I'll help you."

She looked into his eyes. "Why?"

"Because it means being near you and after seeing you in a wet T-shirt, I don't want to let you out of my sight."

He'd meant it to be light and teasing, but the raw truth of it was in his voice. Her eyes widened and then dropped down to her clinging wet shirt. She tried to step away, but he kept her face in his hands and his body close to hers. A hot flush climbed up her neck. He felt the heat of it beneath his palms before he saw it color her cheeks.

She looked at him like she might say something, but she didn't. Reilly took that for a yes. He lowered his face until his mouth hovered just over hers and for a moment, their breath mingled and the anticipation of breathing her in, of tasting her, nearly made him groan. He closed the distance and kissed her. He tried for gentle, tentative. He wanted to give her the chance to set the pace. But the minute his mouth touched hers, he wanted more. A hell of a lot more. And he wanted it fast. He gathered her up hard against him, urging her mouth to open for him. Her soft gasp of surprise was all the invitation he needed to touch her tongue with his, to deepen the kiss. To deepen everything.

She made a small satisfied noise in her throat that set off a million reactions in his body. He pressed her tighter against him and she responded by twining her arms up to his neck. She couldn't miss how happy he was to be holding her, but she didn't back off. She came up on tiptoe so that the hard length of him nudged the softness of her belly. Was there a lock on the porch door? If he got her that far, could he lock out the rest of the world for an hour?

As if in answer to the thought, the porch door slowly swung open with a loud squeal. Surprised, they paused and looked at it. And then it slammed shut hard enough to rattle the window. They both jumped back and Gracie gave a small yelp.

"What was—"

But before she could finish her sentence it opened again—quickly this time—and slammed even harder. And again, until it sounded like a machine gun firing into a rampant crowd. The windows rattled and the noise escalated like explosions rocking the house. The dogs barked in frightened high-pitched yips that contrasted with their bared teeth and massive bodies. Zach and Analise burst into the kitchen with Brendan a step behind. The porch door swung open one last time, the squeal of rusted hinges raising the hair on his body, and then slammed shut so hard that the glass inset shattered.

Analise screamed and ran to her mother. Gracie broke from Reilly's arms and met her halfway, wrapping her in a protective hug as they stared with horrified eyes at the glittering shards on the floor.

"What the fuck was that?" Brendan asked.

Zach stepped forward and circled gingerly around the door. He looked at Reilly and his eyes seemed like black coals against the pale of his face.

"It was the storm," Reilly said, ignoring him. "The door must not have been latched." He reached for the knob and pulled the door open, looking out. The wind howled across the desert until it looked like the rain came sideways in huge, wet gusts. Lightning spackled the sky in a hundred directions and thunder added voice to the show.

Reilly stepped back in. "The storm. We should double-check all the windows and doors. Gracie, do you know where there's a broom?"

The calm certainty in his voice didn't match the blast of adrenaline in his blood or the sixth sense that had him feeling he should be armed and on guard. But it did what he intended. He saw some of the panic in Gracie's eyes dim. Not vanish, but ease. Hell, he couldn't blame her for being rattled. It had been too weird, like earlier. Freakish.

He took the broom from Gracie, and said, "Go. I'll clean this up."

She looked at him questioningly, but Analise still clung to her and he knew she wanted to get her daughter away from the mess and calm her down. She gave a nod and they all followed her out.

Alone in the kitchen, Reilly closed the porch door and threw the dead bolt testing it to make sure it was secure. He swept the glass, hunted down some tape and a cardboard box from the pantry to cover the hole. Finished, he stood back. The simple task had calmed him. It was stupid to let a slamming door bother him, no matter how weird it was. He took the broom back to the closet where Gracie had found it and put it away. From the kitchen, he heard a strange sound. It froze him momentarily as his brain clicked through the possibilities while his gut settled on a conclusion.

He felt the burst of damp air and his skin seemed to draw tight. Slowly he turned.

The porch door he'd bolted so carefully was open.

chapter twenty-one

REILLY stepped into the front room as Gracie shepherded Analise up the stairs. Brendan and the dogs followed. Zach looked pasty, and Reilly suspected that, before the night was over, he'd be hurling his insides out. He tried not to be happy about that as Zach dragged himself to his room. From upstairs he could hear raised voices drifting down every once in a while, words like *baby* and *married*, filled with frustration. He couldn't get the image of Gracie's eyes, round and weighted with the burden of her responsibilities from his mind.

The house still smelled like cooking meat. He wondered what Chloe would think about that. But he hadn't seen Chloe or Bill since he'd left the Buckboard. He hadn't seen the priest since last night. Where was he? Had he gone out in the storm? Or was he simply upstairs in his room? He'd check once it quieted down up there.

Reilly moved to the front window. A part of him considered getting back in the Jeep and going out to see if Chloe and Bill needed help, but he didn't. He wasn't their keeper and he didn't want to end up with the job by default either. He heard footsteps on the stairs and turned to find the priest hovering halfway down.

"Have they returned?" he asked.

Reilly shook his head. "Not yet."

The priest nodded and then turned to go back up.

"Wait," Reilly said. "Did you . . . Were you cooking while we were gone?"

The priest paused and looked back at Reilly with an expression of resignation Reilly didn't understand. "No," he said after a long moment. "It just started smelling like roast right after everyone left."

"Did you check it out?"

"There was no need," the priest said softly.

"What does that mean?"

"It means I knew there was no one in the kitchen, Mr. Alexander."

He went back up the stairs before Reilly could think of what to ask next. The soft click of his door closing drifted down.

Reilly paced the ground floor a couple of times before discovering an ancient-looking guitar leaning against the stairway wall. He stared at it for a moment, wondering where it had come from. If it had been there all along, he would have seen it. Or maybe not. Hell, if it wasn't attached to Gracie Beck, he wouldn't have noticed a tank parked in the front yard.

He picked up the guitar and turned it in his hands for a while. It was a pretty thing, though obviously it had seen more years than he had. It had an intricate mother-of-pearl inlay on the rosette and, if he was guessing, he'd say the tuning pegs were all handmade. He strummed his fingers across the strings, smiling at the sound. Tuned, even. Bemused, he sat on the settee and let his fingers take over.

A little while later, he was back at the window, looking for the van. Chloe and Bill should have been back by now. He let out a deep breath and checked his watch. He'd give them ten more minutes and if they hadn't shown up, he'd go. He went to the kitchen and stared out those windows for a few minutes, thinking about the priest's words. *I knew there was no one in the kitchen . . .*

Back on the couch, he once again picked up the guitar. The sound of music had always soothed him. When he'd been a part of Badlands, he'd been happy. For a while. Until Matt started shit with everyone else, showed up drunk and stoned, sometimes whacked beyond recognition. It hadn't been fun then. It had almost been a relief to leave it behind. There were times when he'd wished he could leave

Matt behind as well. But he owed Matt. Dead or not, he still owed Matt.

"Nathan." Chloe's voice almost scared him out of his skin.

His head jerked up to find her standing well into the room. "Jesus, where did you come from?"

"Upstairs," she said.

"I didn't think you were back."

"We just returned a little while ago. You must have been in the kitchen when we came in. We had to leave the van down the street and walk. There'll be no getting out of town until the rain stops."

Reilly nodded, angry at himself for the sudden guilt he felt at not watching out for them more carefully. They were not his responsibility, he repeated to himself. He ran his fingers over the guitar strings and said nothing.

"May I talk to you for a moment, Nathan?"

"Don't call me Nathan."

"I'm sorry. I know it bothers you, but when I see you, the name is always in your mind. Did you know that?"

Reilly strummed a discordant note and ignored her.

"You hate it because it was your father's name and you hated him."

He changed up the fingering and played another chord.

"And now you resent me, because I've made you see it."

"Chloe, what do you want?"

"I want you to help me."

"Help you what?"

"Your brother, Matthew, when was it he began to change?"

Despite his determination not to, Reilly glanced up and locked eyes with her. How did she know he had a brother? More important, how did she know about the change?

Chloe hovered near the settee, looking frailer than he'd ever seen. He remembered that he'd thought her in her fifties the first time they'd met. Now she looked closer to seventy. How old was she really?

"He wasn't always such a monster, was he?" she asked. Her smug assurance was gone and the question came across as beseeching.

"You never understood what happened, did you? And when he killed your father—"

Reilly stood abruptly, setting the guitar aside. "You're crazy, lady." But suddenly his heart was doing a jackhammer in his chest and his hands clenched into fists. Chloe stared back at him nervously, like a rabbit that'd been spotted by a predator in an open field. Reilly tried to tone down the hostility and said, "Matt didn't kill our dad."

She swallowed loud enough for him to hear, and he suddenly felt bad for scaring an old woman. But her next words didn't hold the same sense of fear her expression did.

"Covering up for him has always been a way of life for you, Nathan. You lied to protect him, even though he still had blood on his hands."

Reilly was breathing hard and it took everything not to shout at her. Not to tell her to shut the hell up.

"I'm not trying to hurt you. You were the good son. Then you were the good brother. Now it's time to be a good man. Be a hero, Nathan."

"Lady, you've got the wrong guy. I'm nobody's hero."

She gave him another of those leveling looks. He wanted to stride out of the room. He wanted to get in the Jeep and plow through the river-filled roads until he could go no farther. But he couldn't make his legs and feet cooperate. He stood there, like an insect trapped beneath glass, while she studied him.

"My father was an abuser as well," she said. She walked over to the picture hanging above the mantel and pointed at it. Each step seemed to cause her pain. How had she aged so much in so little time? Reilly found himself glancing around, looking for Bill. If something happened, like if she keeled over, he wanted Bill around. But for once Chloe La-Monte was alone.

"That is my grandfather," she said, pointing to a man who stood just at the corner of the picture.

The statement blew every other thought out of Reilly's head. Her grandfather? Why would Carolina Beck have a picture of *Chloe's* grandfather hanging in her house? He came to stand beside her and stare at the tidy man in the pinstriped suit standing just shy of the background. But examination of the old sepia print made her claim impossible to discount. She watched him as he noted the similarities she shared with the white man in the portrait. The shape of their eyes, the small, tucked ears, the pointed chin.

"He is my grandfather." She waited for a baited moment. Then she said, "And he is my father."

"What?" Reilly asked. "He can't be both . . ."

But even as he said it, Reilly realized that he was wrong. It was possible that he could be both grandfather and father, it just wasn't right.

"You ask yourself, how could a man violate his own daughter? The answer is worse than you can imagine. In his mind, my mother was an animal, as was her mother. Animals do not have the rights of parentage. They have no rights at all."

Reilly didn't know what to say, but she didn't seem to expect a response.

"He was old when he came for me. But his hate and anger had turned him into something stronger than a man half his age."

It took a moment for Reilly to register what she'd just said. *He was old when he came for me* . . . The bastard had impregnated her grandmother, her mother, and he'd come back for Chloe? It was sick beyond his understanding, but he didn't think for a moment that she was lying. The raw shame in her voice was too real.

"I was a young woman, still in school when it happened. It killed my mother, knowing what he'd done. Eventually, she died of her despair."

A logical part of Reilly wanted to argue that someone couldn't die of despair, but the night he'd stood in front of the mirror and shaved his head, his own anguish had felt great enough to kill him, hadn't it?

"Why are you telling me this?" he asked.

"Hear me out. Please."

Reluctantly, Reilly nodded.

"For generations my family has told stories about this man. We thought he was dead once, but it was merely misplaced hope. My mother believed he could not be killed and that he haunts our family still."

Reilly looked at the picture and back at Chloe. He didn't know what to say.

"My grandmother lived in this very place. Here, at the Diablo."

Her pause felt more than weighted. It felt of things he couldn't understand, things she didn't want to explain. The heaviness of it filled the stillness until it seemed like sand, shifting, but so dense it held them both in place.

"Why are you here, Chloe?"

She moved to the settee and sat down with an exhausted sound. Age hunched her shoulders and darkened the crescents beneath her eyes. When she spoke, it wasn't to answer his question.

"Even before I understood what there was to be afraid of, I knew my mother was frightened. It was in the way she'd watch the horizon, the way she checked the locks after dark during a time when people didn't lock their doors. It was in the shadows of her eyes. We were like animals in a cage, trapped by our own fears. Our family stories told of how we'd tried to get away from him and how he always tracked us down and made us pay." She looked at him. "Do you know what my mother's name was? Misery. They named her Misery. She was a child born of pain and my grandmother wanted her to always remember that."

"That doesn't make sense."

"No, it doesn't. Sometimes sense cannot be made from violence. You, of all people, should know that."

He nodded in acknowledgment, but he couldn't quite meet her steady gaze.

"I know that he still plagues my family. I know he plagues Gracie's as well."

"Plagues? He can't still be alive?"

"Can't he?"

Reilly finally broke free of the paralysis that held him. He took a step away from her, wanting to take several more. "If he was old when you were a girl, then he'd be over a hundred, hundred and twenty by now."

"His body, yes. But his spirit does not age."

"You're talking about ghosts, now. You know I don't buy it. I believe what you say about this sick bastard. But he has to be dead. He can't hurt you or anyone else anymore."

"Believe what you like, but there is another world, Nathan Reilly Alexander, and it exists within our own. I have not the same gift as others—there is one who travels with me now who can see the past, sometimes even the future, just by touching another."

"The priest with the gloves?"

"That's right. My gift, my curse, is that I *feel* the spirits around me. Sometimes I can help them find the resolutions they seek. Sometimes I can only suffer alongside them."

"And you're feeling these spirits here?"

"Yes, Nathan. There are many here."

Reilly couldn't help the sound of disbelief that came from him.

"That is not my only gift, though. I have visions. Terrible visions. I saw the murder of Gracie's mother."

"She died in an accident, Chloe. You heard Gracie today."

"I heard her question how her mother had come to be there. I heard her marvel that her grandmother had known where to find her."

Yeah, he'd heard that too. It was the kind of thing that gave Diablo Springs its haunted reputation.

"I came here to warn Carolina before it happened. To warn her that her daughter was in danger."

Reilly's eyes widened. He knew Carolina Beck would not have taken kindly to this crazy old bat warning her about some vision of death. "She threw you out," he said.

"Yes. And after her daughter and the baby Gracie disappeared, it was I who told her where they would be found."

"And you're trying to tell me that your grandfather"— Reilly paused and pointed at the picture—"that man there is the one who killed her?"

"Yes."

That brought another lengthy silence. Reilly liked the

direction of this conversation less and less. And yet he felt compelled to learn more the way drivers feel compelled to look at an accident as they drive past.

"Diablo Springs has been haunted by evil for years, Nathan. Your people talk of the Dead Lights as if they are some phenomena of steam and moonbeams. But I know why they are called that. There are more bodies in those caverns than you can believe."

She was wrong there—he did believe the ruins were filled with dead bodies. Bodies, yes. But ghostly spirits . . .

"For years, in my youth," she went on, "I tried to block out this place, the legends that were passed down through my family . . . the pain that so marked us. I nearly succeeded. I nearly managed to wipe it all away."

The wistful throb in her voice struck Reilly deep. Hadn't he tried to forget Diablo Springs in the same way? Hadn't he found a way to survive by wiping his memory of everything that had happened prior to his leaving here? It wasn't that he forgot; it was that he didn't choose to remember. And being back now was like peeling the scab off a festered wound.

Chloe said, "When he came and raped your Gracie, I knew I could not pretend any longer."

"I hate to burst your bubble there, Chloe. But your ghost didn't touch Gracie. Someone else did."

Chloe's face filled with pity, and Reilly had the uncomfortable suspicion that she was feeling sorry for him. He stared back with neutral eyes.

"I think even Carolina sensed it was going to happen. When I came to warn her again, she was waiting for me. But she refused to hear me and she refused to heed my warning."

"Do you have any idea how crazy you sound?" he asked.

"Believe me or don't believe me, Nathan. The truth is that I saw it. I felt it. He covered his face to hide his shame, but he couldn't hide it. I know because I saw it. I still see it. And I live with the knowledge that I might have changed it."

She stared into his eyes, refusing to let him look away.

"Chloe, you are so far off-base that I don't even know what game you're playing. You asked about my brother, so I know you have some knowledge of what he did. He raped Gracie. I know it, she knows it, and God help him, he knew it. I'm willing to accept that maybe you're for real. Maybe you have visions. Maybe you see the future or the past or whatever. But I don't get why you'd bring this up when you know what really happened."

"I know you do not understand me, Nathan, but make no mistake, I understand you."

"Which means?"

"That you will not believe until you see it with your own eyes. And even then you will doubt."

He didn't say anything to that. What could he say? "You asked me to help you, Chloe. Help you do what?"

"Three months ago my mother came to me in a vision."

She watched him closely, watched a reaction he couldn't stop sweep across his face. Three months ago Matt had died.

"Every night since she has come. Last night she was joined by Carolina Beck. Nathan, your Gracie and her daughter are both in danger."

"Because of your visions?"

Chloe sighed, as if the frustration of communicating with him were too taxing to endure.

"I warned Carolina that her granddaughter would be raped. The next night it happened. Now I ask you again, when did the changes begin in your brother?"

Reilly didn't have to think about it. He knew. The night his father had beaten his mother to death. The night Matt had returned the favor.

"You took him to the springs," Chloe said. Her voice seemed distant. As if she were watching his memory, watching as he pulled Matt off his father's bloody, broken body. They'd taken their dad up to Dead Lights Road and rigged his car to drive off it. As long as he lived, Reilly would remember the sight of the old Buick breaking through the railing and arcing across the pitch-black sky into the caverns that still surrounded the old springs. The car had hit with a boom that should have been much louder. Reilly had looked into his brother's face then and he'd seen it. He'd seen the change.

Reilly shoved his hands into his pockets and looked away. He knew what came next. He knew he wouldn't be able to stop Chloe from prying deeper any more than he could have stopped that night from happening. He strode over to the window and stared out at the storm.

He said, "Yeah, Matt changed after that. So what? Who wouldn't change after what we saw, what we lived through?"

"You didn't."

"How do you know?"

She stood, bracing herself against the back of a chair as she faced him. "I know what's in your heart, Nathan. I know you yearn to remember your brother as a good man. You don't blame him for your father's death. The law was willing to believe your story; this town was willing to turn a blind eye to what was obvious because they knew about him and they'd done nothing to help you boys or your mother against him. But after that . . . after that, Matt changed. . . . He wasn't a monster before, but he became one. Wouldn't you like to know why? Wouldn't you like to release his spirit from the guilt of this world? Wouldn't you like to release yourself from the feelings of failing him?"

Reilly swallowed around a lump of emotion. He didn't answer. He didn't move a muscle. He couldn't.

"I want to do a séance, Nathan. Tonight. I need Gracie and Analise in my circle. And you. We are all connected in ways I don't understand. My mother, your brother, Gracie, and now Analise. I have to know what happened. I need to see the past so I can protect against the future."

"Look, you may have a few of the facts right, but that doesn't mean I believe a goddamned thing you've said. I think you're spouting so much mumbo jumbo you actually think it's all true. But it's not. Yeah, my brother changed. And goddamn him, he raped Gracie. But it's not connected to anything that happened to you fifty, sixty years ago. And even if it was, Gracie's never going to go for a séance. Not with you, not with anyone."

"She will if you ask her."

"There's a lot of history between me and Gracie, Chloe. None of it inspires the kind of faith in me you're imagining."

"Yes, history," she said, missing the rest of his point. "The history between you is what will make her see reason."

"You think a séance is reason? I think it's lunacy. I'm going to pass on this, Chloe. Gracie's got enough on her plate without you adding a séance to the mix."

"You heard her say it today, Nathan. Why will you not believe? What sent Carolina to the springs to search for her missing daughter and granddaughter? It was I. I saw it before it happened. From hundreds of miles away, I saw it. And though I couldn't prevent it, I led Carolina to her daughter's body."

He couldn't keep himself from asking, "So you're saying you know *what* happened to Gracie's mother?"

Chloe nodded. She looked back at the picture of her grandfather standing behind the four women. But when she answered, it was with another question.

"Do you know why your father beat your mother?"

"Because he could."

"Yes, because he owned her. And nothing in this world would ever change that. If she'd left him, he'd have followed. No matter where she went, he would have found her."

Reilly swallowed, staring at a point over her shoulder, fighting to keep the tide of emotion within him from spilling over. Spilling out.

"My grandfather felt the same about these women," she said, gesturing to the picture again. "He still does. You've recognized the woman in the middle, haven't you? You see the resemblance between her and Gracie. She's Gracie's great-grandmother, Ella."

"If you say so."

"She's the one he wants."

"Well, that should make it easy then. She's dead, he's dead. Let him have her."

The look on Chloe's face made him regret the words as soon as they were spoken. "Would you condemn your *brother's* soul to hell so easily?"

She didn't wait for an answer. He supposed his expression was answer enough. If he could save Matt's soul, he'd do whatever it took.

"There are only women in the Beck family. You've noted this, I'm sure."

Yeah, he'd noted it.

"Each generation is another chance for my grandfather to have his precious Ella."

For a moment, something like hatred flashed across her face. Before he could fully understand it, Chloe said, "He lured Gracie's mother to the springs."

"How?"

"He can make himself seen."

"That's bullshit."

"Ask your Gracie. She's seen him."

Reilly shook his head, but then he thought of last night. Her scream. Her pale and frightened face. The way she kept glancing at the corner by the window. Had she seen something? Someone? Was it possible that Chloe was telling the truth?

He paused, the answer to the question clear in his mind. No. It wasn't. Because there were no ghosts. Granted the Diablo had a lot of weird shit happening in it, but ghosts that could materialize? That could lure someone to plunge to their death in the deep caverns of the springs? No way. Chloe didn't know any more than anyone else about what happened to Gracie's mother. She'd fallen and broken her back, but why she was out there in the first place . . .

"For the sake of argument, let's say it's all true," he said. "Your grandfather is a ghost who's out to get the Becks. That still doesn't tell me why you are here. And why you wanted me along."

"I wondered when you'd ask. I told you last night, *you* are part of the story. And I gave you the excuse you needed to come. I'm here to end the cycle, Nathan. I'm here to send my grandfather to the other side."

"Oo-kay," he said. "And how are you going to do that?"

"There are two reasons why he won't leave. The first, as I've told you, is Ella and her lineage. He considers the Beck women his possessions. He wants them back."

"And the second reason?"

"He is searching for something. Something lost. Again, something he believes belongs to him."

"And what is that?"

She looked guarded for a moment. "I don't know."

"I think you do."

"That is because you don't believe what I'm telling you. You're looking for a concrete *thing* that will explain it all in a tidy way."

Fair enough. "So how do you plan to accomplish the ending of this cycle?"

She sighed impatiently. "I've told you already. I want to do a séance."

Reilly shook his head. "You almost had me, Chloe."

Chloe's smile was resigned. She shook her head and took a step away. Like magic, Bill chose that moment to appear. She leaned heavily on him as he led her to the stairway.

"You don't have to believe me, Reilly, but think about the séance. If I'm right, it could bring closure to years of pain. And if I'm wrong . . ." She shrugged. "Think how good it would be in your new book. The atmosphere alone would be mesmerizing. And should I prove true and raise a spirit or two, my, my, wouldn't that be something."

Oh, she was manipulative. She cast that hook effortlessly and snagged him with her sly bait. But he didn't bite. Chloe stared at him for a moment, surprise widening her eyes just a little. She thought she'd have him that easily. What made him angry, though, was the desire to sink his teeth into her hook. She was right. Without him even being aware, the structure of a story had been building and linking in his head and suddenly he saw it, standing like the plywood framework of a house, waiting for the walls, the windows, the paint. It was huge and precise. And if she delivered on a séance tonight, and he could capture that in words and mood . . .

"You've let her down before, Nathan," she said, the eyes now sparkling with an inner knowledge he resented more than he could say. "What if I'm right? What if this time you could help?"

"You've been listening to your own crazy stories for too long, Chloe. You're not right. I won't play your game."

She nodded and the sparkle dimmed. But the tiny smile tilting her lips didn't waver. She thought she knew him better than he knew himself. Well she was wrong.

"I don't think so," she said, answering his thought. And then she let Bill lead her up the stairs.

Angry, Reilly turned and moved away. His steps took him back to the mantel and the picture. He stared at it, seeing more than he had before. From the start, there'd been no missing the resemblance of Gracie to the woman seated in the center of the picture. That alone had dominated his attention. Now the tidy man in the background became a young, pasty version of the woman who'd just left. But as he stared from one face to another, he saw more. Beside the pinstriped suit was another man, one nearly concealed by the shadows and the smoke. Reilly moved closer, staring into the man's face, prying his features from the faded picture. Like an optical illusion where the image is hidden until you stare at it long enough, the man's face suddenly jumped into focus. Reilly took a step back. Then another. But now that he'd seen it, he couldn't ignore what his eyes told him. Couldn't believe it, couldn't dismiss it.

The man looked like Reilly.

chapter twenty-two

May 1896

I stared at Lonnie Smith's face and I was struck still by the rush of my hate. There was no questioning what he had or hadn't done. I'd seen it with my own eyes. Seen him laugh as he murdered my father in cold blood. Seen him slaughter my little brother and then calmly sit down to eat my mother's stew. I felt as if time slowed to an unbearable measure. I saw a spark pop from the fire and hover in the air. Beside me, Sawyer had stood alert but still.

Aiken moved to his seat at the card table, his smile as oily as the gleaming black hair on his head. "Welcome," he said.

But in response to the weapons drawn by Lonnie Smith and his riders, the rough and ready man sitting to Aiken's left had drawn his gun and pointed it at Lonnie. I saw others move their hands closer to their weapons.

Lonnie swung the barrel of his pistol to the man's chest. "Don't be a dummy," he said, smiling to show tobacco-stained teeth. "Drop your gun right there by your feet."

The man shook his head. "No, I don't believe I will."

"We don't want any trouble here," Aiken said. "Why don't you put away that pistol and come down for a drink? We're all friends."

Lonnie's smile was cold and condescending. I looked to my right and saw Sawyer standing close, hand resting lightly on the butt of his gun. On his saddle was a rifle. He looked me in the eye, letting me know he was watching me. I searched for the same cold-blooded ruthlessness that gleamed from Lonnie, but I saw none. Just warning. With his eyes, he told me to keep my head.

"You all look good and friendly," Lonnie was saying as he scanned the campsite and tent.

Behind him another man stepped down from his horse and then two others. The riders who had killed my family. They all had their weapons drawn.

"Why don't you all come on out in the light where I can see you," Lonnie called in the direction of the tent.

My rage swelled inside me until I didn't think I could control it. Sawyer reached out and took my hand. He used it to haul me back and then he stepped in front of me. The look that passed between us was dark with the flickering fire.

"I said, come on out," Lonnie repeated, raising his voice. One of his riders went to the flapping white tent. He pulled up the side revealing the bare behinds of two men who'd been so engrossed in their pleasure, they hadn't heard or noticed the intrusion. Laughing, Lonnie's man jabbed the butt closest to him with the end of his rifle hard enough to make the man squeal and turn in outrage. When he saw all the guns pulled and aimed, he scrambled off Meaira and struggled to get his pants on. When he reached for his gun, Lonnie fired at it and sent the weapon dancing across the dirt.

Hands in the air, the men in the tent joined the circle made by the Smith riders. Meaira, Chick, and Honey remained where they were, barely dressed as they huddled on one low pallet, looking out of the open tent with fear. I could not see Athena, but I knew she would be close by.

"You girls just stay right there," Lonnie said, grinning. "We'll be with you in a moment."

Lonnie turned his attention back to the cluster of men standing at the makeshift card table. He gave Aiken's solicitous face a dismissive glance and moved on to the next man. He stopped when he reached Sawyer. I saw him stiffen, saw the tautness like a fine sheen that went down his body. I felt the bead of it vibrate through Sawyer.

"Didn't expect to see you here, McCready," Lonnie said.

"I could say the same."

Lonnie's eyes flicked to me and I braced myself for recognition, for he had seen me with my family the day my daddy testified against them. The tension in Sawyer matched my own until it was painful to stand so still. Lonnie's cold eyes stayed on me for a moment that seemed to last forever. Suddenly he smiled. "I don't believe it. I just don't believe it. Boys, boys, looky here. Look who we found. Looks like we hit the jackpot."

His brother and men had us surrounded and stood with guns pointed, waiting for their orders.

Lonnie leaned forward in his saddle and said, "You'll be coming with us, Miss Beck." He gave Sawyer another challenging look, noting that he stood close to me, noting that his gun was not yet aimed. But when he spoke, it was to Aiken. "Push that money out to the middle of the table," Lonnie told him. "Jake will be happy to relieve you of it as well as the little miss there."

Again, time seemed to move slower than possible. I saw Aiken's face tighten. Knew in an instant that he would not surrender his winnings. The same knowledge passed over Lonnie's face and for a moment he looked away from me to level the barrel of his gun at Aiken's chest. I didn't wait for him to do more. I lunged forward, grabbing the gun from the holster of the slack-faced man standing nearby and turning it on Lonnie. I pulled the trigger without hesitation and the gun blasted in a sound that sucked all other noise from the air. It bucked me backward just as another gun fired. I saw cards and money sail through the air and had a second to understand that Aiken had fired through the table at Lonnie, who was already dropping from the saddle, but I didn't know if he'd been shot or was taking cover.

I saw another man stagger, clutching a red stain that spread with hypnotizing speed across his stomach as all around me guns went off like firecrackers on the Fourth of July. Gun drawn, Sawyer shoved me hard to the ground, but he was too late. A red-hot pain sliced through my shoulder and I knew I'd been shot. I screamed as the ground rushed up at me, and then my head hit something hard and all went black.

I woke to utter silence, the kind that comes only in the deepest hours of night. But it wasn't night. I could tell by the coolness of the air, the freshness of the breeze that it was near dawn. I looked around, not recognizing where we were. The last I remembered, we set camp by the river. The miners' tent town had been close enough to see, far enough not to smell. We were no longer near it.

I raised my head, looking around at the unfamiliar terrain. We must have moved. I frowned. Why had we moved? And then it all came rushing back. The Smith brothers, the men, the gunshots.

I sat quickly and pain sliced through my shoulder and tried to split my head. I winced, putting one hand to the lump beneath my hair while I stared at the thick bandage wrapped around my blood-stained shoulder with shock. I'd been shot. Carefully I pushed to my feet, pulling the blanket I'd been covered with around me. I stood. My legs felt shaky and my stomach none too strong, but I didn't fall over. That was good.

Beside me the other women slept in a row under the tarp that stretched from the wagon. There was no tent, no pallets, no sign of the violence of last night. I staggered to the water barrel strapped to the back of the wagon and got a drink. The horses were tied up not far away. That meant that Aiken was still near. And what of Sawyer? As if in answer, I heard a shuffling behind me and turned to see him by the fire.

He was dressed in the same clothes he'd worn last night, but his hat was off, revealing golden brown hair that looked darker in the predawn glow. He didn't look as if he'd slept and his beard was heavy on his cheeks.

He watched me as he rose and I saw that he winced. There was a dark stain on his sleeve. I was not the only one to be wounded last night.

Without a word he rolled his blanket tightly and tied it to the back of his saddle.

"What are you doing?" I asked.

"What's it look like?"

"Like you're packing."

He lifted the saddle skirt and adjusted his cinch, ignoring me.

"What happened last night?" I tried again.

He paused, running a hand down his horse's neck. The animal gave a low nicker and tossed its head.

"What happened last night?" he repeated softly. "Well, you blew a hole the size of a dinner plate through Lonnie Smith. Guess you won't have to worry about him anymore."

I caught my breath as the memory rushed in, with it the smell of blood and gunpowder and fear that still clung to me. I steadied myself against the wagon.

"I killed him?"

"Wasn't that what you were trying to do?"

Yes, I'd wanted him dead; I'd wanted it so badly, I'd pulled the trigger without thinking beyond the act. And I wasn't sorry he was dead. He'd deserved to die for what he did to my family. Justice had failed to make him pay for his crimes, but I had not. I would not shed tears for ridding the world of the likes of Lonnie Smith.

"What about everyone else?" I asked.

Sawyer shook his head. "Can't say who shot who, but five men are dead for it. Two of Smith's boys, three of the miners. Dead. All of them."

"What about Jake Smith?"

"Last I saw he was riding hell bent for leather. Don't know if he'll be coming back."

The blood drained from my face. It left me dizzy and swaying. Lonnie's brother would be out for revenge.

"Your shoulder hurt?" he asked, nodding at the bandage.

"I was shot," I said, as if he didn't know.

"Barely. Flesh wound. Shouldn't give you too much grief."

"How about you?"

He shrugged. "I'll live."

I nodded, watching as he filled his saddlebags then moved to the other side of his huge horse.

"Where is Aiken?" I asked at last, though I really didn't want to know.

"Took off as soon as he saw what he'd done. You weren't the only one trigger happy last night."

His voice was mired in sarcasm, and yet I heard something else there. A note of admiration, an understanding that I would not be the same for what I had done—no matter what my reasons, a bit of awe at my tenacity. I deserved none of his regard, and yet I thirsted for the reassurance it gave me.

But as I watched him continue to pack his horse, it suddenly occurred to me just what he was doing.

"You're leaving?" I said.

He gave me a cold and steady look. "We left five dead men back there, and I'll be damned if I'll take the fall for killing I didn't do."

"So you're going to just leave us here? Just like that?"

"Just like that," he answered.

I looked around at the great nothingness. We could be anywhere. "You know we'll probably die out here."

"I know nothing of the sort. I watched you blow a man into eternity last night. I don't think a few days in the wild will get the best of you."

I sucked in a sharp breath and pulled the blanket around my shoulders tighter. Tears stung my eyes. "I did what I had to do."

"I'm a firm believer in that motto. I think I'll do the same now."

"But . . . but you could take us with you. . . ."

"With me? Why? So you can scalp me in my sleep? I'll be perfectly honest, before—" He shook his head. "I didn't think you had it in you. But now I know different."

"No, I'm not . . ." What? A murderer? "You didn't see what they did to my momma, my grandma, my daddy . . . my little brother. You didn't see." My chest was tight and painful from holding back the tears I refused to shed. He stood, staring at me like I was a unique species of bug. As if he couldn't decide whether to stomp me into the ground or capture me in a jar.

I was breathing heavy with the effort to rein my emotions. He watched me, shifting his weight, looking as awkward as I felt. At last I managed to say, "You're going to Arizona territory. To take over a saloon."

"How do you know that?"

"I may be crazy but I'm not deaf."

He snorted at that, stopping the smile before it reached his lips.

"I ain't taking you with me. Sure as hell there's a posse already forming up, coming looking for us."

"So you'll just ante us up to them. Is that it?"

"You're a bunch of whor—women stranded in the middle of nowhere. They'll follow your tracks easy enough, but they won't think you had anything to do with it. Tell them Lonnie did the killing. Tell them the miners started firing blind. They'll believe you."

"A bunch of whores?"

"I didn't mean that. I know you're not a whore."

"But for the grace of God I'm not. What do you think Aiken had in mind for me when you rode up last night?"

Sawyer swallowed as I locked eyes with him. If he hadn't arrived when he had, if the Smith riders hadn't appeared . . . Just a few more moments, and I'd have been the strongest man's prize. I let him see that in my face, see how terrified I'd been, and I knew it bothered him more than he cared to admit.

"I don't owe you anything, lady. I'm real sorry about your family. But you got your pound of flesh. Lonnie's every bit as dead as they are now. I never had nothing to do with what they did though. I ain't a killer."

"But I am."

He squatted down to clean his horse's feet. "Only if that's how you're going to see it. From my point of view, I saw Lonnie get killed by one of the miners."

I looked over my shoulder at the sleeping women. If he left us here, it would be my fault. The sun peeked over the horizon in a blaze of muted gold. As far as the eye could see, now, there was nothing but scrub and cactus. Not even a tree in sight. No river to follow. No game darting in the trees. And what if it was Jake that found us, not the posse? What if he came first? I'd killed his brother, and he wouldn't let that go. He'd hunt me. And he'd do more than kill me when he caught me. And what about the others? I'd be foolish to think he'd spare the others. I took a deep breath, trying to hold back my panic.

"We could help you." The words were out before I'd considered them, but it was true. We could.

"Help me? Into an early grave maybe."

"What's a saloon without women? I thought Aiken had convinced you that you needed them."

"You bartering out their flesh these days?"

"At least give them the choice. Give them the chance. They've been doing this to save their lives. Maybe they've been doing it because they didn't have a choice. But if they knew they were working toward freedom . . ."

He looked at me from where he crouched down, inspecting the hooves of his horse. I stared back, trying to make myself appear earnest, beseeching . . . obliging.

"They would work for you, Sawyer. They think you're a good man."

His eyes narrowed as he watched me. "What about you?" he said at last, and his voice was low and deep. It made something in my belly tighten.

"What do you mean?"

"You think I'm a good man?"

Dry-mouthed, I nodded. He made a derisive sound that mocked me. He didn't believe it.

"I can't see you taking on customers," he said.

I hadn't meant that I would, but I saw from his face how hypocritical that made me. I was trying to keep us alive, but I was using their bodies for payment.

"I'll do what I have to do to stay alive," I said, wondering where the fierce words came from. Could I, would I really? I couldn't say what I might have done had the burly man hauled me into that tent. To survive, would I have complied?

Sawyer watched my thoughts flash across my face. Then he stood and approached me, his steps slow and measured. I thought of a wolf, moving silently through the underbrush. What was I doing negotiating with this outlaw? He'd helped me last night, but what made me think I could depend upon him? He was no gentleman, no knight in shining armor.

A shiver went through me, sending a fine tremor up as the wind teased a strand of my hair across my face. His hand beat mine to brush it back.

"I don't believe you," he said.

I turned defiant eyes up to meet his. It mattered not that I didn't believe me either. I knew I couldn't let him leave us out here, miles from any sign of civilization, prey waiting to be taken. I had brought this on these women who had taken me in. I was responsible for their being stranded. Yes, they'd been at Aiken's mercy before, but even he couldn't compare to dying of thirst and hunger. That would be our fate out here in the middle of nowhere with barely enough supplies to last a week. That or Jake Smith, who now had the murder of his brother to add to his reasons for vengeance. I'd seen what he'd done to my family. I could only imagine the torture he could inflict on us.

I lifted my chin, showing Sawyer that I would not back down. I would face him and any other man.

"You'd bed a man for them," he asked, his voice tight and dangerous.

He was testing me. I swallowed and nodded. "For us. If it meant you'll see us safely back to civilization."

"What if that man was me?"

My eyes widened as he stepped closer still. The hand that clutched the blanket around me was white-knuckled, but I didn't back up. If I gave an inch to him now, he would ride off and leave us. Just like that. I felt my breath coming in short bursts, but I didn't move, even when his hands settled on my arms.

"What if that man was me, Ella?"

I tipped my head back so he could see my determination, but the sight of those Mississippi eyes so close, so turbulent and filled with swirling need wiped the rebel from me. I watched as if hypnotized as he lowered his face—watched and did nothing to stop him. His lips touched mine and the shock of it went through me like the bullet had last night. Only pain didn't follow. Heat did. It raced through my veins and lit a fire within me, burning like it had that day so long ago in town. My world had been different then, but not the sensations he caused. Not the spiraling tightness inside me.

A part of my mind spoke in warning even as my body responded. Suddenly life had come so close to the edge of death that right and wrong no longer seemed valid. I'd killed a man last night. This morning I was in another's arms. It didn't seem real, and yet every touch, every sense told me it was more real than anything I'd ever experienced.

Sawyer tasted of power and potency. He'd drunk coffee with sugar and it was on his lips, hot as the feelings moving inside of me. My hands let loose the blanket and it slipped to my feet as I moved my arms up the wall of his chest to wrap around his neck. It never occurred to me to push him away.

His hands slid across my back to the curve of my spine and he hauled me up hard against him. His mustache was soft against my skin and his mouth felt like heated satin. His tongue touched my lips, teasing and insisting until they parted and I opened for him. He deepened the kiss, moving his tongue against mine in a caress more intimate than anything I'd ever known. Low inside me everything became hot and liquid. I curled my hands into his shoulders and held on as I rode the wave of feeling that washed over me.

When his hands began to roam again, I didn't protest. My body became a stranger that welcomed any touch he offered. His fingers slid up my ribs and then closed over the soft flesh of my breasts. I caught my breath and held it as awareness emptied me of everything but feeling.

The sound I made stilled him and for an instant we were like statues, frozen in a moment of intimacy. Then slowly he lifted his head and looked into my eyes. I saw wonder and need in the deep flecked swirls but then it changed and became something else. He pushed me back roughly, glaring at me as his chest rose and fell with his labored breathing. I staggered and caught my balance, looking at him with hooded eyes. I knew my lips were red and full from his kisses as his were from mine. But the look he gave me was angry, and I felt the need drain as red heat climbed my neck.

"I don't need a whore," he said coldly.

The words whipped through me and I couldn't conceal the sting they left behind. I wanted to hide my face from him, I wanted to snatch up the blanket and huddle beneath it so he couldn't see me, but I didn't. Once again I lifted my chin and stared him in the eye.

He looked away. Turning his back, he picked up one of his bags and threw it across the camp with a low rumble of anger. "Damn it," he growled.

The muscles in his shoulders bunched tightly and he stared away from me, cursing under his breath. But I wasn't afraid. It was foolish to believe, but I sensed that I was winning. He quieted, shook his head, and made a sound of laughter, though nothing was funny. Finally he turned around and looked at me, still shaking his head.

"Wake 'em up," he said. "Before I change my mind."

chapter twenty-three

.

I was trembling as I moved to the slumbering women and bent to gently wake them up. When I reached Athena, her eyes were wide and black in the glowing light of dawn. She stared hard at me, backing me up as she sat.

"You think you in charge of us now? That what you think?"

"No—"

"No? You makin' deals wit Captain for us. I hear you. What happen to killin' him? You sure changed from killin' to kissin' quick enough."

"What you talking about, Athena? Who kissin'?" Chick asked.

"Ask her," Athena said, bottom lip protruding and eyes hard like ball bearings.

I looked at the expectant faces, some still heavy with sleep, some wide-eyed and waiting.

"Look around you," I said. "Do any of you know where we are?"

Chick frowned and shook her head. "We never do."

"But you always have someone guiding you."

"Or dragging, more's the like," Meaira said.

"She gone and tol' Captain we work for him," Athena said.

Meaira's head snapped back. Honey said, "Is that true?"

I caught my lip between my teeth as I nodded. "Aiken is gone and even if he does come back, I don't think any of us wants to be here. The Captain was saddling up—he was going to leave us. Leave us here with nothing but a wagon, a horse, and a good wish. At least if we go with him, we'll end up at a town. Some place we can find our way home from."

"This wagon my home," Chick said.

"She tell him we his," Athena said.

"You'd planned to go when Aiken was taking you," I told them. "The only difference now is we go with the Captain. You think he's a good man. Honey, you said he was, didn't you?"

Honey nodded, watching me with narrowed eyes.

I shrugged. "You've been doing . . . what you've been doing for Aiken and you haven't gotten anything but more of the same for it. Isn't that right?"

"That's right," Honey said.

"With Sawyer—the Captain, you'll have a choice. You'll have a chance to make some money. Money that can help you start over if that's what you want."

"How 'bout you?" Athena demanded. "What choice you get?"

I held my head up. "The same as you."

"You gon' work for Captain?" Chick exclaimed.

"She gon' work under Captain. She kissin' up with him."

Honey's eyes rounded. "You were kissing the Captain?"

My face was burning, but I nodded. "I had to prove I meant what I said. I told him we would be an asset."

"He know we got asses."

Meaira snorted. "That he does."

"Well now he knows I have one too."

"And you gon' use it?" Athena said with disdain.

I thought I might throw up. I found myself repeating my words to Sawyer. They tasted no better with time. "I will do what I must to survive."

They each exchanged glances in silence.

I was banking that somewhere in Sawyer was a man whose honor would not allow him to use me that way. I was betting that he'd put me on the first train east. But where would I go? I had no family. No money. All I could do was return to Alamosa and give myself to the charity of the people there. I thought they would take me in, but what if Jake Smith decided to hunt me even there?

I shook my head. I could not think about that now. I needed to get beyond this moment, this day, this problem.

"We need to hurry," I said. "He'll leave us if we're not ready."

They jumped up and began gathering things together. By the time Sawyer had returned from watering the horses, the women were up and ready. He gave them each a steady look, ending with me.

"I ain't no babysitter," he growled at them. "I'd as soon as part ways here. Any of you want that, you just say so."

"Ella say you gon' let us work in your saloon and keep some of our money," Chick said, her voice high and thin and clear.

Sawyer looked at me with an expression of such disbelief I might have laughed. But I didn't.

"That's right," he said. "If that's what you want."

I was as surprised as they, but I didn't let it show.

"But I ain't guaranteeing that Aiken won't be in Diablo Springs by the time we get there. If he is, well, you ain't my responsibility."

He gave a nod that spoke the rest. I could see from their faces that none of the women needed it spelled out. They'd said it themselves—they belonged to Aiken. Sawyer would not fight for their freedom. That they had to do alone.

Sawyer's eyes lingered on me for another moment and just the look brought a fresh wave of awareness to me. An anticipation I was ashamed to feel, but couldn't deny. How I'd gone from wanting him dead, to begging for help, to hoping for his touch, I didn't know. But there it was.

He tossed Athena the harness. "You gotta earn your keep, though. I ain't waiting for none of you." The last said to me. "You fall behind, I leave you."

He couldn't have been much clearer than that. Looking at the faces around me, I realized he didn't need to be. We all understood.

"Would you like some breakfast before we go, Captain?" I asked.

He stood, hands on his hips, looking as if he wanted nothing less.

"And some coffee," Honey said with her pearly smile. "A man needs his coffee in the morning."

"You sit by the fire, Captain. Just go on," Chick said. "Athena and me, we get the horses ready. We get it all ready. Ain't that right?"

Athena was still glaring at me. "What she gon' do?"

"She gon' take care of Captain's breakfast. Make sure he don't need nothing."

I swallowed. "That's right. I believe we still have bacon, Captain. And biscuits. May I bring you some?"

He looked like he'd been poleaxed. "You going to shoot me with my mouth full?"

"Where would be the benefit of that? We need you, Captain McCready."

I couldn't make out the words he said under his breath, but I was sure they were curses. Reluctantly he let Chick take the saddlebags from his hands and Meaira and Honey set about packing things up as I prepared a quick breakfast, served without hesitation.

chapter twenty-four

WITH Sawyer hurrying us, we left just as the sun rose up over the horizon in a brilliant shower of reds and gold. It chased back the violet of predawn with a radiance that brought hope. Still, we could not ignore the anxious watch Sawyer kept at our back or the way his gun stayed close at hand. I was worried too. Though Lonnie Smith had been the leader of their gang, Jake was the one most feared. I was sure it was Jake who had violated my mother before shooting her. I was sure he would not hesitate to do the same to me or the others.

Chick drew near me and paced me in silence for a while. We had yet to speak of what had happened last night. I didn't want to talk about it now, but I could see she wouldn't let it go.

"Thems last night was who got your family," she said.

"Yes."

"They done shot holes through everything. We's lucky we was low. Your shoulder hurt?"

"Not much."

"I's glad you get Captain to take us. Athena, she just mad. She just mad 'bout a lot of things. She glad too."

I glanced back at Athena on the wagon bench, stern and straight and looking like she might not have ever been glad about anything.

"I wish Aiken got shot," Chick said softly.

I had to agree, though not out loud. Justified or not, I had enough blood on my hands without wishing for more.

Honey stepped in time with us. She smiled at me and said, "That was brave what you did."

"I didn't even think first. All I knew was what I'd seen him do to my family." I looked down. "I've never killed anyone—anything—before. Not even a chicken."

Honey took my hand in hers. Chick took the other. "You did what you had to. That's not what I was talking about, though," Honey said. "What you did with the Captain. It was brave. But don't worry, Ella. You won't have to make good on it. I'll see to that."

"How?" Chick asked before I could.

"I'll do her share."

"Me too," Chick immediately agreed.

"I can't ask that," I said. "I made the bargain."

"You didn't ask. And you don't have a choice. You find yourself something useful to do when we get there and I'll take care of the rest. Something that doesn't involve the men. Can you cook?"

"Not like Athena. And I don't think she'd let me in her kitchen anyway."

Honey nodded.

"I can sew."

"She good at that," Chick said.

"And I know cards." The last was true, but surprising to be offered as a skill. Though as soon as I said it, I realized it might be my salvation. I could play as well as any man.

Honey raised her brows. "Can you deal?"

I smiled and nodded. "I'm quite good, actually."

"Let me tell the Captain," Honey said. "I'll tell him to-night."

Something in the tone of her voice implied the conversation would take place under intimate circumstances. A stab that could be nothing but jealousy hit me at the thought of Sawyer and Honey locked together. Of his lips on hers, of his tongue tasting her the way he'd tasted me.

When I looked back at Honey, she was smiling. "Like that, is it?" she asked softly.

"Like what?" Chick wanted to know.

"Don't worry yourself. I see the way he watches you. Even when you're trying to stick him like a pig."

I knew my face had turned an ugly shade of red.

"Like what?" Chick said again.

"Like things are looking up for us, Chick," Honey said. "Maybe Aiken will get lost or shot somewhere."

Chick giggled. "I say my prayers."

The sun felt good on my skin, and the companionship of Chick and Honey warmed my heart. I was moved by their generosity and caring.

"Honey," I asked, "how did you come to be here?"

Once, the question might have held a hint of censure. Most likely when I'd asked Chick that note of disapproval had been there. But just this morning I had joined the ranks of those whose fate was decided for them. I understood that choice did not always make itself available.

It took a moment for Honey to answer me. She looked down at her feet as she gathered her thoughts.

"I'm sorry," I said. "It's not my business."

"You have a right, I think," she said. "You may wish you hadn't asked, though, once you hear it."

She seemed to be waiting for something and I nodded. She nodded back, as if we'd sealed a pact.

"Used to be I lived with a white family. My grandma had been their slave, though they were kind and fair. When my momma was born, they raised her with their daughter. And when Miss Hazel grew up and got married, my momma went with her. Even after the war was over, my momma and daddy kept working for them. I was born the same year Miss Hazel had Elizabeth. Elizabeth and I were brought up like sisters. We shared everything. When her tutor came to teach her, he taught me too. I loved her and she loved me."

Honey's voice was low and it seemed to vibrate with pain as she spoke. Chick and I stayed quiet, waiting for her to continue.

"Miss Hazel died when I was twelve. She left my momma and daddy part of her land to work for their own and a house to live in. Her husband, Mr. Walton, asked my momma if she would let me stay with him and Elizabeth. She agreed and I was happy to stay. Mr. Walton used to take me and Elizabeth everywhere. We were like dolls that he'd dress up and parade around. He never got over losing Miss Hazel, but he poured all his love into me and Elizabeth. I remember once we went into a restaurant and they wouldn't serve Negroes. I told Mr. Walton I'd wait outside, but he wouldn't hear of it. He was like that. I was a person to him."

She grew quiet and I thought perhaps this tale was too painful for her to continue.

"We were in Atlanta where Mr. Walton had frequent business, when Aiken saw me."

"I remember," Chick said. "First time he lay eyes on Honey, he say, I gon' have her."

"How old were you, Honey?"

"I was fourteen. He arranged to meet with Mr. Walton and then casually commented on his beautiful daughter and his Negro. Mr. Walton took offense right off. I was not his Negro. I was his daughter's cherished friend." She paused. "Aiken talked circles for a time, trying to find out just how it was. He figured Mr. Walton was doing dirty by me and using Elizabeth to hide his deeds. But Mr. Walton was a pure man. I've never met another with such honor. Aiken offered money for me, and Mr. Walton told him no. I was not a possession to be bartered or sold."

"I 'member Aiken come back and he so mad he spittin'," Chick said.

Honey looked down. "I don't think I slept right until we left Atlanta. I knew, even then, that Aiken would not take no for an answer. A few weeks later, we returned to Atlanta and it was as if Aiken had been laying in wait for us. Once again he approached Mr. Walton and made pleasant small talk. He then invited us to dinner. He said his sister was in town and it would give him great pleasure to entertain us. He felt badly for causing offense, so he said, and wanted to make it up. Mr. Walton was too polite to decline, though I knew he would have liked to."

Chick squeezed Honey's hand gently.

"We met at a restaurant and had a fine dinner. Aiken's sister was quiet and subdued. She seemed almost unaware of us and barely touched her food. Later I would learn her name was Meaira and she was not his sister. I've seen her many times after her dose of laudanum, but she's never been as gone as she was that night."

"I don't understand," I said.

Honey went on as if I hadn't spoken. "The next day Elizabeth became ill. We called the doctor who could not determine what ailed her. Her lips turned a dark purple and her skin so white she seemed to glow. I stayed by her side, but there was nothing I could do. She was taken by fits and then she died."

The silence that followed those words was deafening. "What did she have?" I asked.

"The doctor could not determine the cause. Mr. Walton was stricken with grief so deep he could not get up in the morning. I tried to tend to him, but he refused all comfort. He wouldn't take food or water. Within a few weeks he too was dead."

A sick feeling came over me as I listened.

"I returned to Raleigh, where my family and Mr. Walton's home was and buried both of them there. Aiken came to the funeral. He told me then that he would have me, and I realized what he'd done to my Elizabeth. I accused him, but I had no proof. The doctor had seen no wrongdoing. I was a Negro woman in the South accusing a white man of murdering my friend."

She shrugged as if nothing else needed to be said. In truth, nothing else did. My horror was so overwhelming I couldn't have responded anyway.

"He told me I would regret not taking his offer. I told him I would not." She looked down and I saw that tears were in her eyes. "The next morning we found my nine-year-old brother's body on our porch. He'd been dragged by a horse until there was nothing left of him to recognize but the shoes on his feet. I have five other brothers and one sister. When Aiken came again, I went."

chapter twenty-five

REILLY was sitting on the screened porch, watching the rain sluice from the sky and the rivers become an ocean. The water table in the desert could not absorb so much in so little time. The earth was too hard, too much like stone. Through the gray shroud, he could see the decaying bridge, railing, and platforms that surrounded the springs. There the rain slithered down into underground canyons, but it wouldn't be long until those too filled and the pools would once again flow with water. It was too much like the resurrection of something long dead for it not to be disturbing.

Eddie's sandbagging hadn't helped the businesses on lower ground. The flooding battered front doors and poured through the gaps until a foot or more covered the floors. And still it came down. The Diablo was up on a rise, but even here the water would soon reach its floorboards. It was as if God had a mission to wipe out the entire town.

He leaned his head back, tossing his notebook on the bench beside him. He'd been writing nonstop for two hours. Not since he'd written *Nowhere,* Badlands' number-one single, had he written so fast. And the words weren't draft, disjointed thoughts or sketches. They were pages. Handwritten pages that could be lifted and typeset. Taken from pencil to ink without a change. He'd never had thoughts translate to story so concisely, so vividly.

Behind him the door opened and Gracie stepped out with one of the horse-dogs right behind her. He hadn't seen her since she'd ushered her clan up the stairs. She looked pale and her eyes were red-rimmed, but she seemed stable. Nothing weak about Gracie Beck. And despite everything

that weighed on his mind, despite the nagging anxiety that
Chloe's revelations had left him with, once again the
minute she walked in, all he could think of was to touch her.
More than touch her. He wanted to reach out and smooth
the worry from her brow. He wanted to let his hands trail
down, over the softness and the curves. He wanted to taste
the dark mystery of her mouth.

"Hey," he said softly.

"Hey," she said back, staring out at the rain.

He pushed to his feet and went to stand beside her.
"How are you?"

She looked at him for a minute and then shrugged.
"Numb."

The word seemed to cover it all. It made him want to
open his arms and pull her in even more. But he didn't. His
conversation with Chloe had left him feeling as if he'd betrayed Gracie yet again though he couldn't have said exactly why.

She moved to the grouping of ancient patio furniture
where he'd been sitting. "Writing?" she asked.

He nodded, resisting the urge to turn the page and hide it
from her. Again, he didn't know why. The story coming out
of him had nothing to do with Gracie, but it centered on Matt
and Diablo Springs in the way his own life had centered on
both. The characters he created came from a mishmash of
people he'd known—people from L.A., Denver, Pittsburgh,
Dallas—everywhere he'd ever been. And people from here.
No one specific but there were similarities that left him feeling like he was hiding something, when he wasn't.

Irritated with himself for the rash of introspection he
seemed to be crippled with since coming home, he sat
down next to her, elbows to knees, hands dangling between. The dog made a warning sound.

"Juliet, be nice," Gracie scolded. She perched at the
edge of her seat, looking like she might bolt at any minute.
Juliet put her nose on Gracie's lap and watched Reilly's
every move. Nice, but watchful.

"How did it go up there?" he asked, looking over his
shoulder and up toward the second floor.

She shrugged. "They're convinced they know what's right. I'm just as convinced they don't."

He nodded. "Brendan is a strange kid, isn't he?"

"He's nice enough. Comes from a hard background, though. He's been on his own since he was fifteen." She shrugged. "And he's devoted to Analise."

"But you don't like him?" Reilly said.

"It's not that. He's just changed her course so radically—how can I not resent him for that? Analise had her hands filled with opportunities and now—now she's going to be a mother. She's not even out of high school, Reilly."

He looked at her, not sure if this was the place to butt in or butt out. "Your circumstances were a hell of a lot worse at her age, and you still turned out pretty good."

"Appearances can be deceiving."

"I don't think so. Look, I know a teenage pregnancy isn't what you wanted for her, but she'll have you to help her. From what I've seen so far, I'd say she's lucky."

Gracie's eyes shimmered for a moment before she looked away. "You didn't used to be such a nice guy."

"Yeah, I didn't used to be a lot of things."

He'd said it lightly, but the words seemed to open a door inside him. The conversation he'd had with Chloe weighed on his mind. Should he bring it up? Should he even mention it to Gracie? Chloe had said it was time to be a good man. What would a good man do in his shoes?

"What do you know about your family, Reilly?" Gracie asked.

The question seemed as turned inward as out, but it paralleled his train of thought too closely.

"Not much more than you know about yours. My mother's family was from the East. After she married my dad, they pretty much disowned her. They thought he was trash. They were right. My dad's parents were killed in a car accident—I think around the time he and Mom got married. He had a little sister once, but she drowned in a neighbor's pool when they were kids. And that's it. My folks went on to have me and Matt and my dad spent his last breath torturing the three of us for loving him."

"I remember when he died. And your mom. It was awful."

He looked down, shaking his head. "Awful. Yeah. It was that."

She was watching him. He felt her eyes, felt her waiting for him to go on. And funny thing, he wanted to. He'd been furious with Chloe for prying the lid off the horror of his family life. But now that the wound was exposed, he wanted to talk.

"I remember, he'd been on a binge for a good week. He got laid off from the construction job he had, and he was burning mad about it. He had it out with the foreman, almost beat him to death before the other guys pulled him off. And then he came home and stewed. The first day he just drank. And then he started looking for a fight. He picked on my mom because she wouldn't defend herself and he knew that it would get to me and Matt. It was a pattern and we knew it, but no one ever seemed to be able to stop it."

Reilly stood and moved to the edge of the porch. The rain splattered him there, but he didn't care. It felt good. Clean. From her seat Gracie watched him, still and silent. But he felt her presence. Felt her attention and it made it easier to go on.

"That time, though, my mom saw it coming and she pleaded with me and Matt to just stay out of it. She said he'd quit if he didn't get a rise out of us."

"Why did she stay with him?"

"Why does anyone stay where they don't belong? God knows we begged her enough times to take us away from here. When you're a kid you don't see the reality of things. She didn't have anywhere to go. She didn't have any money. He barely gave her enough for groceries, never enough to save. And after a while, I guess you start to think it's normal. It doesn't even strike you strange that everyone in the house tiptoes around the monster in the living room. It's just how it is. But that day . . . God, I can still hear him. He was on her about everything, but she just kept ignoring him. And then he started hitting her. Matt and I were in our room, listening. Thinking he'd stop. Thinking if we just did what she told us . . . I still don't understand it—to this day I don't know. She was so quiet and he was too—usually he'd be ranting and shouting. But not that time. I swear, it didn't sound like he was killing her. She never even screamed. She never cried. But he beat her to death while we waited in the next room doing nothing."

He took a deep breath and let it out. "After a while, we thought she'd been right and he'd quit. We thought it was over. We came out, wondering what was for dinner. I remember that. Thinking, wonder what Mom's cooking tonight. And then we found him sitting on the kitchen floor with her blood all over him and her body just lying there next to him."

"My God." Gracie breathed.

He faced her, leaning against the damp pole behind him. She had her hands up over her mouth and her eyes were a shiny gray that matched the pouring rain. He swallowed, not sure if he could keep going. Silently she stood and came to stand beside him. Juliet gave a whine and lay down by her chair, apparently accepting that Gracie was safe with him.

"You'll get wet," he said.

"I'll dry."

He nodded once, tried to smile, then realized he was close to tears. He couldn't cry in front of Gracie Beck. He wouldn't. He took a deep breath and looked away, forcing himself to continue.

"Matt . . . I've never seen anything like it. He went nuts. She was dead—no doubt about it. Half her face was caved in, like he'd hit her with something hard. I saw the iron and realized she'd been trying to press his shirts, thinking if she just pretended he wasn't a crazy man, he wouldn't hurt her. It didn't work that way, though. I picked Mom up off the floor and then I didn't know what to do with her. I just stood there, holding her thinking, what now? I don't know how long I stood that way before I realized that Matt was pounding my dad's head against the counter until his skull fractured."

"But . . . he drove off the road, into the canyon. I thought . . . He killed himself."

Reilly shook his head. "Not without help he didn't."

"My God."

Reilly covered his face with his hands, fighting to keep control of the waves of emotion that rose like the water outside. He didn't want to look at her. He didn't want to see the disgust on her face or the revulsion in her eyes. Chloe was right. He'd done nothing to stop it and then he'd helped his brother hide the murder.

He fought it. He might have won, but then Gracie touched him and everything he held back spilled over. She put her arms around him and pulled him into her. He held her tightly and buried his face in the soft skin of her neck. Tears scalded his cheeks as they poured from his eyes. He held her and rocked as she soothed him, as she murmured soft words that told him it was okay and to let it out. He hadn't cried that day, he hadn't cried after, ever. But he couldn't stop now. He cried for the child who'd watched his mother beaten by the one person she should be able to trust, he cried for the teenager who was covered in blood as he dragged his daddy out to the car. He cried for the man who'd lost every member of his family and was now alone in the world. And Gracie held him, weathering his emotion with a strength he'd never had in his lifetime.

He didn't know how long it lasted, but he felt empty when it was done. Slowly, he pulled away, embarrassed by the abandonment of his torrent. What did he say now? But as he glanced at Gracie's face, he saw such complete under-standing that he realized words weren't necessary. Not at all. He was stunned by the miracle of it, of Gracie. He brushed her cheek with his fingerstips then let them curl beneath her hair. She stood on tiptoes, holding his face as she brought her mouth to his.

The gentle touch of her lips against his, the acceptance in their sweet taste, knocked down some barrier within him. He gathered her up to him and kissed her like his life depended on it. And that's how it felt. As if he wouldn't be breathing unless he touched her.

A feeling he didn't understand grew in him. A sense that he'd been here, done this before and that it had been taken away from him, too young. The feel of her skin, the touch of her breath, the smell of her perfume, wove in his mind to create a tie that bound him. She tasted of things so dear they should never be lost. Of memories he'd never had. Of feelings he needed to share.

His hands found the hem of her shirt and slipped under to glide across the warm satin of her ribs up to her lace-covered breasts. There they stopped, overwhelmed by the soft delicateness of her. She was fragile, no matter how strong she was, here, at her core, there was a fragility that he yearned to protect. She wrapped her arms around him tighter and the sound of the pouring rain seemed to blend with the pounding of his pulse as it beat through every nerve in his body.

His feelings were a knot of confusion inside him, but he fought to find one that he could ride. He thought it would be desire, but it was something more and he was grateful, grateful that he was capable of more than need and that Gracie was the woman to bring it to him.

She pulled back then, as if reading his mind, as if wanting to see for herself what he was giving. For a moment she stared deeply into his eyes, and everything in him wanted to cover those feelings, but he didn't. He looked back and her eyes widened with surprise. He rested his forehead against hers and breathed in the scent of her.

They stayed that way for a long time, neither one moving or questioning or attempting to explain. It was the sound of the door opening that broke them apart. But he caught her hand before she could step away, holding her to him by that small gesture. She looked surprised, but she smiled. That moment would stay burned on his mind forever.

Brendan stood at the open door, looking embarrassed to have interrupted. He cleared his throat and said, "Analise needs you."

Reluctantly, Reilly let Gracie go.

chapter twenty-six

ANALISE was physically and emotionally drained but too exhausted to sleep. Gracie gave her some tea and calmed her down enough to sleep. Her daughter looked young and defenseless in her exhaustion and Gracie yearned to scoop her up and take her away from her uncertain future. But of course she couldn't. She could only do what she did now—watch and pray.

Once Analise had drifted off, Gracie found an empty box in the pantry and took it up to her grandmother's room. Brendan was downstairs helping Reilly stack sandbags outside the entrances, and she was alone but for her sentry, Juliet. She tried not to think too much about anything, especially Reilly, as she cleared items off Grandma Beck's dresser and packed them.

She had her back to the door when she heard a tentative knock. She turned to find the priest hovering just at the threshold with an apologetic look on his face.

"I'm sorry to disturb you, Miss Beck. But I wondered if I could speak with you for a moment?"

Gracie nodded, but her reluctance must have shown on her face.

"I won't keep you from your packing," he said. He had a kindly smile and warm eyes. Had he not arrived with Chloe, Gracie might have liked him on sight. He came in, sat on the straight-back chair at the desk, and said, "I wanted to offer my services."

"I'm not a very religious person, Father. I don't need—"

He held up a hand. "Call me Jonathan. I am not ordained by any church. I am a man of God, though, and I wear this collar to remind myself of that." He looked around him for a moment, as if unsure how to continue. Juliet padded over to him, sniffed his feet, and then flopped on the floor, completely at ease with his presence. Jonathan reached down and scratched her behind the ear before continuing.

"My father was a Baptist reverend and my mother an Episcopalian priest," he said. "There were always heated conversations in my house about theology and worship, but never about some things. Never about faith or God. And it was a given in my house that people like Chloe LaMonte, people with psychic abilities, were nothing more than heathens. The devil's children. There were no exceptions. When I realized that I was one of them, I believed that made me an abomination. Chloe taught me that we have a gift, not a curse. Through Chloe I was able to come to terms with what I do and still consider myself a man of God's love."

Gracie didn't know why he was telling her this, but the gentle sincerity of his words kept her quiet and listening as she wrapped frames in paper and put them in her box.

"You see," he said. "My gift is that I can see things that happened a long time ago. And sometimes I see things that haven't happened yet."

"And this is the service you're offering me? I appreciate the gesture, Jonathan, but I've had a glimpse of my future. I think that's all I can take right now."

"The baby?" he said.

She nodded, beyond questioning how he knew.

"Miss Beck, there is a reason why Chloe has brought us here."

"And you know what that reason is?"

"She tells me she wants to end a cycle, a curse that has been on her family and yours for over a hundred years."

"But you don't think that's true?"

"On the contrary, I think it's very true. But I also think there is more. I would like to know what that more is, before I become a participant in it."

Gracie nodded. "How do you intend to find out?"

"If I could touch you—just your hand—and also an object of this house? Something your grandmother owned, perhaps? One of these pictures?"

Gracie had found one on the dresser, of her mother holding Gracie. Grandma Beck stood just at her shoulder, smiling down at them both. She swallowed a lump of emotion and handed it to Jonathan. "Will this do?"

Jonathan nodded. He set the picture in his lap while he carefully removed his gloves and put them aside. Then, with a shy smile, he lifted the picture in one hand and reached for Gracie's fingers with the other.

She didn't know what she'd expected, but the gentle warmth was not invasive and she found herself at ease. She perched on the edge of the bed and watched his face as he closed his eyes and began to speak in a rapid, stream-of-conscious flow.

"Her name is Carolina and she's at a funeral. Her mother's funeral. Ella? Yes. Carolina is crying, but inside she's relieved. She's glad her mother is dead."

"Why?" Gracie asked.

Jonathan went on as if she hadn't spoken and Gracie realized he'd put himself in some sort of a trance.

"Ella was always fearful. Superstitious. She kept such a tight watch that Carolina was afraid to breathe sometimes. She was crazy. That's what she's thinking. Her mother was crazy. Even on her deathbed, she'd been screaming about a curse. A family curse. A man named . . . Jason . . . Macon . . . Aiken? Yes, Aiken. Carolina is frightened. Ella said he was in the Dead Lights. He didn't stay dead. He didn't stay dead."

Goosebumps covered every inch of Gracie's body. Who didn't stay dead? Who was Aiken? What was he talking about? Jonathan's voice rose and fell, becoming more strained, tortured.

"She's in the Diablo now," he said. "She doesn't think of Ella any more. She's forgotten that he didn't stay dead. Business is good." A strange smile curved his lips. "Oh," he said. "She has famous guests. Eleanor Roosevelt is here.

She's thinking that the president's wife is sleeping in a room once used by prostitutes and it makes her laugh." The smile dimmed. "There's a man now. His name is Jimmy and she likes him. He wants to marry her. She is happy. Happier than she's ever been. He tells her about another place . . ."

Jonathan paused. Gracie could see his eyes moving beneath his closed lids. It was like REM, only he wasn't asleep. He still held her hand, his fingers cool and dry.

"Glenwood Springs," he said triumphantly. "He tells her about Glenwood Springs and how business is booming there. He wants to expand. He wants to make the Diablo like that. There's to be a wedding . . . and a baby. Jimmy's baby. She's so happy. Happy. She's making wedding plans . . . but . . ."

His pause stretched and Gracie waited impatiently, wanting to press him, knowing it would do no good.

"Chloe is here now."

At first she thought he meant Chloe was in the room with them and she glanced over her shoulder, expecting to see the old woman. But then he began speaking again.

"She's come to warn Carolina. She . . . Chloe says there's a curse and a man who didn't stay dead. There's a curse. We're cursed. Carolina wants her to leave. Go away . . . go away . . . She's at a funeral again. Jimmy is dead now. The springs . . . underground caverns . . . dynamite. An explosion . . . it opened up a cavern and the water moved underground. Disappeared. Jimmy went with it. Dead. He's dead. Dead Lights. The Dead Lights come. Every night they come. They're looking for something. He's looking for something. Has to find it. Has to find it. Looking for . . . someone . . . It's his. She's his. Dead Lights. Dead Lights. Again and again. Dead Lights. He didn't stay dead. It's true. It's true. Everything Ella said. The curse, the fear. He—"

"What's going on?" Zach asked, stepping into the room and scaring Gracie to death. She jumped to her feet with a yelp, yanking her hand out of Jonathan's light grasp. The trance he'd been in was broken instantly. He came up and out of the chair, the picture frame he'd held slipping from his hand and falling to the braid rug at his feet. Gracie bent to pick it up, feeling dizzy and frightened. *Dead Lights. Looking for something.* What did it mean?

"What are you guys doing?" Zach asked, staring back and forth between them.

"Just talking," Gracie said.

"With *him*?"

Gracie gave Zach a hard look. "Yes. With Jonathan." She smiled at Jonathan. "Thank you."

His gentle eyes looked worried now. He nodded, leaned in and whispered, "In the Dead Lights."

As if that should answer her questions. He was almost through the door before she could think to stop him. Zach grabbed his wrist as he passed. Jonathan's gloves were still clutched in his hand and he recoiled from the contact of Zach's skin against his. He didn't like to be touched unaware, Gracie realized. It was why he wore his gloves all the time. Zach let go as if he'd been burned and Jonathan hurried away.

Gracie stood awkwardly for a minute, too overloaded to think, to speak. What had he meant, *In the Dead Lights*? What had any of it meant?

"What was he saying?" Zach asked.

"He told me who my grandfather was, I think. A man named Jimmy."

"You didn't know?"

Gracie shook her head. "My grandma was a very secretive woman. There was a lot she never told me."

"Why?"

"I don't know. I've never known."

"I heard him say he was looking for something."

"He was talking about . . ." She let out a breath and a half laugh. "To tell you the truth, I don't know what he was talking about. He skipped around a lot, from my great-grandmother to my grandmother. I think this Jimmy must have been looking for the Dead Lights." She shrugged. "Maybe they weren't around back then."

Zach's eyes widened.

"None of it made much sense."

"Well, I'm sorry I interrupted. I thought . . . I wanted to make sure you were okay."

He looked very boyish when he said it, but the gleam in his eyes was very much man. Gracie shifted uncomfortably. "How are you feeling?" she asked.

"I'll live."

"You don't look so good, though. You should go back to bed."

He nodded, but said, "You want to tuck me in?"

Gracie laughed. "I think I'll pass."

"Next time," he joked, but there was more than a hint of seriousness in the comment.

Gracie let her breath out in a *whoosh* as he left. She looked at Juliet on the floor. "Yeah, right. That's all I need," she said.

IT was at least an hour later when Reilly came to find her. Analise still slept peacefully in Gracie's old bedroom and the house was tomb quiet. She didn't know where everyone else was, but for now, she didn't care.

"How's it going?" Reilly asked, stepping in to sit on the edge of her bed.

"Making progress, I suppose. She had a lot of pictures of my mom in here. I'd never seen any of them. It was like she'd tried to erase my mother after she died."

Gracie picked up the one taken when she was a baby. She'd put it in her box and taken it out a dozen times. She couldn't seem to bring herself to pack it away. She held it out to Reilly but instead of taking the picture he used her outstretched hand to tow her closer. Only after she'd sat down next to him, did he look at it.

"Jonathan came in and talked to me earlier," Gracie said.

"About what?"

Gracie told him about the bizarre trance and the disjointed story he'd told. "In the end he kept repeating Dead

Lights and saying he was looking for something. I have no idea what it all meant."

"Huh," Reilly said. When she tilted her head in question, he explained, "Zach had this crazy idea that there's a pot of gold buried in your backyard. He thinks that's why Chloe is here."

"Why do you think she's here?"

"Funny you should ask. She and I had a little heart-to-heart earlier. Although I don't think there's all that much heart left in Chloe LaMonte. She has some interesting theories, though." He set the picture on the bed beside them and put his arms around Gracie's shoulders, pulling her close as he spoke. His voice rumbled in his chest and created a comfort that eased her anxiety. "She was telling me—"

The sound of heavy footsteps in the hallway stopped Reilly in mid-sentence. He stood and went to the door. Gracie followed. Bill was moving up the hall, peering in every door.

"What's up?" Reilly asked him.

"Have you seen Jonathan?"

"An hour or two ago," Gracie said. "He came to talk to me."

Bill's jaw dropped and his eyes widened. "He spoke to you?"

"That's what I said."

"About what?"

"About—Why are you asking?"

"Jonathan is missing," Bill said.

Reilly shrugged. "Well, he couldn't have gone too far."

"Yes, I realize that. But the fact remains that I've checked every room in the house, with the exception of this room and your daughter's room, Gracie. He's nowhere to be found."

"I just looked in on Analise," Gracie said. "He's definitely not in there. And he's not in here, obviously."

"You checked the porches?" Reilly asked.

"Front and back."

"Okay," Reilly said calmly. "Let's start over, go through the house again. He's got to be here."

But thirty minutes later they'd gone through every room upstairs and down and there was no sign of Jonathan. His bag was still in his room, his bed neatly made, a Bible on the nightstand. But the man himself was gone.

"What about the cellar?" Reilly said. "It's the only place we haven't checked."

Gracie led them downstairs to the narrow door in the kitchen that opened onto a steep stairway. "It's not really a cellar—it's more a crawl space than anything," she said, reaching for the string attached to the bare bulb that dangled overhead. The light came on, illuminating twelve rough wooden steps leading down to a pit as black as ink. "This is crazy. He's not down there."

There was a flashlight in a wall mount by the door. Bill pulled it free and switched it on. Juliet nudged in between their legs and started into the dark. The three were halfway down when the overhead bulb suddenly brightened and then dimmed, brightened and dimmed again. They paused looking up. The kitchen phone began to ring.

"Hold on," Gracie said and hurried up to answer it. But when she lifted the receiver the phone was dead. She tapped the hook switch and listened again. Nothing. Slowly she replaced the receiver and turned back to the waiting men. "It's dead."

But it began to ring again and each peal grew louder and louder. At the same time the kitchen lights blinked off and then on. Through the open door she could see the lamps in the front room doing the same. She lifted the receiver, but the ringing didn't stop, if anything, it grew louder and faster.

"What's happening?" she said.

Reilly came up the stairs and took the receiver from her hand, listened, then hung it up, but it kept ringing until Gracie felt like her eardrums would pop. Reilly pulled the phone off the wall and disconnected the line that went in the back, but the ringing kept on.

"What the . . ."

The bare bulb in the stairway exploded, sending shards of glass in a rain over Bill. And the ringing stopped.

In the silence that followed, one by one, all of the lights that were on began to switch off until the gathering gloom of the late afternoon cloaked the first floor of the Diablo.

Gracie looked at Bill who stood frozen on the cellar stairs. "Are you okay?" she asked.

The hand that clutched the flashlight looked very white against the darkness, but Bill nodded.

"That was weird," Reilly said.

The understatement caught Gracie off-guard. She gave a shaky laugh. "Yeah."

"Come on," Reilly said. "Let's see what's down there."

The quiet had become ominous and Gracie didn't want to go down into the darkness below. But somehow she managed to take the first step and then another, concentrating on the weak flashlight beam as she followed the two men down.

chapter twenty-seven

June 1896
Arizona Territory

WE'D been on the move since daybreak, following the sun as it arched across the sky. Sawyer kept us off the road, though how he navigated through the great openness I'll never know. He seemed certain we were heading in the right direction, however, and none of us thought to question him. He could have led us to hell and we'd have followed.

I spent much of the time playing in my mind the kiss he'd given me, blushing at my own detailed memory. Inside, I was knotted up by recollections of the way his touch had moved me, had made me respond to feelings I didn't even fully understand. It was as if I had two minds, one that kept me on this path and moving forward, another that wanted only to return to his arms and be held and kissed and awakened to the wonders of flesh.

My face grew hot again. I tried not to think of the way our passion had ended or the sting of his cold words. *I don't need a whore.* Well I wasn't one, but I'd offered myself as if I were, hadn't I? I thought about this and wondered if perhaps I'd confused him as much as he'd confused me. I thought he'd pushed me away because I was acting like a whore. But as I examined each nuance of those moments together, I began to see another possibility. When he'd pulled back and looked at me, I know I saw the same startled ardor in his eyes that must surely have been in my own. But what had he been thinking? I'd just told him I would join the girls in their profession. Had he imagined that I was playacting while I was in his arms? Pretending to be carried away by the tide of needs that pulled us together? Performing to prove my point?

It would explain his anger and his cruelty. He had no way to know that the desires he'd fanned inside me had managed to completely disable my brain. There hadn't been a thought in my head beyond what I would feel next. Even as I considered all of this, I acknowledged the ridiculousness of it. So what if we had both felt the same consuming passion? Nothing could come of it. Sawyer was not the kind of man a banker's daughter settled down with.

After we rested the horses and ate, Sawyer slowed our pace. I hoped that meant he felt we were safe from whoever might be following, but I knew that was a child's way of thinking and I no longer had the liberty of comforting myself with falsehoods. My world revolved around harder, colder realities now. I had killed a man and though I felt fear when I thought of it, I did not feel shame. Lonnie Smith deserved my bullet, and should I be found by a posse I would not deny it. If it was not for Jake Smith, who I was certain hunted me now, I would turn myself in and face the consequences rather than live life on the run. But I would not bring peril or the unwanted eyes of the law into this makeshift family of mine. I had put Sawyer McCready in danger twice now—once when I tried to kill him myself and then again when I'd shot Lonnie Smith.

A strange bubble of laughter rose in me. It would be a justified irony if Sawyer were as afraid of my violent nature as I was of his shady past.

I looked for him ahead and found him riding not far away. He was watching me from beneath the shadows of his hat and my face grew hot imagining he could read my mind. He looked away and so did I, but many times after I found his gaze on me. Many times I found mine on him.

We didn't speak until the midafternoon, when he dismounted and fell into step beside me. Startled, I looked around and realized I'd been moving fast and I was a good distance ahead of the others. I hadn't been aware of it.

"How's your shoulder feel?" he asked.

"Sore, but not unbearable."

"Athena did a good job patching you up."

"Athena did?" I asked. My voice betrayed my surprise.

He raised his brows in question. "Athena's a good woman."

"I know. I just didn't think she liked me much."

He grinned. "I don't think she's so wild about me either."

"Oh but she is," I argued. "I've never seen her so warm and friendly around any of the rest of us."

I think he was pleased, but he didn't say as much. I liked him better for his words about Athena. It's easy to care about people like Honey and Chick and even Meaira. But it took character to find the good in someone who looked at the world through her anger.

We walked in silence for a few moments. Our feet made a soft thump against the hard ground. In the distance I saw a coyote race across the rugged terrain. Sawyer saw it too and quietly tracked its path until it disappeared. I saw in his eyes a kinship with the predator, in the simple act of hunting to survive.

I cleared my throat and looked away. I needed to break the silence. I asked, "This town where your saloon is, this Diablo Springs. Have you been there before?"

"Nope."

"Did you know diablo means devil? Why is it called Devil Springs?"

Sawyer shrugged. "The man who sold it to me—"

"Lost it to you in cards."

"That's right," he said, looking at me out of the corner of his eye. "Lost it fair and square. He said that some people think the town is cursed."

"Why?"

"Used to be Apache land, but they got run off."

"And they cursed it?"

"That's what they say. Others say it was named because of the hot spring. Hot-hell-devil. That's how they named it."

"A natural hot spring? I've heard of them."

"He said the town wasn't much yet, but it's growing

like a weed. The more he drank the more he talked. He had big plans. Not sure what we'll find when we get there, though."

I hoped for the best and he saw it on my face. He grinned.

His mouth caught my attention and brought a rush of memory. I could still feel how my heart seemed to stop somewhere between beats as he stepped closer. How my breathing ceased as he trapped me in his gaze and held me tight. His voice had been low, low enough to brush against my senses like suede against my skin. The greens and browns of his eyes had darkened, like water with a deep undertow.

"You feeling sick?" he asked.

"No. Why?"

"Your face got red all of a sudden. You feel all right?"

"I . . . yes, yes, I'm just warm."

"You can ride," he offered, hooking a thumb at his horse.

"You'd give me your horse?" I said.

He frowned. "Not to keep."

His seriousness made me laugh. "I didn't mean to keep. I just . . . well, we haven't actually been friendly."

His gaze made an imperceptible shift to my mouth and I read his mind. For a moment, we'd been more than friendly.

What if he took me up on my offer? What if there was no "what if " in that question. He'd made it clear the women were all a burden. He didn't want us and he damned sure wasn't doing us any favors. We'd be expected to work for our keep. That included me. And if he came to me, what would I do? I'd committed us all to this path.

I squared my shoulders. I had not been raised to sell myself to a man, but I had not been raised to let another shoulder my burdens either. I peeked up at Sawyer through my lashes. Although if I was honest, was the burden as heavy as I thought?

I realized he'd stopped walking and was looking from me to his horse.

"No, thank you," I said, more forcibly than I'd intended. "I will walk."

Sawyer frowned at my sudden rigidness and I saw our friendly camaraderie vanish. I was both happy and sad to see it. I would do well to keep my distance from Sawyer McCready.

MY first impression of Diablo Springs was of the dirt. I'd become adjusted to the thick layers of dust, sand, and grit many days ago when the trees and grasslands became a faded memory, replaced by low scrub, spiky yucca, and short barrel cactus that wore rings of bright yellow fruit on their tops. There were also towering green man-shaped cacti with hats of tiny bell-like blossoms. Sawyer called them saguaros and told us they were the smartest plants alive. They stored water in their tall trunks and when the wind blew them off balance, they'd grow an appendage to straighten themselves out. We saw clever little birds living in holes they'd drilled in the meaty flesh of the giants. Sawyer said if you ever got lost in the desert, the liquid in the cactus's skin could keep you alive.

After we crossed into the foothills, Sawyer consulted a hand-drawn map and then we found a trail, which followed the steep incline. As the sun rode low in the west, we crested a peak and looked down at Diablo Springs. We were each silent as we viewed the lone street and the houses and tents sprawled haphazardly in the valley. From our vantage point, I could count five buildings, two on either side of the narrow roadway and the biggest on a rise at the end. It seemed that there were more people walking to and fro than there were residences to house them. The man Sawyer had beaten at cards was apparently right. Diablo Springs was growing like a weed.

"Ain't as bad as the last place," Chick said with a bright smile.

But it wasn't as good as we'd hoped. Like the other mining town we'd visited, it appeared to be the kind of place where stagecoaches did not stop. Where men shot one another over cards and urinated in the streets. Where sheriffs were appointed because they were mean, not ethical; where outlaws felt safe and honest men frightened. And where women were more rare than the ore that was mined. I could not make out a single skirt moving in the streets. Perhaps the women were inside, avoiding the mud and filth.

What Sawyer thought of his new town, I didn't know. His face remained closed as he stared at the dirty encampment.

He asked us to climb into the wagon so as not to start a riot when we got there. We jumped to obey. Only Athena could be seen at the reins as our wagon lumbered into town. Still, men stopped to watch us pass as they mingled in and out of the few establishments. From the back of the wagon, I saw the assayer's office, a tent with the word *food* painted on the side, another selling tools, and beside it, a general merchandise store.

A man was hawking the personal belongings of his partner who'd been shot the night before next to a carpenter hard at work on a coffin. Scattered on the hillside beyond we saw grave markers, several of them fresh. The young town was no stranger to death.

The street was muddy from horse urine and droppings, and the town stank as badly as the mining camp had two nights ago. I didn't understand how people could live in such filth, but without women to guide them, I was beginning to think men reverted to bovine behaviors.

"Lord in heaven," I heard Athena mutter.

A large matronly woman stepped out from a tent and stared. Behind her was a table spread with bread and pies, and as we passed a whiff of something freshly baked overcame the less pleasant smells. Two men sat at a table inside, eating. Though her eyes were cold, I felt better knowing there was at least one other woman here. Another tent like we'd seen in the mining camp ran a boisterous business of selling liquor to intoxicated men. There were few places to sit and most stood shoulder to shoulder, lifting their glasses and watching us pass.

A young man raced out beside Sawyer's horse and shouted to him, "Hey, you the captain?"

Sawyer frowned. "Who wants to know?"

"Who wants to know?" the man yelled, walking beside him. "Hell, just everybody. We been waiting for you to get here and open the damn saloon."

Laughter came from up and down the street and Sawyer smiled back.

"Angus told us you'd be here a week ago."

"Well, I'm here now."

"And thank God in heaven. We've been drinking old Hank's piss water. Angus promised the best liquor in the West and then he never even poured a goddammed drink. How long until you open? I guarantee you'll have a line awaitin'."

"Hate to disappoint you, but there's nothing to drink in there yet. It's going to be a day or two before my first shipment of whiskey is in."

That brought mixed reactions. Some of them cheered for the whiskey, others moaned for the delay.

"Which one of these places is it, anyway?" Sawyer asked.

The young man laughed and said, "Are you blind as well as slow? It's right there."

From the shadowed interior I saw the stunned expression on Sawyer's face, but I couldn't see where the man pointed. Sawyer thanked him and continued down the street. He stopped his horse at a hitching post in front of a surprisingly tall building and I understood his shock. It was the biggest of the buildings we'd seen from above. It was on a natural rise of sorts and so it lorded over the other structures on the road, making it seem enormous. Additionally, it was two, possibly three stories high, and built of sturdy wood with a shingled roof. A sign hung over the door with brilliant red letters painted in the hollowed out channels. THE DIABLO SPRINGS HOTEL AND SALOON.

Though it was nothing more than a wooden building in a town made of canvas and mud, it had a look of permanence about it that was somehow heartening. Steps led up to the railed wooden porch that stretched the length of the first floor. The door was locked tight and the handles chained. Sawyer pulled a large key from his saddlebag and opened up. Only then did he gesture for us to come out. We were all acutely aware of the eyes that followed us as we emerged from the wagon and went inside. You could feel the excitement charge the street and it frightened me. I had not forgotten the mob at the mining camp. Sawyer made a show of checking his rifle before carrying it in with him. I was glad of it.

Inside still smelled of fresh wood. The ceiling and walls were rough paneled, but they were even and mounted with care, as if the builder had planned for it to last forever. The floors had the same rough look but compared to the mud, they seemed as beautiful as marble. A plain staircase hugged the wall to the right. Straight ahead was a wide open room with a handful of tables and a bar against the far side.

The bar had obviously been constructed by a person who loved his craft. We all moved to it, as if beckoned. The wood was rich, golden oak and it gleamed like glass. Ornate carvings marked the supports every few feet and a brass boot rail shone bright as day. Behind the counter, a beveled mirror reflected the five of us standing with identical looks of wonder on our faces. Sawyer let out a low whistle as he surveyed the place.

"You didn't expect this?" I said.

"Hell no. I was half convinced I was going to find a tent and a deck of cards and feel a fool for coming. I had no idea it would be like this. What kind of idiot gambles this away?"

He was so incredulous that I found myself viewing the place through his eyes. I did not know what a saloon should look like, but if the conditions outside were a measurement, the Diablo Springs Hotel and Saloon was opulent. And it belonged to the outlaw Sawyer McCready.

"How much was wagered when you won this place?" I asked.

"Twenty thousand dollars."

My mouth fell open. I could see the same reaction on everyone else's face.

"Where did you get so much money?" I asked without thought to the appropriateness of the question.

"Won most of it. Had some of it."

The way he said it made me think he was lying. It wasn't my business, but I suspected that Sawyer acquired that money by means of a bank holdup. Wisely, I kept my opinion to myself. But I wondered if we had more than Aiken Tate, Jake Smith, and a sheriff's posse to worry about. As if we needed more.

"Aiken put up what I was short."

He said the last as he headed for the stairs. Silently we followed him up to a long hallway with doors opening off it. There were six rooms in all and inside each was a made bed with a mattress and a small table. The whole place smelled clean and unused.

Sawyer grinned, exchanging glances with all of us. "Looks like we're done sleeping on the ground," he said.

"You mean we gets to sleep in here?" Chick exclaimed.

"Hell yes," he said.

Chick squealed with excitement. "Can we pick which we want? Cuz me'n Athena we want here, if that awright?" she said, pointing to two doors across from each other without consulting Athena first. Sawyer shrugged. Taking that as a yes, Chick skipped in and flopped on her bed. She let out a shout of pure joy. "Like laying on a cloud," she said.

Meaira pushed through to the next room and spread out on the mattress. Laughing, Honey did the same. Athena approached the door Chick had claimed for her with hesitant steps, as if she expected to be stopped. She looked back and Sawyer gave her a small nod. She eased her bulk onto the bed and broke into a smile that lit the room.

"This here nice, Captain."

Sawyer turned and started down the hall. "Which one do you want?" he asked, looking at me as he reached my side.

I know my face turned an awful shade of red. I nodded at the next open door and walked stiffly to it. Sawyer came and leaned against the doorframe, watching me with wolf-eyes as I stopped beside the bed.

"Aren't you going to try it?" he asked.

My face grew hotter as I sat down on the edge. The mattress was soft and feather filled. Not hay, not ticking. I smiled and leaned back, more aware of the eyes watching me than the comfort welcoming my body. I turned my head to look at him and our eyes locked for a minute. That look made me glad I was lying down. He made me feel boneless and warmed to the soul.

He pushed away from the door and I thought he would step in. Instead he gave me a knowing smile and walked away. I put my hands over my hot face and tried to slow my heart down, but all I could think of was that look and the promise it held.

It didn't take long for us to unpack the few possessions we'd carried in the wagon. I had nothing but my daddy's gun and hunting knife, both of which Sawyer returned to me. As soon as we'd carried the last item inside, there was a knock on the door.

"Ain't open," Sawyer called out without bothering to answer it. We heard the knocker hesitate and then walk away. A few minutes later another knock came. "Still ain't open," Sawyer said. And so it went until after dark when the last of them decided that Sawyer meant it and really wasn't going to open the door that night. I think he would have if there had been any liquor to serve, but the bar was bare. It was hard to believe it had never opened its doors and served a drink before. The men of the town took their thirst and presumably quenched it at Hank's.

We could hear their hell-raising drifting down the street to the other end from where we were. We'd noticed from our bird's-eye view that the tents and makeshift houses sprawled away from the saloon, so we were somewhat isolated on our plateau at the end of the street.

Later, after Athena had made us something to eat and the dishes were done, we girls were upstairs laughing and enjoying our new rooms. Sawyer came to find us.

"I'm going down to the springs," he said to all of us and none of us at once.

"Where are they?" I asked, standing in my doorway.

He walked into my room and pointed out the window. The other girls came in too and crowded around. The pools of water were dark in the early night, but the moon was bright and cast a glow on their surfaces.

Chick asked what we were all thinking. "Can we come?"

Sawyer's nod elicited another round of squeals and giggles from us. We all seemed to be drunk on our good fortune to be staying beneath a solid roof, unmolested by the men at least for the night, and to lay our bodies on a real mattress when we went to sleep. It was beyond anything I thought I'd see again.

Happily we followed Sawyer down and out the kitchen door to the back of the hotel. There were no tents here, no squatters in sight and I was relieved by that.

"Do you think this is all part of the Diablo's grounds?" I asked.

"It could be. Why else aren't there any tents back here?"

A wooden bridge had been built between the springs and the Diablo, making the short trek easy. As we approached we could see the steam rising off the pools and smell the heavy sulfur that came with it. The planking continued in a sort of deck around the largest of the pools. If we sat on the edge, we could dangle our feet in the water.

It seemed we all thought of it at once and immediately began taking off our shoes. Sawyer reached down and ran his fingers across the surface.

"I'll be damned," he said. "It's like a bath."

The word *bath* brought up all of our heads. Chick got her shoes off first and hiked her skirts up so she could put her feet in. "Ah, Lord, that good."

"I haven't had a bath in ages," Meaira said. "Not a real one."

She had that hazy look about her that I was beginning to understand went with the laudanum. She gave us all a dreamy smile and then without hesitation, she stripped down bare and slid into the water.

"Is it deep?" Chick asked. "I cain't swim good. Athena neither."

"No," Meaira said, and she stood to show them.

That was all the invitation the others needed. They shed their clothes as easily as they had their shoes and jumped in with Meaira. Sawyer watched with interest, I with jealousy. Their sighs of ecstasy filled me with longing. A bath. A hot bath . . .

"Ain't you comin?" Chick asked, splashing merrily. Her golden-brown body gleamed beneath the murky surface.

Beside me Sawyer sat down and took off his boots and socks. As I watched, he stripped his shirt and his pants. His eyes were on me when he reached for his undergarment. Blushing in the dark, I looked away until I heard him splash into the water. I watched with envy as the women frolicked around Sawyer and, each other like sleek seals, wet skin against wet skin until at last my jealousy would not be ignored.

I unbuttoned my blouse and pulled it from the waist of my skirt. I pretended that the dark concealed me, but I knew my skin glowed like pearl in the moonlight. I quickly removed my shirt and my skirt. Dressed only in my chemise, I looked up to find Sawyer watching me from the black waters.

He didn't look away when I caught him, didn't pretend to stare at anything but me. I stood for a moment, knowing I couldn't pull that last garment off with him watching me, but knowing I had no other clothes and I would need these to be dry when I came out. At last I turned my back and stripped the chemise from my shoulders to my waist to the ground. For an instant, I stood naked, wrought with feelings and sensations I'd never known. My breath was coming in shallow gasps that at once hurt and excited me. Before I thought better of it, I turned and ran into the water. The look Sawyer gave me as I skimmed the surface rivaled the steam in its heat.

The girls gathered around me, their skin as slick as the damp heat soaking into my body. They had no modesty, no shame in their nudity and they frolicked like children. Honey swam beneath the surface and suddenly Sawyer went under. He came up laughing, sputtering and launched himself at Honey. The girls screamed with glee and splashed away but the game was on and before I knew it, I was playing too. Our laughter echoed off the thick bank of clouds and seemed as foreign as the hot pool of water in the midst of the desert. We shushed one another in case our voices carried to the tents and men in town, but it felt good to laugh. It felt so very good.

Suddenly Sawyer was there in front of me, low in the water so only his head and shoulders appeared from the surface. I watched him move closer, our eyes level with each other. Our breath joined the rising mist and created a cocoon around us. I was never so aware of my nakedness, of his. He swam closer still, watching me with his unusual eyes, only they seemed darker, like a reflection of the opaque surface of the water. The voices of the others seemed to fade in the mist and it was only me and Sawyer, the shining moon, and a million stars. A light beard covered his cheeks, glinting gold and red in the moonlight. His hair was wet and slicked back from his face, his skin browned by the sun. He was a man who took his shirt off when he worked. My father would have been scandalized by that, but my father was not a survivor.

I caught my bottom lip with my teeth and Sawyer stared at it, like it was the most interesting thing he'd ever seen. His hand came out of the water and he drifted closer to me. His fingers, warm and rough and wet, slid over my jaw and his thumb rubbed up against my mouth.

A small sound escaped my lips, a sound I'd never known myself to produce. It was a sound of satisfaction, a sound of need. I'd wanted him to touch me. I wanted more.

As if I'd voiced it all in that one sound, Sawyer moved closer still, until his bare chest touched mine. His skin felt like hot silk. My hands found their way to his shoulders without my being aware I'd made the decision to touch him back. His went to my waist and in the same movement, he kissed me. His lips were soft and the kiss questioning.

I should have pushed him away, I knew he was not a man to trifle with, but my lips softened beneath his and anything tentative about the kiss vanished. His arms tightened around me, pulling me to the hard muscles of his chest. My legs slipped between his as he held me off the soft bottom of the spring. There was no mistaking the other hardness that pressed against my stomach. But the feel of him sent signals to every part of me, making me want to wrap my legs around his hips and hold on tight.

My own wanton thoughts terrified me and brought me to reason with a rush. I pushed away and swam to the side as quickly as I could. I scrambled awkwardly onto the platform and grabbed my clothes, pulling the chemise I'd hoped to keep dry on over my wet body as swiftly as possible.

My skin was hot now and the damp chill felt good. I was breathing heavily. I tried not to, but I couldn't seem to stop the look back. Sawyer had swum to the other side of the pool. I couldn't see his face through the thick steam, but I could feel his eyes watching me. Enticing me. And truth be told, I wanted to return to him. I wanted to touch him. I wanted to feel him and let him show me the mysteries between a man and a woman.

"You done, Ella?" Chick asked.

"I'm overheated. I think I'll go back."

I heard Sawyer's laughter follow me as I fled inside.

chapter twenty-eight

I was once again in control of myself by the time the others came laughing up the walkway, and I joined into their easy conversation with a composure that surprised even me. I felt Sawyer's eyes watching and I knew inside he was laughing at me, but I ignored him and went on as if he wasn't there. I still had to talk to him before the evening concluded and I needed to seem calm when I did so. There were things to be settled before the doors of the Diablo opened for business.

When the others went upstairs, I decided I wouldn't have a better opportunity to speak with Sawyer alone.

I found him at a table with a ledger book in front of him. He looked up when he saw me.

"I'll ask about a stagecoach tomorrow," he said, his tone serious. "Small place like this, it may not come regularly. May not come at all."

A heady mixture of relief and disappointment coursed through me. He intended to help me get home. Home? The notion seemed foreign to me. I had no home. Home, for me, would be where I made it. But the relief that he did not intend for me to sell my body for him . . . to him, brought a rush of feeling.

"Thank you," I said. I knew he was right about the stagecoach. I'd made the same realization myself. In the best of circumstances, I would be here for a few weeks. In the worst . . . Well, I wouldn't think of that. Either way, I would need money. I had only one dress and though all of the girls had generously shared with me, none of them had much themselves.

I knew my parents would not approve of me earning wages in a saloon, no matter how nice it was, but I think even they would understand that my choices were limited. If I could convince Sawyer of my worth, I might save myself the other, more uncertain fate that awaited me.

I took a deep breath, mustering my courage, and went to sit at his table. He looked up, surprised, and then back down to the ledger book. He turned pages and frowned.

"I found this behind the bar. Looks like his accounting for the cost of this place. I can't make much sense of it though."

I leaned across the table. "May I see it?"

"You understand numbers?" he asked, surprised.

"I am a banker's daughter."

That was good enough for him apparently. He nodded and gave me the book. I studied it for a moment, but it didn't take me long to figure out why the previous owner had gambled the place away.

"He owed," I said. "He owed quite a bit. From the looks of it, he still does. I guess that would be you now. You owe."

Sawyer scowled. "The hell I do."

"Apparently he sold bits of the saloon to any takers that wanted some. Either you pay them their money or they get a share of your profits."

"It says that?"

I showed him the note written on the pages.

"I knew it was too good to be true," he said.

"No, it's not. When you open your doors, you'll be making money hand over fist."

"I'll need to."

"That brings me to something . . ." I took a deep breath and plunged forward. "I have a proposition for you."

"I think we're past that," he said.

I ignored the baited words and the tone that made me feel hot inside. "I assume you'll have gambling here?" I said.

"Hell, I'm not opening a boardinghouse. It's a saloon. Of course there'll be gambling."

I stiffened my back at his sarcasm and continued. "Well, it may surprise you to hear this, but I know how to play cards."

"It won't be pinochle played at the table."

"I realize that. Truth be told, my father was a gambler."

"Your father was a banker."

"And a gambler. A poor one, as luck would have it, but a gambler all the same."

"And you?"

"I am very good."

My voice made a strange hitch over the double meaning of my words, which did not occur to me until midsentence. Sawyer watched me with guarded interest.

"I propose that you bank me into a game," I said.

"And why would I do that?"

"Because I will split my winnings with you."

"Seems to me, that's not one of your better propositions. I'm the only one risking anything."

"I know it seems that way, but I promise you, I won't lose."

Sawyer grinned. "Now there's a bet I'd take. If I had a dollar for every man I'd heard say that one, I'd be richer than God."

I chewed the inside of my lip, wondering what I could do to convince him.

"You got something to put up for collateral? he asked.

I shook my head. "I have only the clothes on my back."

"You willing to wager them?"

Just like that, the temperature in the room rose. The temperature of my blood went with it. Already hot, I felt like steam might rise from my skin at any moment.

"Name the game." My tone was not near so bold as my words, but his smile let me know the meaning was taken. I was playing with fire here and I liked it.

He leaned back in his chair, letting his gaze make a lazy voyage over my body. "I was down south in Texas not too long ago. Learned a game called Hold'em. Ever heard of it?"

I couldn't have been more pleased. "Yes," I said. "My

father played with a banker from Robson, Texas, who taught him. I do know the game."

And it was one I'd had an instant connection with. I understood the strategy and loved the excitement and challenge of it. Sawyer looked suitably impressed and I couldn't help my triumphant smile. Spurred by the small victory, I grew bolder. Leaning across the table, I asked, "If I am wagering my clothing, what will you wager?"

"Every goddamned thing I own," he said softly.

I looked up, startled and jittery. Excited beyond the game at hand.

He sensed my tension and he smiled. My heart seemed to trip over itself at the look he gave me.

"How about we each start with two dollars. We'll see how you do?" he said.

He stood, went to the bar, and got a deck of cards from behind it. Then he poured two cups of coffee, added a splash of whiskey from the small flask he carried to his own and sugar to mine. I blinked with surprise when he set it before me.

"Thank you."

Before sitting down, Sawyer counted out some money and laid it on the table in two piles. He took a sip of his coffee and then slid one pile over to me.

"We'll play quarters," he said.

I took the pile of coins, counted them, then stacked them neatly. Sawyer seemed amused by this, but I didn't let it bother me. I knew I had his full attention now as I dealt us each two cards. He looked at his and threw a coin into the center of the table. I called and turned three cards faceup. There was a king of hearts, a nine of hearts, and queen of spades. In my hand I had both the ace and ten of hearts. Sawyer bet once more and I called again. I turned the two of diamonds out and we bet again. The next card was the five of hearts. I fought to keep my face blank as I studied the cards. He barely glanced at them before tossing another coin in. This time I raised him. His brows shot up and he assessed his cards again. I took a sip of coffee, smiled when I tasted the sugar, and waited. He looked cool as the day was long, but I didn't think he could beat my flush. He called my bet and I happily showed my hand. I'd beat his three kings.

His grin held a hint of surprise and a spark of admiration. I pushed the cards his way and scooped back my winnings. He shuffled and dealt and I won again. The third hand I bluffed him into folding.

As I reached for the winnings, he asked, "What'd you have?"

"A winning hand, Captain."

And with that I mixed my cards in with the others and waited for him to deal. I won that one too. He fished another couple of dollars out of his pocket and put them on the table. I relieved him of those as well.

"Your daddy taught you?" he said when he called and I set down my three jacks to his two pair.

I nodded. "All of us. He so wanted to be good at the game, but his face was open. Always open." I looked down, missing that. "My momma thought it scandalous that he had us playing cards at the kitchen table, but I think she liked it. She wasn't very good, but she laughed a lot when we played. My grandma—now there was someone you didn't want to play cards with. She was lucky too. The cards always came to her."

By the end of my little speech tears were in my eyes and my throat was thick with emotion. "We thought if we played with Daddy, it would help him get better and he wouldn't lose so much."

"Did it work?"

"No. He didn't have the mind for it."

"He was a banker."

"But he never understood odds, even in his investments. He always believed what he saw, not what made sense."

He raised his brows at that. "And you?"

"You have to ask?"

He smiled at me and shook his head. I counted my winnings and then split them into three piles.

"Here is the two dollars you started me with. And here is half of my winnings."

I'd come out two dollars to the black. He jangled the coins in his hand before pocketing them.

"So," I asked. "Will you bank me?"

"Ella, I will bank you."

I smiled, only realizing then how tense I'd been. A lot had depended on my winning his confidence. If Aiken came back now, I would not be so afraid he would force me into another situation like the mining camp.

"I can balance your books as well," I said.

He looked at the green ledger book and back at me. I didn't have to prove anything to him there. He slid it across the table and I picked it up. I stood, aware that he watched every move I made with those Mississippi eyes of his. They sent chills down my spine and heat spiraling through my veins.

"It's been a pleasure doing business with you, Captain," I said.

He reached out and caught my wrist in his hand as I moved to step past him. I paused and looked at him questioningly. I thought he was as surprised by his reaching for me as I, though I couldn't have said exactly why I thought that. I looked down at the place where his sun-browned fingers wrapped around my white skin. His thumb moved across the pulse that beat there and slowly he reeled me closer. I watched the colors in his eyes swirl and darken and I didn't fight him.

When I was standing beside his chair, my legs bumping his thighs, he spoke.

"It's not going to be pretty down here, when it's filled with miners and the likes."

"I know, Captain. I never expected it would be."

"A woman like you isn't used to that."

I faced him then. "I would rather see them over a card table than a bed."

He stood and I stopped myself from backing up. Our shift in vantage points brought his body close to mine. I wondered if he could see the bravado of my words.

"Maybe I'd rather see you in bed."

I caught my breath but moved no other muscle. My silence became an invitation, though. He bent down and took my lips in a kiss that sent my pulse hammering against the thumb he had pressed to my wrist. I still clutched the ledger book and he took it from my unresisting fingers and set it on the table. In a movement as fluid as the needs dancing over my skin, he pulled my free hand up to his chest and settled it over his heart.

He ran his tongue over the softness of my bottom lip and I sighed, opening up to him. My response seemed to light him from within. He deepened the kiss and I breathed in his scent as his hands explored the contours of my back, the slope of my spine, the curve of my shoulders. He cupped my face, holding me while he made me dizzy with the sensation of his tongue against mine, my sugar coffee taste mingling with the whiskey on his breath. I made a sound in my throat that spoke of the havoc he wreaked on my emotions.

He moved from my mouth to my neck. I should have stopped him, but I couldn't bring myself to do it. His roving hands found the roundness of my breasts and I sensed the coiled passion in him waiting to strike. I felt the point of no return rush at me from all sides and I was suddenly frightened by it. As if hearing my thoughts he pulled back and stared into my eyes.

"Ella," he breathed, inches from my mouth.

I looked at him, my eyes heavy with passion, my lips swollen and red from his kisses. He seemed to forget what he was going to say and he simply kissed me again and I was lost. I surrendered reason and gave myself over completely.

There was a loud pounding at the front door. Sawyer lifted his head and shouted, "We ain't open."

The knocking came again, hard and insistent. "The hell you ain't. It's Aiken. Open up."

chapter twenty-nine

WITH each step down to the cellar, the darkness became more complete. Bill led them with the flashlight. Next came Gracie, with Reilly close behind. When they reached the bottom, they stood in a huddle, looking at the cramped space. It was no more than a fifteen-by-fifteen-foot area—nowhere near the length or width of the house. The floor and walls were concrete, spidered with cracks, but it looked dry, for the time being anyway.

"Jonathan? Are you down here?" Bill called. Not a whisper of sound answered.

Shelves used to store jars of vegetables, fruits, and jams Grandma Beck had put up lined the walls. Thick dust covered everything, though, and Gracie wondered how long ago she'd preserved the contents. Years? In the far corner, stacks of old furniture and other junk hunkered in the shadows and cobwebs. To the immediate right, two saddles lay spread on the floor.

The trio moved to investigate as one. Juliet went in the other direction, happily sniffing the sealed jars and dark corners. The flashlight illuminated a small circle in front of them, but everything beyond was shifting and obscure. Reilly squatted down in front of the saddles, running his fingers through the thick layer of dust. Gracie and Bill knelt beside him.

"Close your eyes," he said. "I'm going to blow on it."

When they opened their eyes again, Reilly had cleared a portion of the nearest saddle. It was black, with finely tooled leather. There was a silver inlay on the horn and saddlebags hanging over the side. An ancient-looking rifle stuck out from a holster.

They looked at one another. "Strange place to keep your saddles," Reilly said.

"Especially when we never had any horses," Gracie answered.

A small chest not much bigger than a carry-on suitcase was behind the saddles. It was opened, and the contents looked as if they'd been ripped and then hastily stuffed back in. Reilly looked through the jumble. It was filled with men's clothes that looked to be of the same era as the trunk and rifle. A small round hat and a large cowboy hat sat on the top of the pile. Bill lifted the smaller and turned it in his hands. Inside a white label had been sewn and someone had hand-written a name. *Aiken Tate.*

"Oh my God," Gracie said. "That's—"

Suddenly Juliet began barking loudly and urgently. The three jumped and rushed to see what was the matter. Bill aimed the light at the corner between the shelving and the junk. Gracie saw a foot sticking out. The light beam traveled up the leg to hands, flung out in protest. She saw the white gloves. Her knees wobbled and she braced herself against the shelves.

Bill was next to Jonathan, calling his friend's name, searching for a pulse.

"He's dead?" Gracie asked, but she knew the answer. The light had been on him long enough for her to see the blood, the white matter, the splatter against the wall.

"How did he get down here?" she said. And then, "Who did this to him?"

"There's a gun by his hand," Bill murmured, his voice filled with shock. "He might have done it himself."

"But why? Why come here and . . ."

"Bill, try not to move him. We need to get back upstairs and try to reach Eddie on a cell phone. We shouldn't be touching anything."

Bill looked like he might argue but finally pulled away and followed them back to the kitchen. Analise was standing in the middle of the room when they came through the door.

"Where is everyone?" she cried. "I woke up and I was all alone."

Gracie went to put her arms around her daughter. "I'm sorry, honey, I didn't think you'd wake up so soon."

"I heard the phone. Did you know the lights don't work? And I can't find Brendan and you were gone," she sobbed.

"Shhh, honey. It's okay."

Brendan stepped around the corner as Gracie soothed Analise. "What's up?" he asked.

"Where have you been?" Analise demanded.

Brendan shrugged. "Around."

She looked mad and Gracie wondered if they'd had a fight after the "family discussion" she'd held upstairs. This wasn't the time to worry about it though. "Analise? I need you and Brendan to go get Chloe."

"Why?"

"I'll explain later. Just find her now, please."

Brendan followed Analise as she went upstairs. Reilly used the time to try to place a call to Eddie, but he wasn't getting a signal and the phone lines were still down. Soon it would be full dark and they'd be in the house with a dead man in the cellar and no power. A few minutes later, Brendan and Analise returned with Chloe.

Gracie held her daughter as Bill explained to Chloe what he'd found. Brendan's eyes widened and he paled as he listened. He moved closer to Analise and reached out, as if asking to be included in the circle. Gracie put her other arm around him and let him in.

"I knew something had happened," Chloe said. "I knew it."

"Chloe," Gracie asked softly, "did he do this to himself? Do you know?"

"I only saw his pain. I felt it." Her eyes filled with tears. "I felt it."

"He was always casting his pain out," Bill said, his mouth tightening. "He knew it hurt her and he did it anyway."

There was a flinty edge to Bill's voice that Gracie hadn't heard before.

"He couldn't help it, Bill."

"That's what he wanted you to believe."

"He didn't seem to be in pain when I spoke with him," Gracie said.

Reilly exhaled heavily. "I want to go back downstairs. Maybe we can make some sense out of what happened." He switched on his flashlight and looked at Bill. "You coming?"

Bill followed Reilly back into the cellar. Chloe wrapped her arms around herself, watching them disappear. "I have to know what is happening here," she whispered. "Don't you see? I can't control what I don't know."

Gracie frowned at her and said, "Sometimes you can't control what you do know." The words had no effect on Chloe though.

"Did he ask you?" she said, her face twisted with pain.

"Who? Ask me what?"

"Nathan. Did he ask you about the séance?"

Frowning, Gracie shook her head.

"What séance?" Brendan asked.

"I need to reach the spirit world," Chloe said.

Gracie took a deep breath. Reilly hadn't mentioned a word about it. Was this what he'd been leading up to when Bill had interrupted them to look for Jonathan?

"I think we have enough going on without 'calling the spirits,' " Gracie said.

Chloe gave her a cold look. "You say this because you are afraid."

"Yes," Gracie said. "I'm scared to death. There's a dead man downstairs—no one knows how he got there or how he died, the water's rising about a foot an hour. We have no power, no way to get out, and it's going to be dark soon. So yes, Chloe. I am afraid."

Beside her Analise made a noise that took the vengeance out of her. Gracie instantly regretted her sarcastic response as she looked at her daughter's tight and frightened face. What was it about Chloe LaMonte that made her so angry? Was it the sense that even though Chloe claimed to want to help, Gracie feared just the opposite? That Chloe would hurt her and her family if she could?

"Analise, look at me," Gracie said, holding Analise's

shoulder's between her hands. "Nothing's going to happen to us, okay, sweetie? It looks like Jonathan was a troubled man who ended his own life."

"He was a clairvoyant," Chloe said. "He could never reconcile himself to that. He was made an outcast by his own family for his gift and spent every day after searching for the reason he'd been so cursed. He was afraid to touch another because he could see what was in their hearts."

Chloe wasn't helping Analise's fear with her explanation. Gracie moved to block her daughter's view of the old woman. "Listen to me, Analise. Whatever the reason, he had problems and he most likely killed himself. That's nothing for us to be afraid of, okay? We're safe in the house until the storm stops and then we'll get home. I just don't think a séance is the thing to do tonight. Understand?"

"But Momma," Analise began.

She never called Gracie Momma anymore—it was her childhood name, not the one that went with the teenager. Just the sound of it made her seem so much younger, so much more defenseless. It fanned the need to protect that lived inside of Gracie. She slid her hands down Analise's arms and gave her daughter's fingers a comforting squeeze.

"But Momma, what if she's right?" Analise tried again. "What if there is some crazy ghost running around here, slamming doors and . . . and . . . What about the lights and the phone? What about that?"

"Honey, we're all a little freaked out here. Door slamming—that happens at home. This is an old, old place. There are more drafts in here than out in the storm. And the lights, sweetie, it's the storm."

"But what about the ghosts?"

Gracie took a deep breath. She'd been talking around the real issue because it sounded ridiculous, even in her head. Obviously she needed to say it though, or Analise would keep at her. She was a stubborn child. It had made her a determined and focused young adult, but oh, did she try Gracie's patience sometimes.

"Analise, let's say the impossible is true. Let's say the Diablo has a ghost—which we know it doesn't—but let's say it does. For argument's sake, let's also say Chloe can speak to this ghost. We have no idea what kind of trouble that will bring. None at all. And I'd rather not find out."

Analise looked like she might continue to argue, but the men chose that moment to come back from the cellar. Both of them looked pale and shaken. Bill had blood on his hands. Not just a little, as Reilly had after checking for a pulse. But a lot. As if he'd touched or held the body. Reilly stood beside him, a dark expression on his face.

"There's nothing we can do until we get a hold of Eddie," Reilly said.

"You are certain he's dead?" Chloe asked. A dark look seemed to pass between the old woman and Bill, a look Gracie didn't understand.

"There can be no mistake," he said. "Jonathan is dead."

"You're just going to leave him down there?" Analise asked. Her eyes looked huge in her pale face. She crossed her arms protectively around her middle, and Gracie wondered if she thought of the baby when she did it.

Reilly gave Bill a cold glance. "He's already been disturbed enough. I'm going to try to track Eddie down. Maybe he's back at the municipal building dealing with Corrine. We can't move Jonathan until Eddie's people have been out. He shouldn't have been touched at all."

The last was said with another look at Bill. Surely Bill hadn't moved Jonathan's body? Anyone who had a TV knew you never messed with a crime scene, even if the crime was suicide. What was he thinking?

"He was a friend," Bill said, standing stiffly. "Troubled, but someone I knew, someone I hoped to help one day. I only meant to touch him and let his spirit know to move on."

"Well you should have waited until Eddie gave the okay," Reilly said.

"A spirit trapped in this world is never a good thing," Chloe said.

Reilly shook his head. He pulled his keys from his pocket and glanced at Gracie. "I'll be back as soon as I find Eddie. Stay here and stay together."

Gracie stared at him, incredulous. "Reilly, you can't go

out in this storm. Have you looked outside lately?"

Reilly shook his head and crossed to the front door. He stepped out onto the porch and, like a parade, the rest of them followed.

The front yard was gone.

The fence that had divided the Diablo from the neighboring property was just a shadow beneath the dark brown water. It looked like a lake had swallowed the street whole— no, not a lake, an enormous muddy river that churned and swirled and slammed into obstacles. White caps raced along with the rising current. Reilly's Jeep had been shoved into a leaning mesquite tree, fifty feet down from where he'd parked. Gracie's Honda was nowhere in sight.

"Shit," he said under his breath.

The water rushed the channel of the street, hauling with it the spoils of the storm like prizes raised up to the sky. Branches, a bike, something that might once have been a yard ornament, a lawn chair, a propane tank. And who knew what lurked beneath the swift, dark waters? The water had reached the bottom of the porch steps. If the rain continued to come down, the first floor would be breached by morning, the cellar flooded by noon.

There was nothing they could do but wait it out. Gracie had said as much earlier but standing there, seeing it, brought the reality of the situation into terrifying focus. It seemed to hit all of them at the same time until all they could do was stand, staring at the raging river with a sense of disbelief and rising fear.

THEY told one another that Jonathan Burns had killed himself because the alternative was too much to handle. It was terrible to have a dead person in the cellar; it was unacceptable that his murderer might be under the same roof. None of them spoke of the possibility. The only hint that it was on everyone's mind came from Reilly.

"From here on, until this is over, we should buddy up. No going off alone."

No one questioned the quiet authority in his voice. Like

scared kids they huddled together. Only Zach was missing. They'd checked on him earlier and found him asleep in his room, unaware of anything going on. Looking from one face to another, Gracie realized they'd drive themselves crazy with fear if they didn't do something constructive.

"Brendan? Would you take Analise and see if you can find us candles and matches?" She asked.

Brendan stared at her for a moment and then nodded.

"We'll need them before it gets dark."

That did what she'd hoped. The gathering gloom gave urgency to her request and though she sensed a tension between her daughter and Brendan, neither argued as they went about their task. Tinkerbelle and Romeo followed dutifully at their heels.

Bill suggested that Chloe go upstairs to lie down. She looked frail and haggard and seemed to be aging before their eyes. Though Gracie still didn't trust the old lady, she felt compassion. Chloe's pain and confusion were real, as real as the torrent of emotions inside Gracie. She'd have had to be a much harder, colder woman than she was not to be sympathetic.

"Bill and I are going to search the house, Gracie," Reilly said after the others had left the room.

"For what?"

He looked uneasy. "I want to be sure there's no one hiding out here. If Jonathan stumbled on someone in the cellar and they killed him for it . . ."

Gracie hadn't even considered that they might have a stowaway holed up somewhere in the Diablo.

"We're going to have to go back downstairs and make sure there's no hiding place. We still don't know why he was there in the first place. Do you want to come with us?"

"No," Gracie said, thinking of the dark shadows down there, of the clothes, the hat with *Aiken Tate* written inside, and of Jonathan in a trance, speaking that name in warning . . . "Definitely no. I'll stay here and finish going through these boxes."

"You don't have a buddy," he said.

She smiled. "I have Juliet. She's worth two."

On cue, Juliet raised her head and growled at him. Reilly grinned at the dog and Juliet laid her head back down.

Reilly stepped closer to Gracie and gently touched her face. "Don't worry," he said.

"Why not?" she answered.

"Because I'm not going to let anything happen to you," he said.

The tone of his voice was low and serious. He meant it and a need inside her responded to it. It had been so long— nearly all her life—since she'd felt that someone was watching out for her. The sensation of it washed through her, but she didn't know how to trust such a thing. Reilly's eyes darkened and she suspected her thoughts had shown on her face. He lowered his head until his lips hovered just over hers.

"I swear it," he whispered into her mouth and then he kissed her.

There'd been passion between them before, but this kiss sealed a commitment that neither voiced but both understood. His strong arms circled her back and she molded her softer frame to his. When he lifted his head, it was to stare into her eyes. "Trust me," he said.

And she did.

Long after he and Bill disappeared down the stairs, she remained rooted to the same spot, thinking of that.

The sounds of footsteps above reminded her that everyone else was busy with one task or another. But with the rest of them off on their assigned missions, Gracie was left downstairs with Juliet and a lot of questions. Could there be someone else in the Diablo? If so, that might explain a few of the weird things that had been going on. But with the explanation came a new level of concern. If the choice was a ghost or a murderer, Gracie would take the ghost. There was still the very real possibility that Jonathan had committed suicide, but if he'd taken his own life, why? Why come all the way to Diablo Springs to kill himself? And if that was the case, what had driven him to it? Something must have happened. . . . Could it have had anything to do with the reading he'd done in Grandma Beck's room?

Then, despite her best efforts to keep it away, her mind formed the thought she'd been avoiding. If he hadn't taken his own life, and there wasn't someone hiding out here, that meant that one of the other people staying at the Diablo killed him. Bill had said Jonathan tried to hurt Chloe intentionally, and Bill was nothing if not devoted to her. How faithful was he? Committed enough to kill for her? And what of the look she'd intercepted?

She took a deep breath and tried to get a rein on her thoughts. She could drive herself crazy thinking like this. She needed to take her own advice and do something constructive because, truth be told, she didn't like being down here alone. Not now. A shiver danced over her spine.

Lost in thought, she didn't hear Zach come into the room until he asked, "Where is everyone?"

Gracie let out a yelp of surprise and turned to find him standing right behind her. He had a blanket wrapped around his shoulders, though it was still warm enough to make her skin feel damp and sweaty. His blond hair was flattened, his sea-green eyes framed in red.

"Good Lord, Zach. You look awful."

He gave a halfhearted smile. "Thanks. I'll try not to breathe on you."

"Have you taken anything?" she asked him.

"Tylenol, a while ago."

She nodded. "How about fluids?"

That earned her another smile. She was acting like his mother and it embarrassed her. But she'd rather be embarrassed than have him go into a coma or something from severe dehydration.

"Seriously. You look really bad, Zach. You need to make sure you're getting some fluids in."

"I am. In fact, I've been so thirsty I think I've drunk a gallon of water."

She nodded, not reassured in the least. Did excessive thirst mean anything serious?

"Are you hungry?"

"Nah. I just needed to get up for a while. I've been

passed out since I talked to you. Where is everyone?" he asked again.

Reluctantly, Gracie told him about Jonathan.

"In the cellar?" Zach repeated. "Shit. Didn't anyone hear it?"

"Apparently not."

The sound of footsteps stopped him before he asked his next question. Reilly stepped into the room first. His face was gray and streaked with dirt. Sweat had dampened his shirt and made it stick to his chest. Behind him, Bill looked surprisingly fresh.

"Well?" Gracie asked.

"Nothing," Reilly said. His eyes showed relief and Gracie realized just how worried he'd been about what—or who—they might find.

Bill gave Zach a dismissive glance and said, "Is Chloe still upstairs?"

Gracie nodded. "I haven't seen her since she went up."

"Please excuse me for a moment," Bill said and left to check on her.

"Did you find anything at all?" Gracie asked.

"Just things I can't explain. The saddles, the clothes we saw earlier. It looks like there's bloodstains on the clothes." Reilly shook his head. "Everything's so old, though. It could be cherry pie. I need something to drink," he said, heading for the kitchen.

Zach asked, "What chest?"

Gracie told him about the saddle and the chest they'd found.

"And that's it? A whole cellar and that's all that was in it?"

"All that I could see. That and a dead man."

Reilly came out of the kitchen with a glass of water and seemed to notice Zach for the first time.

"What happened to you?" Reilly asked him, frowning.

"I died," Zach said. "Unfortunately my body doesn't know it yet. Don't worry, I'm not breathing on anyone."

"Good to know. Why don't you quarantine yourself?"

"Reilly," Gracie said. "He's sick."

Reilly ignored her. "You should be in bed, Zach. You look like you're going to fall over and there's no way to get you to a doctor until the storm passes."

"Thanks, Dad," Zach said. "I didn't think you cared."

Beneath the dirt and grime on his face, Reilly's skin darkened. Zach gave a small grin and then gathered his blanket around him and started up the stairs.

chapter thirty

REILLY didn't like having everyone scattered around the house, but he needn't have worried. Gracie gathered up her tribe and camped them where she could see them. Ten minutes after Zach had gone back to bed, her daughter, Brendan, and the dogs were all seated in the front room. A few minutes later, Bill came down with Chloe. She gave Reilly a long, accusing stare, which he did his best to ignore.

"Why haven't you asked her?" she demanded after a moment.

Gracie's head came up like a deer scenting danger. She watched Reilly as he searched for a response.

"You must ask her," Chloe insisted. Bill set a calming hand on her shoulder, but Chloe didn't back down. "Ask her about—"

"Gracie," Reilly interrupted before Chloe could blurt anything else out. "Can we go in the kitchen for a minute?"

"Mom said she wanted us all together," Analise said.

"You are all together," Reilly answered. "And she'll be with me. Just give us a few minutes."

Analise got a stubborn look on her face, but Gracie said, "I'll be right back Analise."

The kitchen door closed behind them, locking them in the dim, fragrant kitchen. The smell of meat permeated everything now. It smelled good and yet, it didn't. Somehow the scent of roasted meat was tainted by the simple fact it shouldn't exist.

Gracie sat at the small table and looked at him expectantly. He took a deep breath, wondering where to start. At last he tried, "Gracie, have you ever heard of Chloe before last night? Did Carolina ever mention her?"

She frowned. Not the question she'd been expecting, obviously. "She didn't like to talk about the past, but I told you what Jonathan said—that Chloe had come here before to give my grandma a warning. It was hard to make sense of what he said, though. I told you he talked about someone named Jimmy too. My grandfather, I think. I'm still not sure if this Jimmy died in the explosion or just vanished when they killed the springs."

"I never knew that's what happened to the springs," Reilly said. "You never heard of this Jimmy guy before?"

"Never. When I'd ask about my grandfather, she'd always say he was killed in the war. It never occurred to me to question the truth of it until today."

Reilly thought on that for a while. What would make Carolina Beck lie about Gracie's grandfather?

"Maybe she lied because she wasn't married to this guy. Maybe she just told everyone she'd married a soldier who was killed to hide the truth," Reilly offered.

"It's likely. She was so private. She would have hated all the gossip of having an illegitimate child. Of course that backfired with my mother. All of us, I guess. People have been talking about the Beck women forever."

He nodded, hearing the note of pain in her voice and knowing there was really nothing he could do to make it go away. In fact, he was going to make it worse. A better man might have chosen not to, but Reilly didn't see a choice.

"Chloe seems to think your family and hers are connected."

"Did she say why she came to see my grandma? Because she wasn't welcome. I got that much out of it."

"She said she came more than once. The first time she told me about was to warn Carolina that your mother was going to be murdered."

"She wasn't murdered. It was an accident. And how did she know my mother?"

"She said she had a vision. She claims that she told Carolina where to find you afterward."

"That's crap."

Reilly nodded. "She said she also came to warn her about the rape."

"You mean, me?" Gracie looked at him, her eyes dark, filled with emotion like the earth was with water. Overflowing because they could absorb no more. "How could my being raped have anything to do with her? Another vision?"

Reilly held up a hand. "I'm the messenger here. I'm just telling you what she said."

"Yeah, well you're what I'd call a selective messenger."

He took that hit without a volley. She was right and wishing she wasn't didn't make it so.

"Chloe seems to think you're in danger. She thinks these connections are generations old. And, she thinks there's more to come."

"What, she senses it?"

"She says her grandmother and your great-grandmother started it all. Don't ask what that means. I don't think she even knows. I don't believe in all her bullshit either. I think she's a nut job. But she's got some . . . hell, proof, I guess. You know the picture over the fireplace? She says one of the men in that picture is her grandfather."

Gracie listened with quiet disbelief as he explained Chloe's history—how her grandfather had raped and tormented her family.

"According to Chloe, her grandfather is the man in the picture."

Gracie's eyes rounded, but it was anger that glinted in them. Not sympathy. Not shock. She pushed from the chair and strode into the front room. He knew she was going to look at the picture. He didn't follow. He waited.

It took a long time before she returned. "Why did she tell you?"

"To explain—"

"No, Reilly, why did she tell *you*?"

"She wants to have a séance tonight. She wants you to be part of it."

"No."

"I told her that."

"Did you? Then why are you spinning this tale for me now?"

He stood, reacting to the accusation in her voice. "You'd rather I just kept it to myself? That would be better, to not tell you what's going on? Let you find out from someone else and know that I chose not to let you in on Chloe's little secret?"

"Well that's exactly what you did. Chloe already told me about it. Now she's sent you in to see if you can change my mind."

"You know that's not true."

"Do I? In all honesty, Reilly, I don't know anything when it comes to you."

That pissed him off. Whether it was true or not, whether she had a right to feel that way or not, it made him mad.

"I think you do, Gracie. I think you know more about me than anyone else alive. If you don't like it, let me know and I'll walk away. But don't play games."

Her jaw dropped and he had a moment to regret the harsh words but he didn't take them back.

She narrowed her eyes and said, "You think a couple of kisses and we're all in tune with each other? You think you've romanced my common sense away? You're a user, Reilly. You always have been. You may have changed in some ways, but not in that. I don't know why, but for some reason you want her to do this séance."

"You don't know what I want," he said.

"No, Reilly, *you* don't know what you want."

The truth in that hit him hard and low. It took the sting from his anger and turned it against him until it whipped and burned. She was right, damn her. He didn't know. He'd never known. He'd simply moved from one convenient place in his life to another, never doing anything meaningful, always opting for the easy way out. Why sit home and struggle to come up with his next storyline when Chloe was going to hand it to him on a platter? Why worry that he might be hurting Gracie Beck when he could justify his motives by saying he needed to know.

Gracie watched him and he realized she was reading his

thoughts as they flashed through him. Her jaw was set and her eyes sparked with anger. Without another word she headed for the door.

"There's more, Gracie," he said, stopping her. "You want to hear or not?"

She spun back around and stared at him. Her breath came quick and angry, but she said, "I want to hear it."

"Chloe seems to think this rapist is some kind of spirit that's trying to get at you."

"That's insane."

"I'm not arguing that. But the death of Jonathan—that's something real. That's something to worry about."

"Are you insinuating that this spirit rapist killed him?"

"Hell no. But what if he didn't kill himself? What if someone else did? What if Chloe wants to prove she's right? Bad enough to kill for it?"

Something flashed across her face that told him she'd thought of that as well.

"She's an old lady."

"Yeah. But what about Bill? Jonathan was shot. Doesn't take Hercules to shoot someone."

"What about Zach?" she said. "Why were you so rude to him? Do you think he's involved somehow?"

Reilly shook his head. "No."

"Then why?"

He ran a hand over the short stubble of hair on his head, trying to look anywhere but at Gracie. A few glib lies popped in and out of his mind, but he let them go. Angry with himself, he told the truth.

"I don't like the way he looks at you."

"And what way is that?"

"He's got a thing for you. Don't tell me you haven't noticed."

Gracie let out an exasperated breath. "He's just a kid, Reilly."

"No, he's not. He may look young, but he's old enough to do everything he's thinking about when he watches you."

Reilly could feel his face grow hot. He felt like an idiot.

"So you don't think Zach . . . and Jonathan . . ."

"No, I don't think he dragged himself out of bed and down the stairs as sick as he is."

Gracie took a long, deep breath and nodded. Worry bunched the skin between her brows. "What else did Chloe tell you?"

Reilly shook his head. He didn't want to relay any more of Chloe's ranting, but Gracie had a right to know what the crazy woman was talking about. She'd probably blame him for it, but he couldn't help that.

"She said we're all connected. You, me, Chloe. She wants to do this séance because she needs to know what happened in the past. According to her, it's the only way she can protect us all against the future."

"That's beyond insane."

"I think so too. But we're all trapped until this flood is over and we have no way of knowing what happened to Jonathan. I could be way off—God I hope I am—but I think we need to consider the possibility that I'm not. If Chloe is crazy enough to do whatever it takes to support her psychic predictions or theories, then we need to be on guard. Maybe if we let her have her séance, it will satisfy her. She won't feel the need to prove that something bad is going on here."

"Do you really think she'd do that, Reilly?"

"Who knows, Gracie? There was tension between her and Jonathan. Bill is so devoted to her that she can do no wrong. Stranger things have happened."

"Yeah, stranger things have happened."

He knew they were both thinking of the doors slamming, lights flashing, and the phone ringing. Of the shattering glass, the smell of dinner still cooking in the cold oven.

"There's one more thing," he said, shoving his hands into his pockets. "Did you really look at that picture in there?"

"What do you mean?"

"Chloe's isn't the only resemblance in it."

"You're talking about me?"

"And me."

She stared at him for a long moment and he looked steadily back. This time when she went, he followed her.

But as soon as she stepped through the swinging door, she froze. Reilly stopped right behind her. He took a deep breath, his chest brushing against her back and he was overly conscious of her nearness. It was if someone had put a spell on him and he couldn't get enough of her.

All faces, human and canine alike, turned to stare at them. He had the dizzying sensation of time seeming to slow to an infinitesimal ping of elongated seconds. The walls around them seemed to draw in. With the heavy aroma of meat, was a thick scent of smoke and malt and a stench of un-washed bodies.

"Mom?" Analise said. Her voice sounded small and dis-tant.

"Do you hear that?" Gracie whispered.

Yeah, he heard it.

Music and laughter, faint, like ice tinkling against glass. It came from all around them. Reilly turned in place, look-ing through the stillness for the source of the sound. Some-thing brushed against his legs, something else teased the sensitive skin behind his ears. The dogs began to bark furi-ously.

The laughter seemed to grow louder, the smoke now a cloud over their heads. And in the sudden gloom, move-ment. People, just out of sight. Shadows danced against the walls, cast by objects he couldn't see. He felt hands move against his shirt, like a woman's touch as she trailed it up his chest to his neck.

He cursed and jumped, but his voice was trapped be-neath the thudding of his heart and the imagined caress be-came bolder and more demanding. The hands skimmed over his back, down below the waist, taunting and seduc-tive and blood-chilling. Christ, what was happening?

"Reilly?" Gracie said. Her eyes were huge, her voice the breath of a whisper. He reached out and grasped her hand, pulling her through the thick, turbid film that held them in place and into his arms.

It was as if that touch triggered a reaction beyond the two of them. In the same instant all the air was sucked from the room with such force their clothes and hair rose to the pull.

Gracie was saying something, but Reilly couldn't hear her. Analise clapped her hands over her ears and Gracie tried to move against the vacuuming pressure but each step seemed only to bring them back to the first.

Then, as suddenly as it had begun, it ended with a whoosh that left their ears ringing and hearts pounding. Gracie stumbled forward and pulled Analise into her arms.

"Momma, what's happening?" Analise cried.

"I don't know, honey. I don't know."

Reilly came to stand beside them. "It's just the storm," he said, knowing it couldn't have been the storm. Whatever was going on in the Diablo had nothing to do with the rain, thunder, or lightning.

Chloe sat still and owl-eyed on the settee, a strange exultance that tripped the line between frightened and fanatic in her expression. Bill stood dutifully at her shoulder, watching them with those calm, dark eyes. What was he thinking behind that mask of placidity?

Gracie made a visible effort to pull herself together. She touched Analise's cheek in a gesture so gentle it moved him. He saw an expression flit across Analise's face, and he realized she'd looked like Matt for just that second. A wave of grief mixed with something that felt like hope hit his raw emotions. Matt was dead, but here was this beautiful girl that could somehow look like him. On the heels of that came a fierce need to protect her. Whatever was going on in this place, whatever was real or contrived, he would make sure it did not touch Gracie or Analise Beck.

Whatever Gracie had said to Analise seemed to work. Reilly met Gracie's eyes as she stepped away from her daughter and moved to the picture over the fireplace. He'd almost forgotten the reason they'd entered the room in the first place.

He came to stand beside her, watching her face as she stared with dread at the picture. There was the woman who looked so much like her she could only be an ancestor, perhaps her great-grandmother. Surrounding her, the other three unknown women. Gracie rubbed her arms, looking beyond them to the men in the background. They all had a look of roughness about them, a suppressed violence that found ways to escape through their eyes, their expressions, their stances. At the edge was the man in the suit with the fussy tie and sly smile. Reilly saw recognition cross Gracie's face as she acknowledged again his uncanny resemblance to Chloe. And then she came to the last man who stood almost in shadow. She stared long and hard. Finally she looked away and into Reilly's eyes.

"I don't understand," she said.

"Neither do I."

chapter thirty-one

June 1896
Diablo Springs

AIKEN pounded on the door again. "You hear me? Open up."

Sawyer looked at me for a long moment and I wanted to shout, "No, don't open the door." I was still in his arms, a part of me still seduced by the touch of him. But the sound of Aiken's voice brought fear low in my belly. I knew now what kind of man he really was. Before I'd thought him cruel and demanding, but I'd not imagined anything that compared to the story Honey had told. I'd been right to feel that Aiken had orchestrated the scene at the miners' camp. Given the chance, he would do it again.

Sawyer stepped away from me and I was overwhelmed by the loss of his touch. I wanted him to hold me and make me feel safe, but the insanity of that was indescribable. Sawyer may desire me, but only because I required nothing in return.

He seemed to hear my thoughts and turned a probing look my way before he unlocked the door. Once again I wanted to plead for him not to let Aiken in, but it was too late. He'd already swung the door open and Aiken swaggered in with a grin.

He was covered in dust and caked with dirt from his small hat to his black boots. He wore the same clothes he'd had on two nights ago at the miners' camp and he smelled rank as the sullied streets. He looked around with bright interest at the gleaming beauty of the saloon. His expression spoke of how far his expectations had been surpassed.

"Damn, look at this," he said softly.

Sawyer couldn't keep the answering smile off his face as Aiken looked around him with wonder. "Hell, man, we hit the jackpot."

I didn't wait to hear more. As quickly as I could, I headed for the stairs.

"You can't even say hello, Ella?" he asked as I passed.

One foot on the bottom step, I paused. "Hello, Mr. Tate."

"I saw you shot the other night. I was worried about you."

I chanced a glance over my shoulder and then quickly back. "It was not serious. Athena patched me up."

"That's good. Glad to hear it."

"Good night, Mr. Tate."

And I hurried upstairs before he could waylay me again. I found the others clustered in the hall, eyes big with worry. I understood their concern. Just having him under the roof was cause to panic.

"He gon' be mad at us," Chick whispered. "He gon' see up here how it is and he be mad."

I hoped it wasn't true, but I feared she was right. Aiken had been sporting his girls in a tent and now Sawyer had moved them to a real hotel with real beds. Aiken was too mean and petty not to perceive that as a threat and be jealous. From downstairs we heard his jovial laughter as he inspected the saloon and none of us felt comforted by it. To say he was pleased would be an understatement and I wondered just how much of the bankroll he'd provided, how much of a partner was he?

We huddled out of sight and listened as he told Sawyer that after the shootout he'd ridden a full day before doubling back. He was certain he hadn't been followed, but Athena made a face as he said it.

"He wouldn't know if a bear breathed down his neck," she muttered.

Honey nodded.

He told Sawyer he'd seen Jake Smith riding northwest. "We seen the last of him," he said.

"I wouldn't bet on it," Sawyer answered.

"So where's my girls?" Aiken asked. "You didn't leave them, did you?"

There was an edge to his voice and I wondered what he would have done had Sawyer left us like he'd planned to do. Sawyer hesitated before telling him we were upstairs.

He'd warned us that if Aiken returned, all deals were off, but we'd hoped it wouldn't come to that. I felt anger at a world that would let a good man like my father be gunned down for no reason and yet let a bad man like Tate cruise through without a scratch. We heard him start up the stairs.

"Go to your room and close the door," Honey whispered to me. "Now."

I didn't hesitate to do as she said. Athena gave me a dark look as I hurried across the hall, but she didn't say what she was thinking. I didn't care if she considered me a coward. After hearing Honey's story, I was terrified of Aiken. I didn't want to be in his sight again if I could help it. Before I closed the door, I saw Meaira step in front of the others and hurry to meet him halfway. She had that tight, jittery look about her that told me she, at least, was glad to have him back and expected that he'd have a present for her.

Their voices drifted through to me, but I did not open my door again. I had secured a means of income with Sawyer and I held hope that he would keep me from Aiken. But I wasn't certain. Whatever was between us, it was not a relationship I understood. His words spoke something different than his actions and I couldn't say which, if either, I could trust.

My door had a flimsy lock, which I engaged before moving to my bed. I sat on the edge, listening to the others until at last they quieted. Meaira's room was next to mine and I knew Aiken had joined her in it. I could not help but listen to the sounds they made as he took his pleasure from her. It made my eyes fill and my heart feel huge and empty. I knew not what had brought Meaira to him, but I understood that he owned her as completely as he did Honey. I only prayed I could escape this place before he set his sights on me.

A delivery wagon arrived early the next morning. I heard it creak and rattle down the rough dirt road and then the driver's boots thudding the boarded walkway in front of the Diablo. I peeked from my window to see him move beneath the awning to the front door.

Quickly I dressed and hurried from my bedroom, just as Sawyer did the same. He'd chosen the room directly across from me and we nearly collided in the hall. He'd been looking down and fastening his pants as he came out. For an awkward moment, we stood still and stared at one another.

I followed him down as he let the man in and stood out of the way while twenty-five cases of whiskey and forty barrels of beer were lugged into a storage room behind the bar. It seemed an enormous amount but what did I know? The sort of men who would be filling the saloon might have unquenchable thirsts.

"You traveling alone?" Sawyer asked the deliveryman as he stepped outside.

The man worked a huge wad of tobacco to the side of his mouth, spat a dark brown stream, and nodded.

"All right then," Sawyer said. "See you in a few weeks?"

The man shot another stream of brown juice and nodded again.

Sawyer looked at me after he left. "Thought maybe you could hitch a ride, but not if he's alone."

I was quietly grateful that Sawyer hadn't made arrangements for me to travel with the foul man. I feared it would have been trading the fire for the frying pan and who knew where I'd have ended up had I left with him.

I went to the kitchen and discovered Athena there already with coffee made and breakfast begun. I asked if I could help her and received a glare for my effort. I wondered if I'd ever know just why she didn't like me.

I found two coffee cups and filled them each under her watchful eyes. I wanted sugar, but didn't dare ask. Instead, I carried them back to where Sawyer was.

He thanked me before saying, "Looks like I can open up today."

"Yes it does."

He nodded, appearing as satisfied as a man could be.

"May I ask you something?" I said.

He shrugged. "Shoot."

"How did you come to be partners with Aiken Tate?"

"We're not partners. Not even close. I owe him payment, not a piece. He gets credit until I pay him back and his girls can do their work out of here. Once we're square, I get a cut of that."

"You'll profit from the women?" I said.

He nodded, looking at me as if he didn't quite understand the question. I couldn't blame him. I'd promised profit from the women as well. But how did I explain the difference in the two ventures?

"Do you know much about Aiken?"

"I know he had four thousand dollars in his pocket when I needed it."

"How did he come to have so much?"

"I'd guess he turns a good business."

"But he is unscrupulous, you know that?"

Sawyer shrugged. "He paid up when he was asked. That's what I know."

"The girls are afraid of him," I said. "I am afraid of him."

He turned on me then, a look of frustration on his face. "I'm not their daddy, Ella. I am not yours either."

"I never said you were."

"I told you already, I'm not here to save anyone. I just want to run my saloon and live my life."

I was stung by the words, though I shouldn't have been. I wanted to earn enough money to go home and get on with *my* life. But I was finding my thoughts more on the way I felt in Sawyer's arms than on the life I would return to. I wanted him to care about what happened to me but I wasn't ready to say just why.

I heard rustling from upstairs and a few moments later, the others started down. Aiken followed at the end like a caboose. I didn't want to face him. Quickly I turned and went through the kitchen, which was empty for once and out the back door. I did not stop until I reached the decking around the hot springs. I took off my shoes and sat on the edge with my feet dangling in the hot water. The day was warm, but not so much that I didn't welcome the feel of the heat on my feet.

I heard a sound behind me and turned to find Chick lying on the sandy area not far from the decking that surrounded the pool. She was curled into a ball, oblivious to me. I stood and carefully stepped over to where she was.

"Chick?" I said. "What's wrong?"

She let out a yelp at the sound of my voice and scrambled to a sit. Her eyes were red-rimmed and her face ravaged by tears.

I sat next to her and asked again what was wrong.

"I cain't tell."

"Why, Chick? What's happened?"

"I cain't tell no one. Not even Athena."

This surprised me. I'd not known Chick to keep anything from Athena. "Is it Aiken? Did he hurt you?"

Chick shook her head, but the tears streamed down her face. Her dress was speckled with their wetness. I no longer owned a handkerchief to give her. She wiped her face with her skirts.

"Chick, I promise I won't tell anyone. Whatever it is. Please let me help."

"Ain't no way to help."

She cast her eyes downward, sniffling as sobs shook her shoulders. I thought she'd never looked younger. There were times when I forgot that she was only fifteen. I pulled her into my arms and let her cry her tears until she was dry. I still didn't know what had upset her so, but I felt her pain. In the short time I'd known her, Chick had become a part of my heart. Her sweet smile and optimism was like sunshine. I wished I could take her with me when I left.

After she quieted, I sat with her in the silence and rubbed her back. I began talking of things that had no importance.

I reminded her of the fun we'd had last night, frolicking like children in the pools. I didn't bring up Sawyer, but my face grew hot just thinking of him and the slick feel of his wet skin.

"I thought Athena gon' box my ears when I dunk her," Chick said, the smallest of smiles curling her lips.

I thought she was going to do worse than that but I knew Athena loved Chick even more than I did. I had yet to learn their relationship, but the older woman watched Chick like a mother would.

"She gon' be crazy when she know," Chick murmured.

"When she knows what?" I asked.

She looked down, plucking at her skirt as she thought about her answer. "You cain't tell," she whispered.

"I won't."

"I gots a baby in me," she said and then burst into tears again.

I didn't know what to say or do. I sat there, stunned, as I considered what Chick had said. She was with child. In the society I had left, she would have been shamed and ostracized or forced into marriage before anyone found out. But here, in this world, what would happen to her?

"Does that mean you'll no longer have to work for Aiken?" I asked hopefully.

She shook her head. "He keep me goin' till I show."

She stopped and I waited. As the moments stretched longer, I began to feel sick with fear of what she'd say next.

"And after you begin to show, Chick? What then?"

"Then he root it out," she said so softly I had to strain to hear.

I stared at her, not wanting to accept the picture those few words drew. "But . . ."

"Ain't no but, Ella. I seen him do it."

"You have? But, who?"

"She ain't wit us no more."

I hoped that meant she'd been set free, but I knew it didn't. Even I was not so naïve.

"What happened to her?"

"He kilt her. She like Meaira. All she care bout was Aiken bring her stuff. That all. He give her the laudanum and then he root around and kilt what inside her. Me and Athena, we try to stop her bleedin' but there no stopping it."

"Perhaps he's learned his lesson," I said, my voice desperate with the need to make it true.

Chick looked at me with pity.

"Why don't you want to tell Athena? Won't she know something to help?"

"She just die if she find out. She know how it be for me. It kill her. I know it kill her."

"But you can't hide it forever. How long do you have until you show?"

She shook her head. "I cain't figure my numbers like that."

"How about the last time you had your bleeding?"

She shrugged.

"Last month?" I prompted. She shook her head. "The month before?"

"It been some time."

I took a deep breath. "You're small, Chick, so maybe you'll be able to hide it until the end, but . . ." But what then?

I wished she would talk to Athena but she seemed determined to bear this burden alone. All I could do was try to help her.

"You know not to tell Meaira, don't you? I don't think she can be trusted."

"I knows that."

I didn't know what else to tell her, but I had to say something to give her hope. I couldn't leave her out here thinking there was nothing that could be done.

"Give me some time," I said. "I'll think of something."

"Like what?" she asked, eyes bright.

I didn't have an answer for her, but I couldn't let the hope drain from her face. "Maybe we can get you away from here. Maybe I can win enough money to help you go someplace else."

"What bout Athena?"

"If you don't want her to know—"

"I cain't leave her. She my sister."

I hadn't known that but it explained so much. I should have guessed it but there was no resemblance between the two.

"I cain't leave her," Chick said again, more fiercely. "Aiken, he do bad things to hurt her. That what he do. When we bad he hurt Athena."

I frowned. "Are you saying if he's angry with you, he punishes her?"

"Not just when he mad at me. Any of us. Honey and Meaira too."

I didn't understand the sense of that. Why punish Athena if it was the other girls who had displeased him?

"He don' want the rest of us messed up, see?"

And suddenly I did see the twisted reasoning behind it. And in my mind I could see how it would work. I might risk his wrath on myself, but I wouldn't when another would receive the punishment.

"Why don't you kill him in his sleep?"

I'd said exactly what I was thinking, but until the words came out I didn't realize just how horrible they sounded. Had I changed so much that I could calmly suggest murder to this young, pregnant girl? Apparently I had.

"We try that," she said, unruffled by my question. "That why he don't sleep there with us no more. Only with Meaira and only sometime. Then he sleep with his eyes open." She widened her eyes in demonstration. "I seen him do it. And he always take the horses so we cain't go at night."

"Did you ever try to run away?"

She nodded, eyes downcast. "He find us. He beat Athena near to death. That why she limp now. She cripple. She cain't run no more. Once we get a boy to help us. Aiken kill him 'fore we got to the next town."

I thought about that and could believe she spoke the truth. Aiken was a lot of things, but a fool was not one of them.

"You think you can help me?" Chick asked. "Cuz I scared, Ella. I scared."

I held her again and rubbed her back as I soothed her. "I'll help you," I said, praying I could make it true. "Just give me time, Chick. A week, maybe two. Can you do that?"

She nodded, wiping the last of her tears away. "I can do that."

Her smile nearly broke my heart. I had no idea how I would help her. I was stranded with no money, one dress, at the mercy of two men I could not trust. How in the world would I assist this young woman? I only knew I had to try.

I helped her to her feet and she gave me a hug. "I lucky you came along," she whispered fiercely.

I felt the weight of responsibility settle on my shoulders. I had failed my own family, but maybe, just maybe I could find a way out for Chick.

chapter thirty-two

AFTER breakfast we all helped Sawyer stock the bar, wash the glasses, and wipe down the tables. By noon Sawyer declared himself nearly ready to open the doors. Aiken sent the girls up to change. I borrowed a dress from Chick that was snug against my fuller figure and made me painfully aware of the scooping neckline. I felt as if miles of skin showed between my throat and the swell of my breasts. I felt at once naughty and beautiful. Chick emerged in the gown we'd made for her, looking so lovely she was breathtaking. She spun and clapped her hands when we admired her. For a quick second, Athena and I exchanged a glance of understanding. She may never like me, but she knew how much I cared for her precious sister.

As I took my place at a table and began to shuffle cards, I was very conscious of Aiken watching me. I did my best to ignore him, but he would not be put off. All I could think of was Chick and what she'd told me. If I'd been a braver woman, I would have killed him myself.

"What do you think you're about?" he asked, sitting down opposite me.

"Nothing, sir. I'm just waiting for a friendly game. Captain McCready has given me a job. I'll be dealing cards at this table."

Aiken laughed at that. "You got money?" I nodded, but my quick glance at the bar where Sawyer usually stood must have revealed my source. "You got him worked around your finger, don't you?"

"No sir. I don't believe that's possible."

"Well what would you say about coming to work for me since you're interested in making some money?"

My sweaty palms made it difficult to shuffle the cards. I didn't know where Sawyer had disappeared to, but I prayed he'd return soon.

"Thank you for the offer, Mr. Tate, but I must decline."

"Ain't no cause to be so formal," he said. His eyes sparkled with humor and he looked to the unsuspecting eye like a kindly soul making innocent small talk. "You can call me Aiken. The other girls do."

"I'm not the other girls, Mr. Tate."

He smiled and reached out to trap one of my hands beneath his. He gave the appearance of being a small man but as I looked at the hand holding mine, I realized it wasn't true. He downplayed his size with his fussy suits and hats, but he was not diminutive by any stretch.

"No, you're most certainly not the others girls," he said softly, watching me. "You're special. I knew that the first time I saw you."

I tried to pull my hand free and he immediately released me. "I'm not special, Mr. Tate. Just different."

"I didn't know about your family," he said. "I am heartsick over what happened. You're lucky to be alive."

I glanced up, frightened by this compassionate façade, but I saw no mockery or deceit in his face. In fact, he seemed to be sincere.

"Yes, I am lucky to be alive," I said. "My family was not so fortunate."

"If I had known, I would have fought harder to keep you safe that night. I assumed . . ." He looked embarrassed for a moment, but I was not fooled. "The other girls have stumbled into my life through one means or another. I thought you'd come to me the same way."

It took a moment to catch his meaning. He imagined I'd joined the ranks of the women intentionally. What a fool. "No, sir," I said.

"I know that now. Meaira set me straight last night. She tells me you're too good for me, but not for the Captain."

Startled, I looked up as a wariness settled deep in my bones. I remembered that Aiken had used Meaira to capture Honey. I felt sorry for her, but I didn't trust her not to betray me if it meant Aiken would give her more of her drug. I would watch what I said around her.

"Is that how it is?" he asked. "You belong to the Captain now?"

I belonged to no one, but for once judgment prevailed over my quick tongue. I was not the Captain's woman, but if Aiken thought it was so, he would tread carefully around me.

"Yes, that's right," I said, feeling the stain of my lie creep up my neck.

His eyes narrowed as he watched me and I knew he didn't believe me. Leaning back, he gave me a slow, satisfied grin. I braced for him to call me out, but instead he switched tactics and caught me once more by surprise.

"Meaira said you bargained with the Captain. You bargained my girls."

Now I saw something hard and flinty in the sparkling eyes. I was already on guard, but this made me even more cautious.

"I merely tried to keep them safe."

"You didn't tell the girls they could work for the Captain?"

My mouth was very dry. I tried several times before I could swallow.

"You didn't tell the girls he'd let them keep their money?"

I opened my mouth to answer, but he shushed me.

"Don't lie, now."

He waited for me to say something so I tried to rationalize. "Is it so unreasonable that the girls get a share of their earnings?"

"Now see, that's what I'm talking about. They never thought of such things before, but now they think they should get something. I feed them. I clothe them. I make sure the men are presentable when they come knocking. That's always been enough."

How could I respond to that? It wasn't enough anymore, and he was a monster to think it was?

"What is it you expect me to say, Mr. Tate?"

He reached for my hand again and I was not quick enough to pull it away before he caught it. This time, he did not release at my tug.

"You're a beautiful woman, Ella," he said, his voice low. That ring of sincerity was back and now it brought a terror I couldn't describe. He gave me a bemused smile and leaned very close. I felt his hot breath at the skin beneath my ear. I could smell his hair tonic and the soap he used. But beneath it, there was something dark in his scent, something that shocked me and made me want to fight free.

"Sometimes when I see a woman, I just have to have her."

"And what if she belongs to another?" I asked when I should have stayed quiet.

"But she doesn't," he said, leaning so close his lips nearly touched my neck.

"I've already told you, Mr. Tate. I belong with Sawyer."

At last he pulled back and leveled those sparkling blue eyes on my face. "I don't think so, Ella."

"I assure you it is true."

"You believe that, girl. But he won't fight for you. He ain't got it in him to fight for something. He'd just as soon turn you over as do that."

I knew the color had drained from my face, but I kept my chin up. "I don't need a man to fight for me, Mr. Tate. I'm capable of doing that myself."

"You going to put a bullet through me?"

"Are you going to force me to do so?" I asked.

He threw his head back and laughed. "You're a sassy one. I like that."

I didn't want him to like it. I wanted him to think me trouble and therefore not worth his time.

"See, you might have gotten away with shooting Lonnie Smith, but you can't just go around killing people and not get caught."

"Can't I?" I said, before I could stop myself.

He cocked his head and said, "No. But some people need things proved to them. I'm sensing you're one of them."

I bit back the challenge that longed to come out. I was smarter than that. I had to be or I would not survive.

"You're thinking hard, girlie. That's good. Because there's nothing you can dream up that I ain't already thought of." He leaned in and whispered, "You don't think Honey's tried to kill me before?"

I hadn't thought her capable of such a thing. She wasn't like me.

"Oh, she has. Ask her what I did. She doesn't try it no more." He winked at me. "You won't either."

With that he stood, leaving me sitting at the table, trembling. He could not just take me, a part of my mind shouted. There was no need to be afraid. But I couldn't stop remembering what Honey had told me. And I realized that nothing in my short life had prepared me to deal with such a man as Aiken Tate.

As he strolled away to the bar, Sawyer came from the back room with a box of whiskey in his hands. He glanced at me and then quickly back as he took note of my new attire. I felt as naked as I had last night at the springs as those Mississippi eyes flowed over my bare skin. The look had a touch and feel that lit something deep inside me and I gave it back, responding from instinct to the desire he roused. For an instant, only he and I existed and the rest of the world fell away. Had my legs not been trembling, I would have stood and gone to him, consequences be damned.

Aiken moved then, breaking the spell that had taken me and distracting Sawyer from his concentrated inspection. Aiken gave me a dark look as he slid onto a barstool in front of Sawyer and lit a cigarette. I shuffled my cards and watched like a nervous bird as he leaned forward and spoke to Sawyer.

Whatever he said made Sawyer look up at him, a frown drawing his brows together. I read his expression and felt the blood rush to my face. Aiken had told him what I'd said. I thought of bolting but couldn't find the courage to move. Sawyer turned his head to look at me once more and I braced myself for his rejection, but what I saw was not that.

Again he let his gaze travel from my eyes to my throat to the bare skin above my breasts. The heat in my face spread throughout my body until the spark he'd started burst into flame. He locked eyes with me and I knew he saw all that I was thinking, feeling.

I'd said I was his woman to protect myself from Aiken. But I realized as I stared back at him, that I wanted it to be true.

chapter thirty-three

IT took some convincing, but Gracie was finally able to escape to the bathroom in Grandma Beck's room. Reilly had been diligent about his buddy system and wanted someone to go with her, but Juliet made it clear that Gracie would be safe in her custody.

"You're a good girl," Gracie said, scratching the dog behind the ears.

Whether it was wise or not, Gracie just needed to be alone, if only for a few minutes.

Once the door was closed, Gracie leaned against it and counted to ten. It didn't help. Somehow the Diablo had become a house of horrors and she didn't know how to escape it. Chloe's latest deranged proclamations only increased the feeling.

She thought of the picture and the likeness to the three of them—herself, Reilly, and Chloe. Even she couldn't call it coincidence. But neither did it substantiate Chloe's wild statements about spirits and links to the past. Still, denial didn't erase the happenings of the past two days. She thought about that. First, Analise taking off for Diablo Springs, then the accident and the strange story she'd told about the cavern and being sucked down. Then there was Grandma Beck, struck by lightning not a hundred feet from where Brendan's truck had gone in. And Brendan, somehow he seemed different now. Gracie couldn't explain it, but she didn't like it either. It was as if he were a different boy from the one who'd had dinner with them just last week.

She sighed and pushed away from the door. And what

about the two phantom people she'd seen? First the old woman under the tree in her front yard and then the man in her room last night. Had she imagined them? Or was Chloe right and the Diablo was haunted by spirits from beyond?

God how crazy could it get? She'd been asking herself that question since she'd seen Reilly standing in the entry of the Diablo. Since the first spark of tension had snapped between them and grown into this electric confusion she felt every time he was near. It all seemed somehow preordained, but she couldn't explain it. She was a modern woman who knew that the world was filled with mysteries she could only guess at. But did she believe in ghosts? Did she think there was another dimension? Was destiny at work here?

She turned on the faucet and held her hands under the water for a long time. The warmth was soothing and yet she was too anxious to truly relax. The only thing she knew for certain was they were trapped here with endless questions and no answers.

As Gracie reached for a towel, Juliet stood and sniffed at the door. She growled. Gracie stilled and listened. Beyond the bathroom was Grandma Beck's room. Had she closed the bedroom door? She couldn't remember. Juliet looked at her, as if waiting for a command.

Slowly Gracie reached for the door and opened it a crack. Grandma Beck's room looked cramped and shadowed, but nothing moved. Juliet wiggled in front of her and pushed out. She sniffed the floor, made a high-pitched noise, and then sat. Her fur was down and she wasn't growling anymore. Gracie took that as a good sign. Deciding she'd had enough alone time, she stepped quickly into the hallway and nearly ran into Zach. She smothered a gasp at the sight of him.

He looked so much better than he had earlier, she almost didn't recognize him. His color had returned to normal and at some point he'd showered. He smelled fresh and made her aware of just how wilted she felt.

"Hey," he said, giving her a gentle smile. "I was looking for you."

"Why?"

"Just wanted to talk to you. See how you were holding up."

"I'm fine. How are you?"

"Good as new. Whatever it was, it went as fast as it came."

"That's great," she said.

"This old place is something else, isn't it?" he said. "You've got your work cut out for you going through everything."

"I know. I'm trying not to think about it."

She looked past him to the stairs. "Are you going down?" she asked.

"Yeah, I just wanted to talk to you."

"About what?"

He smiled shyly and looked at his feet. "You know, talk."

When he looked up, there was something sensuous in his light eyes and Reilly's words came back to her. *He may look young, but he's old enough to do everything he's thinking about when he watches you.*

"I just . . ." He shrugged. "I know my timing sucks, but I'd really like to get to know you, Gracie. I think you're pretty amazing."

Her face felt hot and she knew she was blushing. What could she say that wouldn't offend him? He was a nice guy, but . . . As she struggled to find the right words, he watched her.

"I know what you're thinking," he said. "You think I'm too young. But that's because you don't know me." He took a step closer, entering her personal space, reminding her again that, though she had nearly ten years on him, he was still a man. An attractive man with a look in his eyes that left her little doubt what he was thinking. She put a hand out to stop him from coming any closer. He covered it with his own and pressed it into his chest.

"Can you feel my heart?" he said softly. "It's going a million miles an hour. I've been trying to get you alone since you walked in the front door."

"I don't know what to say, Zach. I think you're very nice, but—"

"Don't dismiss me, Gracie, just because I was born a little late. I'm one of the good guys. I don't lie. I don't cheat. I won't play you."

He said the last as if he knew that someone else *had* played her. Was he thinking of Reilly? The thought distracted her and he took advantage, moved in closer. He wore a cologne that she liked and a dark blue shirt that contrasted the green-blue of his eyes. Still holding her hand to his heart, he moved his other to her face and tilted it up. She realized with a sense of disbelief that he was about to kiss her. While one part of her drew back, another part was curious. Zach was no slouch and she'd have had to be dead not to notice how attractive he was, but that didn't change the fact that she wasn't interested. She was dealing with enough confusion over her feelings for Reilly. She certainly didn't need to add a younger man to the mix.

She pushed against his chest. "Zach, I—"

That's when Reilly rounded the corner, startling a yip out of Juliet who'd been watching them with uncharacteristic calm. Gracie broke away from Zach, feeling at once guilty and angry about it. She didn't owe Reilly anything and yet she knew that wasn't true. They'd made a connection with each other and Gracie was not the kind of woman who took that lightly.

He stared for a moment, looking back and forth between the two of them. Zach leveled his eyes at Reilly and lifted his chin in a quick gesture that was clearly a challenge. Caught in the middle, Gracie didn't know whether to be mad or flattered.

"You look like you're feeling better," Reilly said, giving Zach a cold look.

"Good as new," he said cheerily. "Think I'll go see if there's anything to raid in the kitchen, though. I'm starving."

The last was said with a suggestive look at Gracie that made her face burn with embarrassment. He sauntered away, leaving Reilly, Gracie, and a tension thick enough to cut in his wake.

Gracie bit her bottom lip, looking at Reilly from the corner of her eye. The muscles in his arms and chest were bunched, coiled tight as the rein he had on his anger. He turned and stalked into Grandma Beck's bedroom. She followed, not sure if it was the right thing to do, but certain it was the only thing. As if sensing they might need privacy, Juliet curled up on the floor outside the door. Apparently she had decided that Reilly really was a friend.

"I can't stand him around you," he said, his back still to her.

"I didn't know he was waiting for me," she said softly.

Reilly spun suddenly and she took a step back. He reached forward with such violence that for an instant she thought he would hurt her. But he merely caught the door with his fingertips and pushed it shut. The sound of the *click* sealing them in echoed around them. They stood facing each other in the silence that followed, neither speaking with words, but both communicating in a language of skin and emotions. He took one step forward and she was in his arms, wrapped against the length of him. His mouth closed over hers in the same fluid motion. There was nothing hesitant, nothing questioning there. The kiss was filled with give, and yet it demanded take. That was fine. The knot of emotions firing inside her seemed to match the command of his touch.

His hands were up and under her T-shirt, pulling it over her head and throwing it on the floor. Her bra was next, off in a flash that left her breasts bare against the soft cotton of his shirt. She pulled at the hem and pushed it up over his flat belly. He reached behind his shoulders and finished tugging it up over his head. Then he gathered her to him once more and lifted her on tiptoes.

They stumbled and ended against the wall, his weight pushing her back into the unyielding plaster. Gracie felt possessed and she wrapped her arms around his neck and tried to bring herself closer than their hot skin would allow. She felt as if a flame were burning out of control within her, something that would demolish all she was if she didn't get it under control. But she didn't have the power to stop it from spreading. Already it had lit things deep inside her, starting a chain reaction of heat and need. What was wrong with her?

"Don't, Gracie," he whispered into her mouth.

"Don't what," she breathed back.

"Don't say no."

In voicing it, he gave her the option. It would be her decision to stop and he would honor that. But in giving her the power, he took away the reason.

"Say yes," he whispered against the sensitive skin behind her ear. "Please say yes."

And she did. She took his face between her hands and pulled it up so she could look deeply into his eyes. He stared back, letting her see the tight leash he had on his control, letting her know that the thought of her had haunted him in the same way thoughts of him had haunted her. She pulled him down and said, "Yes."

She felt the muscles of his shoulders and chest bunch, and then he was lifting her in his arms. Her legs went around his hips, settling against the long hardness of him as he carried her to the narrow bed. They bounced as he followed her down. Her hands were at his waist, fumbling with the buttons of his jeans and his were pushing her skirt up so they could slide beneath the elastic of her panties. They tangled with each other, neither managing to reach the destination they desired. Finally he pulled back a bit, resting his forehead on hers as he smiled.

"I feel like a teenager with you."

She did too. Awkward and unsure. But then again, she'd never felt this kind of consuming passion. This need that carried her beyond reason, beyond rationale. She wanted. She needed. She had to have. That was all she knew. He rolled on his back, unfastened his jeans, hooked his thumbs through to the waist of his boxers, and skimmed them off in one move. Gracie caught her breath, looking at him naked beside her.

"Lock the door," she said as she reached for the fastenings of her skirt. He stood and did as she said, giving her the full view of the lean length of him. He was beautiful in ways she couldn't describe.

When he settled on the bed beside her, he let his eyes rove over her body, lingering at her breasts, the dip of her waist, the hollow of her belly, and the area below. His hand followed his eyes down and then up as his fingers found their way to the softness between her legs. Gracie sucked in a breath as he parted her thighs and touched her there. For a moment, she was too vulnerable, too exposed, too needy to respond. Reilly leaned forward and pressed his mouth to hers, as if he understood her feelings and knew how to answer them. He kissed her while his fingers slipped inside and moved in a swift in and out that made her arch against him.

She breathed his name into his mouth and he held it. His tongue teased her lips, brushed the skin inside her mouth, tasted and taunted in a kiss that became the anchor to the rising feelings inside her. The pressure built so quickly it caught her off guard and suddenly she was bucking beneath his hand as a wave of white-hot pleasure washed over her. He pressed her into the mattress with his weight as he shifted to move between her legs. And then he paused, seemed to make a visible effort at control, cursed, and slid off.

"Where are you . . ."

And then she saw him fumbling in his wallet for something, realized what it was with a wash of embarrassment and immediate gratitude. She hadn't even thought of it, so far gone was she. She heard the crackle of plastic, the snap of latex, and then he was deep inside her. He shuddered as he settled himself and looked into her eyes with a wonder that spoke to the awe flashing through every nerve inside her. When had she ever felt this way before? When had she been so carried away by the touch and feel of skin against skin that all other thought left her? Ever?

He began to move in a slow rhythm that started that spiraling tension building in her again. She wrapped her legs around his hips and held on as he brought her to the edge of control. His mouth was hot and demanding, his strokes hard and sure. She reveled in the feel of his muscles beneath her hands. The flexing of his chest against the soft skin of her breasts. And when he brought her, she took him along and they clung to each other as the waves of their climax took them beyond what either had ever known before.

Afterward he rolled onto his back and pulled her into the crook of his arm. They didn't speak, but that was okay. They didn't need to.

chapter thirty-four

REILLY showered and went down first. He'd wanted to pull her in with him, but they both knew where that would lead. Right now there wasn't time, but their lingering kiss told them both there'd be other opportunities. Gracie stepped under the shower alone, but feeling like a different woman from the one who'd woken up that morning. A better woman.

It had grown dark while she was upstairs and now shadows that had hovered benignly in the corners reached out their long fingers to embrace the night. Candles had been lit and placed in holders on the mantel. Analise had found a hurricane lamp that sat on the coffee table, casting a warm and golden glow throughout the room.

Feeling as if everyone knew what she'd been doing, Gracie said, "I think I'll see if there's anything to drink in the kitchen."

She took one of the candles from the table, dipped its wick in a flame, and carried it with her. The shadows parted reluctantly as she passed and quickly gobbled up the light she left behind. Juliet flopped on the floor with the other dogs but Gracie didn't signal her. She wasn't going far and she knew without asking that Reilly would follow her.

The kitchen was silent and still as the heavy air. The scent of meat still simmered in the warmth, and the storm battered against the windows. Where the glass had broken in the back door, cardboard was taped over. The sheltered porch kept it from most of the rain, but there was a dark stain where it had grown wet. Her candle seemed weak in the clustered dark and she wished that she hadn't assumed Reilly would be right behind her. But she didn't want to go back out and admit she was scared of being alone.

She tamped down the anxious fear rising inside her and took another step forward. Something moved to her right. She froze, her startled scream lodged deep in her chest. The man she'd seen in her room last night stood only a foot away. Even by the dim glow of her candle, she recognized him. He was big, taller than Reilly even. His hat cast a dark shadow over his face so she couldn't see his features, but she felt the intensity of his stare.

"Who are you?" she asked.

He tilted his head to the side, as if confused by her words. She sensed a frustration in him and then a pressure that strummed hard against her fear. There was anger too. Cautiously she took a step back. He followed, moving quickly to her. The scream broke free and burst from her lips just as he reached for her. She screamed again, and tried to force her feet to lift, to run, but her limbs were numb from the horror that gripped her. Suddenly the kitchen door burst open and Reilly rushed through.

She stumbled into him and dropped the candle on the floor. It flickered and went out, plunging them into complete darkness.

"What happened?" he asked, pulling her into his arms.

"There's someone here," she whispered, staring in every direction at once. Every shadow was sinister, every corner filled with the unknown. And then a glow started by the door. At first it was no more than a light, weaker than the candle that had been doused. Then it grew and elongated, took form. Gracie's heart seized as she watched it become a shape with legs and arms.

"Shit." Reilly breathed, pulling her closer.

A feeling of menace spread out from the man who hovered, lit from within. Gracie heard a high-pitched noise and realized it came from her own throat.

"Who is it?" she whispered.

Because there was no doubt it was a person, a man with old-world clothes and a gun in his hand.

chapter thirty-five

THE night passed in a blur that left no time to think about Sawyer and what he may or may not be thinking about me. I told myself I was relieved, but I knew it was a lie. And each time I caught my breath and looked up, it was to find him doing the same. Aiken remained at my table through most of the night, gambling with skill but no luck. A rough-voiced miner sat to his right and trumped him at every hand. A smarter man would have left the table, but Aiken seemed determined to be the last player of the night. He nearly was. The men who had burst through the doors in the early afternoon seemed disinclined to leave the same way. They stayed and drank until the drunken rowdiness created a din all around us. For the most part they were respectful around me and the other girls but I was not fool enough to think that would last once they grew used to our presence.

It was well after three in the morning when the final man stumbled from the saloon into the street. Aiken stayed at my table watching with narrowed eyes as Sawyer locked the doors and pulled out the money he'd collected that night. I stood and brought my winnings to the bar as well. Sawyer looked up as I crossed and once again I felt hot from the gaze that traveled my body.

"Made yourself a fortune tonight, looks like," Aiken said amiably, watching as Sawyer sorted through the money.

"Did all right."

Aiken's pockets should have been bulging as well, but

he'd lost his money faster than the girls could earn it. Not an easy feat when all of them, right down to Athena, had been servicing the customers without pause since business had begun. I couldn't allow myself to think of the hours they'd spent upstairs or the exhaustion they must feel right now.

Sawyer counted out the money I'd delivered, took his cut and pushed what was left back to me.

"You did fine tonight," he said.

"She cheated, is what she did. She's going to get us both shot if she's not careful."

Sawyer's eyes snapped to my face. "I did not cheat," I said angrily. "You are simply unlucky, Mr. Tate."

His face reddened at that and I knew I should have kept the last jibe to myself. But he infuriated me. How dare he accuse me of cheating?

"You best check on your own business," Sawyer said, his voice calm but deep enough to tell me he hadn't liked what Aiken said. He hadn't exactly defended my honor, but I knew he believed me over Aiken and that only added to the jumble of mixed-up feelings inside me.

He pulled out his ledger and handed it to me.

"She doing your books too?" Aiken said. "A piece of tail like her? She'll rob you blind and you'll deserve it."

I picked up a pencil and forced my attention to the columns. Ignoring Aiken, Sawyer set two glasses on the bar and splashed three fingers of amber whiskey into each. To my surprise, he pushed one in my direction and took the other himself, leaving Aiken out completely. I'd never drunk whiskey, though after tonight I certainly smelled of it. It had been splashed over my hands, my arms, my dress, my neck, and in my hair at least a dozen times.

"I see how it is," Aiken said when neither of us responded to his insult. "You think you can muscle me out, you're wrong. I ain't no fool you can just set off like I don't own a bit of what's what."

Sawyer looked at him then. "You don't own any of it, Tate."

Aiken frowned. "I was good enough to borrow from when you needed it."

"And I'm good enough to pay you back. Nobody's questioning that. You got your girls working under a roof. You got your business. Don't mess with mine."

Aiken looked at me as if I were to blame for what Sawyer said. "I thought we was partners."

"I never said that. Never did."

"But I was good enough to borrow from."

Sawyer picked up the stack of money beside him and counted out five hundred dollars. I knew we'd been busy, but I'd no idea that he'd brought in so much. When he was done, there were still small satchels of gold and coins piled beside him. I estimated over a thousand dollars had been made in the one night. I, myself, had close to thirty dollars of winnings that were mine. I didn't know how much it would cost to send Chick and Athena on their way, but it was a good start.

Aiken looked at me as if he'd read my mind, reminding me that tickets to somewhere else were not all I needed for them. They would have to disappear, vanish without a trace. How would I accomplish that?

"Aiken?" Meaira called from upstairs. "Are you comin'?"

I'd learned that Aiken kept Meaira on short supply when there was work to be done. I could hear the yearning in her voice now, the raw need to have her awareness dulled. I couldn't blame her.

Sawyer pushed the five hundred dollars at Aiken. "I'll have you paid before the month is out."

"I never said you had to do it all at once," Aiken said, trying to push it back.

"No, but I can see it'll be for the best."

Aiken looked back and forth between me and Sawyer, and I knew he wanted to argue. I knew he liked having Sawyer owe him. I wanted to plop my thirty on top of Sawyer's hundreds, but I knew that the gesture would incite Aiken more than anything, and I was smart enough, for once, to restrain myself. I had an idea though. I counted ten dollars from my pile and handed it to Sawyer.

"My rent," I said.

He had a poker face I could not fault and only a flicker of his eyes gave him away. Beside me Aiken shifted uncomfortably, reminding me of a street dog backed into a corner with a bone.

"Your girls are using four rooms, that right?" Sawyer asked.

Aiken nodded suspiciously.

"You want to pay cash or you want your room and board to go against the debt?"

I saw understanding dawn for Aiken and with it anger that crept up his face and stained it a dirty red. "We didn't never talk about rent."

"I could be letting those rooms," Sawyer said, taking a drink of whiskey. "I already got the other two going tomorrow. Won't charge you what I charge them—not by half, but I expect you to keep that between us."

Sawyer's voice rang clear and honest and I knew he meant it. He would not swindle Aiken, though I wished he would. He took another drink and then played his ace, which I had not suspected he held.

"To show you I'm fair, you can play your cards with house credit as well until my debt is squared."

This, I saw, was a generosity Aiken did not expect. It went long in appeasing the insult of paying rent. But what I knew and Aiken did not, was that Sawyer had set a trap of his own making. For Aiken could not resist the cards, nor, if he was forced to play by the rules, could he win. He'd been cheating at his own table for so long, that he believed he had a gift for gamble. But he was no better than my father. By giving him his bankroll up-front, Aiken would play more daringly and he would lose. I knew it without a doubt.

I felt Aiken's eyes shift to me and I quickly lifted the glass of whiskey Sawyer had given me and took a small sip. The alcohol burned my throat and set me to coughing. Aiken laughed meanly.

"That's a deal. Against your debt, all of it."

"I'll need your mark before you have any of it."

"I'll give it."

And with another mean glance my way, he turned toward the stairs as Meaira's pitiful voice called out again. He paused as he set his foot to the first riser. "Almost forgot to tell you," he said. "I heard Jake Smith is still hunting for her. If I was you, I'd turn her over before he finds her."

I'd almost brought the coughing under control but his threatening words started me anew until I felt I would choke on the burn the liquid left in my throat and the fear his words seared in my thoughts. Sawyer came around the bar and patted awkwardly on my back until the coughing subsided. Tears were in my eyes as I struggled to draw a breath. Sawyer stood beside me until I got myself under control again.

"All right?" he asked.

It seemed an insane question to me when Aiken's words still rang in my ears. Sawyer didn't wait for me to answer. He went back behind the bar, scooped all the money and the ledger into a box, and disappeared into the storeroom. I heard thumping and sliding, as if he were moving something heavy out of the way. I stayed where he'd left me, unsure of what to do next.

He stepped from the back room and slowly I stood. I smoothed the fabric of my dress with nervous hands. I didn't know what he was thinking, but I felt him watching my every movement.

"Jake ain't going to touch you," he said softly.

Surprised, I jerked my gaze from the floor to his face. "What did you say?"

"No one's going to touch you but me."

In two steps he was beside me. Without waiting to hear my response, he scooped me from my feet and cradled me against his chest. My arms circled his neck and I held on as he carried me toward the stairs. A million thoughts flashed through my head, but not one of them was no. Not one.

He carried me as if I were a child and I let him. It seemed like years had passed since anyone had taken care of me or sheltered me from the world beyond, yet only a few weeks ago my father had been alive and watching over my family. How different my life was now. But as I looked into Sawyer's face, I realized I felt no fear. In fact, somehow I'd come to trust him. Whatever happened next, I knew my trust would not be shaken.

He carried me into his room and kicked the door shut. Neither of us had spoken since he'd lifted me into his arms, but words seemed unnecessary. My heart was pounding like the hooves of a stampeding herd and my dress seemed suddenly four sizes too small instead of only two.

Sawyer dropped the arm beneath my legs and let me slide slowly down his body until I was standing in front of him with less than a breath of air between us. The moonlight fell across the floor and turned our world into a silver-edged cocoon where only the two of us and the tension that trembled between our bodies existed. He lifted a hand and placed it on the swell of my breasts and I inhaled sharply at the heat of the contact. Slowly he moved the hand down, watching my face as his fingers cupped my breast. I couldn't seem to catch my breath but I didn't care. I only wanted more.

Amazed at my boldness, I leaned into him and raised my mouth to his. My small gesture of surrender, or perhaps aggression, seemed to unleash the need he'd trapped inside. His arms circled me and pulled me tight against his chest. The buttons of his shirt pressed into my skin, but I didn't care. I ran my hand through his soft hair, and opened my mouth to his kiss. He lifted my feet from the floor and moved closer to the bed. I braced myself for something rough, something taking and unknown. I'd seen in glimpses through the tent flaps what happened next and I was afraid of it. I expected things to go quickly now, for him to act as the men I'd seen had—as if they couldn't believe their good fortune and they wanted to press their advantage before minds could be changed and opportunities lost.

But Sawyer's arms loosened and I had the matching fear that he would let me go and I would be the one left with chances ended before they'd begun. Once again my body slid down his until I stood in front of him, the top of my head beneath his chin. I was afraid to look up, embarrassed now by my behavior, more so by the lust that surely showed on my face. I kept my eyes fixed on his chest and my splayed fingers. The fabric of his shirt was worn and soft, warm from his skin, which I longed to touch. His throat was golden-brown from hours in the sun.

I looked higher at the strong line of his chin and the gold-flecked stubble that had grown since he'd last shaved. His lips were soft and dusky beneath the mustache, moist from my kisses. His face was weathered, creased from squinting his eyes as he looked across a horizon. White filled in the lines that fanned from their corners where the sun could not reach. And then I was looking into those green-flecked brown eyes of his, and what I saw made my heart somehow stumble. There was the need that I felt in myself but with it was an uncertainty, not that he wanted me, but that I wanted him. I understood instinctively and it made me feel bold and sure when I had no right, no experience to validate the feeling.

He saw the wonder as my emotions played on my face and then he smiled, a slow, alluring smile that made everything inside me feel hot and pliable, like melting wax. His hands moved up and around from my back to my ribs to just below the swell of my breasts. He moved his thumbs lightly over my nipples, watching my face as reaction went through me. I arched against him without meaning to and slid my arms around his neck, pulling his head down so I could kiss him. His mouth hovered over mine for a moment that was at once exquisite and torture. Our breath mingled and I breathed him in, wanting to keep the scent and taste of him in my memory forever.

And then his mouth was over mine, his tongue against my lips, which parted without hesitation. I'd never known anything could feel like this total surrender. His fingers fumbled with the buttons down my back but mine had no trouble freeing his shirt fastenings.

I'd pulled the two sides open and pressed my mouth to his chest before he'd freed the first of the tiny pearl-like fastenings that ran down my spine. He made a sound of frustration and turned me. I reached back and started with the last of them as he struggled with the top. After the first came free, the others followed willingly and before I knew it, he was pushing the shoulders down and the dress became a pool at my feet. My heavy breasts swung free from the confines and I was grateful. His touch had made them swell and feel trapped by the tightness of the bodice. He turned me again like a doll and I stood between his large, workingman's hands in only my chemise. He had no troubles with the lacings and before I knew it, he'd loosened them. His hands were indescribably gentle as he smoothed the cotton down until it fell at my feet where my dress still lay like a colorful pool.

His breath seemed ragged and uneven and I was suddenly shy after so much boldness. But Sawyer seemed to understand. He slid his hand across my chest and up my throat until it cupped my face. He titled my chin until I looked into his eyes.

"I've been wondering how to get you out of that since I saw you," he said softly.

And he kissed me again. My bare breasts pressed against his chest, skin against skin, heat fusing us together. I pushed his shirt off his shoulders and we pulled and freed and fumbled until we both stood naked. Sawyer smiled at me again and the look in his eyes spoke of passion and possession. I was his now and I let him see that he would be mine in exchange. He lifted me in his strong arms and set me on the bed, following me down to the softness of the mattress. It was too late to turn back, but the thought of it didn't cross my mind. I wanted him. I think I loved him. It didn't matter what reasoning or sense belonged to the feelings.

I sensed the dark danger inside him. The ruthlessness of a man who lived outside the boundaries of civilization, who slept beneath the stars because walls were too confining. I felt his desire to change that, to become one with a life more gentle, more willing to give and less likely to take. In his own way, he sought after stability here, with the saloon. If not an acceptable way of society, then at least a predictable one.

And I realized that my needs had changed so that I wanted it too. I couldn't go back to the confines of my old life. To marry one of the boys back home and live life like I'd been raised to do. In too short a time I'd been changed, and that forging of a new woman could not be undone. I belonged here now, in the arms of Sawyer McCready and I would do everything in my power to stay there.

He didn't ask me if I was sure in my giving. I saw from the look in his eyes that he knew already. There was power there, the power of knowing I was his to take, to love, to pleasure. His hands slid over my body and my skin seemed to light wherever he touched. I wanted my own dose of the heady stuff shadowing his eyes. I ran my fingertips down his spine as I pressed my mouth to his collarbone and the hollows beneath it. When I reached his bare buttocks, I froze for a moment. The intimacy of touching him here, where the skin was white against the sun-darkened waist, somehow matched any we'd had so far. He felt my uncertainty, and looked up from my breast. The cool air where his mouth had been warm and wet added yet another sensation to the thousands assaulting my senses in a delicious rush.

For a moment I thought he might ask if I'd changed my mind. I thought he might play the honorable gentleman and leave me with my virtue. But when I looked into his eyes I realized he had no intentions of the kind. His smile was slow and seductive as he shifted his weight so he lay right beside me, his chest, hips, and thighs a burning magnet down the length of my body. He propped his head up and looked at my nakedness with bold possession.

I was breathing hard and fast as his fingers moved to parts of me that no fingers had touched before. The shock of skin on skin, of the gentle exploration of his fingers, wet from the need inside me arched my body into his. He watched my face as he touched and teased, and this, I realized, was more intimate, more consuming than the feel of his hands. He stared deeply into my eyes, refusing to let me turn away, refusing to let me hide the tide of emotion, sensation, overwhelming longing that hit me with each gentle movement. When he slipped a finger inside that tight place no one had ever invaded, I caught my breath and nearly released it in a high moan that sounded alien and excited and wanting.

He teased me until his fingers were slick and then he placed them in his mouth and licked them. I was crazy with feelings I couldn't describe or decipher, feelings that had me pulling him down to me, that had me shifting so he could lie between my spread legs. I turned my face to kiss him and tasted myself on his lips. My frenzied positioning seemed to work its own magic and drive him to the place he'd trapped me. I felt the nudge of him against me and then the slow insistent pressure as he moved inside. There was pain, but in some unfathomable way, it was good pain. For a moment concern darkened his eyes and he held still, watching me for a signal. I took in a shaky breath and kissed him, pulling the breath of him into my lungs as he moved again, long and slow, then deep, then shallow. The rhythm of it excited me in the same way plunging heights and dizzying falls could.

I kept my mouth to his, so he would taste the fear and the thrill of my emotions while I drank the dark mystery he unveiled for me. Our bodies were slick with sweat as he struggled to please me while not hurting me and I fought to drive him beyond the ability to tell. I felt a building deep inside, a pounding of pressure, a swirling of tension that rose up and melted down until I was hot and trembling. My body arched in a dance Sawyer knew well and he shifted, changing the rhythm of his music to make me writhe and tighten around him until we were both unleashed by the song. I heard my own cry and then his lower moan of release. He collapsed on top of me, his weight welcome in the aftermath of pleasure. I knew then that I would willingly spend the rest of my life seeking another chance to move him this way.

chapter thirty-six

THE kitchen door swung open with a bang and Bill came through, holding the hurricane lamp in his hands. The bright light chased back the dark and illuminated the room. Reilly stood with Gracie held protectively in his arms, centered in the large kitchen, staring at the place where the man had materialized. He grappled with what he'd seen, knowing that his eyes hadn't played tricks, but not believing the image they'd brought back to him.

"There was a man," Gracie whispered. "I saw him. He came after me and then . . ." She looked at Reilly with shock-rounded eyes. "Did you see him too?"

Reilly tucked her close, avoiding those searching eyes. Inside him the need to protect her was so strong it hummed in his blood. He wanted to tell her no, he hadn't seen a thing. He wanted to appease her fear with denial. But instead he told the truth. "I saw him too."

She sagged against him with relief, as if it was better to have seen an apparition that went against all belief than it was to have imagined it in the midst of a dark and stormy night.

He stroked her hair, tucking a stray strand behind her ear as he murmured again, "I saw it too."

She pressed her face into this chest and he knew she felt the erratic pounding of his heart. He was scared and that bothered him as much as anything else. It had been a long time since fear had found a way to penetrate his mind. Not since he'd watched his father's car careen off Dead Lights Road.

Bill held up the lamp as he walked the perimeter of the kitchen but the man was gone. Not surprising, because it hadn't been a man. But what he'd seen he couldn't put to words. He couldn't say it out loud, ghost . . . phantom . . . spirit. It was too ludicrous. But he had seen someone, something, and there'd been nothing earthly about it.

Analise, Brendan, and Zach clustered at the door, peering in with wide eyes. At their feet the dogs tried to get through and at last Juliet made the break and rushed to Gracie's side, body wagging with anxiety and ears held flat against her head. She snuffled Gracie's hand and then moved to Reilly. He braced himself for her growl, but she only whined and licked his fingertips. Before he could get over that, they heard Chloe's voice coming from the other room.

"It's time," she said.

As if that explained it all, Bill turned and left the kitchen. Reilly and Gracie followed the light if not the command. In the front room they found Chloe had moved chairs into a loose circle. She sat directly beneath the portrait of the women and men from another era. To her right, Bill took a seat. There were four empty chairs in her circle of six.

Reilly, Gracie, and the rest of them stood on the outside.

"Will no one embrace the unknown and learn what it has to share?" Chloe said softly. "Is none of you brave enough to step beyond the here and now? To join our circle of enlightenment?"

The room was so quiet they could hear the candles sputter.

Chloe leveled a dark look at Gracie. "He is calling to you. Why do you refuse to hear what he has to say?"

Reilly sensed Gracie's resistance, sensed that she wanted nothing more than to ignore Chloe's question.

Her voice was strained when she said, "Who is calling me?"

"I cannot know until he speaks to us."

"He wanted to hurt me," Gracie said.

"He wanted to reach you," Chloe contradicted.

"You weren't even there. He came at me. And then we saw him again and he had a gun."

"He is defending what he thinks is his," Chloe said.

"Who is he?" Analise repeated her mother's question.

Chloe didn't answer, but Reilly thought he knew. There was only one reason why Chloe would want to make contact with this . . . this ghost as badly as she did. She thought it was her grandfather—the man who had raped her, her mother, and her grandmother. Had he been haunting her all these years? Was the story she'd told earlier about visions and Gracie's family just a ruse? Had she tracked him down through the history of Diablo Springs? The town's past was filled with just such disreputable men. It was no stretch to think this molester of women was one of them.

"Who are you talking about?" Analise demanded again. "The guy who killed the priest?"

From the expressions on the faces around him, Reilly knew that none of them had considered this. He himself didn't believe it, and yet . . . perhaps Jonathan had been driven to take his own life by the insanity of seeing this spirit walking the earth.

"We have only questions," Chloe said. "We search for answers, but our circle is not complete. He who wanders the halls of the Diablo knows all. Let us call him."

"You mean call him and ask what he's doing here?" Zach said.

"Ask him what he seeks to protect. Ask him why he hasn't moved on."

A strange expression flitted over Zach's face. He looked back at Gracie, his eyes narrowed and considering. What was he thinking? What did he want from Gracie?

Reilly still held her in the circle of his arms. He pulled her closer.

"I'll play," Zach said suddenly, moving forward. He hooked the chair around and straddled it from behind. "What do I do?"

The look Chloe gave him was cold and angry. "It is not a game."

Zach grinned and held up his hands in surrender. "Sorry."

She wasn't appeased but she didn't protest when he remained in the empty seat. Her circle wasn't complete and yet Reilly realized that just by being there, they might be filling it in.

Outside the wind blasted against the hotel, rattling windows and doors, slamming the branches of the giant mesquite into the exterior walls. Lightning crackled through the downpour and moments later thunder rocked the foundation. Juliet began to bark. Tinkerbelle and Romeo joined in, yapping furiously at the storm.

"Gracie," Bill said, looking at her with kindly eyes. "We must be able to focus. Could you remove the dogs?"

Reilly could tell that she wanted to argue, but she finally nodded when the din they made rose to eardrum-busting proportions. He didn't know if it was the storm or something else that had them so upset, but they wouldn't be calmed. Brendan stepped forward.

"I'll put them in a bedroom, Ms. Beck," he said.

Without being asked, Analise moved to help him. They all watched as the two urged the unhappy animals up the stairs, Romeo yapping furiously in Brendan's arms. After a moment the sounds were muffled by a closed door. Brendan and Analise came back down and stood beside Gracie and Reilly. Thunder exploded, shaking the house and driving the caged animals to a new level of fury. But the thick walls trapped the volume and let only a hint of it down the stairs.

In contrast to the storm outside the room grew so quiet that Reilly could hear Gracie's soft breathing beside him. Chloe's voice vibrated through the room, deep and melodic as she asked if there was a spirit who would answer. The sound of it crept across his skin like ants.

Analise stepped nearer to her mother, leaving her boyfriend an arms-length away. "Mom, I don't like this."

Chloe raised her voice and asked again, "Is there a spirit who would join us?"

Hands clasped, Chloe and Bill bowed their heads in anticipation of the answer. If Reilly hadn't known better, he'd have thought they were praying. It was warm in the room.

Too warm and that roasting meat smell had become heavier until it seemed to weight the very air they breathed.

Chloe and Bill bent in concentration but Zach took it all in with a cynical expression. Reilly watched him knowing at a gut-level that Zach was not what he pretended to be. An uncomfortable feeling came over Reilly, a feeling that he was missing something, something big. But before he could put the pieces together, Chloe started making a sound. It was deep and hollow, filled with tones—like music—yet somehow indefinable. It was the sound, not the cool air that suddenly blew from the vents above, that raised the hairs on his body right down to the short stubble on his scalp. The shifty shadows and glowing light that pried its way through the darkness seemed sinister.

"Christ, what's that sound she's making?" Brendan mumbled.

Bill looked up and glared.

The tones shifted, rose, dropped, and thrummed around them. They drew Reilly in like a haunting song, but there was nothing sweet or melodic about it. He looked down at Gracie. She'd stepped away from him and stood next to her daughter, watching Chloe with wide eyes.

Chloe murmured something else and then a voice came out of her that hit him like icy water. It forced the air from his lungs and made him reach for the back of the chair in front of him. It was a man's voice, not an impersonation of one, but a true man's voice coming from the frail old woman. And he recognized it. It belonged to his brother, Matt.

chapter thirty-seven

REILLY felt Gracie touch his arm and he knew she recognized the voice as well. He tried to focus on what it said, but it seemed to be a string of sounds, disjointed words, like a signal interrupted. And then at last, one word that could not be mistaken.

"Reilly?"

The voice that had reached across the room between their twin beds when they'd been boys. The voice that had matured with their years until it rumbled deep and tormented.

"Reilly? You there?" Chloe said again in Matt's voice. Her face was slack, her eyes closed. "You there, man?"

He had no choice but to answer though every cell in his body urged him to bolt. "I'm here, Matt."

Bill spoke then, taking over the questions while Chloe channeled Reilly's brother into the room.

"Why are you with us, Matt?"

Reilly swallowed, waiting for the answer.

"I shouldn't've done it," Matt's voice said. "She was always yours."

"Who are you talking about?" Reilly asked.

"She was always yours. I'm sorry."

"Who, Matt? Who was mine?"

"I found something out there," he said. "It found me."

"What'dya find?" Zach asked, leaning forward. "Where?"

Chloe did the stuttering thing again, a static sound that could have been Matt, could have been anyone.

Bill said, "Why are you still of this world, spirit of Matt? What peace do you seek?"

"What did you find?" Zach asked again.

Chloe frowned, tilting her head as if to understand what was being asked. They confused him, Reilly thought, and then felt foolish for it. Matt was dead. Whatever trick this was, it wasn't Matt, and dead people didn't get confused.

"Stop it," Reilly said. "Right now, this is over."

Chloe's frown faded. She spoke again, still using Matt's voice. It was filled with emotion, filled with the pain that Reilly knew had been his companion for all those years since he'd killed their father. It was so real, so exact that he felt tears in his eyes, clouding his vision.

"I'm sorry," Matt's voice said. "I'm sorry."

Angry, Reilly wiped his eyes and looked away. This was a mind game. A sick trick. But some piece of his heart responded to the agonized voice.

"It's okay, man," Reilly whispered. "It's okay."

After a moment, Bill said, "Spirit of Matt, the other world awaits you. You have fulfilled your destiny here. It is time to move on."

Reilly watched intently, thinking for a moment that he might see the light everyone talked about, might see what Matt moved on to, might have that small comfort of knowing his brother was free from the agony this life had offered. But only the candles flickered as the wind howled and rocked the house.

He shook his head, trying to bend his mind around what had just happened. He didn't believe this shit and he was pissed. He clenched his fists and turned to find Gracie staring at him with huge eyes. Her fear kept him from leaving the room. From raging out into the storm. She looked like she might ask him something, but Chloe began to make the noise again.

It wasn't a hum, not a moan, but it grew and pulsed around their jarred nerves like a vibration. It was uncanny, inhuman, unreal. It traveled the room like a flame on a fuse, hissing and sparking and raising the anxiety to a screaming pitch. The feeling of being watched made Reilly look back over his shoulder as the tension rose higher and higher and Chloe's tonal song reached a crescendo. Then it dropped to silence. When she spoke it was her own voice once again.

"Are there spirits who would join us?"

The quiet crackled with the strain of holding it. Gracie wrapped an arm around both Analise and Brendan, holding the two of them protectively. The pressure increased in the room until it seemed that each of them leaned forward, waiting to catch whatever came next. Reilly's skin felt too tight for his body.

A dull light formed just behind Chloe's head. At first it was just a glow, like the flame from a large candle that waned and brightened in the stillness. It shivered as thunder rolled from the sky and exploded in the hush. Then it grew larger as they stood transfixed, watching it change and morph into the shape of a man.

"Is that Matt?" Analise whispered to Gracie.

No. It wasn't. This was someone, something, new. Gracie shook her head but didn't seem able to answer her daughter.

"Aiken, is that you?" Chloe asked.

Gracie visibly jumped at the question. Reilly turned to her, watching the blood drain from her face in the dim light.

"Will you speak with us, Aiken? Will you let us lay to rest the curse that follows us?"

"What curse?" Analise asked.

As they watched, the form took on substance until it was a solid, glowing light that throbbed before them.

"Daddy, it is time for you to move on. Leave this world. Leave our family," Chloe said, her voice softer, weaker. There was a pleading quality that Reilly felt as much as he heard.

The light began to waver and Chloe's face took on a hopeful glow. In that instant, Reilly understood that she'd been telling the truth all along. She wanted only to lay her ghosts to rest. But why had she needed him for that? And why had Matt's voice filled her?

"There is nothing here for you anymore, Aiken. It is time for you to leave this world."

The glowing shape winked and dimmed. Reilly realized it was listening. As crazy as this all was, it was listening. The scratchy feel of the air seemed to diminish as the shape faded. But then suddenly Zach stood.

"No," he said. "You promised me the money, you crazy old bitch. You can't let him go until he tells us where it is."

The light flared, as if excited by the anger in Zach's voice. Bill surged to his feet as well, glaring at Zach with clenched fists. The light grew brighter and brighter until it was nearly blinding. They stared at it as it began to move away.

"Where's it going?" Zach demanded. He marched over to Chloe and yanked her up. "I said, where is it going?"

"It's not Aiken," she whispered. "God help us, it's not Aiken."

"What the hell is going on?" Reilly said. "Who are you?"

"It's none of your damn business," Zach said. He pulled a tiny handgun from the back of his pants and pointed it at Chloe. "Follow the light."

"It's not Aiken," she whispered again, her face gray beneath her skin.

"I don't give a fuck who it is," Zach shouted. "I want the money. Now follow it or I swear to God I'll kill you."

"Like Jonathan?" Bill asked. "Why, Jonathan? He was a troubled man, just looking for answers."

"Well, I'm looking for answers too. I'm looking for answers she said I'd find. And I want the money."

Reilly felt the shock of that confession hit him. Zach had killed Jonathan.

"He knew," Gracie whispered. "When he touched you, he knew what you were doing. He saw it."

Zach glanced at Gracie, but he kept the gun on Chloe.

"Too bad for him he didn't see what was coming, huh? Too bad he didn't know where the fucking money is."

Reilly closed his eyes, thinking of the questions that Zach had asked in his "interview" that morning. He'd wanted to know about the Diablo's secrets. And what of Zach's sudden sickness on the way home and miraculous recovery this evening? Just a ploy to deflect attention while he murdered the man who had seen into his future?

Another thought hit Reilly. At the Buckboard, Bud Bowman had asked him about Hollywood . . . Reilly opened his eyes as dawning comprehension washed over him. Bud had said, *What happened to Hollywood?* Zach played it off, but now Reilly understood. Zach had been here before and Bud recognized him. He'd hunted Reilly down not to interview him about his past, but about Diablo Springs. He'd assumed if Chloe wanted him here, it was because he knew something. Not because he was part of this cycle she was determined to end. But what was his connection to all of it? To Chloe? To Gracie? It didn't make sense.

Chloe came unsteadily to her feet. Zach held her arm at an angle that had to hurt, but she didn't complain. Her voice was quiet now, but her lips kept moving over the same words. "It's not Aiken."

Gracie seemed to have been struck silent by the events. Now she stepped forward. "What money are you talking about? There's no money here."

Zach looked at her, his eyes considering. Reilly read the thoughts going through his mind without problem. He would use Gracie, if he could.

"There's no money," she repeated. "Look around you. Does this look like a place where someone with money would live?"

"She said there's money," Zach said, jabbing the end of his small gun into Chloe's side. "She said this Aiken would tell us where."

"How do you know Aiken?" Gracie demanded, looking at Chloe. "Jonathan said you warned my grandmother about him. Who is he?"

"They lied," Chloe whispered. "They told her he was dead, but it was a lie. All a lie."

Once again Chloe's voice was strangely disembodied, but it wasn't a spirit she channeled. It was a memory.

Gracie opened her mouth to ask more, but it was Bill who spoke. He started to move toward the fireplace. Zach swung the gun around to track him. The suppressed violence vibrating over them made everyone step back until they looked like an audience around the frail old woman and the crazy gunman.

Bill cleared his throat and pointed to the picture over the mantel. "That is Aiken."

Reilly stared at the man who so resembled Chloe.

"Why does she think he's here?" Reilly asked.

"Because they tried to murder him here, but they failed."

"They—" Gracie started to ask, but Zach interrupted.

"Tell me where the money is," he repeated.

Chloe whispered, "I don't know."

And without hesitation, Zach pulled the trigger and blew a hole through Bill. Before the tall man had hit the ground, Zach turned the gun on Analise.

"She's next."

chapter thirty-eight

July 1896
Diablo Springs

TWO weeks had passed since Sawyer swung me into his arms and claimed me forever. Two weeks that seemed a lifetime of learning. There was no question after that where I would sleep or who I belonged to. The girls giggled among themselves and teased me about the look he'd put in my eye, but I didn't care. I loved him and though the words were not spoken, I felt he loved me back. What a strange world that had brought me to this place and time.

I had not forgotten about Chick during my bliss, however, though I was no closer to finding a solution to her problem. I worried on it constantly and each time I saw a man take her up the stairs, I felt sickened. She was too much child to be a woman, too much woman to be a child. When I thought of her fear, I knew it was justified.

I'd done my best to avoid Aiken but he had done his best to see that I didn't. Each night he sat at my table and each night I beat him at cards, praying as I did that I would break him and force him to move on. He played on credit, still banked against his loan to Sawyer. Each time he drew on it, I made him put his mark on the ledger showing his growing use and Sawyer's diminishing debt. I wondered if he understood numbers enough to know just how much he'd lost at the tables. There was no limit to the betting and the miners seemed as determined to lose their winnings as to find it. Many a hand I'd dealt had stakes high enough to make my heart flutter. One game at a table such as this could have reduced my father to a pauper. I had no trouble envisioning the high-stakes hand that had won Sawyer this very saloon I'd come to call home.

I was torn about one thing, though. While I wanted Aiken gone with all my heart, I knew that should he leave, he would take the women with him, and that I could not abide. I tempered my desire to influence Sawyer, if I could, to force him out. There had to be a way to free my friends of his domination.

There were no more than a hundred men living in Diablo Springs when we arrived, but each day more swarmed the small town until their white canvas tents dotted the hillside like the boulders from a landslide. Each morning I awoke to the sounds of hammers and picks striking stone like the rhythmic chiming of a discordant bell. The silver was hard to find and slow to be had, but apparently, enough had been mined that others were drawn to the search. I grew accustomed, if not agreeable, to the smell of sweat and unwashed men. It might have been worse if Aiken had not insisted that they bathe before bedding any of the girls. Of all the things I loathed about Aiken, this one redeeming characteristic went far on his short list of good.

Ever the entrepreneur, Aiken set up a tub in a tent beside the Diablo and charged two dollars for a bath. The men could have easily bathed for free in the warm springs, but I'd learned that in addition to being a superstitious lot, most of them were afraid of the water. It seemed that legends about the "devil springs" surpassed even those about the silver to be found in the surrounding mountains. I had heard that the springs were haunted, cursed, damned. I had yet to see evidence of it with my own eyes, and for me it would always be the wonderful place Sawyer and I escaped to sometimes in the early hours of the morning when the smell of smoke and the layers of spilled whiskey were too thick to take to bed. Though I will admit that at times I felt the mist swirl like a phantom and I was glad not to be alone there.

Even Aiken was afraid of it. Once I'd heard Meaira try to tempt him out, and he'd refused with a vengeance that betrayed his absolute terror. Later I'd learned that he couldn't swim, but it still seemed to me that his fear went deeper than drowning.

Whatever the reason, few would go near the springs and so they washed themselves in Aiken's bathing tent, using water many times over until I wondered how it could clean. Athena's job was to watch them and make sure they used soap, especially in those private areas. When the water became more mud the liquid, she would dump it and start fresh. I did not envy her the work, especially knowing that her chores did not end there or in the kitchen, because she was used by the worst of them in the bed as well. I could not imagine her exhaustion and my heart was sick for her, but she would not appreciate my sympathy so I did not offer it. When she would allow, I assisted her with the household jobs, but usually my offers were thrown in my face.

One day a man came and took our pictures. He gathered us up and arranged us like jewels in a setting. Later he came back and showed us our likeness frozen forever behind glass. Sawyer bought the picture and hung it on the wall.

Each night as the wee hours of morning came and went, business at last began to dwindle. The last man stumbled down the stairs looking as if he ascended from a part of heaven only he could know and the last drunken miner was carried from the saloon and laid out on the boardwalk until he woke and found his way back to his tent.

I'd been particularly lucky of late and even after Sawyer's cut of my winnings, I thought I just might have enough to get Chick and Athena away from here. But where would they go? How would they live afterward? And what if Aiken chased them down? From everything I knew about him, he would not let a possession of his go so easily, and that's what the girls were—his possessions.

All this I thought of as the night wound down and Sawyer locked the door behind the last customer. As usual, he wiped his bar with the pride of ownership and then went to the storage room where he kept his money chest. Aiken watched him go with an expression I didn't like.

I stood, intending to follow Sawyer and speak with him. I had yet to confide in him about Chick's secret, but I knew

I would need his help. Besides, there were other issues to discuss before we retired for the night and the words exchanged between us became those whispered over our naked bodies.

Aiken stood when I did though and moved close enough that his legs brushed my skirts. I was wearing Chick's dress again and I was acutely aware of the tight and swooping neck and all the bare skin above it. I knew Aiken was too.

"You sure smell sweet, Ella. Must be all them winnings. What you going to do with them?"

"That's none of your concern, Mr. Tate."

"Oh, but it is. I think you've got something up your sleeves, or maybe down here." He ran his finger over the neckline of the dress, touching the tops of my breasts in a slow, unnerving stroke. I slapped his hand and took a step away. He followed, standing too close. Sawyer was still in the other room and I was alone with Aiken. I tried to keep my wits about me. It wouldn't do to show this man fear.

"The Captain will not like your touching me any more than I do, Mr. Tate. Please keep your hands to yourself."

I heard the rustle and thump as Sawyer moved some heavy object—a sound I heard each night when he put up the money he'd made. I knew Aiken heard it too and had surmised that Sawyer was hiding his profits in the storeroom. This was something else I planned to discuss with him.

"Sounds like the Captain got a little hidey-hole back there," he said, smiling. "How about you girl? You got yourself a hidey-hole? You think you're smart enough to keep it from me?" He reached for me again, this time skimming his hand up my chest to my throat. I had only a second to guess his intentions and then his fingers were tightening, blocking off my scream before it could escape.

"I know you're thinking you can force me out. I know you talk against me to the Captain at night when he's fucking you. But ain't no one makes me do what I don't want. I'll leave you for dead and won't no one care. You hear me?"

I couldn't move or speak to disagree. I could barely breathe and my fear worked against me, lodging in my constricted throat until I saw spots behind my eyes. I tried to pry his fingers away, but he was strong, much stronger than he looked, and he was furious.

"See I know all about the Captain. I know what kind of man he is. You think he wants you forever? You think he'll fight for you?" Aiken breathed in my ear. I felt his mouth against the skin there and I shuddered with revulsion. "He won't. He's not a man to fight for what don't come easy. You keep your legs spread and your mouth closed, he'll keep you fine. You talk against me and my girls, and I'll make you dead and he won't do a thing about it."

With that he shoved me away and started up the stairs. I leaned against the bar, breathing heavily, feeling his threat roll over me. He'd hit upon my uncertainties with deadly precision. Would Sawyer fight to defend me? Did he care more for the convenience of my body than he did who I was? If I told him about Chick and her baby, would he help us? Or turn us away? I realized the answer that formed in my head was more telling than anything. I didn't really know what Sawyer would do.

I had only a moment to pull myself together. I looked in the mirror behind the bar. Only a slight red mark showed where Aiken had gripped my throat. I felt as if I should be black and blue, though.

Sawyer emerged and smiled when he saw me and gave me a playful spank.

"What are you thinking on so hard, Ella?"

I was thinking that I was out of time. That Chick had only a week or two before her condition would be visible to all. Already I could see the swell of her belly and the heaviness of her breasts. Had Aiken not been so busy tormenting me, I was sure he would have noticed by now. I wondered that the others hadn't seen it, but then I knew how exhausted Athena was and how Chick took care to wear her loose gowns when she was with everyone else.

"I was thinking about banks, actually," I said.

He laughed. "You thinking on a holdup?"

I forced a smile. "Not exactly. But I do think you're asking to be robbed by stashing your money in the storeroom."

He looked stunned for a moment, as if it hadn't occurred to him that anyone noticed what he did each night. I was willing to wager that every one of the girls knew exactly where the money was kept. Yes, he locked it up, but locks could be broken.

"You need to put your profits in a bank, Sawyer, or you risk losing all of it."

My legs still felt shaky, so I moved to a barstool and turned it so I faced him when I sat. Sawyer crossed to me and leaned one hand against the bar on either side of the stool. The position brought his face close to mine. I could see the flecks of gold and amber in the depths of his eyes and I could smell the scent of soap on his skin. I wished he were my husband and this, our business that we would grow together. I wished there were no danger. I wished for a dream.

"You remember who I am?" he said softly, those beautiful eyes crinkled with a smile.

I remembered. He was an outlaw who'd robbed banks until his gang turned to murder.

"I don't trust banks," he said.

"Keeping your money here is like declaring the Diablo a repository. It's foolish."

He considered what I said.

"Maybe you're right."

I was surprised by his agreement though we both knew I was right. I'd seen the desperate sort that came through our doors. There was no law out here. It would be only a matter of time before my words became prophesy.

He grinned at me then and scooped me off the chair into his arms. "You worry too much, Ella."

Did I? Or was it that he didn't worry enough? He carried me up to his room and closed the door. It seemed I could not get enough of him nor he of me, but my thoughts tonight were too heavy. Did I dare tell him about Aiken's threats? Did I dare not?

He sat down on the bed and pulled off his boots and

shirt, looking at me quizzically when I simply hovered beside him instead of undressing. He tugged at my sleeve and raised his brows in question. "You going to sleep in that?"

I shook my head. "Sawyer, if I was in trouble, would you help me?"

"I've been doing that all along."

The simple truth of it bolstered my courage. Yes, he had. But what I was about to ask was different and I knew it. "Yes, I know. But . . ."

He looked at me. "But?"

"I'm afraid of Aiken," I said at last. "He threatens me."

Sawyer frowned. "Threatens you how?"

"He thinks I have plans that involve the women."

"Do you?"

I kept my eyes cast down and didn't answer. Sawyer took my chin in his hands and turned my face to his. "Do you?" he asked again.

My throat was dry and it was difficult to swallow. At last I nodded. "Chick is with child," I said.

Sawyer's eyes widened.

"She's afraid when Aiken finds out he'll try to do away with the baby."

I told him about Aiken's methods and the girl who had died because of them. It seemed once I began, I couldn't stop. I told him about Honey and her sad tale as well and how the night I'd shot Lonnie Smith, Aiken had talked out of both sides of his mouth, telling the men to leave me alone and have me if they would at the same time.

"He's a slave master," I said in conclusion. "An evil one."

Sawyer looked troubled by what I'd told him, but I knew before he spoke that his answer would not be what I hoped for.

"What Aiken does with his women, that's his business. I'm sorry, but that's how it is."

"And what about me?"

"You stay out of his way and he'll stay out of yours."

"That's all you have to say?"

"Ella, I told you once. I'm not their daddy. I'm not here to take care of them."

"And me?"

"You're different."

"How, Sawyer? How am I different? Because I sleep with you? Go ask Honey or Chick or even Athena. Any one of them would take you to their bed."

The words burned in my throat but they were true. He narrowed his eyes at me as I stood before him, waiting for an answer. Waiting for him to say I was different because he loved me. Because we loved each other. But those words never came.

"They're Aiken's problem, not mine."

"And what does that make me? Your problem?"

"Evidently," he answered.

I knew he meant to tease, but my emotions were raw and I couldn't take it that way. I was hurt and I was scared for my friends, scared for myself.

"I am sorry I've become such a burden," I said stiffly.

He stood, forcing me to step back. His bare chest gleamed in the candlelight and I knew his skin would feel like warm silk. I knew if I touched him now, if I slipped my hands around his waist and pulled him close, our argument would be over. Sawyer didn't like to fight and it was I who'd picked this battle. But I also knew that ending it would not include a resolution. I would be in the same state of distress as I'd begun.

Hands on his hips, he made a noise deep in his throat that sounded like a growl. "Become a burden?" he repeated angrily. "Lady you've been nothing but trouble since the first time I set eyes on you."

I inhaled sharply, willing my tears back. "You don't know how much trouble I can be, Sawyer McCready. I will not see my friends tortured and used anymore. If it means I bring the sheriff here, then I will do that."

Sawyer laughed out loud. "Good plan, but did you forget about Lonnie Smith?"

I hadn't forgotten him, but I hadn't been thinking about him when I'd made my empty threat. I'd only wanted to hurt Sawyer as he was hurting me.

"I can see we have nothing else to say," I said.

"You're wrong there, but I'll let it go. Just stay out of Aiken's business. I mean that."

I lifted my chin. "I will be sure to stay out of yours as well."

He looked like he might argue, but then he turned his back on me. I bit the inside of my lip as I opened the door and left him alone.

I'D cried myself to sleep and awoke feeling angry and foolish. What had I expected of Sawyer? That he would suddenly don shining armor and rescue us all? My love for him was not conditional, so why had I forced him to make a choice between me and the others? I had vowed to help Chick and I would, but it was not fair that I force Sawyer into such an alliance. He'd invested so much of himself in the Diablo, how could I think he would risk it all?

It was early when I came downstairs. His bedroom door was open, his bed empty. I expected to find him having coffee at the bar or perhaps taking stock of supplies. But though I found an empty cup on a table, I saw no sign of Sawyer. I went to the kitchen where I knew Athena would be and asked if she'd seen him.

"He gone afore sunrise," she told me. Her eyes were angry. Her eyes were always angry.

Had I not been so disappointed, I might have left then. But I wanted to know if he'd told her where he'd gone, and I knew she would keep it from me because she could.

"Why do you hate me, Athena?"

I thought my forthrightness would catch her off-guard, but she didn't miss a beat of the eggs in her giant bowl.

"You bring pain to my Chick."

"I do no such thing."

She narrowed her eyes. "You will. I see it."

"You see it?"

"All the time I see trouble come our way and I don't see no face. But you, I see you. I see you bring death."

I was shaking my head, but she glared at me with dark certainty.

"You are wrong. It's not me that brings death. It's Aiken."

"It you."

With that she turned her back and carried her bowl to the stove. There would be no more conversation. Still, I had to ask, "Do you know where Sawyer went?"

"To the bank," she said, not turning.

My surprise couldn't have been greater. I left the kitchen and hurried to the storeroom where he kept the money. The lock was still on the door so I could not look inside, not that I would know where exactly he hid it, but I wanted confirmation that this was indeed where he'd gone. A dark feeling had gathered in my belly and I knew that until I'd seen him and held him and apologized it would not go away.

I poured myself a cup of coffee and sipped it quietly while the girls meandered down the stairs. I braced myself for the moment when Aiken would appear, but he did not follow this morning. The anxiety I felt tightened.

When Meaira plopped down with that distant look about her, I asked, "Where is Aiken?"

"Don't know. He said something about finding Jake Smith though. You made him mad." She hummed for a minute, distancing herself from the world with the simple sound. "You made him mad," she repeated in a sort of sing-song.

It took a long moment for her words to sink in, but once they did I came to a horrifying conclusion. Aiken must have known where Sawyer was going. He must have decided what better opportunity to do away with me than when Sawyer was gone. For he knew that I was the reason behind Sawyer's change of heart about their "partnership."

I stood so quickly my chair fell over. "He's bringing Jake here," I said, though I'd heard her clearly enough the first time.

"To hurt you."

I looked at Chick's stricken face and Honey's widened eyes. "I must leave. Chick, we must leave. All of us."

As soon as I spoke, I realized what I'd done. Meaira looked placidly back at me but I knew she'd betray us at the first opportunity. There was nothing I could do about it now. I wouldn't tell her more though.

I hurried to the kitchen, gesturing for Chick and Honey to follow. Athena looked up coldly as we entered.

"We must go," I said. "Aiken is bringing Jake Smith here."

"That ain't our business," she said.

"He'll kill me."

"We leave, Aiken kill us," Athena told me.

"He'll kill Chick either way," I said.

Athena's eyes widened. Honey asked, "Why do you say that?"

I looked into Chick's sweet face, silently apologizing for revealing her secret. But it could not be kept any longer. Surely she must see that?

"I gots a baby in me," Chick said.

The silence that covered the room was chilling. Athena put her hands over her mouth, her eyes widened with pain.

"No," she said.

Chick nodded. "You know what he do to me. Ella right, we gots to go."

Athena shook her head again, refusing to hear the reason in Chick's words.

"I can't," Honey said. "He'll find me or he'll kill everyone I love."

My heart broke for wanting to help her. But I saw the truth of what she said. I wasn't sure any of us would survive this. I would be lucky to help myself and Chick.

"Go get your things," I told her. "I have enough money to buy horses for all of us. We'll go as far as we can and then we'll figure out what to do next. You too, Athena. She won't go without you."

Athena slowly sank to a chair, hands still over her face, head shaking in denial. "Not my Chick," she moaned. "Not my baby Chick."

I realized there'd be no reasoning with her until she recovered. All I could do was leave her to Chick while I went to procure horses.

On my way out, I saw Meaira still sitting where we'd left her, humming that tuneless melody and staring out at nothing at all. My common sense told me to keep walking, to say nothing more to her. But the way I lived now aside, I'd been raised a Christian and I could not turn my back on someone so obviously lost.

"Meaira," I said. "You heard us, earlier?"

"You'll be going."

"You can come with us."

A soft light entered her eyes, a light that spoke of the woman she'd been before Aiken Tate. "No place left for me, lass."

"Will you tell him?" I asked, when I meant, will you betray us?

The light wavered and became murky, like the woman herself. "I canna promise you I won't."

That was as much as I would get, and I knew it.

The livery was filled with animals that had been bartered for money to buy mining equipment and I was fortunate enough to have a pick of three of the heartiest. The expense took a toll on my savings, but there was no choice. I had to get away. I would leave a note for Sawyer under the storeroom door where only he could find it. I would explain where I'd gone and why. I would beg for him to understand. I would make amends. But I could do nothing if Jake showed up to kill me and so I had to make haste.

When I returned, Athena and Chick were waiting. I took the horses to the back and we loaded them, knowing that we might not make it through another day. I shuddered when I imagined Aiken's reaction to finding us gone. I wished that Honey would come too, but I knew for her, death was preferable to being responsible for what he'd do to her family.

"I'll take care of Meaira," Honey told us as she hugged me good-bye.

"And I'll take care of Chick and Athena," I whispered, so Athena wouldn't hear. She'd like as not have my head for such a presumption.

"You're the bravest woman I've ever met," Honey said as she held me tight.

Before she could step away, Aiken rounded the corner and with him was Jake Smith.

It all happened fast, yet each moment imprinted in my mind. Aiken yanked Chick off her horse and pushed her back against the rail. Athena and I had yet to mount and Athena rushed to Chick's side only to be dealt a leveling blow from Aiken. Jake had his gun pointed at my heart before I saw it clear the leather of his holster. I stared down the barrel of it, knowing my last breath was about to be drawn.

"You killed my brother," he said.

"You killed mine first," I said back, nearly laughing at the childish exchange. But there was nothing funny about dying. Nothing funny about having your body riddled with bullets. From the corner of my eye, I saw Athena, sprawled at Aiken's feet. He had one boot pressed against her face, and was grinding her cheek into the gravel. He held Chick by the throat, as he had me last night, but there was more restraint than intent in his grip. She was sobbing, begging that he forgive her.

The weight of my failure nearly overwhelmed me. Whatever I'd intended, I'd most certainly sealed our fates with my brash plan. Had I really thought I could outsmart Aiken Tate?

"It your baby, Aiken," Chick sobbed. "It yours cuz ain't no one else wit me then. We was away on the trail. You 'member?"

Aiken looked dumbfounded and I had a moment to wonder if Chick told the truth. Why hadn't she said so before? Would it make a difference?

Aiken frowned at her. "Baby?" he sneered. "Ain't no baby of mine." He faced Jake again and said, "Are you going to kill her or fuck her?"

Glaring at me, Jake snorted. "Both."

He lowered the gun and then whipped my face with it. It felt as if my cheek exploded and I reeled back, crying out with the pain. I realized as I lay crumpled on the ground, that I was calling Sawyer's name.

Jake leaned over me. "He ain't going to save you, girlie."

Then he yanked my skirts up and tore my undergarments away. My rage became something wild and living.

I had survived too much to give in to this monster. Aiken stood watching with cold enjoyment as Jake fumbled his britches open. I felt the hardness of his belt, the stiff leather of his holster and something . . . my hands were pinned at my side, but Jake's knife sheath was just at the tips of my fingers.

He loosened his pants and pulled himself free. I forced myself to relax against the rocky ground and spread my legs so that he slipped between them, bringing my hands within gripping range. My fingers curled around the smooth hilt of his knife and I slid it free just as he shoved into me. My shout was of humiliation, of violation, but most of all, of rage. I came up hard with the knife, slamming it into his side just beneath his ribs and then yanking it out as he sat straight up, reaching for the wound. Before he could react, I'd buried it to the hilt in his heart. His face contorted with pain and shock. He wavered, still between my legs, his erection not yet aware that the rest of him was dead. I pushed him back and wiggled away as he fell over.

Aiken stared at me like he couldn't believe what he'd seen. Well, I couldn't believe it either, but I would cower under no man, not Jake Smith and not Aiken Tate. I faced him brave and bold and utterly defenseless. I realized too late I'd left Jake's knife embedded in his chest.

Time simply stopped.

His foot still ground Athena's face into the dirt. He still held Chick's throat clenched in his left hand. And I stood before him.

"Let her go," I ordered.

A bemused smile tipped his mouth. "No," he said, but then he pushed Chick away and pulled his gun in one swift movement. All sense of time and place left me as I saw Chick stumble over Athena's inert body at the same moment Aiken cocked his pistol. I heard the sound of the shot crack the air, smelled the smoke, tasted the gunpowder at the back of my throat, and then something slammed into me with a force that knocked me backward. I felt as if I was being smothered. My skirts had somehow tangled around my face as I fell and I fought to get free, waiting all the while for the paralyzing pain and the blood that would spill with my life.

I heard a sound I didn't understand as at last I tore free of the fabrics that caught me like a web. I struggled up and out and only then did I realize what had happened. Chick lay sprawled beside me, the back of her blue dress stained with blood. The sound I heard was Athena, keening like an animal as she clawed her way out from under Aiken's foot. Her face was bloody where she'd sacrificed the skin of her cheek to get free.

I heard myself screaming, "No, no," over and over.

I spun to face Aiken, thinking I would rip him apart with my bare hands for what he had done. He didn't hesitate or mourn the sweet girl that lay at our feet. He raised his gun again and pointed at my chest.

"Don't do it, Aiken."

I heard Honey's voice in the same instant the gunshot boomed loud around me. My hands went instinctively to my heart, trying to protect against the hard flash of death. But there was no blood to hold back. No pain to endure. Stunned, I locked eyes with Aiken. Only then did I understand.

As if rehearsed the two of us turned our heads to face Honey. She stood on the porch, my daddy's rifle in her hands. A small wisp of smoke drifted from the barrel.

"That's for my baby brother," she said. Her hands shook as she struggled to open the chamber and load it again. I saw in Aiken's face the thought to move, to get the rifle away from her, but already the feeling had drained from his fingers and his gun clattered to the ground. Blood spread in a seeping circle from the first bullet she'd put through his shoulder and I knew it was shock more than aggression that kept him standing. She slammed the chamber shut and pointed it again.

"This is for me," she said softly, and pulled the trigger.

chapter thirty-nine

REILLY had seen violence. He'd been raised on it. But he'd never seen cold-blooded murder. Bill lay crumpled on the floor and Zach, the kid Reilly had thought harmless, but not very bright, held the gun pointed at Analise.

"Wait," Gracie said, moving to protect her daughter and finding that Brendan had already shielded Analise with his body. Gracie stopped in front of them both. "There *was* money. A long time ago. My grandmother gave it to me when she threw me out. She gave me a suitcase with close to fifty thousand dollars in it. I never knew where she got it, but she gave it to me to start over. I lived on it. I spent it. It's gone."

The look on Zach's face made Reilly's stomach plunge and a tightness gather in his belly. It was a look of desperation. The look of a man who'd banked everything on door number one, only to find nothing behind it.

"It's not gone," he said through gritted teeth. "Tell me where it is, Grandma. Tell me where it is."

The faces around them mirrored the exact same expression of shock. Chloe turned her eyes to Zach and shook her head. "I don't know. He looked for it. He thought they had it."

Chloe was Zach's grandmother? Reilly stared at the kid, suddenly seeing a resemblance that the youth, the bleached hair, the distance of generations had hidden from him. Zach looked white, but then three generations of his parentage had been the same white man. Why wouldn't he look it?

"Follow the light," he said and pushed Chloe forward. The light had moved to hover over the small crowd. Now it danced and drifted, seemingly without purpose. It dipped down and touched Gracie. Her eyes widened and Reilly sensed that it was more than the brightness she felt.

The storm outside slammed into the house, growing in intensity as they argued within. The rain was more a waterfall than a downpour. It hit the roof in a never-ending sluice. He was afraid it would wash the house right off its moorings, but he didn't say it. They had enough to worry about.

The light passed through the wall and Zach pressed the gun into Chloe's frail body and started after it. "You too," he said waving the gun at the rest of them.

Zach propelled Chloe through the kitchen, pausing as the light went out into the storm. The light hesitated, as if it did, indeed, intend for them to follow it.

Zach kept the gun on Chloe, but looked at Brendan. "Go get me a flashlight. Now."

Brendan glanced at Analise, his expression speaking of love. He was not willing to leave her and Reilly saw the complete devotion in his eyes. He knew Gracie saw it too. The kid had been willing to take a bullet for her. Whether or not they were too young, he loved her.

"I'll kill you first and then her," Zach said, reading Brendan's mind. "I've got nothing to lose now."

He meant it and they all knew it. Brendan nodded, gave Analise the briefest of kisses, and went to find the flashlight.

Chloe spoke to Gracie in the tense silence that followed. "I'm sorry," she said. "For years I've hated you, I've hated Carolina. I've let that hate devour me."

"Why?" Gracie whispered. "Who are you?"

"I am the daughter of Misery," she said. "Bastard child of Aiken Tate." Her eyes filled with tears. "He thought he owned us. And he took and took and took. Everything we had. He raped his own child—who can know the agony of such betrayal? And then when he came for me . . . Our lives have been filled with only hate and now . . ." She paused, glaring suddenly at Zach. "They told us Aiken was dead, but they lied and for all of our lives he tormented and tortured us until this—" She pointed an angry finger at Zach. "This is what we've become. He has made us the thing we hated most."

They heard Brendan searching for the flashlight. Reilly knew it was mounted to the wall by the cellar door, but he didn't offer the information. He had to think of a way to get Chloe away from Zach and he needed the time.

"Who told you he was dead?" Gracie asked.

"He was an evil man and your great-grandmother promised that she'd seen him dead. She said she buried him here, in the springs. I'll never know why she lied. But my mother cursed her and all her family, and I've lived my life by that curse. And now I see it was for nothing. The curse is on us." Her sad eyes turned to Zach. "This is our destiny."

"No," he said, shoving his gun deeper into her side. "Not mine. There's money. There's money here, somewhere." He looked at Gracie. "Her granddaddy told them he'd hunted the man who owned this place. He said there was money somewhere here. He'd never tell where, but it's here and she knows where it is."

Chloe was shaking her head. "If he'd been able, Aiken would have taken the money."

"His spirit knows." Zach's confidence sounded maniacal. He raised his voice and said, "Hurry up with that flashlight."

He looked back out at the hovering light. It looked the same as the Dead Lights people of this town had been following into ravines for over a century. It did seem to be waiting for him.

Brendan reappeared, a flashlight in his hand. He gave it to Zach and then moved back to stand protectively near Analise.

"No way. You come with us."

"No," Analise cried, but Zach had yanked Brendan forward. He pushed Brendan to the porch while pulling Chloe with them onto the planking that was nearly a foot under fast-flowing water.

Reilly shouted, "You're crazy. No one can get through that."

But Zach seemed determined to try. Reilly stared at Gracie and her family and then back at Zach's flashlight as it bounced in the dark.

"I can't let him . . ." he said to Gracie. "I can't."

Gracie shook her head. "You can't go out there, Reilly. It's suicide."

Analise was sobbing, crying Brendan's name over and over.

"I've stood by too many times, Gracie. My mom, my dad . . . Christ, Matt." He pulled her into his arms. "I'll be back," he whispered.

"You won't," she said. "You heard her. We're cursed. I'm going to lose you if you go."

"No. There's no such thing as curses. You're not going to lose me. And I'm not giving you up. Not ever again."

He kissed her hard and quick, hoping what he said was true. And then he went out the door and into the storm.

chapter forty

July 1896
Diablo Springs

AIKEN'S bullet had lodged itself somewhere in Chick's body, but we could not find it to remove it. We were able to staunch the blood and then finally stop it, but her eyes never opened again. Carefully we took her upstairs and laid her in the bed she'd been so proud to call her own. Athena grew silent and protective and refused our help in cleaning Chick's frail body. She wrapped Chick in clean cotton strips and took up vigil beside her bed.

As Honey and I left the room, she looked at me. "Death. That all you is. Death. You take all I live for and kill it. I curse you now. No child of yours will walk proud in this world. No child will be blessed with good, only bad. I curse you."

The words came through tears and pain and hurt so raw it scratched as they left her throat. But the words came and I felt the weight of them settle over my soul.

I wanted to deny the accusation. I wanted to say Chick wasn't dead, that she might recover, but I knew it was a lie. As if in protest though, the small babe she carried moved suddenly in the womb and we saw it skim beneath the surface of her skin like a ripple in water. They both managed to cling to life. Maybe there was hope.

I looked back at Athena. Staring into those angry black eyes, I said the only truth I knew for certain. "Aiken is dead. He'll torment you no more."

Honey and I left her alone with Chick and went down-stairs to take care of business. It was barely nine in the morning and we had two bodies outside our kitchen door. Had this been another town, someone would have come to investigate. But guns were shot at random all through the day and night in Diablo Springs.

We didn't speak as we heaved Jake Smith up and over his saddle. Nor did we talk as we did the same with Aiken. We led the horses out to the hot springs, taking them around to the far edge where the deepest end of the pool was. In the shelter of the jutting rock to the west, we bound their feet, stuffed stones in their clothing, and threw them in.

Perhaps it was guilt, perhaps it was the hurt of all that had happened. The shock that had kept me numb wore off now that the last deed was done. But whatever the reason, as I stood watching Aiken Tate sink, I imagined his eyes opened.

I clapped my hand over my mouth, but even before I could scream, he'd vanished into the murky depths below.

I waited for Sawyer for a month before I let myself even consider that he might not return. During that time I could do little but berate myself. I'd driven him away. Nothing I could do would ever change that. Still I waited for him.

The town of Diablo Springs surged up around us and business continued against all sense and reasoning. I tended bar because I thought it was what Sawyer would want of me. We hired a man to work the tables and throw out the rowdies when necessary. We made money hand over fist, but there was no glory in it. No feeling of building something better. We broke into the storage room and found the place where Sawyer had stashed his money. It was empty now.

Upstairs Chick held on to life with Athena tending to her like a newborn. And two months after we killed Aiken and Jake Smith, Chick's baby was born. The delivery was long and hard, but Chick never seemed aware of it. The daughter she gave birth to was tiny and frail, but otherwise perfect in every way . . . except her resemblance to the animal who'd fathered her. Within hours after she was born, Chick quietly passed on to heaven.

Athena named the baby Misery and as soon as she was able, she packed the squalling newborn up and left us. I gave her all the money I had saved and she threw it back in my face, spat at my feet, and left on foot. I never saw her again.

We found Meaira dead one morning, her wrists cut open and an empty vial of laudanum on the floor beside her. She'd left no note behind, but she didn't need one. We knew. Instinctively I understood that I would lose Honey as well, though not by death. She could at last return to her family, and I wished her the best.

It was not long after we buried Meaira in Digger Young's cemetery that I realized I was with child. I wept for nearly a day afterward, tears of both grief and happiness. There was a part of Sawyer growing inside me and if I hadn't driven him away, I believed he might have rejoiced with me. Despite Athena's curse, I hoped the baby to be a sign that life went on and perhaps Sawyer would come back to me. But though I waited until my dying day, he never did.

chapter forty-one

THE wind tried to pry Reilly from the boardwalk. The rain and floodwaters tried to wash him away. But Reilly would not give in. He could still see Zach's flashlight bobbing up ahead and the Dead Light leading him to a place near the overhang of rock. Though he knew Zach would be pushing her, they could only move as quickly as Chloe's feeble body would allow. Reilly was gaining on them.

The thunder boomed at increasing intervals until it felt like the earth was shaking from a quake. The lightning hissed in the sky above, branching into a thousand tributaries as it lit up the night. If Reilly didn't drown first, the lightning would get him. Not a comforting thought, but then again, nothing about the past forty-eight hours had been comforting.

Reilly held on to the dilapidated railing with one hand and the flashlight with the other until he reached the bend that looped beneath the rock wall. There the stone hillside offered a small bit of shelter. He could see Zach's light, still now and the Dead Light hanging over the swirling black pool of the springs. There were no longer ravines and chasms. The water had turned it all into a solid, churning surface. Brendan sat on the ground nearby. Zach made sure he knew the gun was still on him.

"Ask it," Zach was screaming. "Ask it."

Reilly came up behind him, silent in the deafening squall. Chloe was sobbing, shaking her head as she stared at the light. Reilly didn't have time to decipher her expression. He crouched low, nearly blinded by the pelting rain, and crept closer.

"It's not Aiken," he heard Chloe wail.

He launched himself at Zach, knocking the gun from his hand as they rolled to the edge of the embankment. The gun clattered across the rock and plunged into the water. Reilly was bigger than Zach, but Zach was younger and fierce in his rage. He managed to pin Reilly beneath him. The blows came fast about his head and face until stars joined the spider lightning behind his eyes. Reilly struggled to get his arms free, using his legs to try to unseat the younger man. It wasn't working.

From the corner of his eye, he saw Brendan moving in, saw him pick up a rock and bring it down on Zach's head. For a moment, it dazed Zach and that was all the moment Reilly needed. He shifted and bucked and Zach flew off of him. Quickly he scrambled to his feet, watching Zach do the same. He stood in a foot of water, the Dead Lights right behind him.

Chloe lay crumbled on the ground. She looked up, past Zach, and made a sound that pulled their attention to the light.

It was taking shape again, this time quick and solid. It darkened and became a man, then solidified into someone recognizable. Reilly's mouth fell open. It was the other man in the picture. The one who looked like Reilly.

"Where is it?" Zach screamed at the apparition.

If he lived through this, Reilly thought, he'd never be able to describe it.

The form leaned forward, looking right at Zach. Reilly felt as if the storm itself had begun to throb in time with the glow that surrounded the hovering man. Whatever Zach saw in the shape, it compelled him. He took a step forward, reaching out. Reilly saw greed on his face. Greed and satisfaction. Was this thing communicating with him?

Suddenly the form seemed to close in on itself. One moment it was there. The next it was a thin line of light aimed down at the lake beneath it. And then it rushed into the dark waters, splitting them with its brilliance. Zach screamed something and dove in after it.

Reilly's step forward to stop him came too late. In an

instant Zach had vanished and so had the Dead Lights.

Reilly stumbled over to where Chloe lay on the ground. Gently he lifted her head and looked into her face.

"So many years," she whispered. "But you got him."

Reilly shook his head. "Let me get you back."

"Yes," she nodded. "I got more time. I got lots more time now."

Her eyes glazed over and for a moment he thought it was the end for her.

"Help an old lady up, Nathan. Take me back and I'll tell you a story."

He gave one last look at the dark water, knowing Zach would not surface, knowing that if he did it would be bad, but hoping for the kid all the same. He couldn't imagine a worse death than one in the black water of Diablo Springs.

chapter forty-two

EVEN after Reilly told her the strange story Chloe had revealed, Gracie couldn't quite believe it. Chloe spoke of family legends that dated back to the days of Gracie's great-grandmother Ella. She told of Aiken Tate who had tormented a small band of women and made them slaves long after slavery was a thing of the past. The legends spoke of Ella Beck, who had betrayed them by lying about Aiken's death. About her love for the owner of the Diablo, a man they called Captain. After driving the captain away, Ella had tried to escape Aiken and take Chloe's grandmother, Athena, and her sister, Chick, with her. But things had gone wrong and Ella was responsible. The tragedy that followed Chloe's family forever after had been blamed on Ella and her deceit.

But somehow during the night when her grandson plunged to his death, Chloe had learned the truth. Aiken had killed the man Ella loved, she had not driven him away, nor had she lied about killing Aiken—for she thought she had. But it was Aiken's greed that had given him strength to survive his wounds, to free the tethers Ella had put around him, and escape Diablo Springs.

According to Reilly, Chloe had learned this from the captain's spirit. With a bemused smile that wasn't quite cynical nor quite accepting, Reilly relayed the story. Chloe also said there'd been a great deal of money, which Sawyer had hidden in one of the many caverns beneath the springs.

"She said he'd been a bank robber," Reilly said, finishing the strange tale. "So he wouldn't take his money to the bank, but he'd wanted it hidden and Aiken had followed him. Aiken never figured out where the captain hid it, but he never gave up his search."

"This is so crazy, Reilly. I can't believe it. But Jonathan kept saying, *It was in the Dead Lights* and *He didn't stay dead.* He must have been talking about the money and this Aiken Tate. He said Grandma Beck was glad when Ella died because she was superstitious and always afraid. She thought Ella was crazy. But maybe she wasn't. And you know what? If Grandma Beck had heard all those crazy stories from her mother, and then Chloe showed up and confirmed them, and then when *my* mother died . . . I'm sure she believed we were cursed. After Matt raped me, I thought she went crazy. I thought she was crying, *aching, aching,* and I didn't understand. But now . . ."

"She thought it was Aiken, back from the dead."

Gracie nodded. "She couldn't believe the truth because Chloe had her so convinced it was a curse being fulfilled. She did the only thing she thought she could. She gave me all her money and sent me away. She was trying to protect me."

It all seemed beyond senseless . . . a century of hurt and insanity based on legends and fears.

"What about Zach?" Gracie asked. "Why did they pretend they didn't know each other?"

"Zach had heard her and Bill planning the trip and he knew the legends had included a large amount of money. So he came up with his own plan. Until Chloe saw him at the bookstore, she didn't know what he intended to do, though. And then afterward, she was afraid I'd change my mind if she revealed that he was lying about who he was and oh, by the way, he's my no-good grandson. After he killed Jonathan, she kept quiet because she was scared."

"Why was it important to her that you come back here?"

"She said she saw Brendan and Analise in a vision, she knew the town had called them. In her mind that meant this Tate guy had lured them in. She knew you'd come. But she needed me, she said, because she thought I could defeat Tate."

"How?"

"I don't even think she knew that. I guess it had to do with my resemblance to this captain. But she thought all along that the Dead Lights—the ghost—was Aiken. She never suspected it would be the captain who haunted Diablo Springs."

"So, if this captain was Ella's love, I would guess he was Grandma Beck's father . . . and since you look like him . . . Does that make us related?"

"Nah, it's like everything else—a fluke. The only way you and I are going to be related is by choice."

Gracie smiled at that. After a moment, she asked, "Reilly, what about Matt?"

Reilly let out a breath, shaking his head as if he didn't know where to begin. "I know what he did to you—what we both did—it's not something you'll ever be able to forgive or forget. But, Gracie, I've never been more sorry about something in my life. And I know Matt felt the same."

She nodded. "I know. I heard him too."

"I don't know why he did it. I don't know how he could hurt a woman after what our dad did to our mom, but—"

She stopped him with a touch. "I guess sometimes we can't make sense of the people we love, but we love them anyway."

His shoulders sagged as if with relief. He'd needed her to understand.

"I took his ashes out to our old house this morning and I buried them in the backyard, next to the dog." Reilly's mouth tilted at that. "I think he'll like it there. He always loved that dog."

Gracie wrapped her arms around him and rested her head on his shoulder.

"God, I'm glad it's over," he whispered into her hair.

She looked up at him, wondering if it was true. Wondering if it would truly ever be over. "What about the money Zach was after?"

"I guess we'll never know. Maybe he found it."

Maybe he had. His body was not among the others found floating in the springs. It would be weeks before the water dried up and the full extent of the damage could be accounted for, but more than one body had washed up from the caverns during the storm. The Dead Lights had vanished, though, so maybe Diablo Springs had finally taken its last toll.

"After Bill is released from the hospital, Chloe's going to take him back to Omaha."

"Who is Bill to her?"

"Who knows?" Reilly said. "Maybe just another lost soul looking for answers."

Gracie thought about that, thought about her own life and where she would go now. Would Reilly be a part of it? Did he want to be? Life with her wouldn't be a picnic. Aside from her own issues and quirks, there was Analise and yet another baby coming into the world. She wouldn't have wished it for her daughter, any more than it had been wished for herself, but Analise was a blessing that she wouldn't have missed for anything. Perhaps the same would be true for this baby. And Brendan had proved to have more grit than she's given him credit for. Maybe they would be happy together. Maybe not. But that's what life was, wasn't it? Taking chances and celebrating when they paid off, changing course when they didn't.

"What about us, Gracie?" Reilly asked, reading her mind.

She smiled at him. "I think you and I have a date with destiny," she said, grinning.

He smiled at that. "I think you're right."